SPLENDOR
and
MISERY

D1213429

Also by Faye Levine

The Culture Barons: An Analysis of Power and Money in the Arts
Solomon & Sheba: A Novel

SPLENDOR
and
MISERY

A Novel of Harvard

Faye Levine

St. Martin's/Marek

ATHENS REGIONAL LIBRARY
ATHENS, GEORGIA

The author wishes to express appreciation for permission to quote from the following songs and poems: "Ten Thousand Men of Harvard" by A. Putnam and Murray Taylor, from *The Harvard Song Book*, copyright © 1966 by E. C. Schirmer Music Co., Boston, reprinted with permission. "Gaudeamus Igitur," traditional, from *The Harvard Song Book*, copyright © 1966 by E. C. Schirmer Music Co., Boston, reprinted with permission. "Duke of Earl," words and music by Earl Edwards, Eugene Dixon, and Bernice Williams, copyright © 1961, 1968 by Conrad Music, a division of Arc Music Corp., New York, used by permission. "Black Is the Color of My True Love's Hair," by J. J. Niles, G. Schirmer, Inc. "John Henry," traditional, arrangement by Bill Wood. "All My Trials," traditional, copyright © 1978 by Chandos Music ASCAP, used by permission. "Loop De Loop," by Teddy Vann and Joe Dong, copyright © 1962 by Tobi-Ann Music Publishing Corp., copyright assigned to Morris Music, Inc., Chappell & Co., Administrator, international copyright secured, all rights reserved, used by permission. "A Little Girl Lost," by William Blake, from *The Portable Blake*, Viking Press. "Walk Right In," by Gus Cannon and H. Woods, copyright 1930 by Peer International Corporation, copyright renewed © 1963 by Peer International Corporation, used by permission, all rights reserved. "I Want to Hold Your Hand," words and music by John Lennon and Paul McCartney, copyright © 1963 by Northern Songs, Ltd., London, England, sole selling agent Duchess Music Corporation (MCA), New

Cont'd. on page 278

SPLENDOR AND MISERY: A NOVEL OF HARVARD. Copyright © 1983 by Faye Levine. All rights reserved. Printed in the United States of America. No part of this book may be used or reproduced in any manner whatsoever without written permission except in the case of brief quotations embodied in critical articles or reviews. For information, address St. Martin's/Marek, 175 Fifth Avenue, New York, N.Y. 10010.

Design by Manuela Paul

Library of Congress Cataloging in Publication Data

Levine, Faye.
    Splendor and misery.

    "A St. Martin's/Marek book."
    I. Title.
PS3562.E896S6   1983   813'.54   82-17050
ISBN 0-312-75269-5

First Edition
10   9   8   7   6   5   4   3   2   1

Acknowledgments

My very sincere thanks are due to the members of the Harvard *Crimson,* past and present, who have been many of my dearest friends and who have helped me in innumerable ways. I couldn't possibly mention them all by name, but I would like particularly to thank J. Anthony Lukas, who came to my aid in a freedom-of-the-press case in India; Peter R. Kann, for information in his *Crimson* report on President Kennedy's last visit to Cambridge; R. Andrew Beyer, for permission to use a portion of his *Crimson* article on the Vernal Equinox; Grant M. Ujifusa, A. Douglas Matthews, and so many others, for specific encouragement; and Paul M. Barrett, M. David Tanzer, Wendy Wall, and others on the most recent *Crimson* executive board, for making *Crimson* archives accessible to me.

I would also like to thank Deane Lord of the Harvard News Office, William Bentinck-Smith of Harvard University Press, Nancy Griffin Jackson of *Harvard* magazine, Ann Maitland and Dorothy Kimball of the Radcliffe Club of New York, and Greg Lawless, editor of *The Harvard Crimson Anthology,* for their invaluable assistance and support.

As always, my agent Elaine Markson (and her assistants Geri Thoma and Raymond Bongiovanni) played a major part in bringing my work to light. In the telling of this story, real literary and emotional midwifery was done by Joyce Engelson, editor-in-chief of St. Martin's/Marek, for which I am profoundly grateful.

Thanks, too, to my friends 'Tascha, Pauline, Ken, T., John G., Mayer, JTS, the rest of the Il Nido/Dockery group, the waiters in the Hotel Chelsea restaurant, merchants of the North Village—especially Hank and Billy of Readers' Commercial Stationery on University Place—and members of Local 32B.

New York City
1982

257274

For the old *Crimson* gang

SPLENDOR
and
MISERY

Sarah Galbraeth had never had to worry about schoolwork, or getting dates for basketball games, or where her next meal was coming from, or whether her mom and dad loved each other. She was busy being princess of Mason City High School, in Cerro Gordo County, Iowa, a job which involved a) planning antiromantic themes for class proms, such as the Black Widow Waltz; b) writing satires of teachers to set to music at field days; c) organizing mass student petitions and walk-outs to protest actions by the board of education; and sometimes d) getting perfect test scores, DAR awards, debating championships, and so forth.

Her parents, who were no big achievers (they had met in the business program of Iowa City High, eloped on their second date and quit school together; now he was president of a small home construction company for which she kept the books), took Sarah's success philosophically. They thought she was also a nice kid, and that seemed to make the abnormal stuff all right.

Her teachers doted on her—though her favorite, Dr. Abramson, drew the line at her being school newspaper editor and student council officer at the same time.

And the boys asked her out, and talked to her on the phone, and told each other she led "a charmed life."

The afternoon Sarah was notified of her admission to college in the East, her best friend, Marianne Reuss, went into the girls' bathroom and wept. Marianne's father was a railroad man, her mother a telephone operator, and she was going to marry her boyfriend Dick after graduation and live with him on his farm in Keokuk. On the same day, Sarah's last and best high school boyfriend, Gabriel, the football captain, got himself bombed on Seagram's and popped the question to the captain of the cheerleaders.

Sarah had never been further East than Gary, Indiana. But Miss Demos, who taught a class in Plato, had told her her place was "in the Ivy League." And Sarah's father's lodge brother's wife, Mrs. Crane, had made Sarah a gift of a cherry-red cardigan (the first cashmere sweater the girl had ever touched) and said the best husbands were to be found in Cambridge, Massachusetts, at Harvard.

It was an idyllic time. The economy was stable. An old Harvard man, John Kennedy, was in the White House, having proposed the establishment of a "peace corps" in the week before his election. Sarah had no idea what Harvard was all about, except that it was something good, but she was game to look it over and give it a try.

At the end of a languid Indian summer, Sarah packed her things into a green canvas duffel bag her uncle had used in Korea and got into her father's commercial pickup truck to drive to the train. They rode together through the broad, flat Iowa countryside, past the stately plain silver-gray farmhouses Sarah loved so much. Ben Galbraeth was proud of his little girl; she would be the first in the family to be going off to school. He tipped his felt hat back on his head, and smiled at her with a shy dignity. She smiled back at him.

Sarah had filled a big purse with books and magazines to read on the trip to Boston, but she was too excited even to open it. She sat with her chin on her hand and her elbow on the train's grimy windowsill as the plains of Iowa and Illinois and Indiana and Ohio and Pennsylvania sped past and were replaced by the fishing coastline of New England, and the thrill in her breast kept her from sleeping.

"On your right"—the lad in the crimson V-neck was shouting, walking backward—"the first printing press in America was put into operation, in 1639"—the cluster of parents and freshmen oohed and aahed and made little clicks with their tongues—"and here the first Bible in the New World was printed. In what language, do you suppose?" A man in a vest suggested Dutch. "In Algonquin!" More oohs.

The new boy students in their jackets and ties, nearly overcome with pride, looked around surreptitiously to memorize their surroundings. The new girls sniffed happily. Mothers clutched at daughters, gingerly smoothing the Fair Isle pullovers and the nubbly putty cardigans that were so popular this season.

Sarah Galbraeth, in an outfit that featured purple knee socks, was gazing wide-eyed at the splendiferous panorama all around. Hot and dusty from the long train ride, she had dropped her foot locker and duffel off hastily at Radcliffe Quad, "the girls' part of Harvard," washed her long reddish-brown hair squeaky clean, and come running back down to the Square, and the Yard, and the Houses of Harvard itself.

As the Crimson Key guide pointed out the life-size statue of John Harvard sitting in front of University Hall in his knickers, Sarah turned her head the other way to follow the progress of a young woman in Bermuda shorts on a bicycle. With an effortless motion of the knees, the upperclasswoman bumped her bike down the curb of Harvard Yard and headed up Massachusetts Avenue toward Radcliffe.

"Looks okay," thought Sarah.

The guide was moving quickly now, pointing out white-steepled Memorial Church, warm and pure and inviting as your rural grandmother; the philosophy department, divided between a light building and a dark building; the president's modest residence; the library open only to boys. The year was 1961.

The architecture of the nation's oldest university came as a delicious surprise to the Midwestern high school girl. Bright blue fairy-tale spires and gold-domed bell towers rose along the river. The plain brick of Colonial America abutted every sort of ancestral European stone. In the middle of a half-dozen boring monoliths in the In-

ternational Style, an astounding Moebius-strip building was under construction. There was a Georgian gas station. And a gigantic, multicolored, ornate palace or church, looming magnificently like a Victorian dream of the Crimean War! Just a short walk across the neat paths from John Harvard's unpretentious post, through the tall elms and oaks (and how superbly confident all these walking students looked!), a terracotta monolith jutted above the earth in a shower of steps and a veil of pillars. There John Harvard's four hundred books had become six million.

Sarah looked at the arches, curved and pointed, and she thought about philosophy and science. She looked at the yellow clapboard houses and imagined herself inside, sipping beverages with wise men, discussing language and literature and the affairs of the day. She looked at the pillars and the steps leading up to the collection of six million books and she thought of her own amazing freedom to enter there, to run her country girl's hands along the ancient, tattered, numbered bindings, to sit awhile with youth and time in a little wooden carrel or alongside a great mural or unceremoniously on the floor, and there to Read, and Know.

Ah. This was a step beyond Mason City—!

Her first night in the brick and metal dorm, as Sarah walked back into the disorder of her small bedroom filled with luggage and clothes and unpainted furniture, she came upon her assigned roommate sitting stark naked on the gray plastic wing chair, casually eating currants out of a box.

"Bonsoir, Sarah," said the other girl, yawning and stretching and luxuriating and eating currants. Yvette Serre was from Paris. She had very short black hair in a jagged "pixie" style, languid hazel eyes, and a perfect body.

Sarah gulped. There had been plenty of nakedness in the locker rooms back home, but somehow the Iowa girls had hurried up and

showered and dressed without seeming to notice their own expanses of flesh, as if it were merely a transitional stage.

Sarah smiled, and said, "Hi," and fled downstairs to "the common rooms." There she met a gentler girl named Rosa Doe, a scholarship student from Toronto, who had a graceful, childlike figure, a smudged beauty in her face, and plump brown braids. Rosa whispered that the girl taking her turn at the switchboard this evening was a real live princess from Sweden named Christina.

They observed Christina. Her face was doll-like. Her sweater was sky blue and so soft. Her unspeakably fine blond hair curled around the crown of her head and expired in the most angelic tendrils around her neck. Rosa and Sarah whispered about how pretty she was, and what a thrill to have her in the dorm, and wondered what she was going to study.

Late in the evening a ragtag marching band from Harvard came by with a lot of brass and two glockenspiels, all laughter and high-spirited generosity, and stationed themselves under the living room windows and serenaded the new freshmen.

> Ten Thousand Men of Harvard
> Want victory today
> For they know that o'er old Eli
> Fair Harvard holds sway
> So then we'll conquer old Eli's men
> And when the game ends we'll sing again
> TEN THOUSAND MEN OF HARVARD
> Gained victory today!

"Hey, what's this?" said Sarah enthusiastically.

In answer to her question, a slim, high-colored girl with frizzy hair and a withering pout on her face looked up from *The Canterbury Tales* to reply: "Just Schneider's Band. Ignore them and they'll go away." Sarah wrinkled her nose and looked at this girl with amazement. She would learn that her name was Tui Burne-Jones ("Tui?"), that she came from California and had brought a yellow sports car with her, and that she was easily bored.

The night was clear and cool, the kind of September weather that makes you remember the summer and the lake and the evenings on the porch. All across the Quad girls were settling in, hauling and stowing and tiptoeing among the tin footlockers and green army duffel bags and luggage of every description. But everyone felt the pagan suggestion in the night, and they hung out of windows or looked for excuses to go out on errands. Some organized themselves into foursomes for bridge. Sarah and Rosa curled up in the dormitory dining room to chat. They felt they had a lot in common.

"What are they singing now?" Rosa asked. "It sounds like Latin."

"I can't make it out."

Virginia Morris knew. She had been bred Harvard and Radcliffe. Her grandparents had met here. Her favorite teacher at Miss Porter's had advised her about the various Harvard departments. So when her partner won the bid in diamonds, Virginia graciously ambled over from the near-caller's room to tell Sarah and Rosa that *"Illegitimum non carborundum"* meant "Don't let the bastards grind you down." She stood leaning against the doorjamb as she spoke.

Sarah admired this Virginia Morris. She was wearing ordinary clothes (it seemed to Sarah)—a creamy blouse under a neat sweater, a tweed skirt, loafers—and yet something about her appearance suggested years of special knowledge, enormous foresight, complex rules of coordination. There was something unusual about her broad, confident smile as well. Sarah hadn't known any rich people in Mason City.

Virginia, Sarah, and Rosa exchanged information about hometowns and schools. Then Virginia told the two other girls what they should expect from academic life.

"At the very top of every class," she said, "the brightest student will always be a boy."

"Really?" said Sarah. What an astonishing piece of information!

"Yes. Then after him will come all the girls."

"Hm!"

"Then all the rest of the boys—at the bottom."

"You're just kidding, right?" said Sarah.

Virginia smiled and shook her head no. "That's what they say!" she trilled. By then the hand had been played and Virginia's bridge partners were calling her back, and so she waved her fingers with a deft gesture, and vanished.

Much later that night, as Sarah was buttoning her cotton pajamas and climbing to the upper bunk to sleep, she imagined her entire previous life dropping away from her, and felt vertigo. The great friend of her childhood, Marianne Reuss—how they had danced and sung together!—they had even made up a religion together, blending Catholicism, Presbyterianism, and the evolutionism they had learned in biology class—how far away she was now, with her husband on the farm. Sarah wanted to keep Marianne close forever. But Harvard was a vortex she could no longer escape. From the effort to grasp these new things—Harvard Yard, the six million books, Yvette, the princess, the girl who played bridge and knew so much—Sarah's mind simply stopped. She began to think instead about tomorrow's breakfast.

In the hall outside their small room, Yvette Serre was curled up in a towel whispering into the telephone, its extension cord stretched to full length. The cord followed her out the door like a rumor.

The moon rose over Garden Street. Sarah dreamed she was a tiny girl sitting on the running board of a Studebaker, touching its big front fender. It was Daddy's car. But Daddy was nowhere to be seen. Mommy was driving away, too, in a Model-T stuffed with plywood and linoleum and a big porcelain bathtub. Then all at once Sarah was in a huge room, or barn, or amphitheater, or the place where she had been asked to sign her name fifty times today; and all along its dark walls were rows and rows of the Harvard Classics, dark leather gold-sealed volumes. In one corner of the big room she caught sight of two older people sitting beside a doorway, speaking to each other quietly. Sarah braced herself, and took a breath, and walked through the arching doorway beside which they sat.

She awoke refreshed and happy, smelling the sweet aroma of rolls and coffee from the kitchen two floors below.

When Sarah got back from opening services in the Congregational Church ("Radcliffe, now we *rise* to greet thee—!"), she found Yvette stretched out in the gray plastic chair, a light blue smock covering the liquid firmness of her young breasts, the sullen latency of her hips. The sunlight coming in through the window put strange lights in the French girl's black hair, and made her look like a wood spirit.

"Hi, Yvette," said Sarah, thankful for the other girl's deference to her modesty.

"Hel-lo, Sarah," said Yvette after a moment. She shifted her weight slightly.

Sarah dropped her notebooks with a plunk and settled down onto the bed. "Who was that great-looking man in the sunglasses you were with this morning?" she said.

Yvette lazily righted herself. "You think François is good looking? I don't know . . . But I love to hear him talk. He has such an interesting mind. He makes me feel so stupid. . . ."

Sarah considered this. It sounded, well, queer, to her. But the obvious fact (though they had not broached the subject) that Yvette was *not* a virgin, nor even—as some in Iowa did—*feigned* virginity, vested in the girl an awesome and ultimate authority in the matter of men. Indeed, earlier that day, as Yvette had pasted up Gauguin prints of Pacific islanders on the walls of their room, Sarah had watched her with respect, feeling she was in the presence of ancient wisdom.

"Did you meet him at the freshman mixer?"

"I would not be caught dead at 'the freshman mixer,' " said Yvette with a smile. "I met him on the Cape this summer." She leaned over for her pack of Gaulois on the windowsill.

Sarah thought this sounded okay. She pictured picnics, bonfires (like on Sprout Lake back home), groups, beer, introductions, laughter. The truth was somewhat more exotic. Yvette, finding herself seated next to the hip-looking foreign student at a play in Provincetown, had put her hand on the boy's thigh at the end of Act One and suggested they leave together.

"He's in arch sci," Yvette went on, now warming to the subject, lighting her cigarette. "He wants to build things on a new principle, a chain from above, actually, so that way you can go higher than with steel or concrete . . ."

"A chain from above! What does the chain hang from?"

"Oh, Sarah, don't be so—! I don't understand exactly either.

Maybe it's like a circus tent. Anyway, he's got a friend on the Prix de Rome committee and a tentative offer to build one in Chandigarh. And he's only a junior!"

"Gee . . ."

"I think I may be in love with him."

At this moment Rosa Doe came through the door, a bright yellow sweater on her shoulder. She looked small and round and neat, her clothes soft. And she said, "Hi, Sarah! Hi, Yvette!" so sweetly and cheerfully, though there were great black circles all around her dark eyes.

"Hi, Rosa," said Sarah.

"Whom do you love?" she asked Yvette brightly.

"Nobody, nothing." Yvette had become sullen again.

Rosa lowered her voice. "Oh, I'm sorry. See you both later," she said nearly in a whisper, backing out the door again gracefully.

"Merde. I offended her," said Yvette.

"Yeah. I think maybe," answered Sarah with a frown. "But, uh, you know, she told me this incredible story the other night about why her name is Doe . . ."

Yvette took a drag on the Gaulois. "Yes?"

"Well, she was born right at the end of the war, and when she was just a baby her parents had to run all across Europe with her. They had all these different sets of papers proving that their name was Pasternak, or Ferenczi, or Schmidt, or Pasteur, or whatever, and they had to hide under sacks of potatoes in a farmer's cart and stuff like that. When they finally got to Ellis Island, some American immigration official gave them the American name of Doe."

"Ah, yes. Doe . . . So where was Rosa born in effect?"

"Outside Babi Yar. Where they killed a lot of people. Now she lives in Toronto."

The French girl was silent for some time. "Well, I didn't know that." She extinguished her cigarette. "But you still don't go walking into somebody's room saying, 'Whom do you love?' "

Rosa had retreated downstairs to the room she shared with Carolee Davis. While Carolee lay in the shadow of the bunk poring over *The Revolt of the Masses,* Rosa was sitting with one leg dangling at her desk sewing a button onto her sweater. The two roommates had not spoken for some time when Sarah and Yvette came bursting in, full of smiles and small talk. They hovered about. Sarah asked what courses everyone was going to take.

Carolee snapped her book shut. She intended to major in Chinese or biochemistry, and would definitely take Kissinger's course in "Realpolitik." Carolee was very skinny. She had short nails, scraped knuckles, and a long, tight, blond pigtail down her back that made her look a little like the Chinese she was planning to study.

"I don't know *what* I'm going to take," admitted Rosa.

"Neither do I."

"Me either."

"Why don't we go see if we can get into the dorm kitchen?" Three faces lit up.

And so, with great stealth, Yvette, Sarah, and Rosa (but not Carolee) crept into the aluminum expanses of the now-abandoned dormitory kitchen, accomplishing this feat by means of a spatula slid along the clasp lock. In the kitchen they found only one edible item: three huge vats of dry and drying white bread. They wondered why such a great quantity of stale bread was being saved. But they swallowed their curiosity, and a good quantity of the bread, with a shrug.

This foray was to become a nightly ritual. Sarah, for one, would later look back upon the two years she spent in the brick dorm as having been fueled by dry, bent, absolutely rock-hard Tip-Top.

On a balcony perched precariously over Briggs & Briggs Music, and over J. August, clothiers to maharajahs for three hundred years, and over Leavitt & Peirce, tobacconists and keepers of the sports records, there sat this evening as the traffic wended its way back home to Somerville in the north and Boston in the east and Newton in the west, five sons of men who had wielded enormous power in this civilization and who would themselves wield it before long. Quietly smoking in the blue-gray Cambridge twilight, lifting occasionally the Porcellian Club's crystal for a sip of eighteen-year-old cognac, they had in common a faraway look in their eyes. As members of the most final of the final clubs, it was incumbent upon these carefully selected fellows to contemplate the passing scene without emotion. Handsome, square-jawed, all would have been leaders in any other group. They were from Groton, St. Paul's. One was an army veteran from Virginia, another the president of the motor sports club. A third presided over the Hasty Pudding's annual "theatrical." A fourth was on the *Lampoon*—he alone wore glasses.

Someday perhaps they would take up machine guns for the property owners or throw bombs with the Bolsheviks. But for now, there was time for thought. Below them on Massachusetts Avenue, the little artery between the Yard and the Houses, university life bubbled past innocently. Flâneurs strolled the length of the strip and then turned and strolled back, finally retiring with their *New York Times*es and their *New Republic*s into modest coffee shops. Young men in rubbed blue jeans and tweed jackets, their ties flung over their shoulders, their collars buttoned down, hastened to the mammoth lectures of Ec 1 or Gov 1. Girls rushed by in capes and boots, carrying woven Greek bags bouncing over bicycles.

Fred Aeschuylus (he was the Hasty Pudding theatrical chief) was remembering the last good upheaval. During the Latin Diploma Riots the year before, undergraduates had surged into these streets laughing and shouting to demand that their graduation documents continue to be inscribed in Latin, like the Mass, as they had been for centuries. An admirable cause. And one that had failed. Diplomas were now in English, and doubtless would be forever and ever. Aeschuylus sighed an imperceptibly small sigh—which was of course lost in the great geniality of his show business demeanor. Transmuting, as he had learned to do so many years before, even this faintest sigh into something he could use for self-perfection, an emotional muscular strength, he merely raised an eyebrow so very minutely and lifted his cognac.

Aegisthus, Anthony, Alabaster, and Smythe were thinking about riots too, as it happened. It was the kind of thought that often occurred to such men as they rested here overlooking Mass. Ave. at the pinnacle of the eastern American way. This Harvard that spread herself all around them so exquisitely baroque, so charmingly Colonial, so amusingly Gothic—was also modern. And there was the rub. Each year more pubbies were being admitted, more Jews, more foreigners, more girls, more of them. This would be Harvard's legacy to the future. A precious thing, precious beyond measure, handed over to a simian. When they thought of this, a rare fire burned behind those carefully trained glances. Apes in the Halls of Caracalla! Perhaps they would have to riot themselves.

But for now there was still smoke, there was still wine, there were still the clean and lovely girls who knew what to wear to look like women and be beautiful, and who knew what their role would be should they be so lucky as to inherit one of us; there was still some kind of work to be done, some kind of money to be made.

Sarah Galbraeth was standing for a moment across the street at the gates of Widener Library, from which spot she could glance up at the balcony where the Porcellians sat. She could see the tall, handsome boys etched like gods against the darkening sky, the latest generation bred to nobility, silent. She could try to fathom what was in their hearts. And, like them, she could dream of the ineffable values of Harvard, and try to embrace them, for a moment.

But perhaps Sarah should not stand there too long. Perhaps she should leave the Porcellians to themselves, stealing away quickly, and be about her own course—lest she fall under their spell, and remain at their feet.

Sarah had her hands full figuring out what to make of a different sort of aristocrat. In her honors gen ed class she had met one Billy Clemens, the son of a very famous American writer. He was a small boy, given to swathing himself in many extraneous layers of clothing, who had a delightfully funny wit and a knack for understanding the arcane requirements of the writing instructor. When Sarah got the chance to meet Billy Clemens's two roommates one day at lunch in the Yard, she had a sudden and strong first impression that these boys might have grown up to be Porcellians themselves, but for an extra gene or reflex they bore for morality.

Billy's roommates were strikingly different from him physically, being tall and blond and athletic. Robin Palmer, introduced as "Robbo," had a cherubic pink and fair complexion and a mop of golden curls. James Winthrop DeWitt, called "Jims," was an elongated version of Robbo: taller and thinner, his hair a paler yellow, his eyes a paler blue, his skin almost translucent.

Like Billy, his two roommates came from illustrious families—diplomats and jurists, spokesmen for the civic and the literary. And the burden of tradition weighed significantly upon them, and the Great Chain of Being rested on their shoulders, and they felt themselves at one with the directions that had been set out for them, at home on the planet and in Cambridge.

And yet, even in these days when it was considered legitimate to be virile and strong, this particular group of friends thought a great deal about the dominance of one man over another, and worried themselves considerably about how the cruder and more awful manifestations of this unavoidable reality might be ameliorated. They sought to defend in their own minds their right to the wealth they possessed—by means of constant self-examination: an ardent and sometimes even painful quest for their responsibility to others. They sat together having lunch under the falling elm leaves discussing the proper uses of wealth and power, the ethics of economics. And all this they did with an elaborate respectful courtesy that Billy and Robbo had learned in a series of progressive boarding schools, and had taught to their friend Jims from Andover one hectic summer bicycling through England.

Indeed, these three boys, different as they were in appearance, had something strongly in common, a certain quality of character. Or perhaps it was the high, fine vibrations of sensibility they gave off when deeply engrossed in conversation together in the Freshman Union that had already caused some of the other boys in their class to nickname them the "Ariels." Though Sarah was not to run into them again until later in her college career, she was intrigued by them, and now and then wondered about them, and asked herself how they would fit into the scheme of things in Mason City.

October. Monday morning. Ten o'clock. The eager, confused, pompous, assured, cynical, conscientious, ambitious, hungry, sated, dissenting, idolatrous, miserable, curious, sober, and arrogant students of Harvard have gathered themselves to within earshot of the thought experts, their shining blank notebooks open in front of them like protective charms. The drizzly October wind ruffles the last few leaves in the Yard and the scarf of a latecomer, running.

Rosa Doe was sitting in the front row of Erik Erikson's course in the life cycle, in the astounding Moebius-strip building. Her smoky eyes were on the professor's flowing white hair and beard, his face a cross between Santa Claus and the bogeyman. The class was listening attentively. The topic of discussion today was to be "the difference between boys and girls."

Billy, Robbo, and Jims were seated next to one another listening to Professor Jameson discuss the Byzantine Empire from A.D. 284 to A.D. 1453. Today they were hearing about how the piety of the Byzantines had led them to riot in the streets over the nature of God and man. Something about Byzantium appealed to the Ariels. The three boys took sparse notes in a minimalist hand, with distant, humorous, altruistic smiles on their faces.

Sarah Galbraeth was high up in the back of a steep amphitheater amid a contingent of girls from Holmes Hall. Below, Nobel laureate George Wald was scribbling on a board the chemical equations for breathing, and for the interaction of sunlight and plants, and for heredity. The girls were scribbling same into their notebooks, many with grimaces on their faces. They hated nat sci. Nightly they would gather in desperate groups around the dormitory dining room tables to try collectively to decipher the dictated diagrams.

Sarah loved it. She loved George Wald.

"I do not denigrate man!" he was exclaiming now exuberantly, his eyes blazing and his cheeks flushed. "I celebrate the molecule!"

After class Sarah bumped into Yvette shopping in the Coop. Yvette was not happy with the survey introduction to French literature. "It's stupid to be dividing things into 'Romanticism,' and 'Classicism,' and 'Parnassians,' " she grumbled. "There's no art within an art movement!"

"How's François?" said Sarah.

"We just had coffee. He thinks I'm a racist because I don't want to marry him and go live in Dakar."

Together they picked out some brightly colored burlap to make curtains out of.

Carolee was practicing her Chinese aloud in the dormitory basement, sitting in a wired-off cubicle in the concrete netherdom, making eerie sounds.

Tui Burne-Jones had not yet decided to go to classes.

Rosa Doe and Billy Clemens were both members of the Bach Society, and even though they were freshmen they were given parts on the cello and violin respectively. It was not long before Billy fell in love with Rosa's interpretation of the "Wachet Auf." They went out for coffee, and then to a couple of concerts, and then Billy asked Rosa to go to the theater.

"Some people think the theater has no relation to our lives," he apologized. "But other people think it's a code for life, an encapsulation of the culture and affects all of us, you know what I mean?"

Rosa didn't know, really, but she was delighted to go to the theater. It was Cambridge's most formal public social activity.

Billy arrived at the girls' dorm too early and paced around the near-callers' room for a while until Yvette discovered him and sailed upstairs to fetch Rosa. Rosa had been ready for a half-hour, nestled into a window seat reading Weber's *Theory of Social and Economic Organization*. At the sight of Rosa's beautiful bosom in a fuzzy yellow sweater, Billy became quieter than usual.

The evening was cold, dry, and sparkling. The wind buffeted them in common. But they gave the temper of the air different meanings. Billy was thinking of glamorous New York City winter, of the Plaza Hotel. Rosa was thinking about Mommy and Daddy cold in Canada. They might have been two statues in the middle of a frozen lake.

At the Loeb they sat through *The Beggar's Opera* happily, laughing and applauding, and saying things like, "Look, there's the *Crimson* reviewer. He always comes late." And, "What I'd like to know is how these reviewers would perform themselves." And, "Everyone said it was so good I was sure I'd hate it, but no, it really is good."

After a cup of coffee in the Blue Parrot in Harvard Square they walked back to Radcliffe in awkward silence, having chewed through the enamel of their date, the raw nerve hanging in the air before them, scarifying their thoughts. It had gotten late and dark. The moment was coming. It seemed everyone had deserted the little residential street and left them utterly alone, with nothing to say, their footsteps not jibing.

As they passed the old Continental Hotel at the edge of the Common, Billy took a drastic step. "Come here, I want to show you something," he mumbled, propelling Rosa (who was startled but favorably impressed by the bold deed) into the hotel lobby and on through to a deserted ballroom where upended chairs were stacked upon tables. Rosa looked at Billy. She felt as though she'd been dropped onto a desert island with Alfred E. Newman. It was a curious but not unappealing sensation.

Billy drew Rosa closer to him and kissed her with a terrible gentleness, as if each kiss were transmitting a whole complete sentence of endearment.

"Is this the fuzzy yellow bliss I have been dreaming about? Can she really be here and now in my arms?" he thought.

"Um, of course I think you're very sweet and smart and nice and everything. But I just don't feel that way about you," she thought.

Soon his arms, wound gingerly around her, began to close in. He put his hand on her neck. She felt his breath. In a flash his touch had become repellent.

"No! Stop!" she said, pulling herself away.

"But why?" he said, apologetic, understanding, hurt. As soon as the words were out he knew it was the wrong thing to say. Desire had churned up inside of him. But his tenderness and intelligence made any further approach unthinkable.

Rosa said nothing.

"Okay," Billy answered himself softly. He walked away. An

immense relief washed through the girl. She felt she could easily re-
sume the flow of conversation now. But he didn't seem to want to.

They returned to the Quad in silence. Billy was in awe of sex. It
was more than just a manifestation of romantic love, it was a primeval,
bestial force or law, always promising to devour and destroy polite
civilization.

"I'll call you sometime—if I'm in the mood," he said gruffly
when they reached the dorm, and stalked off. Rosa felt a momentary
pang that Billy seemed to be mad at her. She preferred his blissful
adoration. But she entered the cozy girls' residence filled with light and
activity and didn't think of him again that night.

A
t Harvard in those days there
were more than four boys for every one girl at Radcliffe. This had its
inevitable bizarre social and sexual effects. "There aren't enough girls
to go around!" a freshman boy would observe unhappily. "Oh, yes
there are," an upperclass wit would reply. "You just have to share."

Sarah Galbraeth was not beautiful. But boys didn't seem to
notice this when they listened to her laugh or saw her stand up in class
to say some quite outlandish thing with perfect ingenuousness. She had
her Irish mother's wonderful conviction that everything was going to
turn out all right, and her kind-hearted Scottish father's deceptive
facade. Neutral, even drab at first glance, like a Harris tweed, Sarah
revealed upon closer attention a personality that twinkled pink, yellow,
purple, bright blue, teal, loden green, khaki, olive, slate, red, rust.

"The image of the Renaissance," she piped up in a hum section,
"was the image of a giant man. *The Prince. The Courtier. Gargantua.* And
this giant man was homosexual." She got a D in the course, and made
three coffee dates.

With her new friends, Sarah strolled through the merchants'
bustle of Mass. Ave., ending up in Albiani's or the Waldorf, to sit long

hours comparing backgrounds, ideas, impressions, goals, over chipped china cups of black coffee.

And oh, those touching conversations: breathless, bright, all faculties poised like Rough Riders on San Juan Hill at the face, in the eyes. A hand with a gold watch would make a gesture to mark or decorate an effect. There would be some business with the cups and later with the bill. Throughout, there was speech: tripping, continuous, defensive, melodious speech, the fragile equilibrium of the presenting of arms. And so it went, this game of youth, through the space of an hour or a few hours, a date or a few dates, until some kind of death obliterated the hope of love. And then it was all over. Though the closing salvos might take up quite a bit of additional time.

That fall Sarah flurried around campus meeting people and doing things with a wonderful unself-consciousness that crowned all her efforts with pleasure. She sponsored a resolution in the Freshman Council supporting the Peace Corps; she was defeated, but the debate was lively. She joined the student liberal wing of the Democratic party. She attended open houses and mixers where she met so quickly and so easily so many young men that her parents would have considered good beaus that she quite reeled from the abundance of it all. A former JV cheerleader for the Mason City Mohawks, Sarah went to every Harvard home football game.

In some ways those Saturday afternoons were the season's noblest times of all. The crowds crossing the bridge to Soldiers Field made a solemn procession, and even if Sarah were on the arm of a fellow from say, Pennypacker, she remained excitedly aware that all these thousands made up one Harvard. She and her date would sit high in the stands in the freshman section and cheer for the yards won and the punts that drove deep, and thrill at the drum rolls and music of the touchdowns. At halftime the marching band arranged itself in silly shapes: a dollar sign, a hypodermic needle. Their shows were funny—but still Sarah enjoyed best her bird's-eye view of the game itself: the distant eroticism of huge men in fight-smeared uniforms, their faces smudged with grease. As the season wore on, the collegians consoled themselves for the cold with thick knit mufflers, little silver flasks of rum, and Elsie's Specials dripping Thousand Island dressing into white waxed paper.

When she crossed with the ten thousand other Harvardmen

back over Anderson bridge heading for aftergame parties in boisterous suites, a certain phrase of music would always come into Sarah's head:

> *Gaudeamus igitur*
> Eb   Fm

> *Juvenes   dum   sumus.*
> BbEbBb Eb   Eb

Brahms had put this melody into his *Academic Festival Overture,* but the song and the sentiment were far older.

> *Gaudeamus igitur, juvenes dum sumus.*
> *Gaudeamus igitur, juvenes dum sumus.*
> *Post jucundam juventutem,*
> *Post molestam senectutem,*
> *Nos habebit humus, nos habebit humus.*

> *Vivat academia, vivant professores.*
> *Vivat academia, vivant professores. . . .*

> Let us therefore rejoice while we are young.
> Let us therefore rejoice while we are young.
> After the delight of youth,
> After the vexation of age,
> The earth will have us, the earth will have us.

Strangely enough, the word "academia" rang in Sarah's ears more beautifully even than the word "Harvard." In her mind's eye she saw far older schools caught up in the harmonics of this melody. She saw the stony medieval universities of Paris and Bologna and Krakow, old when fair Harvard, the pride of the Colonies, was young; she saw the old schools where tutors wore high hats and spoke in the name of still older traditions, traditions even then ancient and sacred; she saw the old schools where first the bohemian youth ran wild in cobbled streets among rats and whores to challenge the traditions and the tutors, to kick them out on their ear and try to derive the old values anew. . . .

In Pennypacker or Wigglesworth or Grays there was always beer and cold cuts, joking, necking, *veritas* banners and mugs and cap-

tain's chairs, and someone's roommate cleaning up a spill good-
naturedly.

"I want a woman!" somebody would be shouting, as Sarah
entered with her date.

Nestor Schwarz was lounging
against the door to the Adams House poolroom entertaining the usual
court of the admiring and curious. He knew everyone in the House. He
was a campus figure. Right now he was holding forth on Norman
Mailer and redemption through "intercourse; intercourse with oceanic
climax; coming in waves not of love, but of something between lust
and pure aestheticism . . ." There was a spot of pink in his cheeks and
something evanescent and alluring in his face. The jet black of his hair
was highlighted strikingly, even frightfully, by a streak of white across
one eyebrow, caused, it was said, by a childhood disease. He was wearing a brown and cream Mexican sweater but did not seem to be encap-
sulated by it, as some were by their suit jackets. His lean, flickering
nervousness intruded into the throbbing life of others without warning,
and they either succumbed in a kind of heady ecstasy or hated him. At
the periphery of the entourage a smaller boy in a large, round-shoul-
dered coat and tweed cap was staring at him warily. Nestor focused on
the hat of Billy Clemens.

"Nice hat, Billy," he remarked in a different tone. "I saw three
of them today in Lowell Lec."

The smaller boy frowned, trying to think of a response.

Nestor went on immediately. "But yours is the most authentic."

Billy brightened, giddy on the vapor of Nestor's changing
attitudes.

Nestor had an instinct for manipulation. He did it without
thought. He tackled great Harvard itself with the same kind of attitude dancing—and scarcely a care for the great enterprise of informa-
tion-gathering or the cultivation of scholarship. He managed the
extraordinary feat of getting all A's by attending only the first few

lectures of a course, scribbling down the professor's pet phrases and jargon, and then regurgitating these key words into his exam books strung together with connectives and transitional remarks. It was an effective system. It flattered the faculty into temporary idiocy. Of course Nestor learned nothing. What he knew of the history of drama he knew from conversations with other scoffers in the field. He never went to the library. It was too lonely.

But there was plenty of company in the Adams House poolroom, and when Nestor wasn't acting in a play on the Loeb main stage he could generally be found there. Now he decided to settle down to a game and a bet. Some of his audience dispersed. The hard-core pool players bantered as Nestor chalked up his cue and peered down its length. Tall, thin, bent over the table, all his considerable charisma now engrossed in the laws of felt-covered geometry, he cut a compelling figure. Sometimes a half-smile would play over his sensuous mouth. But always there was a feeling of flickering darkness in his eyes and something threatening in his slump, so different from the muscular exuberance of the athlete. Nestor was adept at pool. He often won money from an upperclassman known as the Snake. But this only rankled him the more. What he wanted was to be perfect, to run all the balls forever and have people drop dead in cosmic envy orgasm at his feet. He wanted victory at this subterranean game and all games, victory total and illicit, at whatever cost.

Sarah had heard of the "final clubs," but she didn't give them much thought. At Yale, they said, the secret societies of Skull and Bones and the rest were housed in buildings that resembled nothing so much as tombs, the better to inspire dread and submission. But at Harvard the private little male social groupings arranged themselves inconspicuously behind locked unmarked doors at street level, and, as far as Sarah could tell, inspired derision as often as respect.

A public schoolie from the Midwest, Sarah found herself being "rushed" by the campus media organizations, plied with beer and pretzels, and encouraged to "come out for the competition." The radio station wanted her. But, beamed from the basement of the funny-looking Civil War Memorial and received as often as not on dormitory radiators and pipes, WHRB seemed to be a bit ephemeral. The year-book was also interesting, and admirably permanent. But it had a limited circulation and a slowish pace.

When Sarah entered by chance the brick and stone *Crimson* building at 14 Plympton Street, she knew from the first moment that she had found her place. Energy rippled through the ramshackle news-room, its floors littered with crumpled yellow scratch sheets, its walls an amazement of graffiti, engravings, posted notices, complex internal communications. The editor standing on a desk beside one of many heavy office typewriters, talking to the assembled crowd, was solid. He wore thick glasses, from behind which his eyes twinkled. "You'd have to be crazy to come out for this rag . . ." he began, and continued in like vein, wonderfully crabby and satirical, the perfect image of the hardened journalist.

"You come out for the *Crimson,*" rasped Eddie O'Brien, "and you throw away all possibility of a formal education. Your fellow stu-dents will mistrust you. Your professors will wonder why you slept through their exams. The deans will make a note to watch you. And why? I ask you. For what?" He winked at Sarah.

"Since 1873 the *Crimson* has been gathering and repeating hear-say. That's the news board. On the ed board they do more important things, like write scathing attacks on compulsory sophomore tutorial for credit in the geography department. On 'the busy board' they solicit advertising and line their pockets. And if there's anyone dumber and less principled than a news reporter, it's a news-photo type.

"Interested in any of these fields? Mentally unbalanced? Re-jected by the Fly? Then the *Crimson* is for you. Have some beer."

Eddie O'Brien stepped down from the desk and helped himself to a Bud, falling in easily with a group of older reporters and editors. By this time Sarah had fallen in love with the wry managing editor—and had decided to go out for the paper.

And so for the next three months Sarah abandoned all else and threw herself, with all her old princess-of-Mason-City-High-School in-tensity, into the *Crimson* "comp." She learned an imposing array of acronyms relating to newspaper work (such as RIITPOTME, meaning "red ink is the prerogative of the managing editor"), hung out day and night in the irremediably sloppy newsroom, and fetched as seldom as chivalry would allow the sandwiches that the older editors required. Her first printed item was about Schneider's Band. It contained four mistakes of fact in three inches of copy. But the fellow who was night editor for the evening doted on it, and her, anyway, since (as he said) she was just so sweet and impressionable and naive.

Sarah didn't want to let it go at that. She sat down next to her mentor Eddie, the managing editor, who often began his sports stories with the words "Hey, gang!"

"Why is it so important to get the *facts* right," she asked him, "as long as you get the *idea* right?"

"The thing about facts, Sarah Galbraeth," replied Eddie, twinkling, "is that we can never know what *really* happened. So getting 'the facts' right is just a good bet on the truth. An accurate fact will suggest something to your readers—we can't know exactly what, of course—which will be in some way harmonious with what really happened. Their conclusions based on your report will be more or less sound."

"You can count on EOB for the answer," remarked a tall reporter in a cowboy hat admiringly. "EOB is OOTG."

Sarah wrinkled her nose.

"One of the greats."

The girls in her dorm had elected Sarah to the Freshman Council, but Sarah had found that all-female activity tedious. Now the girls were beginning to grow suspicious of her other life on the newspaper. Yvette complained to a boy she'd met in Phil 1, Nestor Schwarz, that her roommate was a square.

Sarah was undaunted. Her feelings for the *Crimson* were in the realm of the absolute. The boys (and the few girls) she had met there seemed to her superlatively dashing and brilliant. Of a sociological turn of mind, she quickly separated them into subgroups. There was the self-styled "shadow cabinet," the intellectual elite, who made believe they had no real powers but rather stood behind a secret, mystical, diplomatic throne of Christendom. Then there was an aristocratic left, chummy with Kennedy and Camelot, who spoke confidently of national affairs and would soon be moving into positions of public responsibility. Then there were the future publishers and *New York Times* reporters, a fourth estate, eternally in competition with the forces of government. And then there were the swashbuckling reds. Sarah loved them all, every one. She loved them with an exuberant, charmed innocence. When she looked at a boy, ego and skin and perhaps even a layer of muscle fell away in a consummation of pure union. She loved George Durbey, who had the most terrible stammer and lisp, and was generally treated badly on that account, and talked with him for hours—for George was as intelligent and gritty as the rest, and, a captain in Army ROTC, he rewarded Sarah's sympathy with anecdotes of military first-aid tricks.

"Oh, yes, you're right, Sarah," said Eddie O'Brien one afternoon. "All these big healthy guys think they're going to rule the world." She nodded, her eyes shining. "But," Eddie went on, "is that good?"

In counterpoint to this metaphysical orgy there was, indeed, the business of putting out a paper. "Do you guys want to play around, or do want to put out a paper?" The man who said that would be Art Hopkins, ageless and venerable linotyper, the last of a generation to work with hot lead smelted anew each evening, the repository of the *Crimson*'s operative wisdom.

"Eddie!" Sarah yelled. "Do we want to put out a paper?"

"Oh, we have to put out a paper," O'Brien replied solemnly. "People need to read the notice column."

"Come on, EOB," chided the tall reporter. "You know nobody reads anything but the sports page."

"This is not true," said Eddie. "People also like to know which plays have pretty girls in them."

There were of course a few who believed that the main function of the *Crimson* was to monitor university policy. The outgoing editorial chairman was running a major series of editorials criticizing Nathan Pusey, the college president. Earlier in his career, the same fellow had engineered the removal of the chapel doors at Exeter. These behaviors were seen by Eddie O'Brien and the rest of the *Crimson* as only mildly amusing stunts or games, or disapproved of outright. Nowhere in the country at this time did college students truly believe they could talk back to adults.

In the days of Eddie O'Brien the *Crimson* was famous mostly for its satire. The *Lampoon,* the official college humor magazine, had degenerated into a mannered, sissyish nihilism. But in the *Crimson,* Eddie wrote: "Yale. Say it loud and there's music playing. Say it soft and it's almost like praying." A classics major made up a crossword puzzle with esoteric Greek and Latin definitions. And the rival *Lampoon*'s treasured totem, an ibis, was mysteriously stolen from *Lampoon* Castle, only to appear in the pages of the *Crimson* photographed in front of exotic international backgrounds. The *Crimson* also either uncovered or invented complementary Find-a-Bird and Lose-a-Bird conspiracies, the doings of which were reported on in great detail.

Sarah's first triumph followed upon her stationing herself conspicuously in an orange jersey in the Freshman Union, the lone girl among twelve hundred boys, where she asked as many as would stop whether they approved or disapproved of the laundry and linen distribution system. Her report in the paper the next day under the euphonious headline "Half Freshmen Questioned Veto Depots" provoked some merriment. The tall reporter from the far West given to wearing cowboy hats and boots fell in love with her.

Sarah and the cowboy went out on dates in his rattly '53 Chevy. They went to drive-in movies in the opposite direction from Boston and then stopped and drank coffee from paper cups. He didn't like Harvard particularly, or Boston, or the Northeast. He told her he couldn't stand *Crimson* faculty parties, but always stood around tongue-tied. Sarah understood what he was talking about. Cocktail parties made her tongue-tied too. But as to whether she loved Harvard or not, she thought maybe she did.

And always in his car, on Storrow Drive and on the ride back home—racing to beat the one o'clock curfew like Cinderella—they listened to the AM radio. A certain zanily confident tune had been number one in the Boston area for more than a month.

Duuk Duuk Duuk
Duuk of Earl Duuk Duuk
Duuk of Earl Duuk Duuk
Duuk of Earl Duuk Duuk . . .

and on like that in the background, while in the foreground Gene
Chandler sang:

> As I wander through this land
> Nothing can stop
> Duke of Earl.

The cowboy and Sarah loved that song. It reminded them of
home (Harvard students didn't listen to popular music) and gave
Sarah an idea. For two days she stationed herself in front of the wide
arched doorway to Sever Hall, beyond which academic schedules and
notices covered the walls of the old brown wood corridor, and there, in
a mock-serious tone and with a distraught face, she said to every student who passed by, "Excuse me, but can you tell me who is the Duke
of Earl?" Their answers were riotously funny. They made up whole
British lineages. They begged pardon for being in physics. Out of three
hundred and fifty Harvard types, fewer than a hundred recognized the
peer for a tune. To complete her study, Sarah collared somewhat more
than one hundred teenagers from Rindge Tech and Cambridge High
and Latin, the neighborhood high schools, who daily cut through the
Yard on their way to the subway—and sure enough, just about a hundred percent of them were familiar with the famous Duke.

When her Duke of Earl article appeared in the *Crimson*, Sarah
suddenly found herself a celebrity. Ph.D. candidates incorporated her
work into their theses. Everyone was glad to see her when she walked
through the *Crimson* door. The hardened journalist Eddie O'Brien was
even a little concerned about it. Proud of his protégé, he looked at her
from his managing editor's chair in the corner, scratched his slightly
balding head, and said, "If you're a legend when you're a freshman,
Sarah Galbraeth, what are you going to be when you're a senior? An
institution?"

As he said this he was dummying another story of hers onto the
page. Sarah was so happy she bumped into the wall on her way out.

Blissful, ecstatic, riding her bicycle through the snow, Sarah
wrote a continuous stream of stories about Halloween and Christmas
and Exam Period, about the World Not Ending Yet This Morning
(contrary to astrologers' predictions), about Radcliffe business and
Teddy Kennedy. She wrote little sonnets about daylight savings time

and to announce new *Crimson* competitions. She couldn't ask Yvette in all innocence how French 20 was without Yvette backing away and replying sullenly, "Why do you want to know? Are you going to write an article about it?"

And when it was time, Sarah was initiated into the ranks in a formal ceremony. Paralyzed with terror, she was to be night editor of the paper for the first time, alone till dawn with all the responsibility for getting the stories together and safely into print so that six big folded pages could fall with a dull thud against the doors of sleeping Harvard students the next morning. This was the test.

Or so she thought. Frightened enough by the work to be done, Sarah, wearing her best Hawaiian blouse, took her place at 7:00 P.M. behind the round table in the corner by the stairs to the print shop. Almost immediately, she started thinking about Eddie. He had made the dummy she was to execute this evening, and would return later to write a sports story. Now Eddie had a longstanding mock feud with the football team. He liked to impugn both their intellect and athletic ability. Once he had sworn they had no chance (against Dartmouth), and offered to eat his words if they proved him wrong. Well, the Crimson eleven beat Dartmouth, and the next day Eddie O'Brien obligingly printed a big picture of himself chomping on his own front page. Sarah wished he were back, so he could help. But Eddie did not return.

Sarah kept glancing at the clock on the newsroom wall. Nine o'clock. *Crimson* editors and reporters were wandering in and out of the building to write, eat, hang out, browse in the Comment Books, pitch wads of yellow paper into the wastebaskets. But no Eddie. Ten o'clock. People settled into the ratty leather sofas to talk seriously. Still no Eddie. Eleven o'clock! Quite aside from the story he was supposed to be writing and the hole there would be in the page without it, where the hell was he?

Around midnight the cowboy ran in with a couple of other editors.

"EOB's been beaten up! Some jocks got him! He's in the hospital!"

Sarah froze. Trembling, she held on to the ruled page in front of her, but no more work was forthcoming. The story was plausible. A vision of Eddie wrapped up in gauze, his arms and legs in traction, filled her imagination. She loved this man, though she had never told anyone about it. No one on the *Crimson* knew. No one in the dorm knew.

Elizabeth Chase, a senior editor Sarah much admired and a good friend of Eddie's, whispered to her, "Go to the ladies room." Obediently, she went.

In the dark, graffiti'd bathroom Sarah wept with all her heart. She wept so hard she didn't look in the mirror, she didn't sit down on the hard couch. She just stood there and wept, forgetful of the *Crimson* and its rituals, forgetful of what this evening was supposed to signify. In a few minutes Elizabeth Chase came in and pulled her out. There, walking down the angled stairs from the sanctum, typewriter and yellow paper in his arms, was a sheepish Eddie.

"I'm okay, Sarah," he said.

"He's okay," they all said. "Ha ha."

"You are not! I don't believe it!" she gasped. And then they were all hugging her, Elizabeth and the cowboy and the two other editors. Eddie put his hand on her arm. They knew, they must have all known, Sarah thought, her tears rushing out once again. But the shock of this most intimate exposure was made right somehow by the equally strong and unexpected realization of the *Crimson* editors' collective understanding and love. And Sarah was moved by this and filled with a strange joy and confidence. Her tears dried into a smile and she guessed she had been initiated.

The *Crimson* was put to bed that night with no further mishap, and the next day's paper carried a nice long sports story by Eddie O'Brien (which he had written in the sanctum during his supposed hospitalization) and a brief note announcing the election to the staff of Sarah Galbraeth.

One day Jims DeWitt had stuck his pale blond head into the *Crimson* newsroom, and gone back to his friends with the news that the place was "unwarm." Pressed for details by Robin Palmer, the boy reported that the editor acted awfully self-important, that the people had a repellent "gung-ho" attitude, that status seemed to be a major concern.

Of all the three Ariels, James Winthrop DeWitt was, in some ways, the fiercest moralizer. He came from the wealthiest background among them, and had grown up and summered and vacationed in neighborhoods his fellow students at Andover had found prestigious. And yet he had stood back from his classmates at that high-pressured preparatory school, had noted with disapproval that the grandson of an exceedingly renowned World War I general was a bully and a homosexual, and somehow he had become a dissenter. He refused to take a seat in a crowded train or bus until every other person in the car was seated. He abhorred "self-indulgence" in play as in food and drink. He was deeply embarrassed that a relative had caused a Harvard building to be named after himself. His roommates guessed that some of this might be a throwback to Jims's Puritan ancestry. But Jims himself laughingly referred to his own predilections as "just Jims being perverse."

Robbo was in agreement with him as to this matter of the *Crimson*. School in the Berkshires had been nothing if not warm. Both boys understood the heartbreak of the prestige structure.

They had heard something about *Crimson* "initiations" as well, and agreed that they were cruel. "I would never subject myself to something like that," remarked Jims.

"And yet I suppose they're not actually inhuman," said Robbo, sitting on the arm of the sofa. "I mean, they don't get naked or put on animal masks over their heads or sing nasty songs or do things they would be ashamed to talk about later. . . ."

When Billy Clemens came in from class and ascertained what they were talking about, he too agreed. Billy was a Taoist. "He who is fearless in being timid will stay alive," he said. And the curlicue lines under his blue eyes made their special, carnival smile.

After a while Sarah came around to the opinion that the *Crimson* wasn't really in the business of printing news at all. It was a medium for arcane outpourings of stream of consciousness oracles every night for the eyes only of fifty or so scribal initiates. On the esoteric level there were, to be sure, the mundane writings in the daily pages. But much more important than these were the dialogues and colloquia and feuds that burgeoned from every topic that appeared in print, and were expounded upon and developed in signed comments each day at length by the other *Crimson* writers. And so every topic of interest to even one of their group exfoliated in all the various Open and Closed Comment Books ranged on the ledge under the clock, and in the brains of all their number. And these written discussions and debates were characterized by all the wit and pathos and frightening brilliance of a set of minds still young and healthy and free from the obligations of family and domicile.

The *Crimson* was no newspaper, it was the house organ of the Pythagorean temple.

Its interests were Truth, Beauty, and Virtue.

You smile?

Well, yes, there was always Foote.

On the street below the Porcellian balcony walked Thaddeus P. Foote in an Edwardian-cut Sherlock Holmes cap and cape and goatskin gloves. He was a red man, with a mane of wiry red hair on his head and an enormous bushy red beard and mustache, a physical anomaly of a man such as did not often appear in a Harvard class and never looked quite in place there.

This afternoon he was as usual hatching a plot.

Poring over his own thoughts methodically, a dim pleasure veiling his green eyes, he considered scaring the gullible readers of the *Crimson* with a story that the squirrels in Harvard Yard were rabid, warning them to carry umbrellas in self-defense. That way every nervous umbrella spotted the next day would be a token of his power. What fun!

In less than a year in Cambridge Thaddeus P. Foote had, through diverse means, won for himself the reputation of shaman. Once he had sent a letter to the University Health Services signed with the name of the president of the *Lampoon,* begging for psychiatric help. Since he was majoring in Ancient Indo-European Languages he was good at producing babble that sounded like speech; on the strength of this Foote enjoyed putting on a turban, setting himself up with a phony "interpreter," and passing himself off as a maharaja or yogi, à la the Marx Brothers. His friends in the psychology and botany departments were helpful too. He had adeptly structured more than one route by which he could legally obtain marijuana from the federal government for "experimental" and "testing" purposes.

There was no end to the man's imaginative duplicity. He could mesmerize with stolen stationery. He played practical jokes on an epic scale. It was said around Harvard, at this time, that if World War III should (God forbid) break out, there would be a whole generation whose first reaction would be jocular disbelief. "Another Foote prank!" they would incant, punching one another on the arm, not wanting to be fooled again.

The letter from Marianne Reuss made Sarah cry. It was so funny, so alive, so full of sweat and energy and good will. Marianne's little sister was in the hospital dying, but Marianne wrote: "Happiness is just one speck in the linoleum of life."

All the people from Iowa jumped off the page. Their beloved mutual friend Dr. Abramson had encouraged Marianne to take classes at the experimental farm near Keokuk, as he had encouraged Sarah to write. The Plato teacher had inquired how "the philosopher queen" was doing.

Sarah was amazed to see the name of Pythagoras (misspelled)

next to a little diagram in the corner of one of Marianne's profusely
illustrated pages. She and Marianne always seemed to be thinking
about the same thing at the same time. On the long walks from school
they had speculated together on what thought and memory look like in
the nerves of the brain. Then they had sat on a fence giggling and
daydreaming about boys.

That her friend Sarah was so distant from her rankled Marianne, but only in the most transformed, muted, funny, kind way. "Ask
not what you can do for your college. Ask what your college can do for
you," she wrote. "After all, you're paying for it." And under that she
had drawn a little cartoon of Sarah talking to a Harvard boy. "How
can I ever love a girl" (said the balloon) "who only got 760 on her
college boards?"

"Dick is fine," wrote Marianne, "and I'm pregnant."

In every group of men working or
playing together there is always one young brave at the center by
virtue of grace, prowess, and beauty, one young man who loves women
and is loved by the other men. On the Harvard *Crimson* of the early
sixties that man was Michael Hart Verhoeven. Michael was the de-
scendant of Scandinavian socialists and American colonists and, far
back along the line, an Iroquois chief; and he counted a world-class
architect among his uncles. Like all the heroes of the past he was finely
honed, muscular, gentle, and full of humor. Sarah fell in love with him
when she saw him behind home plate.

The occasion was the *Crimson-Lampoon* baseball game, fresh and
spicy as the first days of April, the ground outside Soldiers Field a little
puddled with melted snow, a good-sized crowd of hecklers come to
cheer. Of course the satisfactions at stake for the two teams were different. The humor magazine could hope for merely moral and physical
victory. The campus newspaper had official victory in the bag. Come
what may the *Crimson* would report itself to have won by a score of
23–2 in the next morning's edition.

This understood, the annual sport was undertaken with zest and glee and less than one might expect of kidding. The *Crimson* and the *Lampoon* were archenemies after all, more ferociously so than any two universities. One might even have said it was a confrontation between Pythagoreans, who worship measure, and Delphics, who bend the knee before absurdity.

The bat was handed up.

The *Crimson* came up first.

The heir to the nation's semiofficial government newspaper smashed out a triple.

There were loud cheers. The tall, stoical chap managed a modest smile from third. On the *Crimson* he was sports editor.

The cowboy popped out, cursing colorfully.

A photo board girl struck out.

The *Lampoon* pitcher paused, smiling like a cat, spit on the ball, made a flourish with his arms, and threw.

Eddie O'Brien, his sleeves rolled up, hurled the bat across his body and connected for a solid double, bringing the sports editor home. *Crimson* fans yelled all kinds of strange things, jumped up and down, made bubbles with their gum and popped them.

Franklin P. Haas III, the *Crimson* manager, intended to call a time-out at this point, but the Poonies shouted him down.

Next up was Schulte. He was a little plump, with sad eyes, and didn't look the type of an athlete, but he returned the first pitch high and deep into centerfield. Out there a Poonie—the one who had drawn a single giant phallus over page after page of *Lampoon* comment books—slid on a small patch of snow mud and fell. But right behind him another Poonie caught the ball. This was the fellow who had brought the ibis back to its perch afore and atop Poon Castle. Schulte was out, the side retired.

Sarah turned away to talk to Haas, paying scant attention to the chaps now stepping up to bat. One after another they arose with their little hats and their natty gray baseball jodhpurs and swung their sticks in the air, laughing and insulting one another the while. A fair-faced Poonie got a base hit, being a leader among Poons, who had thought of forty-eight different puns on "See the merino standing there, with his long shaggy hair." But his lads couldn't support him and the *Crimson* was shortly running back to the bench.

Haas wanted at that moment to utter some team encouragement in a literary vein. But the perfectly clear, cool Cambridge afternoon, invigorating and damp, and the spectacle of the ancient ritual in its hot-dog fresh American form, stopped the words in his throat. He could only puff on his pipe approvingly. Haas was from Sun Valley, Idaho, homeland of hunters and skiers. He also knew most of Shakespeare by heart. He was a misplaced aesthete and a serious drinker.

Now he turned to Sarah and pointed out to her the newest member of the *Crimson* staff coming to bat, his steps surrounded by cheers, who seemed to have friends on both sides. The pitcher-baiting increased. "Attaboy, Smitty, hey, Smits. Take it easy! Don't choke in the clutch, Smitty baby!"

Michael Verhoeven, wearing a big red sweater and blue jeans, stepped up to the plate with a jaunty, faintly stiff sailor's gait. His open face was sweet with confidence, and he waved at friend and foe on all sides. Sandy hair just a little longer than was fashionable grazed the top of his neck, and freckles across his nose made him look the very brother of Huck Finn.

The boy picked up one of the bats and swung it, picked up another, swung that, and chose it. Then motioning to the pitcher with an economical gesture to wait, he took a battered pack of Camels out of his hip pocket, lit one, replaced the pack, and put the cigarette in the side of his mouth before signaling to the pitcher to go ahead.

The throw came. High and outside.

Another! Low and inside. Michael didn't blink.

A third. Perfect. A beauty. Michael swung. The bat cracked. Out, out, out of the park.

Michael smiled over at Franklin P. Haas III, inhaled, snuffed his Camel leisurely on the plate, and loped around the diamond for a score.

Sarah walked back over the bridge with Haas, nursing her secret love. Michael and the other Crimeds who had played this afternoon were bringing up the rear, pleasantly sweaty. The red-bearded Thaddeus Foote placed his arm around Michael's shoulders. "Well done!" he exclaimed.

Foote was in the unique position of being on the staffs of both the *Crimson* and the *Lampoon*. In this respect he was probably unique in history. He had managed to convince both archenemies that he was a double agent, loyal really only to them. He played baseball for neither.

Michael laughed with Foote and accepted his congratulations. The great interest he felt in the extraordinary fellow was always tempered by skepticism. He walked his awkwardly graceful walk, Foote by his side, in the center of the *Crimson* cortege, as they crossed back over to their own side of the Charles. Cars streamed by up Boylston Street and around the loop in front of Eliot House.

It was the soft end of an April day, that time of year when suddenly everyone throws his coat off and looks around and feels the first stirrings of new lust.

Despite the weather, the cowboy was despondent. Sarah didn't love him. Even after going to see *The Four Horsemen of the Apocalypse* together three times. Even after a winterful of basketball games. Even after the Duuk of Earl. . . . He couldn't help snatching little glances at her as she bounced so merrily, so arrogantly about, up there at the head of the *Crimson* line, talking to Haas. Then he thought of a new scheme to win her affection. An Elephant Race!

It seemed some Californians out in Orange County had developed an in-joke based on an apocryphal Elephant Racing Society. Well the cowboy would make that joke real! Elephants would really and truly run around the track over in Fullerton (it could never happen on *this* benighted coast), and college kids would race them, and he, the cowboy, would be a mahout! As much as he enjoyed contemplating this prospect, the cowboy relished equally the thought of the oration he could make from the library steps exhorting the students of crummy Harvard to lend financial support to the distant pachyderm gambol. A little cheered up, he trudged lighter in his ostrich-skin boots across the bridge and home.

That night as he was sneaking with his date exuberantly out of Dunster House long, long after the time for legal visits from the opposite sex had passed, the cowboy was stopped in his tracks by resident tutor Erich Segal. Expecting the worst he began to stammer an excuse, but Segal only invited the two of them, rumpled and flushed, up to his suite for a drink.

In the classics scholar's well-appointed suite they relaxed and smiled together about Harvard's rules. Segal was funny and literate, the author of a couple of musical comedies on classical themes. The cowboy liked him a lot, and was always glad to get a poke in at the big H.

The cowboy told the tutor about his Elephant Race. Segal laughed and toasted him.

The talk turned to novels about Harvard. The one from the 1930s was appealing but too long. Another was about being Jewish—and the main character was unfortunately rather unpleasant. Then there was, of course, the one about the professorial suicide. *Love with a Harvard Accent* was just out and being well circulated . . . but who really cared about the comp lit department?

"I read it," said the cowboy's date. "But I hid it behind a copy of *Scientific American.*"

The cowboy was leaning back in Segal's leather chair puffing on a cigar and sipping his sherry. "Well, Erich," he drawled, "what would you write about this damp, dingy, cobbled little city?"

The small neat man stood and put his foot up on an ottoman, the better to display his Italian leather boot in softest maroon. He was delighted to be asked. In his opinion the correct Harvard novel would be a very simple story. A preppy and a poor but beautiful girl: she dies.

"You'd make a fucking million dollars!" exclaimed the cowboy.

The weather was really too hot now to study and Sarah thought it must be some kind of accident that there were still exams to be taken. After realizing that she had been reading page after page without absorbing anything, she finally gave up, and went to see her first Bogart film at the Brattle.

Alone in the room, Yvette stood for a long time before the full-length mirror, turning and moving slightly, gazing approvingly at the whiteness that interrupted her glorious late-spring tan in infinitesimally small patches. Then she tied on two tiny pieces of polka-dotted purple cotton, picked up a thick volume of literary criticism, and went out on the grass behind Stanton House to pretend to study.

Between the clothesline and the high hedge, Yvette spread a towel beside the voluptuous Kievskaya and the slender Katha. Smoothing on oil, they spoke lazily of exams, of boys, of Yvette's latest date, the Chilean wrestler. Browning and turning, deliriously warm, engrossed in their fine bodies, they were all three swept more or less by the angst of failing to live up to an ambiguous standard. Soon summer would take them away from here. But were they here even now? Were they really here? When they came back, would they feel any better about this strange, competitive, masculine place than they felt right now?

After a while Yvette and Katha rose and stretched and agreed to have a run around the Quad. Slipping through the hedge, they came out upon the big open field, dotted with other girls in small groups. And as they laughingly ran and skipped—past Barnard and Bertram and Eliot and Whitman and Cabot and 124 Walker and Comstock and Moors and Holmes and Briggs—they looked back and forth at each other and they saw that their bikinis were very much alike, and that their bodies were very much alike; and in the round tautness of their young flesh they saw their mirrored selves. And they felt a pang, as if they were beautiful Amazons together, or maidens about to be sacrificed for their perfection, in some wooded world of the long-distant past. . . .

Sarah got a job that summer in a convent-reform school sleep-away camp, where she taught swimming and French and the first five ballet positions to the bad girls of Iowa. She bused down to Keokuk and embraced her old friend Marianne and goo-gooed at Marianne's new baby, and the two of them couldn't stop talking for three days about the emotions they had had over the past year. And she went out for pizza and 7 and 7s with one of her old Mason City sweethearts, and sat in his car later and kissed him, and found that the old, sweet, poignant necessity had gone out of the kisses.

That same summer, some sixty kids got together at a lakeside United Auto Workers camp outside Detroit to speak for the newly formed Students for a Democratic Society. Led by Tom Hayden, editor of the campus newspaper at the University of Michigan, they drafted a paper called "The Port Huron Statement" that deplored "the military-industrial complex" and supported instead "participatory democracy," "an end to the Cold War," "an acceptance of variants on socialism in the Third World," "civil rights," "welfare," "a sense of community," and "the quality of life." Inconspicuously, the New Left was born.

The last rains of an autumn evening blazed in the streets, reflecting orange and red and gold and white the lights from the Cambridge Savings Bank and the Harvard Trust and the Waldorf Cafeteria and the MTA Rapid Transit To All Points and the Coop. Blue shadows played on the bricked sidewalks and in the road, as the buses from Boston swept around the corner of the Yard and parked, their last stop. Students in rubbery green army poncho raingear and round-the-Horn yellow oilcloth slickers rushed about the wet Square to late lectures and concerts and events picked out of the *Crimson* notice column.

Tui Burne-Jones was seen very little around the Square these days. She had developed a mad passion for Nestor Schwarz, the actor, and was dining and feting and playing snooker with him in her prep school roommate's palatial home on the North shore. "Ah," she thought deliciously, "how angry it would make Daddy the Admiral if he knew. . . ."

Rosa Doe was unhappy with the sociology department. The professors were always assuming they had to rebut previously received truths. Where the other students had received these truths—at Exeter, Andover, Brearley, or Chapin perhaps—Rosa didn't know. But she certainly hadn't, and she wished her courses would start from the beginning.

Yvette Serre, on the other hand, was beginning to get a kick out of the idea of Western civilization. After her beloved France, the high cultures of Germany, England, Italy, and Russia also appealed to her. She felt the presence of the great nineteenth-century bourgeoisie all around. But she was not one of them. Oh, no! She was part of that bohemianism that had begun in the fifteenth century as an anticleri-cal, anti-imperialist, nationalist movement, and had produced over the centuries since such fire-eating specimens as the spasmodics, the decadents, the haschishien-assassins—all of whom could be seen around Cambridge these days, if one knew where to look. The vis stud depart-

ment was full of them. Like Tui, Yvette was rarely seen around the
dorm. She was spending a lot of time across the river in a Boston
apartment with a very ugly man who wore a monocle.

The debutante Virginia Morris had chosen to major in fine arts
because she found its faculty the most charming, just as they had said
at Miss Porter's. She was putting in long afternoons at the Fogg and
the Busch-Reisinger Museums, and going out every Saturday night
with a Harvard prelaw named Strothfeld Geilich who was president of
the Verein Turmwachter. They made a wonderful couple: she with
pure silk stockings over a perfectly turned calf, he in a natural-shoulder
three-and-three-quarter-inch-lapel twelve-ounce navy pinstripe wor-
sted with side vents and dull horn buttons.

"Ruhully, it's great to see you, Virginia," he would say each
week at 8:00 P.M. "You look ruhully great." And she would flash him
that persuasive, well-designed smile, that smile it was her lifework to
perfect.

As Sarah and her friends were lin-
gering over their afterdinner coffee in Holmes Hall one evening, Carolee Davis came running into the dining room with a transistor radio.

"Listen!" she commanded, setting the small machine down on
the round polished wood table, knocking over the salt.

. . . to recap: President Kennedy has announced a
naval and air blockade on the shipment of offensive military
equipment to Cuba. This announcement follows White House
intelligence confirmation that the Soviets have built missile
bases on the island of Cuba, only ninety miles off the coast of
Florida, with a capability of nuclear attack reaching two thousand miles. The Organization of American States has responded to an appeal from Secretary of State Rusk with a
unanimous vote of approval for the use of armed force to carry
out the blockade. From Moscow, the Soviet Union has challenged this government's right to impose the blockade. Secre-

tary of Defense McNamara has announced that U.S. planes have spotted twenty-five Russian ships on the high seas . . . on the way to Cuba. . . .

Repeating the headlines once again: President Kennedy has declared a military quarantine of Cuba. In apparent defiance of the quarantine, Russian ships have been sighted in the Atlantic heading in this direction. The Russians have warned that America is risking nuclear war.

Carolee snapped off the radio and for a long moment the dining room was silent. Rain was beginning to fall diagonally past the dormitory window, beyond the crisp white curtains.

"What does it mean?" said Rosa.

Sarah didn't know what to make of it either. President Kennedy was her hero.

"It's brinksmanship," Carolee told them definitively. "The closest we've come so far. I just got a phone call from Tom in Florida. He says he wishes he were with me. Now that we're near death . . ." The thin girl, intensity blazing in her eyes, was so certain, so angry. The others felt only confusion and a vague fear. They looked at her. They knew very little about her except that she had been born on an army base in the deep South, that her mother was an artist, that her grandmother had been a communist.

Carolee stayed around Holmes Hall for a while earnestly talking, giving the girls her interpretation of events, referring often to data from *The New York Times,* which she read devotedly every day from front page to back. But soon she fled the dorm and, throwing a ragged scarf around her neck, biked at full speed the two miles to Dunster House, to see Dan Matlaw.

Dan and his roommates and pals were making angry remarks abut the UN debate on television when Carolee walked in. She took off her scarf and sat down with them, though their attitude wasn't what she had expected. She had made a

stop at the Radcliffe Library on her way over and taken out some
books on recognizing edible wild plants, setting up elementary plumb-
ing systems, and the like, and now she bantered uneasily with a couple
of Dan's pals about getting into a car and heading for New Hampshire. To the Balkans!

But Danny was staying right where he was, in his army boots
and blue jeans and worn flannel shirt, his Gibson guitar resting easily
on his lap. Every once in a while he would strum it and come out with
a verse, calypso-style:

> Ada-lie Steven-sin
> he look like a penga-win
>
> Speak for Mr. Kennedy
> not for you and not for me . . .

Dan Matlaw was a radical. But not the kind of radical who spat
on tradition, the kind who thought the Second International was a
dictionary, who believed their own impulses negated history. Dan's
mother had lost her job as New York City school teacher in 1952 for
belonging to the Communist Party. She had always encouraged her
son to a) change this horrendous, unjust society; and b) succeed within
the society as it stands.

So Dan worked hard getting into Harvard, and, at Harvard,
studying economics (though it never did make any sense to him, the
way they taught it), and on his own he read Marx and Lenin and
Trotsky and Mao; he read Tom Paine and Lillian Hellman and the
classics of English and American poetry; he followed the careers of
Bertholt Brecht and the major sports figures of the day. And though he
was familiar with the dogmas of the various factions on the left, he
joined no party, and belonged to no organizations but the *Crimson*. For
the campus newspaper he wrote editorials blasting American foreign
policy. And for his soul, he wrote songs and plays.

One night in the *Crimson* sanctum Dan had described to Sarah
Galbraeth how out of place he felt in Cambridge. First of all, there
were all those impossible preppies, with their last names that you know
you've heard somewhere before. But that wasn't even the worst of it.
The worst was that he felt isolated from people he considered his politi-

cal allies. How could he admit to Carolee Davis that he struggled to get through the writings of the thinkers on the left? And the left-leaning disarmament group, with whom he felt himself in some sympathy, didn't ask him to their Thursday lunches in Quincy House with government advisors on·the faculty. "They sense I would do something rude," he told Sarah, "like hold a knife real close to Dr. Kissinger's throat. . . . "

His self-doubts were lost, however, on Sarah. She did not guess that Dan Matlaw was wondering whether his mother's demands upon him were irreconcilable. To her he was a revolutionary of the most beautiful and romantic sort. He seemed to Sarah at least as artistic as he was dialectical or materialist, and she pictured him liberating the Bastille, appropriating the streets in the name of the Commune, drinking wine under the sky alongside beautiful and strong women. At the very least, she imagined him in cafés in Jerusalem or Istanbul or Tangier, and she wished him long cool bohemian eyelashes, black coffee, and victory.

Putting aside her survival books, Carolee brought out a draft of a statement she had written opposing the blockade of Cuba. Dan put away his guitar and read what she had written. A few changes were suggested; she accepted most of them. Then the two of them rushed off together through the dark and rainy streets of Cambridge to the *Crimson* building, to demand, plead, lobby, cajole, and fight to see their statement published. They felt they owed the effort to the Cuban people and the international working class. And they fantasized about the reaction it would provoke among Kennedy's *Crimson*-reading advisors— McGeorge Bundy, Arthur Schlesinger, Jr., and the rest.

Carolee had both inspired and terrified Sarah, who now wandered alone down to the Square in an oilcloth slicker against the rain. Her mind was a blur. She walked past the Out of Town newsstand, past the all-night cafeterias. Turning down one of the tiny side streets, medieval in its dimensions and now

fragrant with the rain on ivied brick, she found her feet had led her to
Club 47.

Inside it was very dark. Students were crowded around small
tables, sitting on folding chairs and wooden stools, slightly damp, uneasy this night, talking softly. She squeezed in. There was some scattered applause. A beautiful, small young woman with luminous eyes
and a delicate sensual mouth and very long black hair had stepped to
the front and was sitting on a wooden stool holding a guitar. Plainly
dressed, the skin of her perfectly turned arms glistening, she seemed to
have the toughness that comes with extreme sensitivity.

The sound of her guitar was like gypsies.

> Black black black
> Is the color of my true love's hair. . . .

But it was the tone of her soprano that was so startling. It was pure,
unearthly, deep as autumn, compelling, sibylline.

Sarah listened, drank a beer. The boys at her table were discussing the singer after each song softly and eagerly, as if they were all
quite smitten.

> *Plaisir d'amour*
> *Ne dure qu'un instant.*
> *Chagrin d'amour*
> *Endure toute la vie. . . .*

"You know she's part Mexican, part Irish?"

"Come on, she's just a beantown college student!"

"No. She's from Palo Alto."

Two men joined her and they began to harmonize on "John
Henry."

"Harvard guys," someone whispered. "The tall one works in
Widener."

> You can't drive steel like me!

Sarah listened and something in her that was ruffled was
soothed. But she could not be easy. Far away this terribly dreary, quiet,

rainy night, a Russian ship was heading across the ocean. Somehow politics had eaten up ethics. There was no justice, just this yawning chasm. Fear. Death. Hope.

> All my trials, Lord
> Soon be over. . . .

In the cavernous and drafty meeting room of Memorial Hall, beyond the stained glass and under scarlet and gold eaves so high above they echoed, the Radcliffe Alumnae Association was having its annual meeting. Women from every class at Radcliffe sat around long bare Adirondack tables. A twenty-five-year-old woman with her hair pinned back in a barrette. A forty-year-old woman severe and tailored. A fifty-five-year-old woman looking well meaning but dyspeptic. A sixty-year-old woman with a square, enduring face. A thoughtful seventy-year-old woman in mother-of-pearl eyeglasses. A seventy-five-year-old woman with a toothache. Several angelic, snowy-headed eighty-year-old women. In front of them, a bespectacled Mary Bunting was speaking about the current relations between the colleges. Harvard would never encroach on the special, valuable independence of Radcliffe, she assured them. There was an attentive silence, for Mrs. Bunting was a popular and imaginative college president who had had an unusually virile career. Just a few of the alumnae representatives whispered together at the rear of the gathering.

Suddenly a young man entered, walked directly to Mrs. Bunting, and interrupted her. He said something in an undertone and handed her a sheet of paper. Mrs. Bunting took a few moments to read it. She poured herself a glass of water.

Then the president of Radcliffe repeated the announcement of the president of the United States with respect to the Cuban missiles, in a clear and steady voice to the assembled Radcliffe Alumnae Association. When she was finished she paused with no comment.

The women were flabbergasted. There was a hush as the horror announced itself to all. Mem Hall was silent. And then, in another moment, there fell the buzz of female conversation, as the women tried to figure out where all this left them.

The great building where they sat might have been the sheltering hulk of Victorian Europe. Its mid-nineteenth–century womb had produced Crimea, revolutions across the Continent, opium war, so much restless, violent nationalism. In the decade that this building was completed, Marx and Engels had published *The Communist Manifesto*. All these ghosts now flapped and moaned and rattled their chains, amid the solemn pomp and self-satisfaction of this huge, proud, supremely majestic edifice.

And Mary Bunting, who would soon be appointed to the Atomic Energy Commission, had no word of solace.

Sarah left the Club at 47 Mount Auburn Street and walked the short block back to the *Crimson*. Her thoughts were jumbled. She had been born just before the bombs had exploded over Japan and all her life politicians had been saying her generation lived in the shadow of annihilation. But only now, in the administration of a young and beautiful president whom she loved—that sweet John F. Kennedy, who only this year had sent out a tureen of hot coffee to student peace marchers shivering in the snow—did she feel vulnerable. She felt six years old again, when she had understood the idea of war for the first time, and had gone running to her father saying, "Daddy, Daddy, I'm so glad we're not at war!" and her father had answered sadly, but with an educating eye, "We are at war." From that day the sound of airplanes that could be bombers had frightened the child, and this feeling had taken a long while to subside. Now she was an adult and the danger was real again. She imagined a bullet like Xeno's arrow headed irrevocably toward her, hanging in space. She knew she could do nothing to stop it but hold up a flesh and bone hand pitifully. Impotence made her nauseous and fear took away her breath.

At the *Crimson* there was a lot of activity. The AP wire had reported that people in Florida were stampeding the supermarket. The Boston radio kept announcing that if a siren went off, it would *not* be a test. An incredible number of people from different political organizations kept coming into the newsroom, asking if the *Crimson* wanted their statements. Eddie O'Brien said yes to them all.

As the AP choked out its ninth lead of the evening on Cuba, Sarah went upstairs to the sanctum. There in the gloom of the large book-lined room, in the shadow of Kipling and Tennyson and Scott, a group had gathered to discuss the next day's editorial. Shoes had been kicked off and the argument was in progress. Sarah settled into a worn leather sofa gratefully. A boy in a blue workshirt and a green silk polka-dot tie and baggy corduroys seemed to be speaking for the general tenor of the meeting; he was spelling out ways Kennedy might have tried to split Castro off from the Russians—might have pointed out to him that it was not in his interest to have Russian missiles on his territory—instead of assuming him to be a puppet and going over his head with the ultimatum to Khrushchev. Many people were nodding. But not everyone.

"I find almost nothing about the United States to command my patriotism," a girl interrupted angrily. "Ideally we may be more meritorious than a totalitarian state. But if we can gamble with . . . with . . . the fate of the earth like this, then we are in actual fact no more humane!"

"John Kennedy *is* in*tell*igent," said a tall man with rosy cheeks named R. R. Hodgson. Hodgson, as editorial chairman, had inherited from his *Crimson* predecessor the traditional "fountain pen of infallibility," and he wore it well. He was able to make even the simplest remark sound exceedingly complex and profound by means of the shadings of his subtle voice. "But he sees too much drama and nobility in his role as a statesman," he said. The tall fellow's smile was minimal, his expression eloquent.

Charlie Schulte was having none of it. Earlier in the evening he had, as he saw it, "vanquished" a "peace wonk," who was "shuffling and bleating" for a page one box on the Tocsin rally. In the sanctum

Schulte was leaning forward on his sofa fidgeting and sputtering. "You do-gooders are wrong as usual! The president's gamble, as you call it, is nothing less than realism. He has a chance of winning. But without a showdown the Soviets will gain momentum—and then where will we be? Their missiles in Cuba have upset the hemispheric balance. . . ."

"Fist-waver!" hissed someone. More emotional comments were exchanged.

It seemed the silk tie/workshirt position would comprise the *Crimson* lead editorial, official and anonymous, running the next day, while the Schulte position would appear the day after that as a signed "On The Other Hand." Modifications and ramifications of this basic agreement continued on into the night.

"The *Crimson* is my idol," thought Sarah Galbraeth. "It can't go crazy. It has such nice solid ecru walls. The sanctum is so nice and maroon and ugly. The hold button on the telephone is so reassuring." And with that she dropped off to sleep in the soft lap of one of the big leather sofas, dozing fitfully through the end of the long meeting and its gradual dispersion. Shortly before dawn she woke, as the first golden lights were breaking over a silent eggshell-gray Cambridge with no one in the streets. The boy in the workshirt and silk tie whose job it was to write the editorial was still there, poring over the yellowing and brittle pages of a bound volume. They went out to the Bick together and breakfasted on eggs and "a rasher of bacon" (as he called it), and then he chivalrously walked her back up to Radcliffe.

That week Sarah volunteered to night-edit, filling her night editor's report with remarks about the rainy weather. Michael Verhoeven night-edited that week as well, dressed in a dapper plaid vest, and laboriously folded papers with the cowboy at 4:00 AM when the folders were late. The usual discussions of which candidates to keep, which to cut, whether to redo the *Crimson* newsroom floor and/or paint the walls, edged the international situation entirely out of the Comment Books.

On October 28 the radio announced that a ship had been intercepted, not boarded, allowed to proceed, apparently carrying oil, not armaments. The crisis was over.

The week after that, Ted Kennedy became junior senator from Massachusetts.

One late afternoon before Christmas with the taste of snow in the air, Sarah stood on Plympton Street in front of the *Crimson* building, pausing before returning to the dorm, thinking nothing much in particular, eating a gigantic yellow apple. She had leaned her bike against the *Crimson*'s low railing, a heavy Palmer's *History of the Modern World* in its rack.

Just at that moment, on his way to the library with a notebook and a newspaper under his arm, Michael Verhoeven came walking up the slight incline of Plympton Street. A few flakes of snow clung to the shoulders of his Danish red jacket. Sarah drank up the sight of him, lean and masculine, as if she had been wishing at that very moment that he would appear.

He gravitated to her and they stood there together outside the *Crimson* this winter day as if they had arranged to meet. A few words passed between them, their first conversation really, and it was as if all the difficult questions of feeling had been resolved long before.

He asked her if she wanted to go to a movie.

The question took its meaning from the fact that it was not eight o'clock on a Saturday evening but just a plain, everyday time. They were outside, unconnected. They would be spared the curses of the past. In Michael's lovely clear voice there was no uncertainty, only dry good humor and joy. And in the question and the voice and the ears that heard them was a passion chaste as the snow now lightly falling on Harvard, as fresh as the first asphodel that blossoms in the Isles of the Blest.

Snow on eyelids, snow on fuzzy cap and red wool jacket, still carrying their books, they went to the University Theater in Harvard Square to see Brigitte Bardot and Marcello Mastroianni in color. It was so beautiful, so passionate, so tragic—it went right over Sarah's

head. But it lifted their spirits the more. When they came out of the
movie into the snowy darkness they scrambled up the fire escape of the
theater and ran up to its roof in a purposeless ecstasy of knowledge of
their situation and contentment to be exactly there.

Michael called out to Sarah something that made her laugh.
They came down and walked, now hand in hand, to the river. Snow
made the slanting shed roof of Weld boathouse silver and slippery, but
they ran and played on it, moving their limbs like children, with
breathless excitement. Until at last they fell into each other's arms on
the slanting boards and Michael kissed Sarah and she kissed him back.

He thought her skin was beautiful.

She thought his hands were beautiful.

After a while they stopped in for café au lait at the Arlecchino,
a few steps down from Boylston Street. Michael told Sarah about the
year he'd spent in Europe. She realized that he was sophisticated. He
listened to jazz and had black friends. By this time the water from the
melting snow was dripping from his sandy hair down onto his face and
he grinned his wide, sunny grin. Sarah grinned back at him with her
secret virgin's pleasure. And they sat there grinning at each other perhaps a moment longer than the breath of time.

At last Michael walked Sarah back to the *Crimson* where she
picked up her bike and sped away.

Snow continued to fall on Harvard
that night as Sarah sneaked into her dormitory illegally, running into
Rosa's room and dancing around, telling her delighted friend that
Michael had had a secret crush on her just like hers on him. Snow fell
deep on the boathouse, and on the roof of the UT, and on the little
Crimson balcony that looks up and down on Harvard. And it stuck in
the topiary of the Quincy House courtyard and laced with stars the
windows of Mather Hall where Michael was talking quietly with his
roommate, a sometimes lumberjack from Yakima, Washington, telling
him that he was very happy.

The next afternoon Sarah told her first blushing desire to Haas. The gentleman in the hunting jacket was in a distracted mood. He was having trouble handing in papers and it looked very much like the university was going to take some serious steps against him. But meanwhile he was busying himself putting together a guide to the cultural resources of the East for Idaho University Press.

Haas had devoted one section of his book to "Young Ladies' Colleges," and for each of two dozen schools he had selected a verse from the bard. Sarah read over his shoulder the triple-spaced lines and broke up. Haas had managed to deride the chastity, intelligence, or looks of virtually every female population, reserving praise only for Wellesley and their own Radcliffe.

"So! You and young Verhoeven have discovered your respective good qualities," remarked Haas. "Well, you won't be sorry."

"Do you think he likes me?" she asked.

"I think he likes you," Haas replied with tenderness. "Why shouldn't he like you? You're a wonderful girl." Pausing. "And, of course, I've put in a good word for you." He winked conspiratorially.

Sarah's mind wandered. In the president's office a radio was playing and she caught the happy refrain:

> Here we go Loop-De-Loop
> Here we go loop-de-li
> Here we go Loop-De-Loop
> All on a Saturday night!

She smiled dimly at the older editor, tall and broad and full of sensibility. "Thank you, Franklin," she said. "Oh, and is CFMcS really going to write something about gambling for your book?"

"Well, we don't know yet, do we," chuckled Haas. "But I suspect his name will appear on the contents page whether he does or not."

While Sarah and Haas talked, leaning up against the wall beside the water fountain, *Crimson* reporters at three big black office typewriters were pounding out an issue of the paper to go to New York City and fill the gap left by the strike of nine major metropolitan

ATHENS REGIONAL LIBRARY
ATHENS, GEORGIA

257274

dailies. They wrote about the launching of a communications satellite and a Venus fly-by; the refusal of Women's Strike for Peace to purge their communists; Rusk's claim to NATO of victory in the Cuban missile crisis; bickering among Yugoslavia, Albania, China, and Russia over whether Russia had retreated in the crisis, or "sold out" Cuba, or been courageously peace loving.

Behind a plastic partition a skinny junior in a bow tie was taking a special pleasure in typing out the local scoop: the FDA was investigating the posible illegal sale in Cambridge of psilocybin, mescaline, and LSD.

Snow drifted past the windows of the old Leverett House library. Inside it was warm, steam-heated, and crowded with students. Discarded boots and parkas dripped slowly into puddles on the parquet floor, darkening the Oriental rug. All the young faces were turned toward a smiling, clean-shaven man with glasses who sat on an armchair between two towering corner windows. His voice was melodic, his manner ingratiating, his idioms articulate and occasionally poetic. He beckoned the assemblage toward enlightenment and consciousness. You might have detected something of the Pied Piper in his manner if you had not been caught up in his spell.

The speaker was assistant professor Stephen Binks of the psychology department and the ed school, lately discovered in the offices of the Center for Research in Personality with lecturer Buster Thatcher, stretched out on Barcaloungers, martinis balanced on their stomachs, strange looks in their eyes. The *Crimson* had printed an article about it. Whereupon the two had been reprimanded for the use of untested chemicals with and on the undergraduates of Harvard in procedures that could generously be described as unorthodox.

But now, curiously, the notoriety that Binks and Thatcher had received in connection with this reprimand had resulted in their being given numerous forums to explain and promote their work—which previously had had to be done on the quiet.

Hanging around the dorm or spying on passers-by from the stone arch of Sever or the glass and chrome corridors of Boylston, Sarah kept busy that winter wrestling with the question, "Who are these people?" She asked Yvette and Rosa and Tui and Carolee and Virginia and everyone else she could corner before fatigue set in, "What one word would be the highest compliment you could give another girl?" She scribbled notes on dress and schools and habits and studies and language in the backs of all her notebooks, thoroughly enjoying herself, pursuing her solitary investigation, and hoping all the time, when it was finally done, she didn't know when, to be able to put together some kind of meta-report on Radcliffe for the people back home.

She tried not to think about Michael. He hadn't called since Christmas even though she'd sent him an intricate silverfoil snowflake. The radio was full of music about the problems of teenage love in its every possible stage—from the first shy meeting to going steady, arguments, suspicions of infidelity, tentative breaking up, learning that life without each other was impossible, making up again, and finally marriage—and everything reminded her of him. Every Doris Day pink telephone movie some other boy took her to made her think of him. Conversations with Yvette and Rosa unfailingly put him into her head.

Finally she settled down to her long-neglected schoolwork. Her sophomore essay was due on Monday. In the soft, yellow-bound book she read: *When I was entirely myself, without alloy, without obstacle, then it was that I can say I truly lived.* She stretched out on her bed in jeans and an ugly shirt, her hair in a ponytail, to think. She had also promised an article to the yearbook: that was due Friday. Everything was behind.

Then Michael called.

"Come to my house for Washington's Birthday," he said.

His voice had the most amazing power over her. It inspired her to great deeds. It demolished her with longing. There he was. Here was all this schoolwork. Sarah ran around the dorm asking everyone what she should do. Everyone said she should stay put and write her sophomore essay. It was an important paper.

At last Sarah went into Yvette's room to ask her old roommate for advice. Yvette was standing in front of an ironing board in her minuscule lace underwear, ironing one of those bright cotton Cubist-design Scandinavian dresses. A bunch of chrysanthemums in a porcelain vase had showered down white petals onto the dresser top. She looked like an advertisement for the benefits of sex. In fact Yvette's very existence—apparently happy, at the very least unpunished—was for Sarah a refutation of the main idea she had had about sex all the time she was growing up. All those high schooly nights she had wept with interrupted desire in the arms of her boyfriend Gabriel—"Why does it have to be like this? It isn't fair!" she had cried. But now that first veil had fallen away, so silently, by the distant inspiration of Michael Verhoeven, under the gaze of Gauguin's *White Horses* and a shower of flower petals, and Sarah knew without having to phrase a question that all the other veils would drop away one by one in their time.

"What were you going to say?"

"Oh, nothing."

Sarah called Michael back and agreed to go.

They flew out of Logan Airport together in a state of advanced bliss. A special Boston to New York shuttle had been introduced that year, and the price seemed right at ten dollars. Indeed, no airplane ride in either of their entire two previous lives had ever seemed such perfection of transport. Side by side in the soft gray cushioned seats, they touched hands and looked at each other and felt like children of a proper pharaoh.

Michael's house was two hours from New York City in an exurb he told her was populated mostly by artists. Inside, his parents' living room was roomy and gracious, full of plants and dark woods, sophisticated but at the same time natural. Along one wall of the kitchen, Michael's mother had installed a linotyper's multidrawered cabinet to keep her things in. There was an herb garden and a grape arbor outside.

Mrs. Verhoeven came down the stairs and introduced herself.

She was a tall, powerful woman of the Katherine Hepburn type. Mr.Verhoeven was still in the city but would be home soon. He was an officer of a labor union.

Sarah had never seen anything like it. Even the bathroom was coolly sensuous. A tall bottle of 4711 stood on a curved marble counter alongside Chagall's *Arabian Nights* in German. (In her folks' bathroom at home one would see instead the *Reader's Digest* and laxatives.) The whole place seemed so clean and elegant, so informed and enlightened. . . . Then Michael laughingly opened the door to the den, where stacks and stacks of newspapers and magazines nestled cozily beside the TV and on a sofabed covered in madras. Five or six cats stole in and out.

Michael and Sarah sat together in the den stroking the oldest cat. The time for discussing emotions had passed. Now the time for discussing technicalities of behavior was past too. They just sat there for a long while making noises and a kind of speech to each other that was not ideas, really, and hardly even emotion, but something corresponding to the chirping and cooing of certain delicate tropical parrots. They listened with all their hearts to the tones of each other's voices, and they watched each other's eyes and bodies, and they felt snug and happy.

They helped Mrs. Verhoeven make a salad in the hugest wooden bowl Sarah had ever seen. Michael's mother put in three varieties of green and red lettuce, endive, fresh dill, real garlic, and oil that came from a golden can. As they were working together in the kitchen Mr. Verhoeven came in, his face all smiles and heartiness, his conversation and manner as refreshing as a charcoal steak.

They sat down together at a big oak table. Sarah was in such rapture she could hardly speak.

"Michael tells us you write for the *Crimson*," said Mrs. Verhoeven.

"Yes. I do," said Sarah, clearing her throat. She couldn't think of anything else to say. She had the feeling her blouse was wrong. It didn't have a collar.

"Mr. Verhoeven and I met in the Chicago stockyards in the thirties," the tall woman continued smoothly, sipping her wine. "I was writing about the meatpackers for the Federal Writers Project, and Mr. Verhoeven was organizing for the CIO."

"The Federal Writers Project was part of the WPA," Michael

explained, obviously proud to share the family liturgy. "Mom was getting twenty dollars a week."

"It was quite enough," Mrs. Verhoeven said. "We believed in what we were doing."

Michael's father picked up the conversational ball, such as it was. "You're studying literature?"

Sarah agreed.

"Of course there's only one novel worth reading," he declared.

Sarah's heart fell. But he was so darling, Mr. Verhoeven, so sweetly stern, like Humphrey Bogart, that she was ready to accept even this verdict. She looked at him with an ambiguous smile, as if to say "Tell me which one that is," and "But of course I know just the one you mean!"

"War and Peace," he announced. He waved at the long wall of books around the fireplace. "That's the only novel I have on my shelves."

Michael was eating his salad eagerly, the watercress, the mint, with an undivided pleasure, as if he believed the beautiful to be the true, and that both were good for him. He was devoted to his father, worshipful of his mother, and had no quarrel with the way they led their lives. His father, the socialist, it turned out, had no use for organized religion—which rather shocked Sarah, who had on occasion taught Sunday school in Mason City. But soon she realized that his position was entirely theoretical. In practice the Stockholm-born first-generation American was the most tolerant person in the world. He even had a religion of sorts, when you got right down to it. Every Fourth of July Mr. Verhoeven would gather his family together at the picnic table in the grape arbor and in hushed, reverential tones would read to them the stirring words of the Declaration of Independence.

Mrs. Verhoeven was talking now about the Iroquois creation myth, which she had heard from her grandmother. Dinner had been superb. The house was heaven. Sarah had the sudden thought that Michael's mother was like the ideal woman described in Scripture. She did so many things with and for her husband. She was so intelligent and talented and strong. "And her children rise up and call her blessed. . . ."

Someday she would tell her so.

Mrs. Verhoeven was speaking now about the present-day Indians' governing councils. Her face was radiant as she talked. And she smiled, when she had made her certain point, a wonderful, broad, illuminated grin.

Michael and Sarah did the dinner dishes. They visited an aged neighbor who pronounced Sarah "beautiful" (much to Sarah's disbelief). They stood in the wintry grape arbor as the moon came up. They drove around for a little while in the VW because Michael loved this woodsy county and wanted to show it off to Sarah. And she loved it all as well.

At last Michael made up the sofabed for two and lay down with her. Sarah, half-dressed, felt that this was not sex as she had known it, not the groping egotism of youth, not anything to do with competition or achievement or whatever outside of just the two of them. It was the threshold of her life. This man, this boy, here with her, was her partner in fate.

The next day was Saturday and in the evening Michael drove Sarah into New York City to a place she had never heard of called Birdland. They went down some red-carpeted steps and sat at a small table with a tablecloth next to a pillar. The waiter brought them two tall Scotch-and-sodas. In the impenetrable darkness Sarah was at first conscious of nothing but the presence of a lot of people, black and white, Michael's thick chocolate-brown sweater outlining his chest, and the soft, low brush of the cymbals.

Then a black man stepped up to the microphone with a long gleaming instrument in his hand, and lifted it to his lips, and began to play, and it was like a revelation. Sarah listened to the voice of his soprano sax (for that was what Michael said it was) running intricately and tenderly over half-familiar melodies. She half closed her eyes and let herself float, uplifted and buoyed by the foam-crests over the profundity of jazz. And the pupil of her heart dilated, and a new kind of light entered her.

Johnny Mathis and Elvis Presley had known something about

love. She and her friends had danced to their music at the high school
after basketball games and in finished basements and in the church.
But this John Coltrane knew everything. He knew all that they had
known about love and lust, loneliness and heartbreak. And he also
knew about strife, effort, and resolution, about the icy peaks and burning valleys of life, about naked existence. This understanding came to
Sarah softly, like the most longed-for, the most unobtrusive, the most
exactly agreeable whisper. And then she remembered that her own
dear friend Michael already existed in this music, in this wisdom, that
it had been here all along in some other room from her life. Here he
was next to her, Apollo in a brown sweater, smiling at her so sweetly,
looking at her so knowingly.

She reached out and touched his woolly sleeve. Birdland was
paradise! How could Harvard compare?

And still the music built up in delicacy, in energy, in force. And
still the black man played on, with the dignity of a saint.

Sunday morning Mr. and Mrs.
Verhoeven put Handel's *Water Music* on the stereo and cooked up a
batch of toast and bacon and eggs expertly and acted as if they knew
and understood and approved of everything.

It was just as she had feared: for
the first time in two years Sarah was not glad to be back in Cambridge.
All these buildings, responsibilities, traditions, rules, crowds, clubs,
classes, were an irritation compared to the immaculately real event
that had occurred somewhere in the ellipse that centered upon herself
and Michael.

"How was it?" asked Rosa and Yvette.

"I can't tell you," said Sarah. "It was perfect. It was marvelous."

She tried to get down to work. But it was a superhuman struggle. All she wanted to do was to see him.

In the last row of her poetry class, not even remotely paying attention to the close textual analysis under way, Sarah sat and doodled on the margins of somebody else's poem. It was about a woman who gradually realizes she wants her husband, who is driving, to kill the dog that is running alongside their car. Sarah was disgruntled. The venerable old poetry professor had as good as forbidden lyrical, romantic poems, and preferred this sort of thing.

The class was a bust. In purple ballpoint she wrote:

> Adlai Stevenson Verhoeven
> John Kennedy Verhoeven
> Ray Charles Verhoeven

made a row of stars and snowflakes, and then added

> Sarah Mary Galbraeth Verhoeven
> Mr. and Mrs. Michael H. Verhoeven.

Abandoning poetry, Sarah got back to work on her inquiry into types of girls at Radcliffe. One day in March soon after the Washington's Birthday excursion, she felt herself in labor with it. She ran to the *Crimson* with her notebooks and banged out a Walt Disneyish synthesis of her year's work in one draft.

"Hey, Haas," she yelled as she was finishing. "What does vanilla connote to you?"

The Idahoan made an appropriately serious face. "Bland. Mild. Smooth. Pleasant."

"Right! Thanks! I mean: no good. What about chocolate?"

"More intense. Difficult. Rich. Meaty. Dirty."

"Fantastic! Perfect!" She typed a few more words. "And what kind of taste or flavor or whatever would connote something exotic and dangerous, sort of cool? . . ."

"An Analysis of Coeds as Ice Cream" appeared in the next

day's paper and was an immediate sensation. It annoyed a few girls
who didn't like being called "peach," but Virginia Morris didn't mind.
Carolee Davis said it was terrific. The boys on the *Crimson* were ecstatic,
and David Riesman called it "brilliant sociology." Word soon came
down that it had become a party game around Cambridge.

This was apparently enough of a constituency. Soon "Coeds as
Ice Cream" started winning prizes, being reprinted here and there.
The wire services picked it up and broadcast a digest of Sarah's thesis
around the country without mentioning Sarah's name. Indeed, the
Associated Press said it was the work of "Harvard men." But this
didn't strike Sarah as at all curious or disagreeable, because she was
too much in love.

Michael had actually got to the
nubbin of Sarah back in Cambridge, in Mather Hall, in the bottom
bunk of a double-decker, his tie on the doorknob to warn away roommates, a come-on cool and sweet as the crème de menthe he took from
his mantel, with his smooth chest and narrow hips showing her the first
she had ever seen of a man's body. But it was not Cambridge they
inhabited. Clinging together after hours of love in the narrow bed next
to the window in the dark, tiny bedroom, Sarah discovered the power
of sex. In those hours nothing else was important, not classes, not going
to sleep early, not writing thank-you letters. They lived as if under a
dome, a bubble charmed and safe, where even the light was different.

Michael had been with one girl before, but he didn't want to
talk about it. This seemed precisely the right amount of sophistication.
His store of knowledge was perfect and wholesome. He brought sweet
articulate reassurance when Sarah's confidence faltered. And his prowess gave her her body. Sarah's baby fat melted away. She had never in
her life been cleaner or softer or smelled so good. Virginia gave her
beauty hints. She bought the colognes and cosmetics that Michael's
mother favored. And she didn't change her style of dressing con-
sciously, or all at once; but one day she realized that she was looking

rather less like a tomboy than she had used to, and rather more like a tasteful Paris streetwalker.

Around the world there were unmistakable signs that something was afoot.

In Egypt the corn god Osiris was plucked from the Nile early in the morning. In Babylon, Tammuz was retrieved from the sea. In the Perilous Chapel, Parsifal located the Grail and thus restored the Fisher King's fertility. It could only mean one thing.

—*The Harvard Crimson,*
on the Vernal Equinox, 1963

One day soon after "Coeds as Ice Cream" and soon after her entire life had turned upside down in Michael's bed, Sarah was walking past the bio labs with their mascot rhinoceroses into the undeveloped section of town between Divinity and Radcliffe where Revlon or someone had constructed a building resembling a giant lipstick, when the gentlest of spring breezes blew through the thin cotton of her jersey. With a feeling that was like ecstasy but calmer, Sarah felt the wind go straight through her flesh and touch her soul. She had never known a spring like this. She understood with absolute certainty that she had dissolved into nature.

When she got back to her room—a Klee print blazing ruby and emerald and topaz on the wall—Sarah threw herself on the bed to catch the feeling and preserve it a moment longer. She could not speak of such happiness: it would make Rosa weep. She savored it alone, exultant. Then she called Michael once again to hear the sound of his voice.

Michael and Sarah made love every day from four to seven as the parietal rules allowed, and then raced downstairs to the House dining hall for dinner. They stood at the end of the line and filled their sky-blue plastic trays with food and carried them across the large room to their customary spot along the glass wall overlooking Mount Auburn. And many people would look at them because they were so much in love and Sarah's cheeks were always pink. And some would feel bitter to see them, and some would say, "The question is not, 'Are they doing it?' but 'Are they enjoying it?' " and some people would just enjoy them. Along another wall of the Quincy House dining room there was a huge nonobjective mural collage that everyone called *The Death and Transfiguration of a Chevrolet*.

Michael took Sarah's silverware out of his jacket pocket and handed it to her. Sarah gave him her potatoes. They set to the nice-looking slabs of beef and the sprawling salad ("I love salad!") and the Brussels sprouts that had been boiled for days. She watched him attack the brick of vanilla ice cream that had been some rich man's legacy to the college, and she demurely sipped black coffee from a beige plastic trumpet-horn cup.

They smiled at each other across the table, saying little. Today Michael was wearing a yellow button-down shirt, one of his thin, dark ties, and slim black chinos. Sarah gazed at the square line of his jaw and sighed to remember the sweet smell of his clean, silky, golden-brown hair. Her own endearingly shiny reddish-brown hair fell past her shoulders and rested on the soft, cherry-red cardigan that had been a gift from Mrs. Crane, the only woman in Mason City who had really been sure Sarah should go to Harvard.

"I wonder what your parents would make of my parents," Sarah said.

Michael laughed. "My parents are radicals. Yours sound like the bourgeoisie. Which reminds me: can I borrow ten dollars?"

"Out of the question," said Sarah. "I gave you five dollars on Monday. What do you do with your money?" She dropped a wrinkled ten-dollar bill on the table.

"Poker," he said seriously.

"Oh, in that case," she said, "it's all right."

At one edge of the crowded, large dining room buzzing with earnest conversations, Sarah and Michael were enveloped in the ribbon of light that passed between them.

When it got warm enough Sarah and Michael lay along the riverbank only half-conscious of the shimmering water, the little strip of grass with other lovers and their discarded books, the two-lane roadway, the moving cars, the bright blue fairy-tale spires of the Houses, the sycamores. . . .

"Your eyes aren't blue after all," he said to her as they half-dozed under the Cambridge sky. "They're gray and silver."

"Gray and silver and blue and green like the North Sea." She picked a few strands of grass and dropped them on his hand. Cars whooshed by in a nice normal curve of sound.

"Did you ever think," she said, "about what an amazing coincidence it is that I love you and you love me back? I mean, it's so amazing that anyone loves anyone else at all in the first place. But what are the odds that the person you love will love you back?"

"I think about it all the time."

Michael kissed her lips and, as if it were the first time, the great old chord inside of her was struck.

It was getting late and the sky was darkening where the sun had abandoned it. Reluctantly they took themselves and their accoutrements back inside the redbrick. There were all kinds of papers they were supposed to be writing. But it was useless to try to do any work when they were together. They would sit on the same couch trying to read and in a few minutes they would be in each other's arms, deliriously mutual, with only the tiniest shrug for what had been flung aside.

And so it went. Books flung aside, then clothes, then the whole rest of the world.

The wind disappeared. The day was long gone. John Coltrane was playing "My Favorite Things." The moon rose over Cahaly's Syrian grocery, recently expanded into a bigger store.

A leaf of the coleus fell into the white candle.

"**I**s this the way it's supposed to be?" said Sarah to an unusually sober Franklin P. Haas. "It's like an interstellar life. Everything else—Harvard, Quincy House, the dining hall, the streets, classes—everything else seems like just a landing platform!"

They were standing on the front steps of the *Crimson* in the spot where Sarah and Michael had first spoken together. A thousand emotions passed in a flash over Haas's face, the final one being, perhaps, that he wished he had a stiff drink.

"You have my complete and entire blessing," he replied gallantly. "Such states are the stuff of song and story, not given to everyone to experience directly. Carry on, old girl! *Carpe diem!*"

Sarah was pleased with Haas's reply. There were very few souls to whom she would entrust such a question. He was a being strangely outside of the social fabric, a type of gnomic godfather.

"But speaking *in loco parentis,*" he went on solemnly, "I must of course remind you not to neglect your Harvard education."

Sarah wrinkled her nose questioningly. This was the first thing he had said that didn't ring true.

"For instance," continued Haas, now gazing off into an indeterminable distance, sniffing the bouquet of an imaginary bourbon and branch, "why don't you take young Verboten to the Bogart flick at the Brattle tonight? I believe they're showing *To Have and Have Not,* a nice little Hemingway-Faulkner collaboration. . . ."

Sarah giggled in relief. Yes, it would be fun to go see *To Have and Have Not* again, to see Hoagy Carmichael playing the piano on "How Little We Know" and "Hong Kong Blues" . . . and laugh with Walter Brennan, the rummy sidekick . . . and hear again the wonderful deep voices of the moral hero and the intelligent heroine being terse about their emotions. . . .

May, and on the Charles the crews were practicing for Yale and the Henley Royal Regatta. The varsity team was undefeated. Eight tall men crowded into each of the lithe crafts. Beneath their sweatshirts their chests were broad and muscled, their bodies taut. They rowed together with a concentration in action that was a kind of trance. Number two oar, a man of finesse, was pulling hard, all his muscles straining, his face resolute. As the boat came up to speed he was conscious of an eerie noiseless rush along the hull and a patterned dripping from the lifted blades. Silhouettes of the Boston skyline danced in his peripheral vision. The launch drew near. On its white stern someone had painted "Class of 1892." A voice shouted: "Draw your hands higher!" The well-born young men, experiencing themselves for a moment as galley slaves, felt its wake. This year they were to do thirty-five strokes a minute with the new European oar. As the stroke moved up imperceptibly, the big man at number five counted to bring himself closer to the end. But he kept forgetting—starting to count again—forgetting again. The pulling continued. Two hours a day, five days a week, a meet on Saturday. They had run, lifted weights, exercised, to be ready. But it was only these two thousand meters that were real. The tension along their arms and legs and across their backs reached an extreme. The little hundred and twenty-pound coxswain was yelling, commanding respect, overcompensating. The expressions on the faces of the rowers had frozen into astonishment, indignation, ferocity. The light fellow at number eight had his tongue out.

There! Done! Over!

As the long oars stopped moving, the number one oarsman closed his eyes and let himself drift. Water ran silently under the boat as they glided to the dock.

In the showers the athletes felt the bliss of undefeated youth. Somebody slapped somebody on the shoulder. Water spray accompanied their pleasured talk like music.

Jims dressed and left Weld Boathouse and walked out into Cambridge's diffident spring. Gray winter had been touched with the faintest, most delicate hope. The elm across from the Henri IV was beginning to bud. Health propelled Jims's limbs and loins and bones. His long clean uncombed yellow hair cried out happily against the

royal blue sweater he had let himself wear. As he strode back to the
House, he could have passed for a young artist on Wanderjahre.

The nascent sensation of happiness surprised him. For though
he had lived a life of the fortunate, he had always troubled his contentment with uncertainties. Sometimes he acted in ways he knew his
forebears would not understand, though he did not doubt himself for
all that; this kind of enjoyment was called "ecstasies of badness." But
simple happiness had for the most part eluded him and he was curious
to search out its plain lines. Today walking up Boylston he asked
himself: "Am I happy? How would the happiness of my life look on a
graph? Who is happy? If you ask someone, 'Are you happy?' is their
answer trustworthy? Is it the job of social orders to make happiness
feasible? Shouldn't I try to find out how happy are the people outside
myself?"

As for today, Jims thought that yes, perhaps he was happy. This
evening he had a date with a perfectly lovely girl, an appropriate girl,
a girl whose family had been importing perfume into the U.S. for two
hundred and fifty years.

The applause was deafening. The
well-bred, well-dressed audience dug its trim leather heels into the
deep-pile carpet of the Loeb Theater and clapped loudly and with no
sign of letting up for Dan Matlaw's play about the fight for space
inside a fallout shelter. The play had first opened more than a year
before, but the scare over the Cuban missiles had brought it back to
the boards.

In the lead role, Nestor Schwarz was bowing deeply and with a
flourish from the center of the mainstage. He was looking extremely
thin these days, had dyed his eyebrow black, and the porkpie hat the
role required gave him something of the charisma of the young J.
Robert Oppenheimer. His ankles were glamorously clad in neon red
socks.

The audience was beginning to rise as the clapping diminished. Proud of themselves, content, uplifted ("There's the *Crimson* reviewer!"), they filed out of the glittery auditorium and congregated in small groups in front of a lobby wall built to resemble a shower of gold coins. It was eleven. The evening's "Square coffee" had yet to be drunk. Garden Street awaited for the final walks home, the girls' high heels catching in the spaces between the bricks, a suggestion of romance in the lilac-heavy night.

Without taking the makeup off his face Nestor breezed out of the theater and strode his distinctive slumping walk to the corner where Tui Burne-Jones had promised to meet him with her car and Rosa Doe. As he walked he whistled "Doe a Deer," in his head—a tune he hated—to keep himself from thinking.

"Heya, Barrymore!" Tui greeted him, screeching on the brakes and simultaneously slapping her left hand on the side of the dusty yellow Jag. The car stopped just short of jumping the traffic island. Crowded in the back, Rosa was wincing.

Nestor threw his head back and laughed, guffawed, his eyes dark with painted lines, ecstatically happy to see his raucous friend; and yet, if one looked deeply into the actor's thigh-slapping, careening-into-side-of-car laugh, one would see a weeping. Tui saw it, and it was why she liked Nestor. He was the first thing she had found in Cambridge that hadn't bored her, not excepting Chaucer; and she intended to stick with him.

"Get in," she commanded. "How was the boop-a-doop?"

Nestor slid into the front seat beside Tui and immediately turned to give wide-eyed Rosa in the back a long, significant look. "My little honey," his look seemed to say. "Are you afraid of me?" And, "I'm dangerous!" All the while he was silent, letting his shadowy eyes and the smells of his body do the work of the irresistible magnetism project. Abruptly, he refocused on Tui.

"It had humor and it had serious," said Nestor gravely, the bad grammar meant to convey an obscure joke on audiences. "Matlaw is a genius. He knows how lost we are. And that those who don't admit they are lost are the most lost of all."

Tui understood that Nestor wanted to talk about how he had played his role tonight and how well the audience had liked him, and she deftly steered the conversation to these matters as her car sped through the stately suburban sections of Cambridge. Nestor chain-smoked as she drove, his arm out of the window grasping the convertible's black vinyl roof. He held forth on the fine points of his art, sometimes directing his remarks at Tui, sometimes at the heavy-leaved elms flying by outside. He was sensitive, he was cultured, he was malicious. The word for him in Tui's mind was "brilliant."

"And how was our friend Fisher tonight?"

"Fisher is a fool! A simpleton! He makes me want to hug him," replied Nestor.

Rosa knew this Fisher slightly, and had always heard that he was smart. She leaned her chin into her hands, so pretty, so round, resting her elbows on the back of the front seat, and said something inconsequential. Nestor regarded her with a start. He couldn't believe how sweet and innocent she looked. He thought she must be playing some kind of game with him. He decided to test her.

"You're something of a simpleton yourself too, aren't you, my dear?" he said to her, all the while smiling his hot, inky, Maybelline smile.

"What?" Rosa was astounded. She sat back abruptly. "What did you say?"

Nestor was disgusted. It was such an uninteresting response.

Tui turned to see, and jumped in on Nestor's side. "Oh, Rosa!" she berated the other girl. "It's so stupid to take Nestor seriously. He was just putting you on!"

Rosa was not crying actually, although there was a trace of water around her eyes. When she spoke her voice was very small. "I'd like to go home," she said. "I, um, don't want to go to the Shore tonight."

"Oh! I don't believe it!" said Tui in exasperation. "We're practically at Revere already! I can't turn the car around now!"

"I don't care," said Rosa, sniffling outright. "I want to go home." She pulled her black sweater from the seat next to her where it was piled haphazardly and wound it tightly across her thin shirt like a shawl, tucking her hands in to stop her breasts from shaking.

Nestor had taken up a noncommittal pose and was exhaling Parliament smoke out the window.

"What do you think, Neddy? We can't turn around now, can we?" Tui appealed to him.

He coughed, took another drag, and then said in a low, father-of-the-leading-man voice, "Well, I guess this is a matter for you two girls to work out."

Tui swung the car around abruptly, making a U-turn that gave Rosa a sensation of giddy relief, and the three of them sped back to Cambridge in the expectant glow of the spring midnight. Rosa was sitting far back in her squeezed-in place wondering why she had agreed to meet this person. Tui was cranky and inconvenienced and worried about Nestor's feelings. Nestor was curiously relieved that things were working out as badly as they always did. And he was ever so slightly fascinated with Rosa.

The car sped up Garden Street, past Virginia Morris walking carefully alongside a tall, stately R. R. Hodgson. They passed many other pairs going north and many single fellows coming back south. With a screech Tui pulled into the driveway that circumambulated the complex of dorms and left Rosa off flat in front of Holmes.

"Good night, dear!" Nestor called out to her as she left, her sweater dangling. She did not answer, nor did she look back.

So Tui and Nestor proceeded once again to their borrowed place on the North Shore as they had planned, and in the large house of Tui's absent roommate they broke out the Beefeater and the macadamia nuts and drank and laughed at how stupid Rosa had been. They sat in the elegant nautical living room in front of the unused fireplace and talked and laughed about plays and people until nearly dawn. And then they retired to the little boy's bedroom upstairs with its blue sailboated sheets and astrolabe clock, and they grappled together with their clothes off (all except Nestor's socks; those he would keep on) until the gentle hours of the morning had been well flouted, taking up with their usual alacrity the theme of assigning fault for their sexual unsuccess—"You're frigid!" "You're impotent!"—until, after an hour or two of shallow sleep, propelled once again into the day by fatigue and black coffee, they got back into the yellow Jag and returned to Cambridge.

Rosa had made herself some tea on the hot plate and gone right to bed, calmed but still wondering, thinking about her family.

It started simply enough. Michael and Sarah were discussing what to do that evening. There was Dan Matlaw's play at the Loeb. There was a *Crimson* faculty dinner. (The cowboy would stand in the background alone, tall and moping, still not at ease with grown-ups. Sarah would go over to the nearest Nobel prizewinner and ask him some brazen question. To Vitamin-A-in-the-eye George Wald she had said, "Why do you study the effects of infra-red light on vision, and not the effects of ultraviolet light?" Wald had given her no answer, but became her fast friend.) And then there was a party being given by a very cute visiting comp lit professor from Heidelberg, who had especially asked Sarah and Michael to be there.

It was the kind of problem that often arose in Cambridge, beehive of the world.

"What do *you* want to do?" said Sarah.

"I don't really care that much. What do you want to do?"

"I don't know! I want to do them all!"

"Well, really, now, it isn't that important, is it?"

"Oh, it is! I just feel so split!"

Sarah's indecision became anxiety. Michael was calm and dispassionate about the evening, willing to let her choose. The hour grew later and later until the time for first the one and then the other party came and went. Michael held Sarah in his arms as she wept, and stroked her hair and smoothed her overloaded circuits with gentle words. And when it was far, far too late for the call of Harvard—drama or journalism or literature or even social life—they went into his bedroom and made love deeply, passionately, and wholeheartedly, spiting all and everything with the terrible hubris of youth.

Tui Burne-Jones was on academic probation due to an unfortunate rash of low marks, unfinished term papers, and one fairly major alleged plagiarism. But she had managed to keep this fact a secret from the other girls in the dorm. Indeed it was widely believed—to the credit of Tui's glib ingenuity and skill in instilling her peers, if not the faculty, with confidence in herself—that her grade report, never actually seen of course, consisted of all A's. Rosa would have sworn to it. Sarah took it for granted.

Tui didn't think twice about being on "pro." She had been the bad girl all through prep school, saving herself time after time at the last minute on the strength of cleverness, charm, and the occasional phone call from Mummy in Bel Air. Having thrown away her virginity with a great flourish the summer before her freshman year, she now compounded her misbehavior eagerly with the help of the yellow sports car. She slept out of the dorm rather more than she slept in it. She quite disregarded the intricate sign-out rules. And when she was waylaid by the real guardians of Radcliffe morals, the Boston Irish cleaning ladies mopping up the dormitory halls and bathrooms at ten or eleven in the morning, watching out for girls just such as Tui returning groggy to their rooms, she was rude to them. The situation was grave indeed. Deans Pomfret, Anderson, and Paine sat down in Fay House to look over her file and consider whether Adeline ("Tui") Burne-Jones might, regrettably, have to be severed.

Two things were on Dean Porlock's mind as he strode from his office in University Hall toward the Wursthaus: sex and drugs. He had asked Health Services Director Lewis Cushing to meet him for lunch because there was a storm in his brain. During a fire scare in the middle of one night this week, a naked girl had come running out of Adams House. The *Crimson* had reported with prim irony that she was "an artist's model." But to Porlock she rankled like a bare-breasted valkyrie at the head of a surging parade unfurling the banner of revolution.

Dean of Harvard College Malcolm Porlock was a manly man, tall, dark, not yet fifty, straight-backed, impeccably dressed, Unitarian, wealthy, a *summa cum laude* graduate of Princeton. His abundant black hair had grayed at the temples, and he wore a neat black mustache over his mouth.

The Adams House girl had affected the ruddy Health Services director in much the same way. Across heavy plates of cold cuts Lew Cushing handed his friend Porlock a report his staff had recently completed on the consequences of student sexual activity. The dean took the thick monograph—statistics, factor analyses, sociological jargon—and skimmed it quickly, sighing.

On its concluding page, the report specified that fifty percent of college women had had sexual intercourse. The figure was so conveniently ambivalent it had to be spurious. This Porlock understood, but he also saw the immediate utility of the report. Its implication was that premarital collegiate sexual activity invariably had bad consequences: academically, psychologically, socially. . . .

"Yes. Here it is," said Porlock to the medical man, giving the report a tap. "This is what we needed."

"But—you don't mean this kind of information should be made public—?" corrected Cushing. It contained, after all, case histories.

"No, of course not. I was thinking we could distribute it in confidence to the freshman proctors, senior tutors, masters, deans. . . . Am I forgetting anyone?"

Cushing touched his neck. "How about their counterparts in New Haven . . . Williamstown? . . ."

"Exactly!" responded the dean. "All the major Eastern colleges." The dean had a daughter who was a sophomore at Bryn Mawr.

"Mm hmm."

The men ate. They drank steins of Bavarian dark beer. At another table someone put a dime into the Seeburg 100 Wall-o-Matic and played an orchestral version of "My Favorite Things" in the style of "Oklahoma!"

What they were not talking about just yet was the drug question. That one was harder to get a grip on, a kind of guerrilla warfare compared to the conventional, Maginot Line fighting oversexuality. Some saw it as even more of a threat to the social fabric. Porlock and Cushing waved this off; "our kind of boys" would not be involved. But just to be sure, the dean and the doctor had sent a letter to the *Crimson* deploring the use of mind-altering drugs and warning that their effects could be dangerous in unpredictable ways.

It was sticky. Last year, someone from the Commonwealth of Massachusetts had come around to make an investigation, asking exactly who was distributing drugs in Cambridge. What a question! The state's senior food and drug inspector, Alfred Murphy, had seemed to want to pin the blame on Harvard University. The deans had been in close touch at that time with Professor Addison Hoakes at the Center for Research in Personality behind the bio labs, the little unit that encompassed Binks and Thatcher and the Harvard drug work. Hoakes had vouched for his young protégé Stephen Binks (who was godfather to two of Hoakes's children) and for Binks's sidekick Buster Thatcher. And so Lewis Cushing in turn had vouchsafed to the Massachusetts authorities that there was "no evidence of any direct harm to any individuals involved." Murphy had gone away grumbling about a Harvard cover-up. This year the federal FDA was asking questions.

Dean Porlock's conscience was not entirely easy. Now he pushed aside his half-eaten deep-dish apple pie. Binks had promised not to use undergraduates as subjects. He had agreed to deposit his entire stock of imported Swiss psychedelics at the Health Center with Cushing, checking them out in library fashion with full particulars as needed. But there was increasing evidence that he was not being, well, truthful.

Cushing brought the subject up first. "Even Hoakes now says that Binks and Thatcher have given up science for the sake of promoting a cult."

Porlock nodded.

Binks and Thatcher were speaking a lot about the "game" of being a Harvard professor. Indeed, everything they said now about the university and its rules was said in tones of rich, redolent derision. They much less frequently referred to their own new pursuits as a "game," but when they did, as they did indeed upon occasion, it was with gentle humor and tender irony, as one might speak of the butterfly-collecting obsession of a small, plump, introverted boy. As scientists, they would have had to pay attention to Harvard as an authority, in some sense or other. But as promoters of a cult, as harvesters of souls, they were a law unto themselves, Neanderthals.

"They've got the first damn organization in the history of the world for the promotion of drug-taking," remarked Cushing sourly. He was thinking of the International Federation for Internal Freedom—or whatever the acronym IFIF might be construed to mean.

The infection had already spread beyond the Center for Research in Personality. Binks and Thatcher had rented two large houses in suburban Newton Centre, where Binks's father still lived, and the houses had quickly filled up with friends and hangers-on. The neighbors had given them some trouble at first over the zoning laws—which stipulated "one family" dwellings—but the elder Binks, a retired millionaire and former president of an oil and chemical conglomerate, had appeared before the town authorities and convinced them that "family" didn't necessarily mean blood relatives.

Besides the Center at Harvard, and the two houses just minutes away in Newton, Porlock knew of another drug office that would soon be opening in the new medical building in downtown Boston, and the grapevine was speaking of drug offices in Los Angeles and on the beach near Acapulco. As it happened, there would be trouble in Mexico. Not long after hearing Buster Thatcher give a lecture on LSD, it would occur to a young Mexican government official that the Harvard professor was absurd, that Mexico had an indigenous drug-taking population of its own, thank you, and that no good could come from this influx of neoprimitives. And so the little clot of American flower children would be summarily expelled from the Catalina Hotel in Zihuatanejo.

In a dittoed report to the Center for Research in Personality, Thatcher and Binks were boasting that in two years they had given psilocybin—the synthetic mushroom extract—to some four hundred people. Of these, they reported, ninety-one percent had had "good trips." That meant of course that nine percent, or thirty-six people, had *not* had good trips. But what did that mean? No one cared to discuss it. It seemed like bad luck even to allow the topic to cross one's mind. Binks and Thatcher certainly weren't worrying. They said again and again that if you had a bad trip it was because you didn't take the drugs with them; or if you did take the drugs with them it was because your attitude and expectations were incorrect. And since there was no way anyone had figured out to determine in advance if a prospective drug-taker's attitudes and expectations ("set and setting," they chanted) were correct or not, well, they just winged it. If you flipped out, you were meant to flip out. Your affairs were just so much melodrama, anyway.

"I don't entirely understand Hoakes's attitude," admitted Porlock. "I know he believes there may be a danger of permanent drug effects . . . but he continues to support the research."

"Well, we'll just have to see," replied Lew Cushing.

The two administrators took leave of each other on the corner outside the restaurant. As he walked back to University Hall, Porlock ground his teeth. He personally wanted to fire the two junior faculty members at the epicenter of this reprehensible activity. But Professor Hoakes, for all his conflict—once Porlock had heard him say "It tears my heart!"—was still officially standing behind them. In terms of protocol, in this community of gentlemen and scholars, there wasn't a whole lot the dean of the college could do.

In a sanitarium in Georgia, a young man who had been recently an honors student at Harvard was concerning himself with the nurses, aides, and orderlies on his locked ward.

Between entreaties to them to let him out, he was praying aloud to "the mystic mushroom."

It seemed to him that all the faces so earnestly surrounding him, speaking platitudes and other reassuring nonsense, were the faces of devils and demons, their voices the voices of demons; and he imagined he heard the howling, sulphurous winds of hell all around him. His agony was terrible.

The doctor came and gave him a shot of one gram of Thorazine.

And as he lay in his bed in a miasma of semiconsciousness, the student decided that by taking psilocybin with Stephen Binks he had enabled the devil to destroy the mind of God and thereby to win, contrary to all forecasts, the battle of Armageddon, so that all good people were damned unto infinite pain infinitely prolonged.

The houses along Brattle Street. Old, Colonial, beautiful, with pleasant lawns. Each one a subtly individuated social and intellectual circle. In this one see Edmund Wilson and the publishers of *The New York Review of Books*. In this one see Tom Lehrer (of "Fight Fiercely, Harvard") and the technocratic psychologists. In this one the boy's parents are not at home and a great throng has raided the icebox, spilt liquor on the floor, and gone upstairs to the bedrooms to pass out.

And yet, different as they are, each is related to all the rest *subterraneo,* through the basements, tunnels, and storm cellars of the mind. Brattle Street. The sum and product is Harvard, control center of Western intellectualism.

Appian Way is something different. Appian Way is still Radcliffe, gritty, old school, feminist Radcliffe. Taking refuge from the storms of competitive Cambridge, in a small and modest white frame house on Appian Way, an English scientist named Francis Crick is handing across a rickety formica kitchen table to Harvard scientist James D. Watson a many-times folded piece of yellow paper upon which rows of initials are scratched, chartlike, in pencil. It is the DNA code.

Sarah Galbraeth, noticing, asks Watson what the last problem science will solve is.

"Love," replies Watson, and asks to see her home.

Dean Porlock went too far when he started writing letters to the *Crimson* about sex. Harvard students were misusing their visiting privileges in the Houses, he complained (the limit was set at three "parietal" hours daily, with slightly more time on weekends). "We are seeing a rise in the incidence of premarital sexual intercourse," the dean wrote, "which is *prima facie* unfortunate. But when this begins to involve the young lady students of the neighboring colleges, we have a phenomenon grievously to be deplored."

The cowboy, incredulous, phoned the dean to ask him if he really wanted his letter to be printed.

The dean replied that he did. He was throwing his full weight behind Cushing's Health Center report. Always the inquiring reporter, the cowboy probed the dean's attitude: Was he really maintaining that sex was "bad?" The dean clarified his position. And the cowboy, hanging up, concluded that what the dean and by implication the university were calling for was a return to simpler times, "the good old days," when Harvard men could blamelessly ravish townies while preserving respect and honor for the virgins who were their social peers.

The cowboy was frankly puzzled. There was a kink in this argument somewhere. Why were good men expected to get a sexual education somehow, and good women to be protected from it? The cowboy-journalist was himself not so very sexually experienced. But in his private religion the madonna Sarah was fully justified in using Harvard real estate for the consummation of her dream love with the boy prince Michael. For her sake, as much as for the mid-century rational individualism of his own background, the cowboy rallied the *Crimson* around the position that sex was probably "all right," but that, in any event, it wasn't the business of the university to worry about it.

The dean's scandal batted about in the pages of the undergraduate newspaper for about a month, precipitating a fall of moral dandruff over the campus. No one could quite figure out where or why the trouble had begun. Witty letters to the editor rebutted Porlock. Long eloquent defenses of sex were printed on the *Crimson* features pages. Some of the chaste became uneasy.

But when, by coincidence, Michael wrote an article about the continuing debate, and used the word "sex" in a headline for the first time (previously the *Crimson* had always referred to the matter of "parietal" hours, which was an in-group term), the Hearst paper in Boston picked it right up.

The next afternoon two thousand copies of the Boston *Record-American*, screaming "Harvard Bares Sex Scandal," were sold in Harvard Square. Night-editing, the cowboy commented wryly in a picture caption: "The market for fiction has improved spectacularly. Here Harvard men" (showing a great crowd grabbing at the papers) "fight to get story on wild parties they never attended."

The wire services jumped on the bandwagon. Under wonderfully clever headlines an account of sex at Harvard was published the following day in New York, Philadelphia, New Haven, Miami, Washington, Dallas, Denver, Phoenix, Minneapolis, and elsewhere. West of Iowa it was printed on the inside pages. In the East it was page one.

In the *Crimson* sanctum the boy in the blue workshirt and green silk polka-dot tie was talking about the sexual revolution. "Telephones are as much to blame as contraceptives," he was saying.

"Wrong again, JHC!" snorted the cowboy, who was stretched out on one of the ratty leather sofas drinking a Coke.

A spot of red appeared in the other speaker's cheeks. "It's true," he said. "People used to marry one another and stay together because they wanted someone to talk to. Now all they have to do is pick up a piece of plastic and they can talk to anyone they want, anywhere, any time."

The cowboy harrumphed.

"Don't blame it on a machine!" said a voice from the direction of a Charlie Chan movie playing at low volume on a black and white TV. "Malcolm is right," this person continued. "It's the fault of the communist free-lovists out to undermine this great nation."

"Very intelligent," said the cowboy. "You can tell this is a former *Crimson* president speaking."

To defend his honor the Charlie Chan fan now swung his armchair around to face the others. Stuffing was coming out of its cushions and arms in little white wisps like puffs of immobilized smoke. When he had repositioned himself, R. LeBaron paused confidently.

He had indeed been president of the *Crimson* some twenty-five years before. Now he was a prominent Wall Street stockbroker. Like many of the old *Crimson* fold, however, he found himself stopping in to the humble establishment on Plympton Street whenever he was remotely in the neighborhood. For here he still found a certain ethos and camaraderie no later glories or wealth or association with the mighty had quite matched.

"Let me tell you about the time I had Kimberly George Todd spread-eagled on my bed," he said.

"Go right ahead," said the cowboy.

"She was only there, you understand, because it was spring vacation. We didn't have all these 'parietal hours' you fellows have now. The houses were off limits to the distaff. But there she was, officially home with mum, in reality all mine, in my McKinlock Hall suite, the roommates gone to the Cape or somewhere. Oh, she was pretty. She was a field hockey player. She was writhing. She wanted me. She wanted it. There was her pretty blond hair all splayed out on my pillow, there were her trim . . . Well, perhaps I'd better not go on."

"Suit yourself," said the boy in the blue workshirt and green tie.

"What do you mean? Go on, you turkey!" thundered the cowboy.

"Well," said LeBaron slowly, former *Crimson* president, prosperous broker—"could I have some of that Coke?—well, there she was, naked as the day she was born. And I just couldn't do it. I made her get up and get dressed and go home."

The cowboy: "What? Are you crazy? Why?"

LeBaron drank up the Coke heartily. "Because she was Kimberly George Todd. She was a big person at Radcliffe. I couldn't do that to her."

"Kimberly George Todd . . ." said JHC. "The name *is* familiar."

"She's the president of Saddletruss State Teachers' College now," said LeBaron, "a fine Midwestern institution."

Then the weight of life and love and the times settled over all three of them for a moment, sitting there in odd and random postures in the reddish shadows of the sanctum.

"So how's life treatin' ya, RL? What's shakin' on the Street?"

W_as LeBaron's attitude outmoded? Not in 1963, no. The slope of the curve may have been about to change but it had not changed yet, and those people who had discovered their own sexual freedom still considered themselves pioneers.

Take Jims, for instance.

Two years earlier during the Christmas deb season in New York, the handsome Jims had met a fabulously beautiful girl from a perfume-importing family who was fortuitously heading for Radcliffe the following fall just as he, himself, was bound for Harvard; and not wanting to waste a good and economical opportunity, Jims had started to date this girl with consistency verging upon the dogged, making complete sports and gameboard friends with all her sisters and brothers and both parents and such grandparents as were available, installing himself in both the summer and winter homes of his "girl friend" ("Is he still hanging around?"); and this he did with a sense of total correctness and propriety he associated with virtue. Yet in all his years in boys' schools, even at such a fine school as Phillips Andover Academy, he had never learned how to talk to a girl or treat her like a pal; she was a beautiful thing, an object, a tool in the struggle of life. Her adorable little green bathing suit hung in the bathhouse of Jims's parents' summer house on Block Island. And he wouldn't consider having sex with her in a million years.

"Harry, which seems worse to you: mediocrity or insanity?" asked Sarah.

"Insanity, of course," replied Harold Weiss. "Doesn't it to you?"

"No," said Sarah thoughtfully. "Mediocrity seems worse."

Harold Weiss was a mathematical genius, the kind of precocious kid you can actually imagine getting a Nobel Prize when he grows up. Crew-cutted, bow-tied, white-shirted, he had an uncanny sense of concentration, though his movements on the overt level were awkward, evasive, even listless.

As the newest member of the *Crimson*'s governing executive board, Weiss took his job very seriously. One of the first tasks he faced was to help put together a position for the paper on Binks and Thatcher. The cowboy was president now, and Schulte managing editor, and they and the other execs worked together long hours in one another's offices wrestling with the drug question. There were long and serious debates about the nature of scientific inquiry, about the ability of undergraduates to judge faculty research, about the quality of the testimony on both sides, and so on. While they all felt an initial repugnance for the idea of research into mind-alteration, they could understand, at the same time, the university's reluctance to put itself in a position of "having turned its back on another Galileo."

And yet whose motivation can be said to be pure? The cowboy had caught the thrilling scent of a police action. Schulte thought about the sad but necessary business of journalism. Among them Weiss was unusual in feeling absolutely no fascination with the subject.

Though he was not actually one of the paper's executives, Thaddeus P. Foote often joined in the drug deliberations. Uniquely in the university, he seemed to have one foot in the drug world and one foot out of it.

Foote had attended a meeting at the Center for Research in Personality and subsequently printed a summary of the Center's business in the *Crimson*, which embarrassed Professor Hoakes. Whether he had "infiltrated" the meeting, as he liked to claim, or merely attended an open meeting, was not entirely clear. But it was clear that Foote had a passionate interest in the case of Binks and Thatcher and more facts than anyone else around. He was to play a key role in their firing.

Barely ten years later he would be making his own fortune as the most popular cable TV talk show host, promoting the very same drugs, in all the ways it was legal to do so.

One afternoon in the spring of 1963 Foote brought it to the attention of the *Crimson* exec board that at least two and possibly as many as a dozen Harvard students had been committed to mental hospitals after having taken Binks's and Thatcher's drugs with them. One of the boys was even claiming that Binks had seduced him, that that was what had driven him mad.

"Holy shee-eet!" responded Weiss.

"So that's what they mean when they call their course 'Existential Transactional Behavior Modification'!" said the cowboy.

"Yeah, and 'Love Engineering,' " added Schulte.

Foote spread out the documentation. Sam they all knew. Randy was the son of one of America's richest Jewish families.

"Holy shee-eet!" said Weiss again. "Those poor guys."

"Page one, column five?" said Schulte, turning to the cowboy.

"Not so fast," interrupted Foote, holding up a white-goatskin-gloved hand. "The university isn't pleased with what Binks and Thatcher are doing, the few who actually know anything about it. But their lawyers tell them they don't have a case. Not based on this, anyway. It can't be proved that the drugs are responsible for the breakdowns."

"Even if they happen on the same day?" interrupted Weiss, pointing to Foote's papers.

"Even if they happen on the same day," repeated Foote, with a shaman's lilt. "It can always be said that these were latent psychotics, that they're just some kids who've messed up their lives and want to blame the university."

"Latent psychotics? That's not a textbook term," mused Weiss.

"Well, look at it this way," continued Foote. "If you have this crazy kid get up on the stand with a funny expression in his eyes, and maybe his hair not combed right, and he points a finger at a tenured Harvard professor—"

"Neither Thatcher nor Binks is a full professor or tenured," objected Schulte.

"—which of them do you think the judge is going to believe?"

The cowboy was convinced. Schulte was silent. Weiss was trying hard to bring law and justice over onto the same side.

But the cowboy was also mad. Standing up, balancing a big hand on a big thigh on a hard, smooth, cut-away writing desk, and reverting for extra emphasis to his full Grand Tetons drawl, the cowboy said: "As *ah* see it, the *Crimson* oughta publish the *hail* outa them mo'fux! Comeon, *man*! Let's go talk to the damn *la' ou'sel!*"

And so they went to the lawyers, the tall cowboy, the round-faced Schulte, the bow-tied Weiss (the red-bearded Foote trailing behind), visiting *Crimson* counsel in Boston that very day; and they found out that the same thing preventing the university from prosecuting the drug miscreants tended to prevent the paper from printing the story. After a long afternoon they settled back into the newsroom with Elsie's Specials and prepared their next move. The worst of it was that, as Foote now told them, the parents of the several drug casualties were apparently no more keen than the university on having anything revealed. The execs ate their roast beef and slurped their Coke (Weiss eating tuna salad because he was kosher), and thought.

As they ruminated, the idea came to Weiss that the problem was in the language of the debate. Naturally, all other things being equal, they had more respect for and confidence in Dean Porlock as a man than in this pair of wise guys from California (Thatcher had taught at Berkeley, Binks at Stanford). But the drug twins' preachings were just so wildly confident and charismatic. They were full of prehistoric yodels ("Ololiuqui!") and stirring theosophy. They said exciting things like: "The drug experience is no more dangerous than four years at Harvard!" They pooh-poohed every kind of authority beyond the realm of drugs with the noisy, directed focus of Joshua shouting down the walls of Jericho.

By contrast the antidrug forces seemd vague, ambiguous, bland, hesitating, qualifying, lacking in conviction. Porlock's letter to the *Crimson* had concluded with a weak: "I don't like anyone urging our undergraduates to use them [drugs]." They spoke of the "misuse" of drugs, but gave no clue to their proper use. It was discouraging.

But when Foote had added to the mix the missing—suppressed—facts about Randy and Sam and the others, the *Crimson* execs' three understandings suddenly transmuted like chunks of dark metal turning multicolored in the fire, and they heard all the old slogans in a new way. Suddenly Porlock's and Cushing's simple statement: "The drugs are dangerous," took on a bony elegance.

It was hard, they agreed, to speak in favor of consciousness nonexpansion, about as hard as to defend democracy.

Michael sat alone in his living room in Mather, his beard overgrown, his clothes raunchy, gazing at the print over the fireplace of Blake's *The Good and Evil Angels Struggling for Possession of a Child*. The child in the good angel's arms had its hands thrown up piteously. The radiant angel carried him with some slight concern over the waters. The evil angel looked worried and also guilty, his hands extending limply out from his cape of fire, his chained legs flung out behind him. Michael's gaze melted into Blake's shimmering, iridescent colors, from the half-sun on the waters to the skins of the three beings, to the hot breathing fire.

He had a paper on Plato due for gov, and he couldn't bring himself to start it. Was Plato a totalitarian?

Sarah had offered to type it.

Sarah was waiting for Michael in the Radcliffe library. He was very late. But she didn't think for a minute to be angry with him. Perhaps he was having a conversation that was difficult to break off, with George, say. He would never tell George, "Well, I gotta go now." She spotted two other lovers on the far side of the reading room. The curves of their arms on each other's chairs were so wonderfully "two." They looked at each other and changed their faces in the partial oblivion of sex. Sarah basked in their beauty.

The cowboy was aglow with a fiery Western fury. He had put on his good ten-gallon hat for the occasion. Schulte, Weiss, and Foote were sequestered in his office, two on the sagging sofa, one on the arm of the threadbare armchair. Outside the closed door cartoonist David Royce '56 had caricatured every *Crimson* president since 1958, and heads decorated the wall like an imperial column of captured kings.

"What we're gonna do," the cowboy snarled, "is demand the immediate firing of Binks and Thatcher."

Foote smiled and cleared his throat, Weiss raised his eyebrows, and Schulte said, "How do we do that?"

"Simple," said the cowboy. "We make old Malc Porlock believe we're about to print the story about the guys who flipped out. It's one thing for him to be on record opposing giving drugs to undergraduates. But he can't get caught turning the other cheek on this kind of horse manure. He'll fire them to keep us quiet."

"Not bad," said Foote, suppressing a real delight. Every kind of deception thrilled him.

And that's exactly what happened.

Two days later the top *Crimson* executives plus Foote trooped over to Dean Porlock's office in University Hall in the calm geographic center of Harvard Yard for their regular weekly press conference. It was not without considerable satisfaction that they paraded along the paths of the Yard, straightening their ties and clearing their throats, for, even in the most mundane of circumstances, these ritual man-to-man confrontations with the dean, no intellectual holds barred, were exhilarating. All four were sons of the middle class. Their parents were teachers, civil servants, modest professionals. But somehow by the miracle of work these boys, Harvard's proudest product, had been promoted into the heady precincts of the ruling elite, enabled to enter, as now, the corridors of real power. Porlock might have—indeed, very likely—felt himself socially superior to the motley undergraduate newspapermen. But he never acted on that feeling.

And today was to be an extraordinary encounter.

Something was troubling the dean even before they entered. The *Crimson* editors had alerted him that they meant to discuss an "urgent" matter. Porlock had been of late quite preoccupied with the rumblings in the social body, and for the first time he looked upon these middle-class young men—now stepping, brimming with self-importance, into his austere office—as if they brought with them a dim portent of cataclysm. His thoughts turned by instinct to the meticulous files, the critical files, in his secretary's office. Perhaps the dean had a fear of being under siege by students not too different from these. But, no. These boys were tied, jacketed. He could see in their eyes and posture that they were respectful. They were not cut from the cloth of the T-shirted troops in the International Federation for Internal Freedom office just down the street. But still . . . The dean feared for the future of morality in the university, in the country. Were the *Crimson* editors going to ask something embarrassing? Demand something impossible?

"Hello, Al," he said to the cowboy, coming around the desk to shake his hand. A muscle in his forehead was working. "Hello, Charles. Hello, Thaddeus. Hello—?"

"This is Harold Weiss, the *Crimson* editorial chairman," said Foote.

"Yes. Pleased to make your acquaintance, Mr. Weiss. Won't you all sit down? Make yourselves comfortable." In the dean's office the leather wing chairs had all their stuffing intact. His desk was a neat mahogany, the walls a pleasant pastel. "What can I do for you today?"

Now Al Coulter, also known as the cowboy, felt that the gun duel mode was the most appropriate for the occasion, and so he sat back in his wing chair till his weight seemed to be balancing on a couple of cervical vertebrae, set one kangaroo-skin boot conspicuously in the air at the end of a long, blue-jeaned leg, crossed, and turned on the full hundred percent drawl.

"We all've got a complaint f' you heah, Mr. Po'lock," he said, his voice a low, hoarse rumble.

Porlock frowned. Foote in his three-piece suit smiled impassively.

"See, Mr. Po'lock," the cowboy went on, "we all've foun' out, nevah you min' how, somethin' you didn't coun' on us findin' out."

Weiss was distinctly uncomfortable. He looked around the room.

"You all have a coupla funny lakh psych-ahl-ogy profes-sors heah, name a Binks, ah think? Thet raht? An' Bustah Thatchah? An' they all've bin goin' roun' givin thet nasty 'dope' stuff to a lot a li'l studen' types. Yeah! Ev'body knows *thet.* But what ev'body *don'* know is thet when yo' big psych-ahl-ogy profes-sors get through with th' dopin' an' th' buggerin' an' th' blowin' a them po' li'l min', wa-a-al" (the cowboy's words were coming out faster and faster), "them li'l cusses' in *no* shape f' gen ed—but go runnin' home t' Mama yellin' so bad even Daddy cain't fix it, and the' they set, lahk po' ol' skunk cabbage o' tumblin' weed o' somethin' useless in some damn funny fa'ms, some god-damned laughin' academies, tryin' t' think: 'Was ah evah up the' in "Fai' Ha'va'd," o' was thet jus' somethin' ah dreamt?' An' you know *all* about it, Mr. Dean Po'lock! An' you been jus' settin' heah keepin' it quiet lahk fo' some two dang ho's-whuppin' possum-playin' yeahs!" The cowboy mock-spat. He was through. "Do you wan' t' give me yo' o-pinion on thet, Mr. *Dean* Po'lock?"

Porlock was suppressing, by long habit, the most violent fury at being addressed in this way. "If gentlemen could not conduct diplomatic sessions in the proper discourse . . ." But the dean was a moral man. He was not going to take a stand against the *Crimson*'s accurate information.

"Well," he said, clearing his throat uneasily, "so there have been some unfortunate occurrences in connection with this controversial drug research . . ." A careful inflection in his words concealed his own prior knowledge or lack of it.

The cowboy didn't distinguish this remark with a reply.

"But even if this is so," continued the dean, "as I have every reason to suppose it may be, how can we be sure that any such—uh, psychiatric difficulties—that have arisen among the drug subjects— stem *from* the drugs, in a direct, causal . . ."

"Damn, Po'lock!" exploded the cowboy. "Those wun't *'drug subjects.'* Those w' ah *frainds!*"

Porlock paused a moment. When he spoke again he directed his gaze at Foote.

"All right, gentlemen, all right," he said uncomfortably. "You are quite right. It is indeed the case that one or two students have left school recently, and the question has been raised as to whether their troubles might possibly relate to their drug experimentation. But this is not a matter for us to discuss. Surely it would benefit neither the boys themselves, nor their families, nor the university, to pursue this matter in all its complexity in the public arena. You can understand the damage it would do—"

"The damage to Harvard, you mean?" This was Weiss, speaking for the first time.

Porlock looked startled. *Et tu?* With a tiny sigh, then, he said, "Well, what would you propose?" now addressing himself to Harold Weiss, a boy he had never seen before. "I know the well-being of the university means something to you all, as does the well-being of these boys." Porlock was a bureaucrat first and last, diplomatic where he could be but always, with eternal vigilance, protecting the system. Strangely, none of the four boys sitting there with him this afternoon disliked him.

"We propose that you fire Thatcher and Binks," said Weiss quietly.

"Well, that is quite impossible," said the dean with resigned exasperation. "No member of the Harvard faculty has been fired in this century. The situation is under control without that. The drugs are in the keeping of the University Health services, and the drug research team must sign out for them when they want to use them, indicating how many doses, and with what subjects. This is a significant control, made on the initiative of Dr. Cushing. In addition the researchers have agreed not to use undergraduates as subjects."

The *Crimson* executives were restless.

Foote took the floor. "Surely, Dean Porlock," he said in a tone of extreme courtesy, "you are aware that assistant professor Binks and lecturer Thatcher have kept a plentiful supply of psilocybin, DMT, and other drugs in their own homes and elsewhere, where they have been quite blatantly flouting the controls you mention. And as for their not giving them out to undergraduates, why! there must be a hundred undergraduates right now who are part of their following!" He paused. "The *Crimson* has documented both of these facts."

It was not clear to the *Crimson* editors whether Dean Porlock was in fact aware of the drug professors' breaches of their agreement with the university. Did he secretly wish that Binks and Thatcher were nothing more than bad boys, who could be straightened out with a reprimand and a promise? Did his gentleman's commitment to Professor Hoakes at the Center for Research in Personality affect his view of the situation?

The dean of the college was stony-faced. Before he had time to respond, the cowboy leapt in again.

"What we' all gonna do, Mr. Dean," said the cowboy, "is we' all gonna *print* thet story 'bout Randy an' Sam an' the resta them flippin' the' damn wigs—unless you do fi' that coupla bad-lookin' coots, and ah mean, lahk, *raht away!* No mattuh what all thet do t' Ha'va'd!"

The *Crimson*'s ace in the hole was that Malcolm Porlock did not know that they were as leery of legal problems as he himself was. He had seen the rising tide of recklessness, and he dreaded it. He felt apprehensive and anxious, and assumed the *Crimson* of 1963 was more radical and impulsive than it was. Their tactic was successful.

The dean of the college took the matter up with the president of the college, who called in Stephen Binks for a *pro forma* conference and faced him off, and a week later the Harvard Corporation met and declared the psychologist-educator's appointments in both departments terminated.

Buster Thatcher was easier to dismiss, as he had dropped out of the game of being a Harvard professor entirely some time back, and was no longer attending classes or giving grades at all, preferring to sit in a straw lifeguard tower and stare at the Pacific Ocean.

Foote and the cowboy coauthored the story of Binks's and Thatcher's dismissal jubilantly. Yes, indeed, this was column five, and with a five-column head! Before printing it they drove out to one of the two drug establishments in Newton Centre to allow the subjects of the story the opportunity to deny or correct any statements made about them.

They found the house in a wooded residential section on the crest of a small hill at the end of a circular driveway. Three youths lolled about a rubber-tire swing in the front yard. Big wooden outer and inner front doors led in through a large entranceway to a lush, thickly carpeted living room with an ornamental fireplace at the far end. Through an arched passage they caught glimpses of what must have been a music room; a grand piano, at any rate, was lying on its side, and cluttered around it were guitars, banjos, and redundant hi-fi speakers. Where the living room branched off toward the kitchen a ladder led up to a small loft. Twelve feet overhead, the boys could see an intricately carved wooden Buddha half the height of a man. From the environs of the Buddha curlicue wisps of scented smoke wafted downward. Mattresses and cushions were scattered about.

But the cowboy could scarcely see the furniture for the girls. Everywhere he looked he saw barefooted, long-haired girls—and long-haired boys, too!—floating around, wearing long, flowing madras sarongs, T-shirts with nothing underneath, tight jeans. A woman stepped out of the kitchen with a ladle in her hand and stared at the newcomers dreamily. Foote pointed out to the cowboy a curious collage on the kitchen door: a dozen or more cutouts of naked women taken from magazines, to which was tacked a real brassiere.

Binks in a black T-shirt, his glasses off, his face more relaxed than it was when they had seen him last in the role of psychological researcher, was sitting in the music room just beyond the hearing of the *Crimson* editors. They could see him, but he hadn't noticed them yet. He was staring into the eyes of a shirtless boy with shoulder-length blond hair. His face and the boy's were about a foot apart.

A boy in a Harvard sweatshirt and a girl in a sarong idled up to Foote and the cowboy at the door, assuming they were friendly (most people were, who came here to "Pala"), and, smiling at them, began to greet and explain. Foote indicated with a discreet gesture that he was interested in Binks's activity.

"Oh, that!" exclaimed the girl in a delighted, breathless whisper. "It's a game we play. Jerry has been pursuaded not to look away from Steve's eyes. Not even for a moment!" She was enjoying the intrigue. "Soon he'll feel he has to reveal everything!" She giggled.

"Is that right? Like reveal what?" said Foote coldly.

She put her hand across her face. "Oh, you know, secrets. Like the other day Diego admitted he thought his thing was too small. Stuff like that!"

"And what did Binks say then?"

"He told him to take his pants off and go with it!" She giggled some more.

By this time Stephen Binks had heard the intruders, recognized them, and was stalking across the big entrance hall of the mansion.

"What do you want?" he demanded.

"We've come with the *Crimson* article, Steve," said Foote, holding out a galley. "Do you want to read it?"

Binks grabbed the galley sheet peremptorily and read it with red-rimmed eyes. The look of relaxation was gone from his face. When he had done he dropped it like something dirty onto the parquet floor and stood staring at the two boys.

"I'm not going to talk to you snakes," he said, with as much power as he could muster.

"You mean you have no comment?" said the cowboy dutifully but uncertainly. He found the abundance of half-dressed people a little dazzling.

"Get out of here!" Binks replied.

Hearing the commotion, Buster Thatcher entered from the kitchen off right. His fit limbs, toned by swims along every coast of North America, were wrapped in a red, gold, and blue silk striped dressing gown. He looked at the two journalists with an expression of faint consternation crossing the distant, angelic, aquiline lines of his face. He had big dreams, but for now he was just a lecturer in psychology about to lose his job. He said nothing.

"Back on the East Coast, Buster? Well, good night," said Foote pleasantly, and the *Crimson* editors turned and left. Before they had shut both doors of their car in the driveway, three of the kids had come running after them, two girls and a boy, little stamen and pistil children.

"You're going to destroy a beautiful thing!" said one of the girls. The cowboy looked at her with longing. But there was no going back now, he thought. It was a case of right and wrong. Runna bastids outa town. With billy clubs bouncing off their heads. Like Father Feeney.

"Pudendum," her tutor had said.
"Pudendum!" That dusty little man in his musty little apartment had read a Blake poem about a rose and had said "the female pudendum" was sick, rotten, and dying because some worm had gotten into it. Sarah couldn't believe her ears. At first she didn't even know what he meant. But quickly enough she figured it out, and the ugly word, combined with the man's pursed-lip expression of distaste—and the whole idea of taking wonderful old Blake and making him out to be saying something so horrible—made her feel positively sick. She wondered what was wrong with her, why she hated poetry tutorial so much. Her tutor didn't like her much either, that was clear. She was glad to finish the hour and get out.

But she couldn't stay angry for long. The brilliant spring day made her feel silly and dizzy and happy again, and she skipped over to the *Crimson* and lugged a big typewriter up to the sanctum. Dusty tutors be damned! How dare he cast aspersions (or asparagus, as Virginia would say, making a pun in French) on the poet who had written—and she banged it out now, herself, as a kind of exorcism:

> Children of a future Age
> Reading this indignant page,
> Know that in a former time
> Love! sweet Love! was thought a crime.

"Do you have to make all that racket?" said a voice from the other end of the long room. The wide-screen black-and-white TV buzzed and twitted as usual from the seat of a deeply carved, high-backed, thronelike wooden chair.

"Yes!" replied Sarah simply from the cocktail-party–peanut-table end of the sanctum, and continued. The TV was turned up a bit. More sure of herself now, even though her mean old poetry tutor always liked least about her what she liked best, Sarah began to compose a sonnet after the manner of Shelley:

> When Summer floats us mindless along
> The billows of her slow sleep-walking stream
> And daylight sharpness melts into a gleam

> Of veiled stars, when June's full-throated song
> Becomes the muted echo of a throng
> Of frogs somewhere, and feverish roses seem
> Asleep in love's surrender to a dream,
> And nowhere in the morning walk the strong:
> 'Tis then, my love, that love belongs to us
> And wordlessly we sleep away our life
> In memories and sounds. What Fall will bring
> Of all the morning world's efficient fuss
> Is yet undreamed. My wanton August wife
> And I are still alone with whispering.

Michael had come up to the sanctum and read the poem over her shoulder before she saw him. He leaned down and kissed her cheek. He liked it. Then he joined the television audience.

Sarah ambled back downstairs.

In the president's office a poker game was in progress. Schulte, four reporters, and an editor from the busy board had accumulated around a coffee table, losing their shoes under the sofa, smoking cigarettes. Caught in the bright lights of destined world leadership, they were gradually succumbing to gravity, sinking lower and lower into the springless old furniture, turning their speech into the limited channels agreed upon for the duration. Sarah watched them with amusement from the newsroom next door.

The plastic-coated cardboard rectangles slapped against the table like the lapping of small concepts against the great ocean-front property of consciousness.

"Three big fellas," said one of the reporters.

"Three ladies, goddamnit!" complained Schulte.

As the sophomore raked in his pile of quarters, dollars, and scrappy IOUs, Charlie McSilver, *Crimson* resident gambling and T.S. Eliot expert, a little green visor on his head, swooshed the cards together for the next deal. He sang as he dealt:

> Walk right in
> Sit yourself down
> Baby let your mind roll on.
> Walk right in

Sit yourself down
Baby let your mind roll on.
Everybody's talkin bout the
New way of walkin—
Do you want to lose your mind?
Walk right in—

"Shut up, McSilver," said Schulte.

"I'm out. I'm going home," said a guy in a T-shirt, rising to light a cigar.

"What's the matter, can't you play for IOUs?"

"Never touch 'em."

"So, let's play for your Harley!"

Guffaws.

"You can't quit," whined GNP, who had gone up twenty-seven dollars in the last two hours.

"Sing 'You're Just a Dumb Little Kid,' someone prompted CFMcS as the cigar-smoker walked out and down the stairs and into the light of day.

From behind the half-closed door of the president's office Sarah could hear McSilver obliging: "Oh oh oh oh oh oh oh oh oh you're just a du-umb little ki-i-i-i-i-i-i-id, you're just a du-umb little stupid little ugly little ki-i-i-i-i—"

"Not as bad as 'Walk Right In,' " said Schulte, who was glad to have an opinion in this arcane business.

The Ariels had not been taken in for a minute by Binks's and Thatcher's rainbow-hued rhetoric. They weren't attracted by the idea of "highness" because they had a deep, almost religious respect for the everyday alternations and vacillations of life. They dismissed the convenient *ex post facto* morality that "set and setting" determined whether you saw God or went mad. They were not interested in the hullabaloo of messianism or the riotous enticement to adventure. They understood that true happiness lay in temperance, prudence, justice, and a courage that rested in silence.

Like most students the three Ariels had already left Cambridge for the term, their exams completed, when the story of the firing of Binks and Thatcher broke on May 28. In touch by phone from the various environs of New York, they wondered over it. The joint by-line was a problem. Al Coulter could be trusted. But Thaddeus P. Foote?

Jims, in particular, felt that if Foote said that Binks and Thatcher had been fired, then the greatest probability was that they had not been fired, that they had never worked for Harvard in the first place, that there was no Harvard at all, much less a *Crimson* to read about their firings in, and that there was no possibility of inquiring into the basic truth of the matter since, if he, Jims, were to inquire, it would not be he, Jims, at all. In short, Jims loathed and detested Foote, and considered his playful little jokes on others' credulity to be the most odious sort of authoritarian aggression. Binks and Thatcher might be immoral, but the Ariels fretted over Foote's amorality harder and longer.

"Well, we've done it," said the cowboy to Foote. "Lurid and Pervert are out! I only wish we could've printed the whole story."

The two newspapermen looked at each other for a long moment. The clock on the *Crimson* wall over the counter of Comment Books ticked one audible tick ahead. Foote's eyes flashed emerald under his red foliage.

"Yeah-up," drawled the cowboy, stamping at something on the floor. "There's only one thing that worries me."

Foote seemed to know what the cowboy had in mind.

"Ah thaink we jes' "—"launched them," finished the two newspapermen in unison, Foote with a pleased, confirming smile, the cowboy with a worried furrow across his brow.

Having been given the boot, Tui was not a girl to stick around for long farewells. "What an awfulization!" was the last thing anyone heard her say, as her sports car laid down rubber and streaked off into new horizons.

Franklin P. Haas III was quite the other way. As befit a man who loves ceremony, he was decidedly put out that his "severance" would prevent him from participating in his class commencement exercises. Harvard commencement was nothing if not ceremonious, blessed by God as by man with fair skies for more than three hundred years, the deep velvet colors of the robes of the doctors of philosophy shimmering like the jewels and coin of a spiritual kingdom.

With ingenuity, aplomb, and unimpeachable Elizabethan diction, Haas managed to convince the young, handsome Massachusetts governor Endicott C. Peabody by phone that he, Franklin P. Haas III, had been selected to be his "student guide" for that day. And so, flawlessly attired, erudite, and proud as one can only be who has crashed a party to find himself the guest of honor, Haas walked and dined and drank his way all through the most luxuriantly ceremonious of the ceremonious activities of Universitas Harvardiensis, Commencement Exercises in the Year of Our Lord 1963, on the arm of the Governor of the Commonwealth of Massachusetts.

Along with Foote and the cowboy, Michael stayed in Cambridge that summer to work on the summer edition of the *Crimson.* Mostly he was thinking about Sarah, who was in Mason City making up an honors curriculum for the high school. His letters went off to her like Christmas gifts every few days, each one more thrilling than the last. Sarah picked the *Crimson* envelopes out of her parents' white tin mailbox with the most palpable joy. She caught her breath just to see the marks he made on paper: his simple, bold hand, in blue fountain pen ink. Beneath the foam of adventure of life in Cambridge there was always the deep surge of his manly, honest, private love.

He told her that Foote had sold the story of Binks and Thatcher to a national magazine for fifteen hundred dollars. He told her that Marilyn Monroe had been sleeping with Bobby Kennedy. He told her about the Newport Jazz Festival, and how Nina Simone singing "I Love You, Porgy" had made him almost die from missing her.

Sarah wrote to Michael about her father's occasional sudden urges to cook up big batches of home fries for the family; about her brother's baby son's thirty-word vocabulary, each word of which seemed to mean the equivalent of about five of our words; about how Marianne Reuss had run after a cow with her bedroom slippers on and gotten a knee as big as a basketball. And Michael, like Sarah, drew erotic delight from the curls his lover's purple ballpoint ink made on white looseleaf pages, and he told her so, again and again.

One night when Sarah had wandered some miles into the cornfield behind Dr. Abramson's and was sitting on a rock looking at the moon, she got a sudden feeling that Michael was thinking about her. She ran home breathlessly.

Her mother was standing at the screen door, a short woman with her hair coming out of its hairpins. "God love ya!" she said. "But what's making you move so fast?"

"Nothing really," said Sarah. "I just had this feeling."

"Sit down. Catch your breath. Your friend Michael called you all the way from Boston. How much does that cost, Ben?"

Sarah's father was sitting in the living room smoking a pipe and reading the papers.

"Michael! He did? When?"

"Just now."

"Oh, no, that must have been it! I'm going to call him back."

Her mother: "You are? I'm sure he'll call you again later this evening or tomorrow."

"Let her call the boy if she wants to," said the man in the living room in an even voice.

With trembling fingers Sarah dialed the *Crimson*, late as it was, because that was the only number she had. Wonder of wonders, he answered!

"Hullo?"

"Michael! It's me! You just called me!"

"Darling! Your mother said you were out in the fields, and I didn't think I could compete with all that Iowa corn."

"It's so wonderful to hear your voice."

"Yours too!"

"So how are you?"

"Well, I'm still getting over Newport. I didn't sleep for three days. But it was fun staying in the sailor's Y. They had these little niches where you could sit and write."

"Oh, darling."

"But the real reason I called is this postcard I got from Iowa."

"What postcard? I didn't send you any postcard."

"No. Well, I know it's stupid to make a thing of it, but somebody sent me this anonymous postcard with an Iowa postmark, saying that you were sleeping with a lot of guys out there."

"Oh, Michael! It's not true! I can't think about anybody but you!"

There was a silence at Michael's end of the line. Sarah could hear someone's running commentary on their own success throwing wads of paper into the wastebasket.

"I know that, Sarah, darling. I guess I just wanted to hear you say it. I love you."

"I love you too."

Now it was Sarah's turn to be silent. "But I don't understand. Who would want to do a thing like that?" she said.

Michael didn't have to think very long about that. He acknowledged the stunt was pretty much up Foote's alley. "He could have done it on Al's behalf. You know," (softly) "he's never stopped loving you."

"I know," said Sarah. The image of the cowboy haunted her. She could see his gigantic mournful frame lingering in doorways to look at her, startled when apprehended. She could see him gulp and turn away awkwardly. There were so many big, empty, dark spaces between Midwest and West. They just didn't meet.

"Oh, Sarah," Michael continued, "I can't wait for the summer to end. Every five minutes I think of some great thing I would say to you if we were together. I'm saving them up. Mostly they revolve around the fact that I love you."

"I love you too, baby. I *really* love you!"

They talked for a few more minutes after that, and then Sarah hung up.

In the fall Michael moved from modern, glass-faced Quincy House, full of peace marchers and Young Democrats and the drone of discussions about international trade policy, into scholarly Lowell House with its traditional Georgian architecture and proud blue bell tower and Russian bells. The lumberjack had returned to Yakima and at the last minute an impersonal housing bureaucracy had assigned Michael to room with an evangelist from Alabama.

Sarah, Rosa, Yvette, Virginia, and some of their friends had moved out of the brick dorm and into one of the big old one-family houses that lined Garden Street, a Victorian suffragist's home with stained-glass windows and a majestic circular stairwell. In Elizabeth Cady Stanton House, Rosa quickly became friends with Kievskaya, a buxom biology major who sang light opera. To Sarah, Kievskaya seemed like the typical Jewish girl, with her large breasts, thick, dark hair, and faintly olive skin. Virginia moved in with the daughter of two federal judges, on the strength of their both believing that you should "put a little Pooh in everything you do." There was a beautiful poetess in the new house too, with waist-length ash blond hair.

Carolee had transferred to an altogether different sort of off-campus house, the kind with four straight sides and a metal fire escape and a number instead of a name. But she didn't lose touch with her old friends, meeting them often in the graduate center for lunch, sometimes in the company of her new pals, the ballerina and the psychologist.

At one of these lunch dates early in the term Carolee handed Sarah a copy of *The Second Sex*. It was a well-worn ninety-five-cent Bantam paperback with a cover picture of a lovely, delicate lady of the Copenhagen harbor posed meditatively in a gold and amber mist. "Gallimard published this in French in 1949 and the Knopf edition came out in 1953," Carolee said. "But when I saw this on the rack in

Gainesville in 1961 with a naked woman on the front, I knew the tide had turned."

"How do you mean?" said Sarah.

"It meant they were ready to sell it," Carolee explained. She looked pleased to be asked. She enjoyed knowing a lot. She positively devoured *The New York Times* each morning, meticulously applying its new information to her theories of the way the world worked. But even more than reading and knowing she enjoyed answering questions, debating, educating. She didn't mind mistakes. Mistakes were merely errors in the operation of the reasoning mechanism and could generally be thrashed out and corrected by honest discussion. But unconsciousness, yawning in her face, forgetting an agreement—these she didn't go for. "You should definitely read it," she was saying now. "Not just for that reason, of course."

"I will," promised Sarah. "I always like books that people give me better than ones we're supposed to read for a course." There was another reason why Sarah would read this book, though shyness kept her from mentioning it. She had had enormous respect for Carolee ever since that first night of the Cuban missile crisis when the sky had been streaked with paralysis and fear, and Carolee had been the only one in the dorm with the calm and the faculties to stand up and speak as if what was happening could be understood.

They finished their grapefruits, putting aside the grapes disguised as maraschino cherries.

"You still seeing that nice boy Michael?"

Sarah nodded, smiling with the degree of beatitude appropriate to a huge room smelling of boiled food.

"He's president of the Liberal Union, right?"

"That's right," said Sarah. "They invite people to come speak."

"Like who?"

"Oh, uh," (Sarah had to think) "Norman Thomas, Martin Luther King, Paul Goodman—"

"Paul Goodman? Why him?"

"Why? What's wrong with him?"

"Oh, it's nothing. I mean, he's most famous for writing about bisexuality."

Sarah wrinkled her little institutional paper napkin into a ball and placed it into the hollow grapefruit half like a pale shadow of the missing pulp. "Is that bad?"

"Well, look," said Carolee, sitting forward, her eyes flashing. "Read Simone de Beauvoir." She tapped the book. "One of the things I think we should be fighting for is for strong men to love strong women. It's easy enough for men not to love women, and just love each other, since they're the richer and more powerful ones in this society anyway. That way they just keep their power and their money among themselves. And for women to go the lesbian route, well, that's a sellout, that's all; it makes it too easy for men. I know it's tricky. But I want to be loved by a man for who I am. It's a nonnegotiable demand!" Carolee shook her head at this last phrase, laughing at its solemnity, setting her pigtail flying across her back.

Sarah's head was swimming. Carolee's argument made sense, but she couldn't completely agree. Nothing she had learned back in Iowa in Sunday school or regular school had any bearing on the subject. Now her happiness with Michael was a kind of religion for her. When she wanted to talk about anything important she talked first with him. And she knew he had no strong feelings for or against bisexuality. . . .

Sarah left Carolee at the gardenia'd door of the graduate center and headed toward the Square and the *Crimson*.

"Next we will be considering Algernon Charles Swinburne, 1837–1909, the youngest of the greater Victorian poets," intoned Professor Hudson from a podium in Sever Hall.

"Why am I taking this course?" thought Rosa. "To be with him. But he doesn't even show up."

"Swinburne attended Eton and Oxford, and at Oxford became attached to the Pre-Raphaelite Brotherhood whose founders had emphatically repudiated the humanistic Renaissance in favor of a return to medieval religiosity understood in a romantic, emotional spirit. From a political point of view the medievalist revival was at first reactionary; but in the end as we shall see, its protest against the temper of the age combined with the spirit of reform."

Rosa was taking notes furiously. In point of fact she was enjoying the course, though it was outside her field. At least Hudson didn't spend the whole hour analyzing the levels of ambiguity in a single phrase, like some professors.

"Swinburne was influenced by French poets Hugo and Baudelaire, and has been called a Hellenist, or neopagan. He is worthy of our attention because of the splendor of his diction, the beauty of his verses, and the spontaneous charm of some of his lyric dramas. His radical defects are his want of balance, restraint, and clarity of mental and moral vision, and the unsubstantial character of his work on the intellectual side."

Hudson was winding up. "For Thursday I'd like you all to have read *Atalanta in Calydon* and *Songs Before Sunrise.* The former is perhaps the finest of all Swinburne's works, and the latter will give us a sense of the poet's attachment to the cause of national liberation in Italy."

Rosa gathered her notebook and books and filed down with the others along the worn beige rubber-tiled steps of the old classroom building, past the dusty palm-and-eggshell-painted walls, holding with one hand onto the smooth polished bannister. She was wearing a light jacket over a virginal pink blouse, a gray pleated skirt, stockings, and black Capezio flats. One tortoise-shell barrette held all her chestnut brown hair in a braided loop. She found her bike in the rack and rolled it out, all the time feeling strange, dissociated, and cut off from other people. She was liked for her sweetness by the girls in the dorm; but sweetness was not a quality Harvard valued very highly.

As she pedaled past the Common toward Radcliffe the thought of Swinburne drifted out of Rosa's head, evaporating in the autumn air, and in its place came the thought of Nestor. Did Nestor have "clarity of moral vision"? What did that even mean? Had the idea been drained of its meaning by the communists and the fascists? Was Professor W. H. Hudson himself a ghost from a more benign era?

It was a little too nippy for the jacket Rosa was wearing and she shivered.

When Rosa reached Stanton House a mile later she parked her bike around in back by the clothesline and then, so as not to disturb the girl who lived in the room by the kitchen, walked around to the front to enter through the three sets of heavy wooden front doors. In her present mood the groan of the heavy doors sounded to her like a protest. They'd rather be letting in princesses, daughters of editors of monopoly newspapers, nonimmigrants. She saw them as a bulwark against herself.

But inside all was familiar and cozy, virtuous, charming, and anachronistic as the cast-iron wood-burning stove in the kitchen. Throwing her books down and loosening her hair with a gesture, Rosa gravitated into the living room where Yvette was lying on the floor in jeans doing homework. Over a threadbare sofa hung a portrait of Elizabeth Cady Stanton herself, surveying the large parlor of the old homestead. In her time it must have been gracious, with chandeliers and drapery, end tables and meeting tables and highboys and secretaries, a rolltop writing desk with pigeonholes perhaps. But all that was gone now, and the room's desolate spaciousness suggested rather less of the gracious parlor and rather more of the sweaty, abandoned gymnasium.

"Hi," said Yvette.

"Hi," said Rosa, still feeling weird and disoriented. "Do you want a cup of tea?"

"Sure."

In a few minutes Rosa returned with a bright red tin pot of spice tea that she set out for Yvette and herself on the floor of the old living room.

"Oh, I feel so terrible!" she said at last, not realizing that that was what she was going to say.

Yvette remained discreetly silent.

"I don't know. It's just no good. I don't know what it means. I don't know what I should do—!"

Yvette sipped from her painted clay mug. "Do about what?"

Then Rosa began crying softly. Yvette felt bad for her, but thought it important not to pry.

Rosa spoke. There didn't seem to be anything else to do. "You know Nestor?" she began.

Now Yvette had a good idea of what was wrong, and a hefty ambivalence.

"Tui's friend?" Rosa continued.

But Yvette was off on her own toot. That creep Nestor Schwarz had gone around telling people about how she'd seduced him in Phil 1 freshman year, and it was just so tacky. He was really impossible. The linguistics department gang had laughed at her about it. He was a good actor and too clever by half, but Yvette had finally decided just to walk away.

Good-bye. The end. And that had been that.

But, oh, God, then Tui had picked him up in some soc rel professor's house and here he was back on the scene, messing things up again.

Yvette realized that Rosa had been talking all this while. "It's a little inconsiderate of her," she thought, "to bring up Nestor to me when she knows I did have *something* to do with him. But maybe she doesn't know? No, she knows." Then she apprehended that Rosa was really quite distraught and talking impulsively. What had she been saying all this time? Oh! That she had stopped seeing Billy Clemens, who was a nice person, and gone to bed for the first time with Nestor, who was a terrible person, and she didn't know why!

Yvette looked at the other girl with softened eyes. True sex transcended ego. "So you picked Nestor to be your first lover?" she said gently.

Rosa wobbled her head up and down. The tears had made her cheeks a couple of different colors. She picked up her mug of tea, sloshing it a little, spilling a drop.

"That wasn't such a good idea," continued Yvette, still gently. "This tea is good. Thank you."

"He said something to me that was so horrible I don't know if I can even tell you," Rosa began, and then stopped and drank some more tea.

Now Yvette was getting weary. Nestor she knew. "You may as well," she said.

"When we were—in the bedroom, he said, 'What's the matter with you? You undress like a Girl Scout!' " And at this Rosa began to cry in earnest.

Yvette half-rose, trudged on her blue-jeaned knees over to

Rosa's side, put her tan arm around the girl's shoulders, and gave her a little squeeze. She tried to think of something reassuring to say. "Don't worry, you'll have another virginity coming around"? "Don't cry just because you gave your love to a jive-ass son-of-a-bitch"? She couldn't think of anything that didn't make her want to cry too, and so she just squeezed Rosa's shoulders a few times.

Finally the tea left in the perky red pot had cooled. "What are you going to do now?" said Yvette.

Rosa shut her eyes and turned her head as if she were in pain. "I don't know. That's the worst part of it. I suppose I should never see him again. But I don't know. I just don't know."

Nestor Schwarz woke from a dream of huge triumph and outrageous embarrassment to the odor of dirty socks and a ringing telephone. It was Tui, calling from California, asking for him. The boy from across the hall, accustomed to dealing with Nestor's girls, told her he was in Willahamsett.

Nestor roomed by himself in a House famous for its student artists and musicians. He longed with all his heart to be able to play Bach like Gould, but could barely stumble through Clementi's first sonatina. Always ill at ease when alone, he had generated an imposing layer of debris over an apartment that was otherwise structurally elegant. Threadbare jackets and dark turtlenecks covered a torn sofa. Hundreds of books, magazines, and notebooks were scattered on the floor and heaped up on the mantel. Remains of sandwiches and full ashtrays were nestled on the seats of chairs. Only the LPs were relatively tidy, housed in numerous packing crates. Contemplating the disorder of his waking life, Nestor spent a long moment in uncomfortable silence. Then it occurred to him that he could hand in his long autobiographical paper to yet another course. He got up slowly.

Nestor stepped over the Mailer and the Salinger paperbacks, kicking the New Directions Ginsberg under the radiator as he passed. In the bathroom he leaned heavily against the sink and peered into the mirror. The jolly flash of the white eyebrow only irritated him. A few days growth of beard had changed his aspect from wolf to bear. Tui was the latest girl to reassure him that he was handsome, but he peered deep into his own black eyes searching for handsomeness. What was that spot he saw in there? He wanted to be perfect. He had to be . . . ! To show them, to show them all! Sometimes playing pool or rehearsing for a new play he would forget his own imperfection for a while, and would achieve a kind of peace. But the end of the game, the ringing down of the final curtain, would bring out the pain again, the horrible constriction around his heart, the stabbing knife that stopped his breath, the choking and the wheezing that embarrassed and mortified him even beyond the terror of asphyxiation. In an agony of shame he grabbed for opiates; for alcohol; for indulgences of food that never seemed to add an ounce; for his syringe and his life-saving inhaler. Now he glared with hatred at the shadow of a beard across his cheeks.

The secret horror of Nestor's life was that another life had been sacrificed for his. Before he was born his mother had been ill. The doctors had said it was unsafe for her to bear. But Nestor's father had so wanted a child that Nestor was born . . . and his mother had become a lifelong invalid. Nestor had spent his earliest years in a dingy two-story attached house in Philadelphia with only his father for companion, a quiet, defeated man who holed up all day long in a second-floor study adjoining the sickroom to work on ambitious, never-completed projects. The family lived hand to mouth on an allowance from a despised relative in the clothing business. And Nestor's mother, as she lingered on, always sinking, always barricaded behind a strange apothecary, became quite mad with rage at the thought of this child who had cost her the blessings of sun and air and movement; and she varied her constant, sullen, scolding reproaches and demands only with periodic outbursts of hysteria that sent Nestor running out of the house choking and in pain, and his father to turning up his little Emerson radio louder, feigning deafness.

Nestor was partly rescued from these unfortunate circumstances when the uncle in the clothing business, making one of his rare visits to the Schwarz household, handed over a sum of money to Nestor's father with the specific instructions that the boy be sent away to school: preferably far away, to an institution in a pleasant landscape, with loving teachers and a gentle regime. Though the elder Schwarz was at first reluctant to spend money in this way, he was prevailed upon, and the boy was dispatched. But Nestor carried the fetid sickroom and his haunted father in his heart, and the smoldering resentment with which he combated his nightmares, and the desire (that was very nearly an oath) to revenge himself on an unjust and cruel fate, established him early, even in his sunny place of refuge, as an enfant terrible.

Well, the story of Nestor's adventures in the mountains would take some time. Suffice it to say that three years later, after his first love affair was past, Nestor had narrowed the blame for his unhappiness down to the female half of humanity, and was looking forward to his next step—Harvard—as a pilgrimage to the homeland of the male, the strong, and the powerful. His pulse leapt at the thought of continuing the dialogue with genius so tenuously begun, so briefly glimpsed, in a stray conversation with a drama teacher under an apple tree.

Nestor snapped himself out of his reverie. He *was* handsome. He *would* starve himself and become thin. He sneered into the mirror.

As he plugged in the electric shaver he noticed a copy of *Partisan Review* lying in the bathtub. With his free hand he plucked it out and hung it respectfully over the towel rack. In the next room the guy had put on Bartok.

In the *Crimson* all was slow-moving hustle and bustle. Michael was looking gracefully hearty in his shirt-sleeves behind the managing editor's desk, concentrating and laughing, dummying the next day's page, in the throes of a grueling eight-week executive competition. He meditated on the ruled mock-ups and upon his scratch pad, and then, in a bold hand, in blue ink, writing with a thick-nibbed fountain pen, he modeled out a quick form for the news. The trick was to determine the relative significance of the different events of the day, and to convey this subliminally to the reader by means of the shape and location and size and style of the headline and text. The pyramid structure was being drilled into candidates. Looking at Michael, Sarah felt as much love and respect for what he was doing as if he were pulling a bullet out of a resistance fighter using only a sharp knife and some alcohol.

Dean Porlock was on the bottom of the front page in a story about getting books to black elementary school students in Roxbury. So was the pending *Fanny Hill* obscenity case. People in the newsroom were laughing about *Fanny Hill* and *Lady Chatterly's Lover,* and a reporter was passing around both the ninety-five cent edition and the newer, printed-in-Paris, covered-with-courtroom-quotations, two dollar edition. When *Crimson* photog Cadwalader saw that Sarah had come in he grabbed her and pulled Michael from where he sat and gestured the two of them down onto the ed chairman's sofa—put a copy of the Paris *Fanny Hill* in Michael's hand—and said, "Okay, you lovebirds, read the book." Michael and Sarah obediently pretended to be reading, and Cadwalader snapped a shot of devilish expansive male glee and offended but fascinated female curiosity.

"I'll be through in a little while," whispered Michael when they were alone. "Do you want to come to my room?"

Sarah looked at him and said, "Oh, yes."

Then he went back to his work and she moved over to read the Comment Books. From long familiarity she knew each Crimed's handwriting, and the pens that they used, and most of all recognized the hieratic little monograms that appeared at the bottom of every comment. As Sarah leaned idly against the ledge and turned the pages of the big blue nineteenth-century ledgers, hearing in encoded form what all the gang had said about integration and coeducation and the new movie at the UT and one another, she felt again as if by some magic or miracle she had stumbled into a room in which golden, brilliant men and women were mingling in conversation, their speech the secret nectar of life, abiding in their ageless court in Cambridge or four hundred and fifty miles east of Srinagar or in a space capsule forever.

She thought of Eddie who had graduated and gone on to the *Chicago Sun-Times.* She missed him. She missed his funny comments. Of course the shadow cabinet was funny too, but in a different way. They had never really got on too well with Eddie. She smiled to see one of R. R. Hodgson's references to "Môle" from *Wind in the Willows.* She hadn't read the book; her childhood reading ran to minor works. But

RRH's frequent references to Môle, Toad, and the rest always made her laugh. He put a circumflex over the O. The circumflex was very funny.

"Mike, are you going to review the Avedon-Baldwin book?" Dan Matlaw asked. He was sitting in one of the straight-backed newsroom typing chairs, his arms on the platen of the old Royal Upright in its shelf.

"Sure," said Michael, walking over. (This particular communist and this particular social democrat liked each other, though they knew they weren't supposed to.) "I have my first sentence worked out already. Want to hear it?"

"Let me guess . . ." Dan held up a hand. " 'The civil rights movement must be getting pretty fuckin' *classy* if Richard Avedon and *The New Yorker* crowd . . .' "

"That's *your* first sentence," Michael cut in. "Some of the pictures are incredible."

"I'm real glad. I just need it for Sunday."

"No problem," said Michael, and ambled away, thinking some more about his own first sentence. . . . "Sometimes what the pictures say is unfair, cruel, or pointless; but more often it is strong and perceptive. . . ."

In the president's office, Bobby Wagner was finishing up a review of a book about New York City.

Dan lifted his arms off the sturdy old machine and with a certain vehemence pulled the yellow copy paper from its carriage, crumpled it, sank it in the wastebasket with a hook shot, and inserted a fresh sheet. He thought a moment and then began to type. He looked like a man playing honky-tonk piano.

Wind at the bedroom window moved the leafy fingers of a poplar. Sarah's smooth nude body fit into the curve of Michael's. "What do you want to be?" she asked softly.

He leaned up on an elbow. It was funny they had never discussed this. "Senator," he said, "from New York."

"I thought you were going to be a newspaperman," she said, almost disappointed. "You're so good at it. You have the most terrific mastery of the forms, and you're such a good writer, and you're so rational, and you always get to the heart of things; and on top of all that: you're casual about it."

"Well maybe when I retire from the Senate I'll get a little high-quality newspaper of my own to edit in New England or somewhere," he said cheerfully. "That would be a gas."

He caressed her arm and shoulder. Miraculously, the touch of his hand never failed to delight her. Was it because of some skill of his, something that related to his skills with the pen and the design of a front page? Had he rather tuned her to his frequency, imprinted the character of his love upon her? Was it youth? Was it the god Cupid?

She touched his toes with her toes.

"You know, I can't think about what I want to do," she said. "I don't want college to end. I see myself as I am now through a kaleidoscope, and it's so interesting."

Michael thought that was funny. "A kaleidoscope? I don't think I'd like that."

"I mean when I read Jane Austen or somebody, I always start thinking how she would have described me. And when I read Dickens, the same thing. And Conrad. Anybody I read. I hardly know which one is the real me."

"I don't know what the hell you're talking about," said Michael genially. "But don't worry about it. You're going to be my wife."

A door bumped softly beyond their room. The evangelist was back.

"Of course I'm going to be your wife. Oh, Michael, my sweet darling, I love you so much!" she whispered, turning and half-raising herself on one hand to cover his ear and his cheek with kisses.

JANE AUSTEN:

"The Galbraeths' younger girl, I believe," said Lady Weathering, "works on a newspaper."

"Well, tut tut, perhaps she'll meet a nice young man

with a forgiving disposition," said Mr. Brooke, doing his best
to avoid seeming startled.

CHARLES DICKENS:

Suddenly the door to our little room burst open, letting
in a hiccough of wind, a few scrawny leaves, and a tall greyish-
brown woman. Once in, she was all motion—tugging at thin
brown leather gloves, opening and closing a dirty grey pocket-
book which seemed to enclose a vast captured army of folded
yellow and grey bits of paper, and straightening (with a barely
audible "tsk") the brown line that ran up the back of each leg;
and all the time so running her pebbly eyes over our room
that I felt Mrs. Merriglove's cheeks grow warm with house-
wifely embarrassment.

Like a cascade of leaves before us the young woman
had begun to shiver all over, making rustling sounds with her
hands as well as her voice. "Number 42 Merriglove residence
husband doctor?" she muttered, running her fingers through a
stack of lined paper, clipboards, spirals, and old greying newspapers that had somehow appeared in her hands. With another hand she scratched furiously at a jagged grey design on
her cheek, a pencil mark from birth probably, coughed a bit
like the dry sound of a kitchen door closing on a crackerjack
and, digging the toe of her scuffed brown shoe into the carpet,
let her little eyes light upon us, exhausted.

"Howdoyoudo I'm from the Browntown Daily Message and Sentinel I'm conducting a survey," she said in one
shallow breath. Her cheeks made some folds that indicated a
smile.

JOSEPH CONRAD:

There was a woman in our group too, I remember. And
on a particularly painful winter night we would all sit together in the carpeted warmth of the Sanctum, smoking and
glancing lazily at the pictures in the old magazines, listening
to the harsh pinching sounds of the wind on the window lintel,
and would draw a kind of heady comfort from her presence,
from her differentness. She wasn't beautiful—oh no! Old Met-

tlehead the printer even said sometimes, "Ah, Sally, I love you
'cause you're so ugly." It always made us shiver a little with
embarrassment, feeling as we did the dignified truth in the
crazy old man's remark, and yet wondering, worrying, with
the lower plane of our consciousness, how a woman feels when
she is called "ugly." We always wanted to ask her, but of
course no one ever dared.

And we kept her, in a way, pure, by never opening the
subject. Like little boys we drank in the winelike richness of
woman secretly, asking nothing. Sitting together on a cold
night, we had only to look up, to glance at her gently curving
brown hair, at her arms that were mysteriously rounder than
ours, to feel again the awe of something great and strange. We
fought the cold outside, the sterile noise of the printing press
below, the nagging boredom of our own existence, by simply
owning Sally, by having a woman as part of our fraternity.

GEORGE MOORE:

I met a crazy, very skinny girl once at a party—named
Sarah or Mary or something like that. So funny! One of those
curious females who take up books and ideas as if they were
fine foods and exult as they devour them. I heard later she had
become a religious recluse in Germany. I never saw her again.

Michael rolled over and drew his
left arm around Sarah and with his right hand began to caress the soft
place where her breasts began.

"I want you," he said huskily.

And Sarah touched him too, and stretched out more deeply
into the bed of their pleasure: far and slowly, out, down, until she had
pushed every last nerve away like a cat, until the last subtle tightness
had melted, been smoothed or coaxed to sleep, and she yawned, sinking. Her arms wound into the warmth of him, her legs so thoughtlessly

moved to meet his legs. And she caressed his satiny muscled body, kissing his face, consoling the flesh familiarly and as one unlike.

And she rejoiced to experience herself in his hands. He was subject, directing force, powers controlled and competent. The country of her hips, her stomach, her breasts, was body, object, the explored. Like a childhood playmate he began to caress her more teasingly, until she laugh-sighed into a still more perfect ease.

Now Michael had given Sarah an Indian holy book called *The Thread of Eros* by some and *The Kama Sutra* by others, that he had heard about from his father; and the two of them had read its wonderfully methodical intricacies, and called upon some one recipe or another now and then to spice their already delicious lovemaking.

And so now, released from fear by a marvelous vision of sacramental lust in a high and cosmopolitan civilization, the sweet dream of a timeless humanity, the lovers became one person again, woman inside turned outside of man. And Sarah rode the motions of her own and Michael's unconsciousness, quiet, submissive, faintly delirious, endlessly, endlessly, endlessly . . . until the fire caught—the Volcano erupted—The Boundaries Dissolved—The Heat Flowed O*U*T!! and she screamed. And she rode the crest of the lava in tumultuous, selfless joy down the side of the mountain until slowly, slowly, she came to an easy gradual rest at the foot of a hill, and there the girl friend found the boyfriend again.

A particle of thought strayed into her brain: "Yes. That's what they meant."

The streaks of green and blue and violet light that had flamed to brilliance behind her closed eyes only a moment before were fading to wispy blues and lavenders, drifting off and out with a soft throbbing water rhythm, blowing away. All that the visual world could offer seemed meager compared with the messages she was receiving along her skin. It was not touch but the parent of touch, a new and fuller sense, involving the fluid communion of her long periphery with the plenteous surrounding universe. The ground below her was no longer bed, comical in its rectangularity, its self-satisfied functionalism. It was Michael, the other part of the mystery, strangely jagged and smooth, complicated and absurdly simple, soft and moving, like herself.

He drew his arm further around her shoulders and like molten metals the two of them flowed together again, dense with life. She felt an emanation coming from him that told her he was feeling as she felt, and a moment later he kissed her, a velvety understated kiss, on the part of her that was nearest him. The emanation had been evidence, the kiss was proof. Of what exactly, Sarah didn't know. But she knew that a great many things suddenly had meaning—like the idea of a kiss—that had been puzzling abstractions before.

Michael's weight, his smell, his breathing. Somehow he had crossed what divided them. He was on the same side of Out There as she was. Perhaps they had not visited the same Oracle, but these returned presences, these shells of themselves, seemed to remember the journey in the same way. The conflagration that had melted them separately into the infinite now smoldered and meandered homily between them.

Oh. God. Sarah leaned up to cover Michael's beautiful face with half-formed, grateful kisses.

His fingers touched her lips. She had received him in her virginity in the spring. But those few drops of blood had been nothing compared with the baptism and marriage that had come later, this autumnal ritual of the two-in-one.

He smiled, almost laughed. Sarah laughed too, and curled against him. The lights had dimmed, but they were still so warm together, so safe. She felt sure that something had been ignited in her that would never in her life be entirely extinguished.

"Oh, darling, *you're* so good," she whispered.

He took her hand. "Your cheeks are red."

She touched them, and closed her eyes a moment to remember.

At seven they rose and dressed. It was too late for a Lowell House dinner, but that didn't bother them, really, because this new House was full of stuffed shirts. They bundled off happily to Tommy's for cheeseburgers and pinball.

One door away, a sluggish fellow with a sallow complexion and a stale smell, too deficient in animal spirits to be quite likable, was scribbling in pencil in his gov notebook.

Now he gritted his teeth as the two lovers exited, letting the door slam. Every afternoon before dinner he was treated to the sound of Sarah's ecstasy and it was driving him crazy. Why couldn't the whore of Babylon just take Michael out to a hotel or somewhere and do her dirty things and leave him in peace? Oh, no, she was a Radcliffe girl, a fellow student of Universitas Harvardiensis, who was engaged in this abomination. The sallow gov student was full of wrath. But his roommate was within the law, and so he was obliged to keep a lid on it.

The only child of a Methodist pastor from rural Alabama, this fellow had, upon achieving manhood, taken his parents' heartfelt moderate Protestantism one step further and become a fundamentalist. It was not a popular position around Cambridge. He had to take the MTA bus out to Dorchester every week to attend the meetings of the Christian Volunteer and Information Agency.

On the wall of his snug bedroom hung a lifelike photo-montage of the head of Christ crowned with thorns, bleeding and weeping.

Sarah and Michael sat at the counter in Tommy's feeling good, clean, and bohemian. He ate a cheeseburger and drank a Coke while she nibbled at a side dish of cole slaw. As usual they could hardly see anyone else in the joint. The memory of bed enveloped them like a rosy cloud.

When they were through with their dinner, Michael played a gleeful game of pinball on the machine in the corner—it was still illegal in New York—as Sarah leaned against the machine with a dreamy, adoring, idle smile on her face.

"Foote wants me to try some morning glory seeds," he remarked.

"Omigod! Why ever would you want to do that?"

"He says morning glory seeds contain the active ingredient in LSD—uh, do I sound like a toothpaste commercial?—but that they're safer because they're natural."

"Oh, don't listen to him."

"I have no intention of taking either morning glory seeds or LSD. But he keeps badgering me about it. He says my inter-hemispheric relations are no good."

"What!?"

"The speech and logic centers in the left hemisphere of my brain don't know what the gestalt center in the right hemisphere of my brain is doing. Says Foote."

"Good Heavens, what crap! There's no one I can think of who's more infinitely cool than you. Your gestalt and your speech and your logic are all fabulous. Foote is the one who's sort of weird. And who would ever want to divide a brain into left and right hemispheres, anyway? It sounds sacrilegious to me."

"You're so sweet, Sarah," said Michael, hugging her. It was a discreet hug—nothing the other Harvard bohemians and preppy rebels eating their cheeseburgers would notice.

"I don't know what he's after. But I have no intention of cooperating."

They sallied out of the greasy spoon into the fresh fall evening. Sarah bought a little scroll of Danish strawberry licorice at Felix's cigar store. Then they wandered into the Yard and sat down on the grass under the dogwoods behind Thayer.

B eneath the tower in Hoare House, Thaddeus Foote was bent over his desk doing something with a stack of packages of Burpee seeds. After some time he threw away the empty packages and shook the jar into which he had poured their contents. A smile was infecting his face like a disease. He had the most wonderful idea! Tonight there would be a discreet little morning glory seed party and afterward . . . ah! just to think of it! Foote's eyes closed in solipsistic ecstasy. "Afterward we shall do the pals' under-the-bed trick and make that poor pre-med wonk from Oxnard think he's going bananas!"

Foote hummed a chantlike ditty to himself as he brushed away the debris of the Heavenly Blues and straightened up his little garret: the issues of *Veda,* the *Psychedelic Reviews,* the syllabary from the American Society for Ancient Indo-European Languages. Then he stroked his red mustache with his fingers, locked all the cupboards and doors with care, and stepped out nattily to extend an invitation.

On October 19, 1963, "our boy Jack" flew into Logan Airport from Bangor, Maine, made a beeline past the official welcomers to a throng of airline mechanics waiting for handshakes, and then ducked out of a side door of the Sheraton-Plaza and sped to Soldiers Field for the Harvard-Columbia game in an unmarked car.

The day was beautifully clear and nippy. Word of the young president on the fifty-yard line between aides Dave Power and Larry O'Brien threw the crowd into ecstasies of clubbiness. What a wonderful world! But it made the teams nervous. As Kennedy smoked a small cigar and chewed on his sunglasses, Harvard lost the ball on fumbles four times in Lion territory. Columbia too made its share of costly mistakes. Neither team seemed to be able to manage a touchdown, and the score stood frustratingly at 3–3.

Of course there were moments. Gene Thompson ran forty-three yards in the first quarter, until his punchy offense was halted by a perfect flying tackle by Harvard's formidable Tom Bilodeau. The president stood up and cheered in the second quarter, when Mike Bassett carried four Columbia linemen on his back for a short gain around right end.

At the half (after laughing at the Band's joke about the planned Kennedy library), JFK left the field to visit his son Patrick's grave in

Brookline. He sipped a butterscotch ice cream soda at Schrafft's in Copley Square, and was mobbed as he walked the few blocks back to his hotel. Mounties drove the people back. But Kennedy stopped to talk to some nuns and a newsboy.

"It's all in a day's work, kid," said a secret service man to a *Crimson* reporter. "Sure we have our problems. But we haven't lost a president in sixty years!"

After the game both teams were embarrassed and silent. The score between Cambridge and New York had remained at 3–3. "A tie is like kissing your kid sister," said Harvard coach John Yovicsin.

It was the Friday before Thanksgiving, an unseasonably warm, seventy-degree New England day. The bells of Memorial Church were tolling.

In the Square the generation was walking about strangely, quietly, their eyes big like Keane paintings of children, looking as though they had been kicked in the stomach by someone they thought was a friend. Hurt, puzzled, lost, foreign emotions played beneath the surface of their faces. Occasionally a smile would break through; embarrassment; a sob. They looked at one another piercingly, angrily, hungrily, uncomprehending, as if to ask, "Was it you?" Rosa ran into Yvette at the Out of Town kiosk and they instinctively stopped to be together—some force held them near, taking mute comfort—but then, still silent, they separated. A large group had gathered around the newsstand, stunned, walking dreamily, restless.

The *Crimson* people had come running from all ends of the campus to gather in the newsroom. They stood by the AP machine, its ticker tape spooling out like the word of an unbelievable God, and looked guilty and ashamed, as if asking, "How did we let this happen?" In the president's office R. R. Hodgson and some others of the shadow cabinet were speaking of civil rights and the peace corps and the Moscow treaty and the moon program and the artfulness of this man who had been hero, lover, Yankee, Harvardman. Someone mentioned Pope John XXIII and his encyclicals—as if they too were part of the Kennedy legacy.

Charlie Schulte was the first to act. As Sarah watched, astonished, he sat himself down behind the m.e.'s desk and started putting out an Extra edition of the paper. "Is this how the world ends?" she thought, "with an Extra?" He assigned George Durbey to cover the postponement of the Yale game. He contacted Professor Sam Beer, who had written speeches for FDR, and got a statement from him. As the others continued to move only in a dreamland of grief, Schulte sketched out a dummy, the little diagonal folds of flesh across the corners of his eyes making him look profoundly, genetically sad.

Sarah and Michael watched Schulte for a while in disbelief and disapproval and then went out into the warm and windy afternoon. They sat at a sidewalk table at the Pamplona and drank café au lait. At the next table three famous Harvard government professors were talking quietly. Sarah and Michael listened. But they didn't say anything. They rambled, childish as everyone else. "Who comes after Speaker of the House?" Hobbes asked McCloskey. Half-heartedly, McCloskey told him.

And so passed the first day after Camelot. Over the weekend it got cooler, more seasonable for November. Monday classes were canceled. Everywhere across the university students had spent the weekend gathered in little groups to watch the assassination being replayed on television. Then the assassination of the assassin, and the replays of that. The networks almost seemed to be focusing more on the killing of Lee Harvey Oswald than on the killing of John Fitzgerald Kennedy— as if that murder were more sensationally horrible, more absurd, more provoking, more commercial.

The commentators' voices droned on, conducting a mass, secular funeral. And the students at their television sets could not tear themselves away. For three days they clung to the hope that they would wake from this dream, that some tiny detail would be revealed that would change everything back to the way they had thought it was always going to be. Their spirits were prostrate before the monolith of communication. But no salvation came from that source.

Sarah and Michael sat close to each other in front of the set in the *Crimson* sanctum as other *Crimson* reporters came and went. For a while Thaddeus Foote stood over them, or strode around the edges of the large room, looking bitter and angry.

"What's burning you up, Thaddeus?" asked Michael at one point.

"Jack Kennedy was not even bright!" replied Foote with surprising savagery, leaning on the back of the sofa. "He was a dull man! Dull, dull, dull! But *this* is going to elevate him to greatness!"

Michael turned scarlet. "You're nuts!" he said. "Kennedy *was* great . . . At least he *would have been* great . . . And he would have written great memoirs!"

"Do you really think that memoirs—" Foote began sarcastically, but Michael interrupted him.

"I don't want to talk about it!" he snapped, his head now turned back to the TV, his jaw muscles working. "I do *not* want to talk about it."

And then the world split up into "Harvard ties" (eight parts crimson, two parts navy, one part light blue, thin white lines) and "Dallas ties" (two parts gold, two parts navy, one part light blue, beige trim, thin black lines), though we didn't know it, most of us, at the time.

Sarah sat at her writing desk and doodled.

> All day we primed the volcano for fun
> And at dusk it erupted,
> Burying the thoughtless capital in fire.
> Trees burnt like men, and men like their houses,
> For the city had still the skeleton of a forest.

The shootings in Dallas had sent a shock through the collective unconscious that was hard to monitor so soon and from so close. Kennedy's right-hand man, thirty-six-year-old Ted Sorenson, had come back to Harvard traumatized and closed-mouthed, to sequester himself in the university's plushest accommodations in Leverett House and work on a book. The South was in turmoil. What was to become of the Kennedy-Khrushchev peace treaty signed in Moscow just that summer by Adlai Stevenson of the electric blue eyes? Kennedy was dead and Krushchev would soon be in exile. Only a hundred and forty Americans had died in the Indochina war—the media still documenting the circumstances of each fatality—but that would change.

Less than a month after Dallas, a new sound came over the air waves. It was called the Beatles, and it was young and beautiful and wholesome and loving and melodious, and the stir that it aroused at Harvard and throughout the country was not trivial. Barely a year and a half before, pop music had been unfashionable among the Ivies; it was the badge of a culture the ruling class rejected. Sarah's poll on "The Duke of Earl" had been evidence of that. But with the coming of these four boys, three Celts and a Saxon, the old guard of the English-speaking world underwent some kind of transformation. Harvard musicologists were going into raptures over the Beatles' use of modal progressions, their mid-melody changes between major and minor. Billy Clemens added Lennon and McCartney to his violin repertoire. The son of the author of *America as a Civilization* wrote an encomium to the Beatles' performance on "The Ed Sullivan Show" in early February.

And Sarah and Michael and the generation young enough to turn on a radio or drive to a movie listened to them and said, "That's us," as the Beatles sang:

> Am
> I want to hold your hand.
>
> Em F   G7   C   Am
> I want to hold your ha-a-a-a-and!
>
> F   G7   F   C
> I want to hold your hand.

Sarah was studying Oliver Cromwell in Soc Sci 2, her favorite course. Her sectionman was big and lazy and authoritative and antiauthoritarian and she loved him. He liked to sit back in his chair and prop his feet up on the seminar table.

Sarah told Michael that Cromwell's Puritanism had been the superstructure of the English Civil War, while the economic transformation of the bourgeoisie of the time was its real structure.

Michael frowned.

"You've been talking like a Marxist ever since you've been taking that damn Soc Sci 2. Why didn't you take Soc Sci 1 and learn something useful like the history of Western civilization?"

They were sitting in the ed chairman's run-down office having one of their usual arguments about politics.

"Theories like Marx's degrade individuals," he went on. He made a big blue ink blot on a stack of yellow newsprint with his fountain pen. "I prefer to believe that conscious motives are the real motives, that men shape history."

Sarah looked at him adoringly. The Sunday school Presbyterianism of her youth still gave her a warm feeling, but it didn't explain as much as Soc Sci 2. VFW high school civics explained even less. Harvard had given her a new vision of people all around the world belonging to one whole, one integral terrestrial community, swept by forces she had never guessed at. But for all her new enthusiasms, she still looked to Michael for guidance. Now she tucked her red-stockinged feet underneath her on the sofa.

Michael was for Sarah the very embodiment of optimistic, confident, positive Harvard. He believed devoutly in democratic socialism and was a fervent anticommunist—a political position that was usually caught in the middle between two enormously powerful opponents and seen by both as an enemy. But he held on to this faith as if it were his birthright. Whether cause or effect of her love for him Sarah didn't know, but she devoutly admired his guts, his open-hearted morality, his intellectual stringency. Though she had left the church group and the VFW and the DAR behind, she felt certain that if and when they knew Michael they would approve of him.

"You talk about Cromwell 'completing' the bourgeois revolu-

tion, for example," he went on. "But don't you see, the important
question is not, 'What do the Marxists say about Cromwell?' but 'If
you were living in the time of Cromwell, would *you* have supported
him?' "

Sarah had been an on-again off-
again member of Tocsin, the disarmament group, ever since her freshman year, when she had joined their march on Washington for
"unilateral peace initiatives." Dan Matlaw thought they were a bunch
of goody-goodies. He told Sarah, "I thought toxin meant, you know,
like a poison. Then Gitlin explained to me it was spelled *t-o-c-s-i-n* and
it meant like a warning bell in old English or something. Where else
but Harvard would they name a peace group 'Tocsin'?" But for all his
sarcasm he attended their meetings frequently in his role as *Crimson*
reporter.

Tonight, when Dan got to the sunken junior common room of
Winthrop House, he saw a couple of hundred students, mostly boys,
milling around waiting for someone to call them to order. He headed
over to the Goldmark-Gitlin-Hochschild circle in the corner. The senior leadership were amusing themselves before the meeting trying to
think of words with five consecutive consonants, like blackstrap and
nightshade.

Something—the missile crisis, the signing of the test ban treaty,
the Kennedy assassination, or the tactics of SNCC in opposing racial
segregation—had had a fundamental effect on the peace group. Previously they had been, by their own admission, "elitists," arguing the
merits of various disarmament proposals directly with State Department officials. Now, Dan gathered, the younger members wanted to
take the case against the arms race directly to the working people
whose jobs and lives it jeopardized.

The new president of Tocsin, who was pushing for this change
of orientation and program, was a redhead named Katy, daughter of a

prominent New York civil liberties lawyer. Dan liked the way she quoted C. Wright Mills and Seymour Melman and I. F. Stone.

When the meeting was through he idled over to her and they talked. He invited Katy out for a drink and she accepted.

They spent the next month uninterruptedly in bed, unable to get enough of each other.

Michael became managing editor of the *Crimson* and settled into an arduous daily routine that made attending classes difficult and doing schoolwork impossible. He accepted the situation fatalistically, enjoying the newspaper work, agonizing only occasionally over the lost academics. But he played more poker than before, slept less, and lived on the edge of exhaustion. It was a peculiarity of Harvard's, he told himself for consolation. At *The Michigan Daily,* for instance, Tom Hayden had gotten course credit for being editor.

Perhaps it was this comparison with Michigan that Michael had in mind when, offered the opportunity to go to Dearborn and pick up a bright red Mustang convertible, free, no strings attached, as a promotional courtesy from Ford to the editor of the *Crimson,* he readily agreed. Sarah was opposed. She thought it positively venal. But Michael went and got the car, and rode in it up and down Harvard Square's tiny streets; and his enjoyment of the silly thing seemed so enthusiastic, so wholesome, so biological, that Sarah finally got in beside him and hushed her doubts and enjoyed being a BMOC too. After a while she told herself that what Michael was was gregarious, and that fastidiousness wouldn't be a very useful trait in the Senate.

Sarah was appointed executive editor of the *Crimson*—a lighter job than Michael's—and was responsible for filling the inside pages of the paper with features and putting together the occasional supplement. She had by-passed the grueling exec comp that Michael and a half-dozen other boys had put themselves through. This she did with-

out giving the matter a second thought. In the same way she had
avoided high school physics, not because of any personal problem with
science (she had gotten 800 on her math boards), but simply because
girls never took it. Sarah took femininity for granted. She couldn't
imagine the social organism functioning without it. She filled her *Crimson* post gently, with tenderness and flirtation, persuading rather than
commanding other members of the staff to write for her. She wrote
frequently herself, including a sociology column she called "Trivia
Writ Large." There was always someone in a class or in the dorm to
laugh at her latest parody or comment on her last political article, and
she felt great. Of course the compliments she got in the Comment
Books from her fellow editors ran to "delicious," "adorable," "crazy,"
"cute," and the like; and she would have preferred to have been seen as
intelligent, logical, and righteous; but that was all right.

M ichael took Sarah to a Spee Club
party during winter reading period. Snow weighed down the catalpa
and the silk and the redwood opposite the Fogg. Snow always gave
Cambridge a portentous hush.

At the door of the Eliot House suite a host with glazed eyes
said, "Coats in there, drinks in there," gesturing loosely. He looked like
a mechanical doll. The girls too looked all of a piece to Sarah: white as
the snow outside, pinkish as the promised spring. On one side of her
she heard people talking about a clambake. On the other side a boy
with blond hair and blue eyes and an extremely square jaw was exclaiming about a weekend bacchanal that had taken place recently in
New York—costing one hundred dollars per person! Michael greeted
R.R. and Virginia from across the room.

"Do I belong here?" thought Sarah.

Virginia looked chaste as Diana, shiny, clean, blooming and
discreet. She was wearing an oatmeal-colored sweater with little rose
and blue squiggles around her neck, framing her pleasant face and

setting off her amber hair. As an antidote to the headiness of the room, Sarah glanced to the window to see the snow still falling, falling, falling, like a thought.

Virginia said, "Hi, Sarah." She didn't speak as much in public as she did in the dorm. She held a tall glass of bourbon and water in a maniacal hand.

R.R. and Michael began to chat. They agreed the wine tasted like crank-case fluid. Someone brought up the subject of the Signet, and R.R. pronounced it "harmless," in his hidden-amusement mandarin way, and Michael listened carefully, and then, suddenly, Sarah interjected. She flippantly dismissed the all-male literary society. She made out that she didn't care a fig that her name had been brought up for membership and shouted down.

R.R. looked at her with amazement and concern. "You live in a strawberry ice cream world, Sarah Galbraeth," he said. "Be careful." Sarah wondered what he meant.

It turned out that although the Spee was not quite at the top of the heap with the Porcellian (Roosevelt), nor had it boasted a Rockefeller, like the Fly, it was the club that JFK had belonged to. And so it was with some little trepidation that Michael told Sarah a few days later that he had been "punched." He was already a member of "the Hasty Pudding Institute of 1770," which enabled him and Sarah to eat mediocre roast beef and stale bread sticks in an echoey dining room decked out with sports relics and posters of transvestite theatricals. But the Spee was more exclusive than that, a final club, something better.

Sarah didn't have to think twice. She forbade Michael to join.

They drove out of Cambridge in the red Mustang to discuss it, the top up against the cold wind, traveling roughly in the direction of New Hampshire. The white pine around Fresh Pond was heavy with clean snow, and the scent of winter came rushing in through the Mustang's open windows. Half a dozen kids in wool caps were skating on the ice.

Michael had mixed feelings about the whole Spee thing. And these feelings were muted in contrast to his feelings about, say, the *Crimson,* or Sarah. But Sarah was sputtering with indignation.

"They're so silly," he began lightly. "Knights of the Square Table, indeed. Porkers. Why should you even care about them?"

But Sarah knew they were not silly and she thought Michael knew it too, or he wouldn't be considering joining. "You know these clubs are taken seriously by the guys on Wall Street and in Washington and all," she stammered. "They look back on the Pork and the Fly and Bones and Keys as the places where they really learned about loyalty and intimacy and friendship. They sit around in their secret lodges after their dates or wives or whoever have gone home, and they tell each other every last thing about their motives, their anxieties, their deepest secrets. And for the rest of their lives they're in bond to one another! I heard that if a clubby is seated on a jury and another clubby is in the dock and signals him—the jurist is sworn to vote for acquittal, no matter whether he thinks the guy is innocent or not!"

"That can't be true!" said Michael. He was a believer in constitutional forms, in the Romans and the peers of the Magna Carta and most especially in Virginia's Tom Jefferson and the congregation of inspired men that had flowered up to illuminate civilization around the year 1800.

"Well, I heard it was. But we have no way of knowing. They sure as hell aren't going to tell *me*. And once you join, you'll be *pledged* not to tell.

"And you know what I think is at the heart of it, really?" Sarah continued. She took a breath and braced herself. Michael was looking at her with interest. "I think what they really are is masturbation societies. With a little sodomy thrown in!"

At this the boy clapped his hands down on the steering wheel and laughed hard. They were speeding along. The nice line of snow-laden highway department trees raced by on both sides.

"Well, it's not impossible!" he said. "And what would you do about that? Set up female counterparts?" He considered. "Speculum insertion and public douching societies?" He continued laughing. "To plant the seeds—I mean nest the eggs—for an old girl network?"

Sarah found this idea repellent, but she said nothing.

"I'm still not entirely convinced that it's wrong," he added thoughtfully after a moment. "Do you have any other arguments?"

"Oh, yes, I forgot to tell you the main one!" she replied eagerly, brushing hair out of her face. "I bet you didn't know this. I read it in a little Harvard pamphlet—"

"But how do I know what you're going to say?"

"Right! Uh, ha ha. Well—before the American Revolution, Harvard College used to keep a formal list of the students' social status. Can you believe it? Theodore Roosevelt IV up there at the top, Michael Verhoeven and Sarah Galbraeth down at the bottom."

"Wait just a minute there. You come on like a hick for the fun of it. You're not at the bottom. Somewhere in the middle, probably. Me, too."

"Bottom. But that doesn't matter. The whole thing, the official social rank list, was abolished at the time of the Revolution. And what do you think made its first appearance right after that, in 1791? To take its place—y' know what I mean?"

"The clubs."

"Porcellian. The first club."

"Well, that *is* interesting." Michael drove a moment in silence. He didn't have a quick answer. The social ranking system of Europe (Jesus! It probably went back to Fooke's Indo-Europeans!) was one thing his people had definitely chosen to leave behind. In Sweden his grandparents and his father had all become socialists. On the other side there had been foot soldiers in the American Revolution; and his well-bred mother had rolled up her sleeves to go get the story on the Chicago stockyards. The Declaration of Independence, with its fantastically great assertion of the equality of human Creation and of men's Deity-endowed Rights, was the closest thing Michael had to a Scripture. He believed in America. It has his grand arena, his just, tranquil, splendidly democratic nation. It was in all his cells and the very blood of his body to defend it and its values.

So he sped the Mustang up a little, and then more and more, until the needle tipped eighty and eighty-five and Sarah got nervous. Then he seemed to think better of that, and pulled off the road into a handy Howard Johnson's. They went inside at the orange and tourquoise and drank hot chocolate and spoke of other things.

A week later Michael made his final decision not to join the Spee Club. It might have helped his career. But he had more important things to think of.

Carolee Davis had a delicate bone structure and the strength of a bull. Her face was classically sculpted. Her long blond hair, in its invariable single pigtail, was arresting. But she didn't dress very well. She favored slacks in a day when slacks were considered inappropriate for women doing anything besides gardening. And these she wore with shapeless T-shirts and old jerseys and what the socialites described with infinite disdain as "dead sweaters." It took a special kind of man to see beyond her offhand exterior and imagine the beautiful woman beneath.

Carolee was one of the first to risk a trip to Cuba under the auspices of the Progressive Labor Movement. Though she was not a member of that group, and disagreed with them in many ways, she was interested in Castro, and scraped up the money for the fare out of what she had earned the previous summer researching mental health and social class for a professor at Yale. In the excitement of Havana she met and fell in love with another American radical who had made the trip. He was six years older than her, and had been number two in his class at Stanford—a Phi Beta—and Carolee thought for a while that he was her ideal man. He knew as much as she did, which was rare to begin with, and more. They made love furiously in the most uncomfortable and exotic places. And as her skinny, wiry body loomed above his big one, she would fantasize about their being "a red couple" together.

But the truth was he didn't love her back, not in the way she wanted. She settled back into Cambridge resigned to misery and study, flirted with and was distantly amused by many men, and cut her long blond hair as short as a boy's. She dug into her work in Chinese, and after a while produced a series of broadsides about the war in Vietnam that were widely read around the Yard. The *Crimson* reprinted them. The broadsides correctly anticipated the coming antiwar mood and its reasoning. But they were prescient by several years, and were not, on that account, readily accepted. Carolee was seen as an interesting eccentric. And Dan, who had had a falling out with her for reasons he could not or would not explain, put it about that she had cribbed her opinions from *National Guardian* journalist Wilfred Burchett. Carolee denied the charge vehemently in another broadside.

Wade LaMar Sterkin had come to Harvard from Amarillo, Texas. Down home he had been discovered by the local Republican Club and had rung a thousand doorbells for Nixon. At Harvard he had hooked up with conservative Howie Phillips, and joined Phillips's newly formed Young Americans for Freedom, and they had worked together on the anti–Peace Corps mailing that went out with an unauthorized Harvard student council endorsement.

Wade LaMar was burly and broad and had played fullback at home, and been president of his high school class. He had big ambitions. The contacts he would make at the Club would help. So would his carefully planned progress up the rungs of Harvard student government. He was conscientious. If he had been born in Eastern Europe he probably would have made his way up to a high position in the Communist party.

On this particular afternoon, having just come in from a game of House football, Wade LaMar was throwing the *Crimson* down on the floor with unusual anger and disgust. Once again the paper was making fun of Harvard student government and of the government of the country in general, and the satire was so pointed, the arguments so well taken, that it was hard for even a patriot like Wade LaMar to ignore.

Wade LaMar, his blond hair still wet from the shower, could hardly stand it. He swore. He gave the punching bag in the corner of his room a fast, powerful cross. And he went to look for his pal, the Alabaman.

Over Billy's firm opposition, Robbo and Jims had decided to go out for the *Crimson*. The two sportsmen had come to feel that the *Crimson*'s political thought on the subjects of war and peace was the most interesting and creative in town. And so they found themselves standing in the building on Plympton

Street for the early spring competition in their junior year, cool and aloof in thrown-open wolverine fur parkas.

They were greeted and given the welcome-to-the-comp pitch by Charles Francis McSilver, resident bookie, expert in horses, cards, newsprint and basketball, T. S. Eliot, and rock. CFMcS was not a favorite of the paper's intellectual elite, the shadow cabinet, because his entire vocabulary consisted of sportscasterese, song lyrics, and *The Waste Land.* Robbo and Jims listened to the fellow thoughtfully and gave each other the subtlest of shrugs. They had decided to put up with most anything in this exciting and disturbing endeavor.

Jims and Robbo felt a little old among the twenty-odd other candidates, and they stole furtive admiring glances at the energetic freshman girls. They made mental notes as Charlie outlined what was in store for them in the coming months—long afternoons of reporting and writing, certain modest privileges, a good deal of rigamarole, and a strict prohibition of access to certain books and certain rooms. As they stood there, Robbo and Jims gradually became aware of the smell of the ink wafting upstairs from the print shop below . . . and of the rhythm of the flatbed press churning like a washing machine, continuous and pleasant.

"Do you hear it—?" asked Jims.

"It's faster than surf," said Robbo.

"But slower than a heartbeat."

They looked at each other with the eyes of men who are facing a force of nature, a high mountain peak gleaming faintly in the mist of dawn, asking them if they and their equipment are ready.

Later that evening they told Billy it had been a positive experience. He was in bed reading, his room piled high with books, music, clothes: it was not exactly a chaos but a delicious mess, like a fudgecake. They could not convince him. First Robbo tried, and then Jims. More than anything, they didn't want to exaggerate. But they were fairly certain, and tried to convey to their friend, that there was something in the *Crimson* that partook of peace and stillness, something that was more like a long-term relationship than like laziness.

"It just surprises me," said Billy, "that the Robin Palmer I have known so long so well should end up on the staff of *The Harvard Crimson.*" The use of his childhood friend's full name expressed the gravity of the situation.

"Yes. Well," replied Robin, "the Dalton Robin and the Berkshire Robin are certainly different from the Cambridge Robin . . . and, of course, our situations change, in ways we have little control over. . . ."

The evening ended with less understanding among the roommates than in many months. Jims had not tried to argue very hard, because he had an even worse dread than Robbo of being self-righteous. But he felt good, and went to bed humming: *"She dances overhead/ On the ceiling, by my bed. . . ."*

Far below the thirty-six foot ceilings of the Widener reading room, Kievskaya was whispering to Harold Weiss, whom she had met in the bio labs. Many ghosts flapped and moaned in the space above their heads, chief among them the ghost of Eugene Gant or of Thomas Wolfe who had imagined him, who had set out to read all six million books in this library. For her part, Kievskaya was in a moral flap. She felt that her Harvard education consisted of making enormous discoveries and then not knowing what to do with them. She had been horrified to learn that the popular Chem 20 professor was also the inventor of napalm—and that one of the college's favorite physics professors had figured out how to detonate the atom bomb at Los Alamos. As the voluptuous girl whispered her findings, Weiss was silently mapping out an essay he would do for he knew just which learned journal: "A Stress Analysis of a Strapless Evening Gown."

"I don't know what you want," he said at last. "For myself, I am interested in the fundamental structure of nature."

"But what about the future of mankind? If *you* don't see it as your obligation to save the world for man—you who have the rare ability actually to help do so—who will?"

Weiss answered in a stately, rhetorical tone: "I comfort myself with the thought that another species will surely inhabit the planet after us."

Kievskaya was stunned. At first she thought he meant that beings from some other planet would colonize the earth. Then she realized that no scientist would say that. Birds were said to have inherited the earth when the dinosaurs became extinct. He must mean . . . insects! . . . and grasses . . .

All around Kievskaya and Weiss, as they sat and whispered in the reading room, there loomed the forest of books. Millions upon millions of books, too many for any one man to read, had been stacked, piled, numbered, classified, and divided like civilization itself into separate domains. The Main Collection. The rare collection. The boys' and the girls' collections. The Houses' collections. The clubs' collections. The fields' collections. In all this endless acreage of word a lonely student might settle into a truncated corridor full of newspapers and magazines—or into a small bookshelf-lined parlorlike space with comfortable chairs and a cozy name—and wander no further. The student would know it was inadequate, laughable, a joke compared with all this great collection of book, this Book, this Bookness; but the student would feel he could do no more.

"I can only speak about what I know," Weiss continued. "I can only report on events where I was present. I'm interested in scientometrics: I'll do a study and tell you whether large or small college laboratories produce the greater scientific output."

"That's not what I'm interested in at all!" moaned Kievskaya. "Men before me have wrapped their minds around time and space. I don't want to measure, I want to reorder."

Weiss smiled. She had the loveliest eyes.

"Tell me about it," he said. "Where would you start?"

Kievskaya glanced around the room. A boy at their table was looking at them with annoyance. She lowered her voice.

"I would start right here at Harvard, and reorganize the departments. Institute the Department of Comparative Imperialisms, the Department of Histories of Continents, the Department of Ancient Servo-Mechanisms, The Department of Criminal Endocrinology, the Departments of Social Physics, of Geomagnetism, of Small Group Economics . . ."

"I see what you're getting at," said Weiss. "But is it operational? After all, the curriculum really comes down to what the faculty wants to teach."

"The faculty!" exclaimed Kievskaya. "That bunch of quarrelsome egomaniacs!" She bit on a fingernail. "What this faculty doesn't realize—no, what Western scientists don't realize—is that, just because they *can* do something, they *should* do it. 'I can make an atom bomb, so I guess I will!' They're obsessed with their own power. They don't understand the power of holding back."

Now the boy at the end of the table was saying "Shh!" loudly and angrily.

Weiss instinctively recoiled from Kievskaya's vehemence. He didn't want to argue. He didn't happen to believe that truth is hammered out on the anvil of debate. Her pious wish that scientists should restrain themselves in order to save the world didn't appear to him to have any evidential backing. In India and the tropics generally there was a lot of withholding of effort, but nothing seemed particularly improved by that. To Weiss the mathematician, science was a beautiful and human way of creating the world, and he could not imagine that it should be interfered with for any arbitrary reason. Certainly not on the basis of an intuition, which was, it seemed to him, nothing but the jumping to a conclusion on logically insufficient grounds.

In America and in the whole of the modern world science was important and powerful and rich. Only here in the ivory tower, science and technology were still considered bastard knowledge. Scientists were socially inferior to aesthetes. Weiss thought of Aristotle, long suppressed, and of da Vinci, alienated from the scholars of his day, who no doubt saw him as grubby and perverse. And he knew he was doing what he had to do. And he wished to God that he could talk to this beautiful girl about it.

But for now he could just look at her, and listen to the way she used concepts, and put sentences together, and tested the truth of those sentences—and he could guess that she would be one of the many who would transfer out of biology to graduate in social relations or psychology or English. What was there to say?

"Don't be too hard on the faculty," he whispered. "Some of them see things the way you do."

"I know," said Kievskaya quietly. "Professor Nash cried. He showed us slides of Hiroshima and Nagasaki and said he never would have dreamed that the work he was doing in chemistry in the thirties would be used to rain down death on millions of people. He showed us the slides, and he cried, and then he walked out of the class in the middle of the hour. If I learned nothing else my whole freshman year, I learned from him to watch and be careful how any work I did was used."

Harold Weiss looked thoughtful.

Kievskaya went on. "But even if there are some good guys—don't the bad guys hold most of the power? Don't they hold fifty-one percent of the power?" She understood as she spoke (and Weiss saw that she understood) that her question, though couched in mathematical language, could not be solved by experiment. She perceived it as lying bubbling and unemancipated in the common matrix of religious myth. And she was content with that.

Nestor believed in disordering the senses, in the adventurous pursuit of the decadent. He was an ardent follower of Susan Sontag's "camp." In music he favored the ornate, nebulous, unnatural, lacy, emotional, textureless Saint-Saens—though when necessary he could hold forth like a fan on the meaning of Motown. Of modern drama he liked Albee, and Artaud, and Beck and Malina's very most current "living theater," which dared its audiences to the starkest of encounters every night (though this last also filled him with a crazy fear). The crowd down at the Loeb Theater called him a "pleasure wonk."

It was with enthusiasm and gratitude, then, that Nestor accepted John Stone's offer to let him taste a hit of DMT. The very next evening the young actor knocked on the door of the under-professor of social relations' modest Central Square apartment. The decor was redwood poverty, with here and there touches of black humor. In the kitchen Stone's wife Hepzibah showed him her collection of cookbooks from different monasteries.

The drug came with a needle. "This is going to be a real treat," said the under-professor. He shot Nestor up, and then himself. The rush was immediate and powerful. Stars, exclamation points, and pin-wheels. A thirty-minute LSD trip.

As Hepzibah served two small cups of stoneseed tea, the hand-some young faculty member grabbed her ass from behind. "Isn't she beautiful?" he gloated. "Do you want her? You can have her!"

Nestor was taken aback. His senses were ariot. This was by far the hardest drug he had ever taken. "But she's your wife!" he gasped. By this time he was sitting on the floor.

The features of John Stone's face were chiseled to the point where hardness becomes beauty or vice versa, and he had worked out the muscles of his long legs and arms and chest and belly until love itself was a ghost sent running ignominiously home.

"Sure, she's my wife," he said. (Were his words ever so slightly slurred? or was it Nestor's imagination?) "But you're my friend!"

Hepzibah looked down at the boy ambiguously.

Nestor looked up at her.

The woman's face seemed to be changing at least ten times a second. Her breasts looked obscenely huge. Her hips under her thin cotton housedress swayed as she walked toward him with a dish towel in her hand . . . as if, he thought, she is about to garrote me! . . .

"What a drug!" he managed to say. He pulled himself with difficulty back up onto the kitchen chair.

John Stone was smiling. "You're my friend!" he said again, or perhaps Nestor only imagined that he said it.

"Yes. We're friends." Nestor stammered, smiling back with hot oceanic love into John's face.

Hepzibah Stone had gone into the bedroom to lie down, the damp dish towel over her eyes.

Sarah opened her eyes to a won-derful gray overcast sky and the steady splash of water on the eaves. Oh, good! Rain always made her want to work, just as sunshine always

made her want to make love. She thought of the book catacomb deep
under the earth of Harvard Yard. She would read one of those books
with uncut pages and in its creamy recesses she would find out why the
Cathedral of Chartres was the first stop on the way to the pyramids.

She rose supremely content and dressed herself in a blue A-line
skirt, a purple jersey, black rubber Polish army boots, and her mother's
olive suede art deco jacket from the thirties. She got her slicker and the
big black umbrella out of the closet and went downstairs.

In the chipping and peeling kitchen of Elizabeth Cady Stanton
House breakfast was being waged with a certain commotion. Several
copies of the morning's *Crimson* were scattered on the table and under-
foot, and the girls were making sarcastic remarks about it. There were
not enough frying pans for everyone to have breakfast at once, nor was
there agreement on whether the window should be open to the rain.
High up on the smokestack of the unfunctional iron stove someone had
taped a mussed print of Matisse's *Red Room*. Virginia was pouring
orange juice into her omelet. Sarah picked up a *Crimson*, skimmed it for
by-lines, and dropped it back on a chair. Nothing by Michael today.
Rosa watched the door closing behind her.

Sarah snapped the snaps of her slicker and opened her umbrella
and picked her way happily through the wet leaves. The mile walk to
the Yard under the tall lilac always pleased her. She enjoyed the re-
spite from sociability. Sometimes she set herself little problems to work
out because their solutions (and she fervently believed there was always a solution) thrilled her so, sent a rush of orgasmic pleasure
through her, made her feel a notch older. Once she had solved to her
own satisfaction the problem of the relationship between ends and
means, she recalled, though she couldn't remember the substance of
the solution. She remembered more vividly the day she had discovered
that apple seeds have a sweet, almondy taste.

This wet morning her mind was drifting loosely, full of pictures
and numbers and designs, gliding across sights, perching fleetingly on
sounds. She became aware of the street's pungent bouquet: the lilac
first, then grass and bridal wreath. She could almost feel the sweet
smells penetrating the brain's worn pathways as far back as memory.
The heavy lilac, more fragrant than usual in the dripping rain, made
her think of mature womanhood. Why was that? Was it cousin Flor-

ence? Did the scholarly old spinster wear lilac dusting powder as she sat on the flowered upholstery of Grandma Galbraeth's couch, her arm on a crocheted antimacassar, telling stories?

Sarah began to think seriously about smells. What was the hierarchy among the senses? No sooner had she thought, provisionally, that, well, sight is more encompassing than sound, then she had a quick second thought declaring the first to be preposterous. Yes and then no. Truth and then falsehood. What was the use of ever beginning? She felt a twinge of discouragement. And then too many ideas flooded into her head for her to follow, a torrential, misunderstood mixture of what she thought must be mystical philosophies. Almost immediately they swept out again, taking the toddling thought with them, leaving only a bit of driftwood and the nice smell. Lilacs. Garden Street. Rain.

When Sarah got to Widener she installed herself in an underground carrel, her slicker and jacket over the opposite chair, no one in sight, Madame deStaël and George Sand and Simone de Beauvoir all around her.

Her lit tutor had suggested she write about the similarities among the three French women writers. All had done novels about women who destroyed themselves for love. But Sarah wanted to write about their differences. DeStaël had codified the distinction between "classic" and "romantic" and been an enemy of Napoleon's. Sand had loved Musset and the great Chopin and worn pants. De Beauvoir, still alive, was Jean-Paul Sartre's longtime companion. She had applied his metaphysics to the question of women.

"Feminism" was a word that sounded fresh and original to Sarah. No feminist structures had been defined in Western Europe or the U.S. since the winning of the vote a good two generations earlier. Nor was de Beauvoir, the existential feminist, fashionable in intellectual circles. The philosophers who exalted her companion Sartre ignored her. The historians and literati carped about her personal life.

All except for Professor Hughes. Now there was a man. Hughes had stepped down from the ivory tower long enough to run for the Senate against Teddy Kennedy and George Cabot Lodge on a touchingly idealistic platform of peace and justice. Radcliffe and the *Crimson* had supported him. Hughes appreciated de Beauvoir. He assigned her book about postwar Paris, *The Mandarins,* to his seminar on ideological fiction, along with novels by Hesse, Forster, Moravia, Malraux, Grass, Sholokhov, and some other men.

Sarah decided she would stay with de Beauvoir.

The Second Sex was a fat book. As she sat there and read, this rainy day deep underground in the stacks, Sarah felt her familiar pang of regret that she was not a better student. Studying was such a fine activity. With admiration verging on amazement she read on, as de Beauvoir cut a slice of womankind along an angle that had never been tried before, and put it under a microscope. De Beauvoir's rejection of Catholicism and Freudianism was agreeable to Sarah. The statement that "condition determines character" sounded right to her. De Beauvoir looked the fact squarely in the face that women had not accomplished as much as men . . . and she suggested some good reasons for this.

When Sarah reached the book's final chapter—after the denial that there had ever in history been female political power, after a dazzling recital of mythologies, after such wonderful facts—Sarah found a heraldic, optimistic prediction of the future. "New relations of flesh and sentiment of which we have no conception will arise between the sexes," de Beauvoir wrote. And: "If society restores her sovereign individuality to women, it will not thereby destroy the power of love's embrace to move the heart." And: "When we abolish the slavery of half of humanity, together with the whole system of hypocrisy that it implies, then the division of humanity will reveal its genuine significance and the human couple will find its true form."

There was nothing better than this. Liberty, equality, fraternity, so beautiful in themselves, now rediscovered. Sarah snapped the book shut, and leaned back and closed her eyes to think. This semester she was required to pick a topic for a major paper, and suddenly she knew what it would be: "Simone de Beauvoir: Prophet of the New Feminism."

She clutched *The Second Sex* like a smoking gun.

Sitting at the managing editor's desk, Michael was turning the pages of the day's *New York Times* back to front. He liked to read the paper that way, so the page one news would come as a wonderful surprise at the end, a dessert.

Sarah dropped in at the *Crimson*. "You know what your friend Virgil said to me?" she began indignantly. Virgil was a black scholarship student from Little Rock who wore expensive three-piece suits.

"No, what?"

"He said James Reston was coming to Eliot House to speak tonight, and I said, good, I'd like to hear him, and he said no, I couldn't, because girls aren't allowed in the Eliot House junior common room."

"Well, that's too bad," said Michael sincerely. "But you know how they are in Eliot House."

"Yes, I know," said Sarah.

What Michael and Sarah and everyone else knew was that Eliot House was the stronghold of misogyny. The House master had arranged to populate his dormitory with boys from the very best clubs, who prided themselves on the precise rightness of their shirt collars, and scorned the company of females as a distraction.

"That's not even what's making me mad!" said Sarah. "See, Virgil got really offended when I said that I thought girls should be allowed to go hear James Reston. We were having coffee in the University Restaurant. And he said, quite seriously, that if I felt that way, he wasn't going to pay my check or hold my coat for me."

"Yeah, so?"

"Yeah, so he didn't do either of those two things and I *still* don't get to go hear James Reston!"

Michael closed the *Times,* fitting it carefully back into its original shape, and looked up at Sarah with as much sympathy as he could. He valued Virgil's friendship and could see both sides of this little squabble. Perhaps the best thing to do was to take Sarah's mind off the inevitable.

"So how did you like Dwight MacDonald?" he said brightly. "Really, he's much more interesting than Scotty Reston."

Sarah didn't answer.

Michael saw she was peeved. But he didn't know, really, what was going on. Women at Harvard had their place. They were no threat to the establishment. They were patronized, condescended to. If a woman had gripes, it was obviously her own problem. If she was more than daintily ambitious, it was called a "personality disorder," and she was disqualified from whatever on that account. There was a new book out defending housewives' right to be human—that was Friedan's *The Feminine Mystique*. Sarah thought *The Feminine Mystique* a watered-down version of *The Second Sex*. But this was neither here nor there. Not too many people had read either one.

"Come on, kid," he said. "Don't take it so seriously. And speaking of not taking things so seriously, what do you know about Nestor Schwarz?"

"Nothing," said Sarah sullenly. "That actor Rosa is going out with? He's some kind of type, I don't know. Yvette and Tui went out with him before Rosa. Why?"

"All I know about him is that he acted in Dan's play. But Foote apparently thinks he's worth some attention."

"Oh, no. What now?"

"Foote has some stationery from *World* magazine. You know how he does it, with all his stationery: the Justice Department, Yale, et cetera, et cetera.

"Yeah, he must have an army of thieves working for him."

"Confederates. Anyway, he's sending Schwarz a letter on *World* stationery, with the editor's forged signature, telling him he's been chosen student actor for the year for the whole country and would he please come to New York at his soonest convenience to be interviewed and photographed and to pick up his Harry."

"His Harry?"

"That's the award Foote made up."

Sarah snorted a little. "Oh, well, *that's* funny."

"Foote is a funny guy."

"Uh, wait a minute. What's supposed to happen?"

Michael looked embarrassed for a fleeting instant. "Well, I guess Schwarz is supposed to go down to the city and bang on the *World* editor's door and get told that no, he isn't the student actor of the year and no, he isn't going to be photographed and interviewed and no, he isn't getting any Harry."

Sarah wrinkled her nose. She had mixed feelings about Foote's

shenanigans. They were always interesting to hear about. They made
you laugh and gasp. But there was also something sneaky and horrible
about them, something that frightened you to the extent that you felt
vulnerable.

She took up a comfortable stance of compassion for the victim.
"Poor Nestor Schwarz!"

By then, the inevitability of Thaddeus Foote and the puzzle of
Nestor Schwarz having driven the Eliot House slur out of her mind,
Sarah brushed the whole thing off, leaving Michael with his newspaper
at the m.e.'s desk.

She stood on the *Crimson* balcony
looking up and down Plympton Street to the Yard, to the river, into
the viney recesses of Apthorp courtyard. Boys and girls hurried up the
narrow street toward their classes, tweed jackets over jeans, ties flying,
mostly alone, some in small clusters. A girl coasted down the incline on
a ten-speed bike, her face white as a rag doll's, wrapped in a huge cape.
Then the famous political theorist Stanley Hoffman walked by with a
green bookbag over his shoulder, his figure fine, meticulous, strong.

After what seemed like a long time Sarah wandered back down
to the newsroom, past a sexy photo of herself on the stairway bulletin
board. The newsroom had filled up in her absence with the commotion
of a new competition. A host of youngsters were scurrying about with
cans of glue or big scissors, pecking away at the office machines, looking pleased with themselves. Charlie McSilver was dejectedly lobbing
wads of yellow paper into the wastebasket; he was mad because a
freshman newsboard candidate had brought in a dart board and stuck
it up on the wall next to the men's room. Michael had gone back to the
House. Sarah noticed a tall, thin, handsome blond boy leaning against
the Comment Book ledge.

"You're Billy Clemens's roommate, right?" she said, walking
over to him. "We had lunch together once freshman year. I'm Sarah
Galbraeth."

Jims smiled back at her, as awkward as the tin woodman, and croaked, "Yeah. Hi. I'm Jim DeWitt." He remembered Sarah—all of Harvard knew who Sarah was by now—but it was important to him not to make any sign to her of her exalted fame, while at the same time not being unfriendly. The result was a confusing mixture of signals, like a shimmer of electricity, that Sarah found endearing.

"Hi, Jim," Sarah said, smiling up at him. She wondered whether tall people acted more honorably than shorter people, since they were always more in the public eye. She watched Jims's Adam's apple traversing the long course of his neck. "How do you like the *Crimson?*"

"Well, er, um, ah—" he said, and looked at her as if she were supposed to understand. She looked back at him as if he were crazy. For him, this particular locution, while, indeed, meant to gain time, was also supposed to convey humor and irony, to be a comment upon itself. It was one of a thousand verbal jokes he had with the Ariels, based on nicknames and puns and malapropisms repeated so often they had become codes for higher understandings.

"Er, that is, I mean—it's very *Crimson*-y."

Sarah, Jims felt, was so closely identified with the paper that he couldn't possibly even consider revealing to her the exciting torment that the *Crimson* was to him, with its Byzantine structures and horrifying pushiness. So he smiled.

She decided to try a different tack. "What are you working on?"

Now a pink blush crossed the boy's face from his yellow hair down to his blue sweater, making him quite colorful. The work issue was impossible to evade. A projection of his father invaded his brain like a shadow: William Winthrop DeWitt, Jr., who had inherited the mantle of wealth—and as an important ambassador and diplomat had worked unceasingly throughout his life to live up to his numerous responsibilities. "Life is work," William Winthrop DeWitt, Jr., had told James Winthrop DeWitt, his only son, when the family was living in Britain.

And Jims had in consequence grown up with a pronounced ambivalence about work. He wanted in his brain to achieve as his father and his grandfather and the whole line of DeWitts and Winthrops had achieved. But something in his guts told him that his manhood depended on running in exactly the opposite direction. And so he achieved—and turned his back on his achievement—like a diffracting electron, interfering with itself.

"Uh, I'm doing a survey on happiness," he admitted shame-facedly.

"What a wonderful idea!" bubbled Sarah. "How are you doing it?"

Jims explained his plan of operation, which involved rather more personal interpretation than standard mean deviations, but which would result in something like a graph.

She was even more delighted. This tall, uneasy, aristocratic fellow gave every appearance of being the sort who would balk at putting people into charts. And yet here he was bravely embarking on this important fact-finding mission. Her opinion of him soared. He was not only cute, he was intelligent. She smiled at him warmly, and he saw the Harris tweed colors in her eyes for the first time.

"Do you like stock car racing?"

"Huh?" said Sarah. "You mean like at Indianapolis? I've never been."

"No, uh," said Jims, discouraged. "What they race at Indy are race cars. Stock cars are drawn from the regular manufacturers' stock. It's more interesting. . . ." He felt very foolish.

So did she. She wished she knew about stock car racing.

"Well, I'll see you later. Good luck with your survey." Sarah disappeared into the corner office to talk to *Crimson* editor-in-chief Christopher Green. Jims watched her for a moment and thought about what a funny and bold girl she was, and then turned back to the Comment Book ledge to work.

Not long after that, a girl and two boys came bursting up the newsroom stairs. The fund-raising was a success! There would definitely be a newspaper to cover Freedom Summer. Bureaus staffed with *Crimson* reporters would be set up in Mississippi, Alabama, and Georgia. A *Crimson* editorial had spoken of "the social revolution erupting in this nation." Now, as the newsroom gang gathered around looking impressed, delighted, timid, or jealous, the girl announced proudly that Eddie O'Brien had agreed to leave his job at the *St. Louis Post-Dispatch* and come on down to Montgomery to edit the thing.

Balanced against the Comment Book ledge, Jims made a grimace. "There is a race war going on in the South," he thought, "and I'd rather stop a war than write about it."

In the University Restaurant Sarah was drinking coffee with Christopher Green, the dimpled and amiable *Crimson* editor-in-chief. They felt close, Sarah and Chris, partly because they had both been elected to the paper at the very start of their freshman year and had consequently logged in many hours together, and partly because they had both come from public schools in the Midwest. In a funny way even their personalities were similar, being male and female versions of the same wholesome provincial.

This afternoon they were discussing who should hold what positions on next year's exec. "So I asked him whether he would rather be managing editor or president," Sarah was saying, "and he made a token gesture of respect for the m.e.-ship. But it was pretty clear he felt his height qualified him for the presidency, and that he really wouldn't mind a year of glory and no work."

Chris smiled at Sarah's definition of the office. It was true, the presidency was something of an honorific, a public relations job, while the managing editor did the real work. But it had its cachet. One felt oneself in a line with Franklin D. Roosevelt. One got one's head caricatured on the newsroom wall by David Royce.

He was about to repeat an anecdote about a famous battle among *Crimson* executive candidates in the fifties when he noticed someone near the door and interrupted himself to call him over. Tommy Cartier had spent a year at Harvard—then a year in Johannesburg putting out a newspaper about apartheid—then another year at Harvard—and was now on his way to Albany, Georgia. He had a square Harvardy face and bony arms sticking out of his T-shirt sleeves and an attractive intensity.

Over some fresh coffee, and looking mostly into Sarah's eyes, Tommy Cartier outlined his philosophy of life. "You shouldn't do anything you don't want to do," he said sternly. "Because you're going to die. And nothing you did halfheartedly will mean anything."

From the next booth they could hear a boy saying, "I don't see what's so great about the Categorical Imperative. You can't really universalize *any* action, because you can always abstract it into language in an endless number of different ways."

Chris had some questions about South Africa and Tommy answered him in detail. Half-moons of sweat formed under the arms of his T-shirt.

After that day Cartier was not seen in Cambridge again.

Nestor Schwarz drove down to New York in John Stone's Porsche, full of piss and vinegar, dressed like double-o-seven with a strapped blue suitcase and an attaché case that looked like it must have a built-in gun. Only things didn't turn out as he had expected. When the third secretary in the *Earth-World* building raised her eyebrows and looked at him questioningly, Nestor a) realized that he had been had, and b) resolved immediately to turn things around and get the last laugh on Foote. Silver-tongued and newly confident with the adrenalin rush that follows adversity, he managed to secure a good, long interview with a senior editor at *World*. Finding the man was less interested in student drama than in drugs, Nestor put himself forward as an expert on the subject. He estimated for the editor that thirty-five percent of Harvard students had used marijuana. The truth was probably closer to one or two percent. But the way Nestor said it, full of subtle emphases and long-practiced rhetorical melodies, made the ridiculous statistic ring true to the old journalist. Pleased to hear that things were as bad up there as he might have thought, the editor scribbled "35 Harv MJ" on his desk calendar.

They parted on excellent terms. When Nestor had one foot out the door he generously offered to keep *World* informed about the drug situation and related issues on the Cambridge campus.

The actor of the year returned triumphant.

A single drop of sweat splashed into the open engine of the Mustang. Michael was leaning over it lovingly, his sleeves rolled up, grease on his jeans. The sun was bright overhead and he felt great. George Durbey had installed himself on the front seat of the convertible, his legs on the Plympton Street pavement, and was providing a running commentary on the glories of the current Harvard season. Dockery was a sure bet to sign with the Jets. Del Rossi had already signed with the Yankees. The runners had swept the heptagonals and socked away the best score against Yale in the history of mankind. Bill Bradley was a deity, of course, but Sedlacek *had* outscored him. . . . Was Michael there?

Michael nodded absentmindedly at George. "Must be the distributor."

A mile away, Sarah was slowly approaching. Her steps led her to the Out of Town newsstand in the throbbing center of Harvard Square. There she paused half conscious on one foot and let her eyes feed on the panoply of newspapers and magazines as if on the effluvia of time that even big Harvard was obliged to respect and make sense of.

And then she crossed to Nini's Corner to admire the piles of great, pompous, swollen, waxed apples in the window. After some deliberation she picked one out for a quarter and bit into it as she continued her walk.

Sarah's ramble took her along the south wall of the Yard where there stretched the thin strip of trade like a membrane of a higher organism: the fancy men's clothing shop, the exotic smokeshop with track and crew schedules in the window, the foreign language bookstore with the postcard collection she liked, the crummy fast-food places that came and went with great rapidity.but had their fiercely loyal clienteles nonetheless. Why did this simple perambulation give her so much pleasure?

Sarah recognized Michael's tutor perambulating like herself, a *Times* under his arm, but she didn't know him well enough to say hello. She thought vaguely of doing some acting.

When she got to Plympton Street she quickened her pace and arrived at Michael and the car and George quite giddy with happiness. "Mike, baby!"

"Darling!"

"Oh, baby!"

"Don't mind m-m-me," grumbled George good-naturedly.

"Let's go see *Dr. Faustus!*" she said.

"At the Loeb you mean? Tonight? Nah, it's a grim story."

"Come on. Nestor's in it. Rosa wants us to go with her."

"The famous Nestor Schwarz? I wonder how he made out in New York." Michael peered back into the engine. He attached the valve gauge to the intake manifold, signaled to George to step on the gas and take her up slowly, and watched, chagrined, as the needle jumped from 7 to 20 and back down to 10.

"Shit!" he said. "A blown head gasket. Gotta yank all the spark plugs and put in a compression whosis."

Sarah was hanging back looking uncomprehending.

"And you best believe that's gonna cost!" he said in his hillbilly accent.

"*Dr. Faustus?*" she repeated.

"All right, if you really want to go."

The main stage had been transformed into the likeness of one huge book, dark and weighted with antiquity, along the thick and heavy spine of which, at stage left, ranged golden letters in a long, polysyllabic title, runelike, not quite intelligible. From backstage could be heard the chill strains of Holst's *Saturn*. As a screen rolled away, three scholars in cap and gown entered from stage right, and simultaneously the figure of Johann Faustus, doctor of divinity at the University of Wittenberg, was revealed sitting in his musty study in the hollowed-out center of the great volume, poring over a smaller book with rapt and unholy attention. Renaissance Germany. Rosa squirmed in her seat.

Nestor lifted his head. Black and silver shadows played around his eyes. A false nose jutted out from under his cleric's fez. In his heavy brown cowl robe decorated with a scholar's small ruff he might have been a nightmare version of Raphael's Pope Leo. Sarah thought he looked quite amazing.

Then Nestor/Faustus vehemently flung his book across the floor, waved the other scholars away (who fled), and in a marvelous, sonorous bass intoned Marlowe's verse:

> "Philosophy is odious and obscure,
> Both law and physic are for petty wits,
> Divinity is basest of the three—
> Unpleasant, harsh, contemptible, and vile.
> 'Tis magic, magic, that hath ravished me!"

Sarah pulled on Rosa's sleeve. "This is terrific!" she said.

"Harry Levin says Faust is an 'overreacher,' " whispered a girl behind them.

The great book dissolved into a gauze. Faustus, still on stage, stood now alone in the middle of a chaos, a confusion, an entropy, a woods with an obscene name. Lifting up his long arms in their draping brown sleeves, he called with all the strength of his great bass voice upon Mephistopheles and Beelzebub—embedding their names in an incantation so blasphemous that shudders ran through the bodies of the entire Harvard and Radcliffe audience.

Stage effects and horrific sounds shook the theater. By some miracle of art, a globe of lightning dropped in a thundering peal from overhead. The radiant ball transformed itself astonishingly into the shape of a fiery creature on the borderline of humanity, and then resolved itself into the form of a gray-clad beggar monk. Nestor/Faustus ostentatiously winked at the miracle, and gave the audience to understand that he did not for a moment believe in God or the devil. Still, here was ripe opportunity for advancement. He laid before the apparition a list of demands.

Michael shivered. Out of the corner of his eye he had spotted Foote a few rows ahead, sitting with his latest accomplice, Briggs Smith. Foote was grinning.

Faustus demanded of the devil that he obey him, that he bring him everything he asked for, and that he answer all questions truthfully.

"That's absurd," whispered Michael. "Of course the devil's not going to speak the truth if it's not in the interests of hell."

In return the devil asked merely for Faustus's body and soul pledged in writing in his blood, and that Faustus renounce Christianity, all Christians, and anyone trying to dissuade him from his bargain. "I shall go even farther," volunteered Nestor/Faustus. "Hereupon I deny all living creatures that bear the shape of God, yea all that lives. And had I as many souls as there be stars, I'd give them all for Mephistopheles!"

Then the gauzy screen descended once again, leaving only the great book. Only now the audience might have wondered if it was a book of divinity, or law, or physics, or philosophy, or one of those books "whose deepness doth entice such forward wits/To practise more than heavenly power permits."

Franciscans' bells signaled the end of the act.

The audience rustled. Michael leaned across Sarah to Rosa. "How do you like it?"

Rosa was too thrilled to speak.

In Act Two the Seven Deadly Sins, which the devil referred to as "pastimes," paraded before Dr. Faustus, distracting him from thoughts of God—and from his worsening symptoms of cold, trembling, and fear of imminent death.

Rosa whispered across to Michael that Faustus had become paranoid.

"What?" he said.

"Shh!" said Sarah.

Rosa leaned back in her chair. The Seven Deadly Sins reminded her of the pathologies they had covered in Psych 401. Pleased by the observation, Rosa whispered to Sarah that Covetousness was kleptomania; that Envy, seeking revengeful equalization, was "sociopathic character disorder"; that Wrath was "uncontrolled hostility"; and that Gluttony, of course, was just the old way of saying "fat"— which word still strikes people as pretty terrifying. Sloth was depression that immobilizes; and Lechery? Well, call it promiscuity, nymphomania, womanizing. As Sarah was smiling at this, and Faustus was watching, fascinated, and Michael was trying to divide his attention between the stage and his companions, came the funniest of all. Of all

the sins the one most attractive to Faustus was Pride—"that disdained
to have any parents." Rosa whispered into her friend's ear that this
was more or less what "normal" modern psychology was about, the
cultivation and development of the demanding, grasping, thrusting
ego.

"What are you saying? It sounds so interesting," whispered
Michael.

"O, how this sight doth delight my soul!" quoth Nestor/
Faustus. And he turned to the devil's book to peruse and learn how to
enjoy in hell all these delicious pastimes.

The next act of the play depicted Faustus bringing low his real
or imagined enemies all over the world—ranging from the Pope, whose
dignity he could hardly dent, to a poor and meager enemy of his
enemy's enemy, a simple knight, whom Faustus ridiculed unmercifully
and drove away into a life of grief.

Then came a short act depicting the lighter side of magic.
Faustus and his valet-disciple and their constant companion the Lord
of Darkness stole food and wine from the lords and innkeepers of Sax-
ony and Bavaria and Salzburg, and clothes from the mercers of
Nuremberg, Augsburg, Frankfurt, and Leipzig. The recitation of the
names of the old German fiefdoms and towns seemed to suggest some
kind of five-hundred-year-old joke on the marketplace, and elicited a
loud laugh from Foote. Michael recalled vaguely that Foote had once
stolen a case of *Crimson* gin and lain about his Hoare House garret for a
week finishing it off.

This was the most congenial type of magic to the various others
in the play who were imitating Faust, and they baffled innkeepers
repeatedly.

Finally, when the last of the monks' bells had tolled, Dr.
Faustus's twenty-four-year pact with the devil came due. In a horrible
scene, Dr. Faustus seemed to be trying to repent, but was unable to do
so, and instead—by the magic of stage art—was torn limb from limb by
a band of prosecuting devils, who dragged the remains of him off to
eternal torment.

"I don't know," said Michael, when the veil had rung down for
the last time. "Do you think those were really Nestor's blood and
brains and eye and tooth that were scattered around the stage?" Sarah

poked him. Rosa was looking at Foote, who was holding forth loudly on the meaning of the play, drawing glances from several directions.

After a bit Nestor appeared at the stage door in the theater's crowded lobby. Almost involuntarily, he hailed Foote first, and then came quickly over to Rosa, Michael, and Sarah. The white eyebrow still had a smudge of silver eyeshadow above it and his smile had an aroused brilliance. He wore shiny black chinos and a black turtleneck under a black nylon jacket with a red-lined hood. The slightly shabby quality of his dress, combined with the excited confidence of his idiosyncratic features, gave him the look of a very exceptional orphan. He had never met Michael or Sarah before, though they had mutual acquaintances. As introductions were being made, his late tormentor Foote stepped over to join their circle as if it were the most natural thing in the world.

"Grats!" exclaimed the red man, slapping Nestor on the shoulder. "Not bad at all!"

"You were wonderful, Neddy," said Rosa, but Foote's voice rode over hers.

"Of course," he added, winking at the company all around, "there were some flaws."

"Flaws?" returned Nestor passionately. "Like what?"

The loiterers in the Loeb were beginning to thin out. Foote's sidekick Briggs Smith, bored, was gazing at the glass front doors.

"Ah, well," said Foote, taking his time. "Far be it from me to denigrate your . . . but . . . I suppose I had better say it—your interpretation of the damnable life and deserved death of Dr. John Faustus was glitteringly vapid. Witty but superficial. Cosmically pretentious. Bombastic . . ."

Nestor took in a sharp breath. He didn't even glance at the others. He just stared at the fine red-haloed face of Foote for two long, silent minutes.

And then he slapped his shiny black thigh and let out the most enormous, gorgeous, heartbreaking laugh, a laugh with eternities of weeping in it, a laugh of fear, of castration, of resignation, of triumph. He grabbed Foote by his dapper lapels and held him for an instant in a clinch.

"You're all right, Foote," he said. "You're okay! . . . I was upset for a moment until I realized what you were doing. You were" (he glanced at the others) " 'putting me through changes!' And then I forgot about happy and sad, which cancel each other out, and returned to the simpler existential confrontation, the Drama of Artaud. Where before there had been only rhythm, you introduced momentum of irregular and interesting pattern. Well done, m'boy! Homage to Sade!"

Michael was staring at the spectacle of the breathless Nestor, the distantly nodding Foote, as if he had just seen a man assume the face of an ape. Sarah was puzzling over the white eyebrow. Rosa appeared to be in pain.

"Let's have a drink on that!" suggested Nestor heartily. And he shepherded the little group out of the theater ("When tragedy becomes comedy, we are forced to think," he was babbling. "Nothing changes, and yet we are different. We have grown!") and down the street a short way to the Club Casablanca.

"I thought it was very good," said Michael to Nestor, with a penetrating gleam in his eye, when the two boys and their dates were seated around a little red checkered table in the underground club. Foote and Smith had excused themselves.

Nestor raised his eyebrows. He lifted his hand to take a long drag on his filtered cigarette, pursing his lips and letting his black-edged fingernails fan out delicately. He stared into the well-modeled face of the boy sitting across from him as if to say, "Just what is it you want from me?"

"Sarah thought so too. Didn't you, baby?" said Michael.

As Sarah agreed ("Oh, yes, it was terrific!"), Nestor looked at her for the first time, and as he did so Rosa saw something awful in his glance. She guessed that Nestor was thinking, "This woman is more famous than I."

"Why, Sarah Galbraeth," he began. "I am honored." He flicked an ash into the little white ceramic tray advertising a Moroccan beer.

Charm fell over his face. "I've followed your work since freshman year, when I was dating Yvette Serre. Your model for Lime," he added explanatorily.

Sarah made a face. "She was not my model for Lime. No individuals were archetypes. It was an abstraction from a lot of individuals: you know, sociology?"

Nestor, smiling, charming, didn't appear to believe her. He liked to tell people about this Yvette being the model for Lime business. It reflected well on him.

Michael was making a "let it go" gesture at Sarah. He changed the subject. LBJ was escalating the war. The Maoist PLM was staging a demonstration against it. But there was good news, too. "They finally got Hoffa."

"Bobby'll never be able to make it stick," retorted Nestor. "The mob's too powerful."

"Speaking of the mob, are Binks and Thatcher under lock and key on that big estate in New Jersey? Or is it some kind of country resort?"

"Oh, they're living it up, all right," answered Nestor. "The story is: they got this place in Red Bank from some young guy with an enormous trust fund they're diddling, and they've set themselves up with a half a dozen adults and half a dozen children and a half a dozen cats and some dogs and a monkey. Plus a lot of these fantastic old Buddhas and statues and antiques and stuff. They're conducting group acid trips, with a guide reading out of the Tibetan *Book of the Dead*. It's really wild . . ."

"Yuk. It sounds horrible," said Sarah.

"Crackpots," said Michael.

Pause. "I'm not so sure about that," said Nestor. On the Casa B jukebox the Vibrations, five Los Angeles blacks, were singing "Hang on Sloopy." In a few months Little Caesar and the Romans would record the same insistent, druggy tune.

"Those guys are creeps," repeated Michael.

Rosa was wondering what Nestor would say to that. She knew he was very interested in the Red Bank doings, but she had never been able to make him justify his feelings to her in words. She looked at him expectantly.

"Buster Thatcher is a little too messianic, it's true," began Nestor. "He can go over the line, and become unacceptable. But Stevie Binks is really quite cute. He has this adorable gleeful toothy grin. When you approach him he always looks so happy to see you, like he's picturing you on his hors-d'oeuvres tray. And you know that even if he were to stab you in the back, it would only be with a one-of-a-kind, absolutely special, antique, barbaric spear.

"I'm thinking of going out to visit them this summer," he finished casually.

Sarah was cleaning appetizer peanuts from between her teeth with her tongue. Nestor's glance caught her off guard and she made an obliging grimace.

"Is that right?" said Michael, and stubbed his cigarette out in the clay dish.

"I thought I—" began Rosa, but Nestor interrupted.

"Any messages for them?"

"Well, no," said Michael, "but you can tell us all about what you see there, next fall."

At this Nestor relaxed, mistaking Michael's professional interest for a personal one.

He gave the other boy another look, and noticed his good bones. "There is wit in that face," he thought.

"Are you going out to Red Bank too?" Sarah asked Rosa.

"Oh, no!"

"Dylan is coming to Cambridge for the Freshman Jubilee," announced Nestor. "Isn't that just too much?" His black eyes flashed merrily on Sarah.

"Who's Dylan?" said Sarah.

"Oh my God," gasped Nestor.

"You know Dylan, honey," said Michael. "Bob Dylan. The folk singer with the scratchy voice."

"Oh," said Sarah. She tried to think.

Michael went on tentatively, glancing from Sarah to Nestor. Michael had gone to the Newport jazz festival last summer, not the folk festival, where Dylan had made such a splash (the sun in that fuzzy hair, that troubled sneer, that skinniness). But word was out that the kid Dylan could write some stirring lyrics about peace, about civil rights. "The Times They Are A-Changin' " was even a sort of anthem for the whole caboodle, the watchamacallit, the "generation." . . .

("Is this hip?" thought Nestor.)

"Oh, you mean Dylan—that Danny Matlaw likes?" said Sarah. Michael nodded. "He says Dylan is always coming out with things he's thinking about just before he does."

("But there is something cute about them, just the same.")

"Do you want to go hear him?"

"A scratchy-voiced folk singer? Nah."

Michael and Sarah bantered for another moment about "the scratchy-voiced folk singer." She laughed prettily. ("But why does she laugh so easily at everything he says?" thought Nestor. "If I said the same thing, she'd say I was dogshit. And I'm much cleverer than he is.")

The talk ranged back to the play of the evening. Rosa was persuaded to tell everyone the clinical equivalents of the Seven Deadly Sins, which she did in a small voice. Michael laughed appreciatively, but Nestor remained blank, jiggling the ice in his glass.

For a moment the orphan showed in Nestor's black and white eyes again. When Rosa finished he began abruptly: "Tell me, though, did you folks think there was any merit to what Foote said?" His voice faltered.

Michael looked at the actor. He knew Foote pretty well, and was generally amused, rather than upset, by the fellow, but he was hard to explain. "No, no, you know Thaddeus," he said. "He was tricking you. You said it yourself. You were great."

"You were. You really were," said Rosa sweetly.

Nestor's eyes rested emptily on Sarah. She sensed that he was waiting to hear it again from her, too.

"Uh huh," she said. "You were great. OOTG. OOTATG."

Michael smiled at the *Crimson* slang. A fund of esoteric knowledge separated the two couples.

("This bitch is right out of *Time of Her Time*," thought Nestor.)

Soon after that Nestor felt compelled to rush back to the House. "Are you ready to go, dear?" he said to Rosa. "Are you finished?" The two of them left the Casa B, Rosa looking back at Sarah and Michael, lifting her hand, smiling sheepishly. Nestor had grabbed her shoulder and was propelling her forward with some insistence.

Yvette couldn't exactly remember how she had gotten here. She had been drinking all night—too much, that was clear; she felt vaguely nauseous, and doubled; the personality that was watching her act had no control over the acting personality. She was in a dingy Boston apartment with Don and his friends. And they were so mean. How had they gotten here from the party in Somerville? Did Don say he had something he had to give someone?

Don and that awful friend of his and the others were still drinking and smoking a lot and talking loudly among themselves, too fast for her to catch everything, and quite often they used phrases she didn't understand. What did she see in Don anyhow? Yvette couldn't remember. Don would yell at her to get something, to bring something from the kitchen—and he would give her a mean look if she didn't do it right away. Yvette wanted to go home, but she felt like an infant, an invalid; she didn't know how to get home from here by herself. So she just waited, and watched Don, and looked at him with suspicion.

They opened another bottle of bourbon. Yvette got the ice. She was wearing a black sweater that showed off her breasts perfectly, and no makeup. Her black hair hung straight on her neck. Her blue jeans were faded to the palest blue-white, and Don and his friend watched her legs as she walked.

Yvette knew she was beautiful. She had learned that long ago. But right now it seemed more like a curse than anything else. She had never felt so unconfident and unstable. Was Don mad at her because she had said hello to Nestor outside the Loeb this evening? Now he was putting a brown and orange capsule in his mouth, handing a drugstore vial to his friend. Yvette's confusion swirled around her like an aura and her tired mind fell back on the thing she was most sure of: her beauty. She padded around the room barefoot, slender, and luscious, and her beauty touched the men's hearts, and maddened them.

Dreaming, alone, beautiful, Yvette let herself be drawn into the men's game. Strip and whip. What was that? It didn't matter. The cards came fast, the men drank more. Unself-conscious, she was naked before she realized that Don was cheating to keep himself dressed. Then he ordered her to perform. He hit her with his belt while the others watched. She realized she was the entertainment. "C'mere, babe," she remembered Don saying, in a low, wheedling, almost apologetic voice. "C'mere, beautiful—" That was the last thing she remembered.

Somehow she had gotten through the rest of this awful night. She had obeyed Don, partly because he had the car keys in his pocket and partly she didn't know why. But she felt unspeakably degraded and angry, and resolved never to let it happen again.

Yvette sat for a long time alone in the Stanton House kitchen, her eyes hollow, drinking cup after cup of coffee and not looking at the newspaper open in front of her. The kitchen was bright and gay, the ripped print of Matisse's *Red Room* was still taped to the old iron stove. But Yvette was cold and frightened, and as the other girls in the dorm arrived home one by one and tried to exchange words with her, she kept silent.

"**N**estor is a damn good actor," said Michael to Sarah as they sat and swung in the glider on the Stanton House porch. "I think I'm going to nominate him for the Signet."

"Why don't you nominate him for the Wagner prize?"

"For best acting. Yes, I could do that. The *Crimson* gets three votes."

"Then Foote's little joke will come true."

"True. Let's see: do I really want to do that? Oh, why not? What the hell. He's a good actor, he's Rosa's boyfriend, he's so absurd, and he seems like he deserves a break."

That night as usual Nestor and Rosa tried to make love in his cluttered suite, and as usual failed. As usual he convinced her that it was her fault. The girl left his room buttoning up her little jacket, pretty and pathetic, a maiden out of Thomas Hardy.

It rankled the hell out of Nestor not to know what OOTG and OOTATG meant. Maybe he could get Foote to tell him.

Reading period, the end of the year. On her way back from the Library Sarah sat down under a big evergreen in Radcliffe Yard, at that point where it comes closest to Harvard Yard. Someone at Harvard had decided there would be no gardens in that school, that the reigning deity was the soul, not nature. But this little garden had sprung up in the sister school nonetheless, on the site of the old "annex," right at the beginning of Garden Street itself. It was a quiet spot of green with ornamental shrubs and flowers and half-hidden fragments of a wall and all the peacefulness of neglect. Few people stopped here very often, perhaps because it was indeed alien in spirit from the rest of the university.

There under the yew Sarah picked up Dwight MacDonald's *Memoirs of a Revolutionist,* a book Michael had given her that she had so far been unable to read. Its thick historical text swam before her eyes: messages of Leon Trotsky and Henry Wallace. Soon she was fast asleep, the paperback sprawled open beside her, her head on a stone wrapped in a sweater.

Sarah dreamed a strange dream, not of revolutions but of trees.

Now one of the oldest trees on the face of the earth was just such as this yew. Who knows?—perhaps its pollen was floating around the universe in smokelike clouds and the yew was older even than the earth itself. At any rate the yew, along with the palm, the pine, the camphor laurel, the fern, dated back to that time we call the Eocene, when electricity was just being born in the form of a resinous amber gel.

Electricity danced in the blood of Sarah's brain. She was dreaming of a time when trees had already matured, but man was still new. An army of trees headed by the alder god Bran was faced

in battle array against an army of trees headed by the ash god Je-
hovah. . . . Before she had slept an hour Sarah was discovered and
rather impudently awakened by Jims. She scrambled to her feet,
brushing the fragrant needles off her dress.

"Hi," he said. "You looked like you needed waking up. It's
known to be very dangerous to remain in an unconscious state for more
than a moment or two in such near proximity to Harvard Square."

Sarah laughed. She was glad to see him. "I don't know what
came over me," she said. "One minute I'm reading this fascinating
political book and the next thing I know the alder god is in danger of
losing his throne to the ash god. Do you think this is a good political
cause to get behind?"

"Well, I prefer something like nobody should be hungry," Jims
admitted.

"That makes sense," said Sarah. "What do you do to help bring
that about?"

"I don't eat," said the boy, wrinkling his forehead violently. He
felt she had caught him again. But he had decided he liked her, so he
was going to let things happen and watch where they went.

"Hm," she was saying, trying to work up a category for him.

"I know what let's do," he said cheerfully. "Do you want to
come with me? I was just going to the Office of Graduate and Career
Plans to look through their book of stuff."

"That sounds like fun," said Sarah. "I haven't even started to
think about what I want to do after next year, but it'll be good for me
to force myself."

"Most everything that's good for you is no fun," said Jims. "But
maybe this will be good for you even if it is fun. I don't know. It's a
possibility."

He smiled at her then with a sudden enthusiasm that surprised
her, but she wrote it off as a momentary trick of the pleasant shade
under the yew tree. He was obviously eager to move, to be "doing"
something, rather than simply "being" together, but she had found a
spot where she felt comfortable and was inclined to linger.

They did eventually walk over to the Office of Graduate and
Career Plans, but only after a long getting-acquainted conversation.
He told her about his father, ambassador to the Court of St. James, a
name known round the world, and about how he had been raised in

elegance in Chappaqua and on Block Island and in St. Croix. He told her about his grandmother who had had a salon that the Impressionists came to, and about his mother who worked all the time raising money for MOMA and the Met. He told her about the kind of music he liked. Sarah told Jims about what she'd liked about high school, and about the home-building business in Iowa. And it turned out they liked the same kind of music, more or less.

And when the last minute arrived to get going to the Office of Graduate and Career Plans before it closed—in that stolen instant of motionlessness leaning against the half-wall (Sarah) and against the yews (Jims)—in that moment James Winthrop DeWitt lowered his voice and looked as all alone as a man can look, the bones of his face dashed by some prehistoric wind, and confessed the deepest secret of his life.

"Sarah," he said, "my father saved the pound."

The cowboy was graduating. From now on he guessed he would be known as just plain old Al Coulter. He had lined up a job in the *Times* San Francisco bureau and was happy about that connection, and happy to be going West again. On his last night in Cambridge he went stomping through the *Crimson* looking for people to say good-bye to.

Thinking he heard noises in the sanctum, Coulter hied himself up those angled stairs for yet another poignant farewell. But at the top he stopped dead, and stood transfixed, and all the blood in all six-four of him drained to his feet and disappeared. For there on a ratty leather *Crimson* sanctum sofa, Al Coulter thought he saw Sarah Galbraeth and Michael Verhoeven making love.

It wasn't true. It was a mirage, a hallucination.

But see it the cowboy did, in some dim recess of his cerebrum or agony-blazed ventricle of his poor heart. And from that dread moment he felt absolutely and profoundly sure that he could never marry anyone else in his life.

Overcome by despair, Coulter turned and went back down the familiar *Crimson* stairs as soundlessly as he could, to go look for a man to drink with.

In late May of 1964 Carolee went to Mississippi with a thousand other volunteers to work with SNCC on voter registration. From the very first, when she was being interviewed by the SNCC command to see if she could be one of the troops, she was aware of the outrageousness of the situation. They were being screened to see if they could do a summer of work at the risk of getting killed, and they had to pay their own expenses. SNCC had no salaries to give out.

When Schwerner, Chaney, and Goodman were murdered in Meridian in June, Carolee heard about it first on SNCC's WATS line. Soon everyone was talking about it. But she was not surprised particularly, nor any more frightened that she had been already. All by herself in an isolated rural town called Itta Bina, Carolee had long ago surrendered to the enormous risk.

She did receive a short letter from Tui, who was working as a congressional intern in Washington. "There's a lot of talk around here from some people," Tui wrote, "that Schwerner, Chaney, and Goodman were just hidden away somewhere by SNCC—so as to provoke . . . etc., etc. I don't believe it for a minute, myself. But how would *you* answer those people?"

Carolee thought the question wrong-headed, but Tui had contributed fifty dollars to the costs of Carolee's summer, and so she wrote back a patient and earnest answer.

What SNCC was officially doing, spread like missionaries throughout the state, was organizing the black community: to register to vote, to build a new political party, to set up community centers and new types of schools. These, and providing for her own survival, were more than enough to keep Carolee busy in Itta Bina. But something was also happening in a deeper stratum of her being. She was falling in love with black people—a phenomenon dubbed The Freedom High—with the ones who could neither read nor write, there in the countryside, but who spoke about their own lives in such clear voices. And with the SNCC leadership: she venerated Bob Moses and his strong wife Dona Richards. As the debate over SNCC's internal organization began to unfold—some calling for more centralization, some less—Carolee felt respect for both factions. She wanted to remain close to the struggle, near the nectar of leadership, to continue to work and fight as necessary.

Carolee dropped out of Radcliffe that fall and spent the next few months in New York City and Alabama organizing for SNCC. All the while she prepared herself to return to Mississippi the following summer to participate in the next phase of the drive.

Tui, freshly psychoanalyzed and with a whole new wardrobe, returned to school.

Sarah flew to Russia and Poland that summer on a student exchange. In Kiev she bought moss- and persimmon-colored illustrations of nineteenth-century Russian fairy tales. Outside the Kremlin she stood gawking, wearing a worn black raincoat, till a Russian passer-by tugged at her sleeve and told her she wasn't dressed properly. She debated with Russians and Poles and Americans whether communism was worse than capitalism—she said it was. The compartmented trans-Europa train from Moscow to Paris was gloriously romantic. Still she rushed back eagerly, stuffed with impressions, to Cambridge, to see Michael. On Labor Day they made love by way of greeting in a tiny off-campus room he had rented. And when she woke by his side the next morning, one keester warm and reassuring against another, she felt at peace and at home.

Diffident, Michael didn't have much to tell about his summer. The Verhoevens had gathered as usual, his sister with her bohemian boyfriend, his parents, the old socialist grandmother, for their Fourth of July party. It had rained on the grape arbor, and they had had to rush inside. Mr. Verhoeven wasn't feeling completely well, but he read the Declaration in the same stirring basso profundo as always, and as always the little ritual sent chills down Michael's spine and brought a fleeting, embarrassed mist to his eyes.

"Your letters were so great," he said. "They actually said something, instead of just being a lot of drivel like mine were."

"No, what you said about your feelings was wonderful," Sarah protested. "I could feel your presence in every word."

Michael pointed out a new print on the wall. "How do you like that? My mother gave it to me for my birthday." It was a pale, spiraling staircase, peopled with diaphanous, radiant beings ascending and descending. *Jacob's Ladder.*

"Blake is so great," said Sarah.

A carton of Camels, a bottle of Glenlivet, and a big jar of peanut butter stood on top of the refrigerator that abutted the bed. The sofa was piled with newspapers, folded meticulously.

"I didn't write you," he said, "but you know that necking we did in the grass at the airport? Well—"

"I know what you're going to say!"

"—I got poison ivy!"

"So did I!" They both laughed until their laugh became a hug.

"That must have been a real drag in Warsaw."

"Are you kidding? I arrived all covered with horrible red blotches. You can imagine what kind of American monster my host family thought I was. But they didn't let on that anything was wrong. They just whisked me away to sleep off my jet lag in the most beautiful bed I've ever seen. Quilts a foot thick. All these lacy, embroidered white blanket covers and pillow covers and stuff. Really. I've never seen a bed like that."

They smiled together, their skins smooth and tan and soft, and leaned back on Michael's hard double bed.

"Did you wind up enjoying it?"

"Well, the people I met were pretty brainwashed. The Polish girl my age referred to their system as 'the road to socialism,' though her parents didn't seem to go along with that; they sort of shrugged and winked. She thought her textbook of Marxist economics was just 'very difficult, very hard to understand.' And she changed the subject whenever I brought up Bill of Rights–type stuff."

"People in a totalitarian country can't afford to be frank. Even with themselves. They reveal themselves indirectly."

"Yeah, I guess. They kept dragging me around to statues and parks. I guess they were nationalists—they weren't afraid to admit that. At least in Moscow I managed to escape Intourist."

"Your letters about that were the most wonderful things I've ever read," said Michael, reaching across to touch her back. "You know, I existed all summer for your letters. I wanted to shout and shout till somehow they brought you back to me again. You don't mind that I went around telling people I'm going to marry you? Oh, Sarah, baby, I know this trip was wonderful for you and that you got a lot out of it and everything, but I never want to be separated from you for as long as a whole summer again! . . ."

Sarah kissed Michael's freckled nose.

"How was your National Student Association thing?"

"Ah, yes, the NSA." Michael propped himself up. "Well, getting there was a complete disaster. United Airlines lost my reservation, so I had to spend the night in O'Hare airport. So there I am reading *Gone with the Wind,* which is very readable and above all very long— when, about two A.M., I go to get a *Tribune,* and some bastard steals the book. So I bought a copy of *Moonraker,* but I couldn't get interested in that. So I slept the rest of the night intermittently" (here Michael pantomimed nodding off, then coming to with a start), "waking to Muzak every couple of hours. I didn't get to the conference until two the next afternoon, about twenty-four hours late."

"Whew," said Sarah.

"Yeah, right," said Michael. "The dorm all the Harvard guys were staying in looked like a Treadway Motor Inn. Without even washing or unpacking or anything, I rushed right over to this high school auditorium where the plenary sessions were in progress."

"And how were they?"

"*Bor*-ing. Mostly parliamentary maneuvering. Only the chairman was okay. His speeches about being quiet and clearing the aisles were the best of the day. This went on until about one A.M."

"What kind of politics do they do?"

"Oh, NSA is mostly liberals. Some of them softies—you know, laughing scornfully every time someone criticizes communism. A few clownish conservatives. A large group of nondescript types. Pretty much all of the white Southern colleges have dropped out this year. On the other hand, in a few places the liberals have dropped NSA because they're more interested in direct action, civil rights, things like that."

"Why doesn't NSA send delegates to the International Union of Students? I heard about them in—"

"Sweetie!" expostulated Michael. "How can you even ask that? The IUS is a Communist front! We can't lend them our prestige. There's nothing we can learn from them . . . Why are you looking at me like that? Am I speaking in clichés? Oh, yeah, well, maybe. We can talk about it more later.

"Here. Wait a minute," Michael said, smiling. "I brought this back for you." With a twist of his lean, broad-shouldered torso, he reached to the far side of the bed and took an object from the dresser top. It was an official NSA name tag, a little piece of folded plastic with a white card inside and the skeleton of a pin on the back. Only Michael had penciled in a heart around the edges of the card, and where the identification should have been he had typed, "Hello! I Love . . . Whom Do You Love?" and then he had written in "Sarah Galbraeth" along the dotted line.

F. Scott Fitzgerald might have said that Michael and Sarah were the top couple at Harvard. Truly they were in their prime, seniors, signaling happiness and joy as they drove around the Square in the red convertible or ambled over to Tommy's for cole slaw and pinball. They had such lavish, delicious confidence in themselves. Michael had a lot of power as managing editor of the *Crimson*, the center of a circle of the brightest boys. And Sarah's *Crimson* writings had given her the keys to the city. "Are you *the* Sarah Galbraeth?" people would ask wherever she went. And when they said it they looked at her with a special look in their eyes, a thrilling look of love and approval.

Michael knew what he was supposed to do with his power. He was supposed to put every possible energy into the *Crimson* and to act like a complete professional in all his dealings with the outside world. Then upon graduation he was supposed to get a job with the *Times* or the *Trib* or *Newsweek* or *Time,* cover Washington, establish a power base, and win a seat in Congress before he was thirty.

Sarah was a little less sure of what she was supposed to do. At different times she had thought of becoming a nurse, a ballet dancer, a philosopher, a minister, a politician, an actress. She had been elected to the Radcliffe student government and had satirized it in the *Crimson*. Once she told a dean that she expected in fifteen years to be married and have two children, to be living in a suburb and teaching and writing.

Now that Sarah had become a star, however, she was liking it. She became restless. None of her old goals seemed adequate. She craved new guides for her behavior and extraordinary models for her life. She read Paul Tillich and Reinhold Niebuhr (and spilled peas on him at a *Crimson* dinner) and George Orwell and Marx and Engels and David Riesman and W. W. Rostow and Czeslaw Milosz and Margaret Mead and V. I. Lenin and Malcolm X and Sigmund Freud and

Bertrand Russell and James B. Conant and all seemed to have bits and pieces for her, but none the whole picture.

She found more immediate clues in literature. Between the lines of fiction and verse, in the actions of characters who were and were not the spokesmen for their creators, Sarah heard a promise of life that was true and authentic in its every detail. Blake, Yeats, Balzac, Tolstoy were closer to her than the news on television. The love between Antony and Cleopatra wrenched her heart more than the little wars and joys of her friends. She wanted to live a life that Byron and Goethe and Mann would have approved of. She wanted to be defiant, strong, avant-garde, a pioneer: like Simone de Beauvoir and her lover Jean-Paul Sartre.

That fall the talk in Cambridge was all about Berkeley. The U Cal administration had banned political organizing and fund-raising from the usual area, Sproul Plaza, the entranceway to the university from busy Telegraph Avenue. Thirty thousand students were up in arms. At Harvard, reaction was mixed. Berkeley was actually in the running for new chief rival, displacing Yale, ever since some impartial study had rated the California school higher than Harvard in certain sciences. The cowboy, in the Frisco *Times* bureau, was sending back funny special dispatches on the Berkeley situation to the *Crimson*. But no one, not even Coulter, seemed to know precisely what had set things off. Was it Free Speech? The great size and impersonality of the university? Its ties with the military and industry? Free-floating rage and grief at the loss of a beloved president less than a year before? The escalating war? In any case, in the middle of it all, a twenty-three-year-old fellow said casually, "You can't trust anyone over thirty," and in a screaming San Francisco *Chronicle* headline the next day a generation gap was born.

The twenty-three-year-old fellow had been shoved into a police car; so the cheeky Berkeley throng had surrounded the car for a solid day and a half to prevent him from being taken to jail. Then came the building sit-ins: first by two hundred students, then four hundred, finally a thousand. And when most of the thousand were removed roughly, the whole university went "on strike" for five days: the first time such a thing had been done at any school.

When the dust settled, all the students' demands had been met. The chancellor of the University of California at Berkeley had been forced out. University deans and trustees across the country shivered. And college students everywhere felt the same shivering thrill, and heard the howls from Berkeley as birth pangs, and wondered if, indeed, it really *was* possible to talk back to grownups.

On the *Crimson* Charlie McSilver was jubilant. The freshman candidate who had had the nerve to introduce the dangerous sport of darts into the newsroom had been cut, and his dart board had disappeared with him. Everyone knew that journalistic acclaim was correlated with wadball prowess, not darts.

"And anyway, he was ugly," said McSilver.

Breakfast had been bad for Rosa. She and Kievskaya had been discussing the injustice of some people's having more than they needed while other people lacked even the necessities of life, when Tui—back in school and full of mischief (she had been quick to reestablish a claim on Nestor)—had remarked that yachts were a necessity for people who had grown up with them. This thought had so upset Rosa that she left the room without further conversation, the phrase "the rich ones" pounding in her head.

Rosa climbed the three flights to her bedroom and got back into bed, tucking the blue quilt around her neck, curling her toes and knees up like a seahorse. She thought of the struggling her parents had done, how they had had to leave everything. She thought about her childhood in the Danforth neighborhood of Toronto, the screams and purse-snatchings outside the door, the boarders taken in for spending money, the clothes that could not be bought. And she felt the old nagging ache to work hard, harder, hardest, so that she would not lose her scholarship. Her parents would never have been able to afford three thousand dollars for tuition and room and board. "Tui doesn't have to worry," she thought. "Her parents will take care of her. And afterward, some rich Harvardman . . ."

Then Rosa's thoughts turned to Nestor, and she took little comfort. She could not seem to break away from him, though he was obviously seeing Tui and other girls now too, but felt united with him in inertial misery because he had been her first lover. Just before the beginning of the term they had gone off to Mount Monadnock together. Rosa had fallen out of their rented canoe and sprained her knee. Whereupon Nestor had violently pinched the hurt little knee, as though to punish her for the injury. Rosa gave him the benefit of the doubt, telling herself that he was only trying to distract her from the pain.

At last she recovered herself, and rose to go about her business. She sniffed at the cool air coming in under an inch of open window. Today or tomorrow at the latest she would stop in at Phillips Brooks House, the social work center, and sign up for the Columbia Point program. It sounded good from what she had heard—the Harvard and Radcliffe volunteers were teaching children in a desperately poor housing project in Boston to make gifts for the neighborhood orphanage.

"Good luck on your hour exam!" called Kievskaya as Rosa passed by the kitchen. Tui was eating cinnamon toast with a haughty expression on her face.

At the end of October, halfback John Dockery set a new record for Harvard Stadium and the Ivy League by running 104 yards down a muddy field, leading the Crimson eleven to a 16–0 win over Cornell. Family and fans watched him breathlessly on the TV in Dockery's Tavern in New York City. But Sarah no longer went to football games. She didn't feel she had the time for them anymore. She was busy applying existential Marxism to all her courses. Compared with Simone de Beauvoir, all the "female psychology" people—Margaret Mead, Erik Erikson, Karen Horney—seemed backward-looking. De Beauvoir helped Sarah discover that women suffrage was only granted in Britain after suffragettes broke windows on fashionable Bond Street, smashed porcelains in the British Museum, and shaved "Votes For Women" in a golf course favored by the House of Lords. Russia under Kerensky had granted women the vote before England or America anyway. What this added up to in terms of her own life, Sarah wasn't sure. But bold, radical, careless, she was getting A's on all her papers.

In the world, political alignments were undergoing one of those occasional major shifts that George Orwell had described in *1984*. Khrushchev had been taken out of the Kremlin and the very next day the Chinese had exploded their first A-bomb, becoming the fifth country in the world with access to nuclear weapons.

While Carolee was in New York working with SNCC, some of the ideas about Vietnam that Sarah had first heard from her came to be embodied in a student organization called the May Second Movement. May 2, 1964, was the date of the first demonstration against the war—sponsored by the pro-Chinese Progressive Labor Movement. By autumn M2M was attracting a lot of attention at Harvard, holding rallies and distributing literature and posters.

One pleasant afternoon Michael and Sarah dropped in on a M2M rally on the steps of Memorial Church. Strictly speaking this site was off limits for political activities, but the deans and administration were letting it pass, wary of setting off "another Berkeley."

Disgruntled boys in work boots and rumpled pants were standing and sitting on the pristine steps, listening to their leaders' harangues. A few carried signs: "Vietnam Needs Social Reform, Not War," and "Why Not $1,800,000 a Day for Negro Freedom?", and

"No U.S. Support of Dictators." A hoarse, crew-cutted fellow Michael knew for a Trotskyite yelled, "Let's get out of Vietnam and take our napalm bombs with us!" A civil rights organizer in tweeds said, "As long as the U.S. supports a repressive dictatorship in South Vietnam, it will continue to force majority sentiment over to the Chinese side."

Then M2M's top man, a tall, lanky senior with heavy sideburns and a Texas twang, said, "Okay, now, here's the Red, the real live Red. Who wants to ask the Red a question?" A few people laughed.

"What do you think about Stalin?" Michael called.

The Texan answered, "I think you'd have had to be a little touched in the head to have had the mentality the left had in the thirties—their uncritical approach to the Soviet Union—the way they changed their views overnight on Stalin's orders."

An argument developed. "How do you *know* he killed thirty million people?" a girl demanded. "It sounds to me like something his enemies would make up—" Several people began shouting at once.

The rally continued, wrenched back to its original subject: the war in Indochina. Michael and Sarah broke off from the group.

As they walked away from the church Michael remarked how different these people were from the liberal peaceniks. Sarah's old friends at Tocsin had hooked up with the faculty. But these guys were always at odds with grownups. More important, this organization was obviously tolerant of communism. Michael couldn't forgive that. Not that they were agents of a foreign power; it was nothing like that; they didn't take orders from anybody. Michael rather admired Maher, the colorful M2M leader. But it was just that they felt—and this the managing editor saw as naively romantic—that a pure, "general will" democracy might be able to exist under some forms of communism. To Michael communism and democracy were unalterably opposed.

They passed through the gate between Widener and Houghton, under the admonition carved in stone to "Depart to Serve Better Thy Country and Thy Kind."

"Yeah, I liked it better when Tocsin was the big thing around here too," said Sarah. "They were so cute. And funny. Remember when I wrote about the peace march and they sent me a telegram saying 'Thank you for a wonderfully uninformative article. The elitists love you. Signed: The Ad Hoc Committee to Assassinate Sarah Galbraeth'?"

"Holy shit!" said Michael. "No, I don't remember that. Were we going together?"

"Oh, I guess not. It was freshman year, before the march. The one where President Kennedy sent the leaders out in the cold some coffee?"

"That was great. Peter Goldmark and President Kennedy."

"Yeah. That was when I discovered that either I didn't want to, or couldn't, write 'hard news.' My article was blatantly pro-Tocsin. But I felt strongly about it. I thought it was more important to be correct, you know, to tell the truth, than to be 'objective.' I mean, what is 'objectivity' anyway, but just another point of view?"

" 'The first casualty when war comes is truth,' " quoted Michael.

"There definitely is something different about these guys, though," she continued. "I agree."

"They're softies," said Michael, clearing his throat. Through the wide front glass of the UR they could see Michael's tutor sitting at a table, reading a newspaper.

"Oh, well, yes, I—I don't know," replied Sarah. "They seem pretty brave to me. I mean, they definitely don't have Tocsin's sense of humor—"

"At least Tocsin was at home with its own elitism."

"—but they have, uh, backbone. Guts. I mean, I'm really embarrassed that I flew halfway around the world this summer instead of going to Mississippi."

"I know what you mean about that," said Michael. Something in his voice made Sarah look at him suspiciously. She didn't remember him even considering going down South. He had stayed in Cambridge to edit the summer *Crimson* because it was expected of him as managing editor.

"I don't think you do know," she retorted. "I mean, it's really something to feel guilty and ashamed about. You should have gone to Mississippi. We both should have gone to Mississippi."

"Come on," said Michael. "I'm a lefty, just like you. I mean, for God's sake, my parents met each other at a packing-house workers' social. How many guys at Harvard do you think can say that?"

"Oh, your parents!" said Sarah. "I love your parents. You know that. But just because they were radicals doesn't mean you're one by inheritance. Every generation has to define radicalism for itself. If you're just doing what they want you to do, you haven't gone far enough."

She went on. "I'm working on my courage. I'm drawn to them. I feel like SDS and SNCC and even M2M and Tocsin, all of them, are playing this incredibly interesting game—"

"Game? What game?"

"Oh—schoolyard basketball. And I'm on the sidelines watching, and it's really absorbing. But also terrifying. Because they're not playing just to make points, they're playing for life and death!"

"Yeah, I suppose so," replied Michael, "though I don't know if all of them are so brave as all that. And you're not necessarily any less brave. You went alone to the Orthodox church in Moscow and picked up that black-marketeer just because he had good stories to tell—"

"And the best English accent."

"—and you could have gotten yourself thrown in jail for that— you know how the Soviets feel about 'economic crimes.' No, I don't think you're deficient in courage. It's sensible, not cowardly, not to be so eager to get mixed up in something like the Mississippi summer project that's just looking to become violent."

"Oh, Michael, I don't know!" Sarah was distraught. She couldn't make sense of this question for herself, and Michael's certainty irritated her. "Isn't it ever a person's duty to fight?"

"Oh course!" the boy replied. "If the fascists have attacked you, it's your duty to defend what you value, and if it comes to that, to defend your life at the expense of someone else's. Take George Orwell. He went to Spain in 1936 and fought in their Civil War, even though it wasn't his, because he knew that the fight was important, that it could be a prelude to the same struggle on a bigger scale. Even after he got shot in the neck, and it looked like he might die, he went on writing about the war there, and its complicated alignments, and his own emotions—with this great, hard, kernel-like truthfulness. He brought back a reliable scorecard. He said what he thought should be done."

Sarah nodded. She knew Michael revered Orwell, that Orwell was one of his political touchstones.

"I've got to get you a copy of *Homage to Catalonia,*" he said. "You'll really love it."

Sarah looked at her handsome Michael and was willing to be

convinced. She believed that she would indeed love Orwell, as Michael did. Indeed, at this moment Michael Verhoeven and George Orwell were indistinguishable in her thoughts.

Straw polls throughout the university in early November gave Lyndon Johnson an overwhelming lead over Barry Goldwater. This was not typical for Harvard, reported Sarah in the *Crimson*'s election supplement. Generally the business school and the freshmen voted Republican, while Radcliffe voted furthest to the left, with the faculty a close second. The last time all parts of Harvard had united against a major party candidate was in 1896, when William Jennings Bryan had, like Goldwater, tried to set Western sectional interests against Eastern.

Sarah also did a two-day study of bumper stickers. LBJ cars, she reported, were nearly all red, white, or blue Fords, Chevys, VWs, and Volvos. Goldwater cars included a Mercedes, a Corvair, and a curtained VW bus, and ran to black, light green, beige, and gray. On the basis of her car poll, Sarah predicted LBJ would win with seventy-nine percent of the vote.

A little cloud of worry hung over Billy Clemens's comical head. He pulled his overcoat tighter across his chest. It was all a misunderstanding. When he had offered "anyone" a ride to Detroit for Christmas, sitting in the Stanton House kitchen, obviously he had had Rosa in mind. Of course he knew she was seeing Nestor Schwarz. He would not presume to have an opinion about that. But he did think . . . that perhaps . . . Instead, who had volunteered to accompany him but Yvette Serre! She had a boyfriend or something in Niagara Falls, and would be glad of a ride that far. . . .

Billy had been waiting for nearly an hour. Sitting restlessly in the dormitory parlor, he tried to keep up an internal conversation about Pericles, about the imperialism of Athens, about the genocide at Melos. But thoughts of Radcliffe kept intruding. He liked it here. His old friendship with Rosa had gotten him used to the place, to the charming gray and brown monotony of the decor, to the guardsmanly stare of Elizabeth Cady Stanton over the hearth. But Yvette Serre! Suddenly a vision of himself alone in this room with all twenty-five of the Stanton House nereids (and they so lightly touching his clothes, floating, cascading, closely knit) caused him to break out in a sweat. He tugged on his scarf.

At last Yvette appeared on the ceremonial stairway, wearing a black reefer coat and a long white silk aviatrix's scarf, holding onto a big valise. "Sorry I'm late!" she called.

"Hello!" said Billy, accentuating the "o" in defense. Why had he gotten himself into this? Why hadn't he had the presence of mind to think of an excuse when she had answered? He had not realized in time that it would mean a twenty-hour car ride alone with her.

They loaded their parcels into the old car, she going back into the kitchen for a bundle of brownies, and pushed off into Cambridge just as its great white and yellow and red and lavender eyes were beginning to open up in the streets. Traffic flowed warm and comradely down to the river, home for Christmas. Heads in fours and fives lined up behind smoky windshields and rearviews, amid bundles of clothes and books that would not be opened, behind plastic decals boasting of Harvard. The bell towers dwindled into a fantasy vision that was their fullest reality. The new Prudential building jutted up behind the Boston skyline. Headlights on Storrow Drive made a gleaming necklace.

Yvette gaily threw her head out of the window. The December air rushed into the car, making Billy grope at his scarf.

"The window, really—?" he implored. She shrugged and raised it halfway.

They drove out of town through signs and tolls and mechanical roads. On the blank superhighway Billy eased the accelerator up to a steady seventy and Yvette pulled off her black beret, letting the spiky points of her damp black hair take the rushing wind from the top of the window.

Billy observed the gesture with awe and admiration. Women's mysteries. He wondered what the two of them could possibly talk about.

"Well," he began bravely. "I'm concentrating in history, and I understand you're in modern history. Is that right?"

Yvette turned to him and nodded without saying anything, the wind still in her hair. "At least," he thought, "she didn't shout at me that I'm a fool for saying that."

"Uh, how does the department define 'modern'?" he continued.

Yvette bit her lower lip. "Modern," she repeated petulantly, "is from 1740 to 1940. Period." She smiled.

"Aha!" said Billy Clemens, enlightened. "From Voltaire to the Hitler-Stalin pact?!"

"You might say so," Yvette replied. "I don't think they would say so. Harvard is stuck in a disciplinary rut. Diplomatic historians and literary historians and the historians of science and sociologists have very little to say to one another. I should have stayed in Paris."

Billy scanned the time line in his head that was his own field of "history," and reflected that "modern" might alternatively be said to have begun when somebody invented the wheel, or in the Age of Pericles, or when da Vinci sketched the first television and airplane, or in 1591, or 1685, or 1865, or 1900, or 1920, or even at the present moment. But then again, if Harvard had chosen the mid-eighteenth century as the starting point, well, there was probably a very good reason for it, and he would go along. They would make conversation about the mid-eighteenth century.

"I suppose you have strong feelings about the French Revolution?" he said pleasantly.

"I suppose so," Yvette conceded. She looked at the driver all bundled up in his winter clothes and at his odd and comical face. He was kind. Though it was rather a silly question, she could see that he was not making fun of her. That in her which dreaded being tiresome and ridiculous was obviated by that in him which was patient, tolerant, and just. She began to say one or two things about the events of 1789 that in ordinary circumstances, speaking with most of the men and boys she knew, she would have withheld. She told him about how she had learned about the Revolution as a child in the Alps outside Grenoble, and how that compared with what she had learned as a teen-ager in Paris after her mother had remarried—

"Your father?"

"Died when I was ten. At Dien Bien Phu." Yvette explained how enormous an issue it still was at home, "like your race question here?" and how her teachers in Paris had persuaded her that the Revolution in the end had resulted in a "general augmentation of happiness for France and for all mankind." Billy listened, fascinated.

"Who is it exactly that doesn't like the Revolution?"

She feigned ignorance. "I really don't know. The Pope?" They laughed. But only in America, she said, and in Cambridge, had she been taught that the terrifying Robespierre had not in fact called for anything more dramatic than the liberals routinely called for today, that the Jacobins were in reality hardly radicals at all. . . .

"Yes, but," Billy interjected, "isn't the point about Robespierre that 'the revolution devours its children'?"

"No," laughed Yvette. "The point is that 'Twas bliss in that morn to be alive/But to be young was very heaven.' "

Billy Clemens and Yvette Serre conversed about this in a jolly way for a long time. Miles and miles of highway sped by, the nighttime cars trailing or passing one another fluidly. As they were turning down toward Albany Billy admitted that his own study of history tended to involve nonspecial individuals, rather than revolutions, say, or big events.

"What do you mean by 'nonspecial'?"

"I can't define it," he said. "People who occupy an important but generally invisible aspect of life. People like . . . post office clerks."

"Ahh!" Yvette was intrigued. This Billy Clemens was an acute fellow. His intelligence had a warm and wavering edge she wasn't used to, but he was quite adorable. With her encouragement he was about to dilate upon mail clerks, when suddenly an eighteen-wheel trailer truck loomed up in the darkness a little out of its lane. She screamed in French. He swerved. They rode on without speaking. It was approaching midnight.

Then Yvette realized that she should have taken a nap if she were going to relieve Billy at the wheel. Not having done so—she had

spent the day as usual, writing letters and baking brownies, and deciding about clothes—her eyes were beginning to tire. She hadn't even
thought to bring No-Doze. Billy was possibly worried about driving all
night too, for he had hitched up his shoulders and wrinkled into his
laugh lines. The car was full of doubt. Yvette rolled down the window
once more and put her head out into the freezing night.

"Let's stop at a motel," she ventured, her voice faint on the
wind. "What do you say?"

"What'd you say?" he choked out.

She pulled back inside and said it again.

He said all right.

Now fear filled the car. They rode on silently for another half
hour.

Then they saw a giant glowing Holiday Inn. "Here!" said
Yvette, and Billy turned obediently up the ramp. He parked. Sat mo-
tionless. By way of preparation for the coming ordeal he rewound his
wool scarf more tightly across his throat.

"Yo, Billy?" said Yvette. He slunk out of the car and followed
her through revolving doors and into a palmy Muzaked reception area.
She stepped aside for him to sign the book, and when the clerk turned
for the key she whispered, "Write Mr and Mrs." He swallowed and
obeyed. They rode upstairs in the elevator.

As they closed the door behind them in the sterilized modern
bedroom—and Yvette threw the last of the brownies, and her suitcase,
and a copy of John Fowles's *The Collector* onto the bed—she could see
there was definitely something wrong with the boy. His hands and face
had red and white blotches. He was sweating. He held onto his suitcase
and stared at inconsequential spots around the room.

"I can't sleep with her," he was thinking. "Our ideologies are
too different."

How had he ever let himself get into this position? he wondered. Here he was full of awkwardness and unbearable mental restrictions in the same motel room as this . . . this . . . sex goddess. "My idea
about sex is not simply prudish and puritanical," he was thinking
fiercely, "though these people might call it that. Perhaps I am more
sophisticated than they are, if the truth be known. Perhaps their
'emancipation' is in actuality something juvenile, animallike. But

whatever it is I can't help it. That's the way I am. If it repels Yvette, then that's just the way it has to be. I'm not going to try to—"

Yvette meanwhile was unpacking her suitcase carelessly. It concerned her to see her riding companion so distraught and after a moment she realized what the matter must be. "If he were only a little more reasonable," she thought, "he would see that stopping at a motel was merely the only thing that we could do under the circumstances, and as for getting separate rooms, that would have been silly and expensive . . ."

"Listen, Billy," she said. "I don't know how you feel about getting explicit about things like this—"

("Yes, yes . . ." he interjected quickly.)

"But I'm not going to sleep with you."

She looked at him carefully for the first time since they had left the car. His face had gone easy again, though a little weak-looking, like after a good vomit. He put his suitcase down on the floor and walked over to the picture window that gave out onto the parking lot.

"Well, I wasn't so sure I wanted to sleep with you," he said.

January was the cruellest month. The streets of the Square were wet and messy with uneven brown mountains of snow along the curb. The sky was leaden. The indiscretions of the term and a guilty Christmas vacation were about to come due. Certain students were prepared, of course, for the week-long barrage of three-hour written examinations. These few spent reading period reviewing their notes one last time, underlining in black, highlighting in yellow. Rather more students worried, or pretended indifference, or indulged in every kind of negative and self-destructive behavior.

At the *Crimson* one ordinary, bleak, fearful day in January, the usual gang had collected to hang out and throw wadded-up newsprint into the green wastepaper baskets. Charlie McSilver was keeping tabs on the wadball scores in sportscasterese. Thaddeus Foote was huddled with Nestor Schwarz in a newsroom cubicle. Christopher Green and his younger brother and his brother's roommate were closeted in Chris's office hatching an ingenious diversion. Joey and Benjamin were, like Chris, ambitious journalists, eager to be liked, likable, aiming at law school and national political careers. The three had been cronies at a well-known experimental public high school in Chicago where academic innovations had been successfully applied to a demographically mixed student body. All three had come effortlessly and with great pleasure to Harvard, to work on the *Crimson*.

Sarah showed up in the newsroom in the late afternoon as was her habit, and was hailed as usual by the pack of idlers. Working over his dummy, Michael winked at her and threw her a kiss. She sat down on the edge of the managing editor's desk brushing snow off her loden coat and dripping, and began to chat with George Durbey. Her reddish-brown hair glistened with snowflakes where her hood had not reached, and hung long down her back, looped up in a silvery barrette.

Hearing her familiar voice, Chris Green stepped out of his office.

"Hey, Sarah," he said with a wide, Great Plains grin, "how would you like to be Class Marshal?" Sarah looked at him a moment in surprise.

"No, really. I mean it," said the *Crimson* editor-in-chief, taking a few steps toward her.

Nestor looked up and snorted.

Chris glanced over at Michael, who was looking up from his dummy and smiling brightly. Sarah looked at Michael and caught the openness in his expression.

"Sure," she said. "Why not?"

At this Foote boomed out from the corner: "Why not, indeed! Because C. Douglas Dillon was Class Marshal! Because Harvard is a men's school!! Because there has not been a female Harvard Class Marshal in three hundred and twenty-nine years, and with luck never shall be!!! Because—"

"Get some sleep, TPF," said Chris Green mildly. "We already have the petition. I thought you'd agree." He nodded to Sarah. "Joey and Benjamin circulated it among seniors at dinner last night and we've got thirty or forty names. More than enough—!"

"Omigod," said Sarah. Michael, still smiling, straightened his collar.

Now the other two boys poked their heads out of the editor-in-chief's office and came into the newsroom all encouragement.

"God, this is cool!" said Joey.

"Cool isn't even the word, man," said his roommate. "This is *nothing-short-of 'BOSS' !*"

"Something for our friends out in Berkeley—?" commented Charlie without interrupting his wadball.

"TASFURIA!" thundered Foote. He squinted at Nestor.

Nestor said nothing. The actor was studying all the faces in the newsroom cannily. A couple of freshmen candidates were just walking in, oblivious. Sarah was smiling dazedly. Chris and Michael seemed to be talking to each other with their eyes, though they said nothing. When Nestor finally did speak, it was to parody all these journalists— from whom he felt himself distanced.

"Sarah retreats to country hideaway," he declaimed. "Has 'no comment' for media."

Charlie McSilver turned on his heel gleefully and hit Nestor on the forehead with a congratulatory wad.

Word of Sarah's challenge to the Class Marshal election reached the student council like a huge spark, like the crackle of heat lightning. Council president Wade LaMar Sterkin (who was running for the office himself) and his good buddy the election committee chairman instinctively turned to the conservative dean of the college, Porlock, and joined forces.

Most of the other thirty-some members of the undergraduate governing body had no strong convictions on the matter. They were good boys, all-American, handsome and muscular, motivated by a desire to do right, to show school spirit, to obey authorities. After Harvard half of them would enlist in the armed forces; several would see active duty in Indochina.

But for now, caught suddenly in the spotlight of the sex question, the student council boys were influenced by the certainty and confidence, even fervor, of their two officers, and the momentous imprimatur of Dean Porlock. They acquiesced. It was the simplest thing to do. It would have taken the presence of a fourth estate or radical mentality on the council to do otherwise.

Sterkin and company proposed that Sarah's name be omitted from the ballot despite the legal petition. The council so voted.

Deep below the earth, in the greenish shadows of the Adams House swimming pool, two boys were communing in a fishy silence.

Some of the more important transactions in the cold war had been effected in this way. But this evening it was only Nestor Schwarz whispering a plan he and Foote had dreamed up into the ear of a compliant lad from the physics department.

If Sarah Galbraeth's candidacy—"this girl thing!"—couldn't be stopped by subtracting her name from the ballot, well, then, she could perhaps be stopped by the addition of a parallel, diversionary element into the election, and the subsequent confusion of the issues.

The physics student, grinning, effeminate, agreed to put himself up for the Class Marshalcy as well . . . in such a way as to defy the establishment, as Sarah had done; perhaps on a "silliness" ticket.

Nestor winked with pleasure.

And there were smiles and laughter in *Lampoon* Castle that night as well, to hear the tale of this excellent trick.

Though the student council's adamant opposition irritated Sarah, she shrugged it off as preposterous. Being nominated for Harvard Class Marshal just didn't seem that odd to her. What was it but a logical extension of having been Sunday school teacher and valedictorian in Mason City? Why shouldn't she be the first female in three hundred or so years to perform this function— whatever it was—carry a baton, perhaps, at graduation? Dun classmates for money forever? She had done a good job at Harvard, she thought.

Chris, Joey, and Benjamin were enthusiastic, but their enthusiasm was not a simple emotion. They didn't care that Sarah was writing a thesis in which she was predicting the emergence of "a new feminism" in America in the next few years. Among them and their friends and the *Crimson* boys generally, "this girl for Class Marshal thing" found its common denominator as "a good joke." The student council opposition excited them. Though Foote was a clear opponent (his "tasfuria" being the *Crimson*'s version of the army's "snafu"), the rest of the gang pretty much understood the Sarah campaign as the kind of thing Foote would have done if he'd had a mind to.

Photography chairman Cadwalader printed a funny, grinning face of Sarah on the official Class Marshal nominating broadside, next to some thirty-three solemn photos of the male candidates. Sarah let the *Crimson* omit the paragraph of qualifications that ran beneath all the other photos, and print only "Hi." She was thrilled simply to be the lone female on the page alongside all those boys flying their proud flags of biography . . . and didn't realize she was politically naked.

Like an aspiring starlet posing for her first nude photo, Sarah felt she could easily separate the immediate expedient from her long-term and more serious goals. Achievement, she reasoned, does not spring full-grown from the head, but proceeds in many steps, complicated, tangential, apparently contradictory, now mistaken, now only apparently mistaken. Back in Mason City it had always been her way to combine a joking, self-deprecating (that is, feminine) tone with real (that is, masculine) achievement, in order to keep people from resenting or being afraid of her. She had believed since she was eight years old that she could be president of the United States. And besides, she thought that Chris Green was such a terrific boy, and the whole thing such a terrific idea, and since her first loyalty was to the *Crimson,* it was only logical to go with the *Crimson* on this, in whatever way it developed.

The national press didn't exactly share the perception that it was a joke. When news of the Harvard student council's opposition to Sarah's candidacy reached the wire services, reporters from all over the country descended on Harvard to cover the story of the threat to male supremacy.

"Tradition Under Fire," wrote the fellow from the Associated Press.

> A slim, dark-haired Radcliffe girl is trying to chip away at Harvard University's traditions. Pretty Sarah Galbraeth, twenty, a senior from Mason City, Iowa, wants to be Class Marshal at Harvard's 329th commencement exercises this June.
>
> The coveted role of Class Marshal has gone to a male without exception since the university was founded sixteen years after the Pilgrims landed on Plymouth Rock.
>
> Miss Galbraeth has been turned down by Harvard student government officials in her bid to have her name placed on the Class Marshal ballot. And college officials say her candidacy is illegal because she is not a male.

The AP and United Press International took some wonderful pictures of Sarah looking beatific, grinning, and wholesome, some with her posing in silent bliss with a phone receiver at her ear. Published in *Stars and Stripes,* one of these shots elicited a handful of marriage proposals. Radio and television reporters came around. An Australian UN delegate's palmist predicted a bright political future for her ("a Star on her Mound of Jupiter"). Clippings from the suburban papers in Boston and New York and DC and Iowa poured in. Sarah was called upon to hold press conferences in the *Crimson* newsroom, and she made four or five impromptu speeches a day, beaming and eloquent, while in the background Chris and Joey and Benjamin and the rest went about their business, smiling more or less benignly, only occasionally paying any attention to the sensation they had created, thrown into eerie eclipse by this unforeseen explosion of radiance.

Naturally the national and international press attention had their effect on Sarah. The idiom of professional journalism, the five W's—who, what, when, where, why, and sometimes how—the pyramid structure, heads and tags, were near and dear to her from long practice. And so when she saw her name, rank, and serial number in the lead of all those pyramidally structured stories, she began to think that something really must be happening, that this was not just another panty raid. The old *Crimson* that she revered so much seemed conservative by comparison with the fourth estate out there in the world.

She and Michael were seeing a lot of Nestor and Rosa now. Ever since the night of Dr. Faustus—and Michael's nomination of Nestor for the Wagner—the two boys had become friends. They'd logged in countless hours of pool and poker together, gone to many movies at the Brattle. Nestor had even taken to hanging around the *Crimson* offices talking now with Foote, now with Michael, poking fun at the earnest journalists. And Sarah and Rosa being friends of long standing, they found many excuses to "double-date" for dinner and little excursions. And so, one night soon after the start of the Class Marshal race, as the four of them were sitting in the Chinese restaurant having a late snack, Nestor declared solemnly that Sarah had become "the most famous person at Harvard." Michael and Rosa, though they did not usually discuss such a matter openly, believing it to be too important or too traumatic, this evening went along with Nestor.

And Sarah agreed as well, blithely. She thought they might be right, because she was beginning to experience that fame in her very body. When people looked at her now, in classes, at dinner in the Houses, in the dorm, she felt a gigantic wave of approval and envy (and a few stray germs of hatred) that she hardly knew what to do with. It undid her, like a kind of megasexuality.

"Just don't start taking yourself too seriously," warned Michael.

In a chilly window-seat niche in the attic of Stanton House, Sarah sat and scribbled excitedly on yellow newsprint. She wrote manifestoes of women's rights, hymns to the liberation of women she perceived as already achieved. She blessed her generation for having sent her to this miraculous place. She wrote odes to the love between new man and new woman.

As she wrote the sky filled gradually with white dots and the snow came, dribbling sideways in diagonal lines across windows bleary with old dirt. She went on writing, ecstatic, wise in her youth, at peace in her innocence. She envisioned a democratic socialist party she would head nationwide, and she scribbled the names of all the people she would invite to this "party," people who would redeem the nation and spread justice. She jotted down procedures to follow in the organizing of such a party, and goals, and planks of a platform. A vision of international peace filled her head, and of honor, and of open covenants. She dated the manifestoes 1984.

The snow was falling heavily by the time she stopped, piling up into white hillocks in the corners of Stanton House's old wooden sides. Big black rubber Polish army boots were a fad this year, and the girls would be getting theirs out of closets and pulling them on, rubbery and persistent, their hands in threadbare woolen gloves. At this very moment Rosa was negotiating the long, icy canyon between the Continental and the Commodore hotels on her way back from the Square, her bike swaying in the storm wind, her eyes tearing in the snow cold.

After a while Rosa came running up the stairs, her cheeks and nose red. "Hi!" she said sweetly to Sarah in the attic.

"Hi!" replied Sarah. "Snowing out?"

Rosa smiled and kicked off her big black rubber boots and dropped her whitened scarf and mittens on a crate, opening her coat and stretching with a lovely grace. She felt so good, so happy. She had taken the MTA to Columbia Point in the morning, and the beautiful little seven- and eight-year-old black girls had climbed into her arms and covered her with affection as she told them a story. They had fought to be closest to her, but she had calmed them and soothed them with her voice and her harmonious and equitable love-distribution system. Such things came naturally to her. It was a kind of dancing.

She asked Sarah what she was working on, and Sarah pushed the yellow pages over to her for her to read.

"We are the free generation," Rosa read, with a thrill. She loved Sarah, and Sarah's writing, and she was so happy for her! . . .

We are the free generation!
We are the daughters of slaves set free in the great city! Behind us, our mothers have never dreamed of our daily lives, they have never felt as we feel, they can only wish us well blindly, with faith.

A beautiful old world is opening up to us, the gathered treasures of the mature race, the rulers. And still tentatively, but with generosity, they beckon to us to join them.

For three hundred years Harvard has nurtured its sons, filled their hearts and minds, and sent them forth into the troubled world to carry on the great task. But we could only watch from the background. Our mothers cleared away the debris of Harvard so that the Harvard scholars could grow in peace. But now we too shall grow. The soul of half of humanity is just now awakening. From Harvard we climb to the summit of the world, to the height from which the depths can be seen. And for the first time in history we stand in the rarefied atmosphere of Truth.

Our mothers were molded, shaped, smoothed over into the model of themselves. They did not live their separate lives, their separate reaching, hungry, violent lives, but bent their heads until they fit their mothers' patterns—from mother to daughter the unbroken chain of flesh, forever limiting, forever subduing. And as they thus held hands across the generations their sons were slaying the fathers, the men were breaking, killing, usurping, and being forever reborn.

Beware now, mothers, for your time has finally come. We your female children will be your death. We disclaim the inevitability of the flesh. We shall seek first ourselves, alone before the universe. To the myth of the Titan slaying his father there shall be added a new myth. Beware, world, for the female sex has discovered violence, and the ecstasy it embraces.

Our mothers never knew our pleasures. They called them evil, feared, denied them. Our sports were their tragedies. They never knew the sweetness of abandon, risk, the snapping elastic thread of emotion. We are free before a world long disguised, overflowing with delight.

They fear our independence, our mothers, our fathers. What will we make of the world they bequeathed us? What will become of the world they knew? And here we cannot answer. The way before us is unknown and perfectly new. Yet we can walk toward it with perfect confidence, the offspring of knowledge our parents never had. Our failure of prescience before our parents' certitude is testimony to our greater wisdom. Like all humanity before us, we will fail, we will tempt the abyss, we will pass through life neither well nor badly, but sometimes humorously, sometimes tragically, depending on how the story is told. But we carry tools our parents never dreamed of. And if we do not far surpass them, then humanity has never made any progress.

We will be better mates to our men than our mothers could ever be, for we will be better human beings. Our men will be more men for our greater existence. In our liberation shall come their emancipation as well. In our birth, the renaissance of all humanity. The world changes when a new beast emerges from the sea depths of thousands of years of sleep. With him comes a brilliant new light over all the existence there was before him. And thus we too, arisen from the depths, shall set our hand on civilization. Who knows what changes shall be wrought by a new touch? The gnarled hand of our mother nurtured, cared for, and preserved us. But it has grown old now, beyond its usefulness. And from it has come a new hand, young and more pure. Shall it rest on the arts, the sciences, the humanities? Like the fairy's hand, it shall spread a magic powder around itself. From divinity and from twice divine humanity shall come our power!

Platform for a New-Women's Party, 1984

1 Optional socialized day nurseries
2 Optional socialized medical care
3 Optional socialized evening baby-sitting
4 Equal pay for equal work regardless of sex, race, age, or nationality
5 Abolition of the draft
6 Stepped-up foreign peace corps
7 Formation of a domestic peace corps with differing lengths of service
8 Formation of a conservation corps
9 Rehabilitation of the cities starting with housing
10 More use of the unemployed in schools, hospitals, city housing, and geriatric services
11 Distribution of all government-owned and warehoused surplus food
12 Curtailment of automobile traffic in central cities
13 Cleaner, quieter, and better-ventilated subway systems
14 Institution of a Cabinet-level secretary of transportation with mandate to strengthen and rationalize public transportation networks
15 Institution of a Cabinet-level ombudsman
16 No restrictions on foreign travel of U.S. citizens
17 Abolition of all immigration quotas
18 Legalized contraception and abortion
19 Divorce outside of courts, with court-appointed arbitration boards to pass on economic settlements
20 Dispensation of all addictive narcotics through public hospitals
21 Education compulsory to age eighteen
22 National Merit Scholarships to be vastly increased in scope; formation also of National Talent Scholarships
23 National Adult Merit Scholarships (also Talent, also Need) to encourage lifelong schooling as desired
24 Several national educational television stations
25 Several national educational radio stations

26 Publication of a Washington, D.C., newsletter edited by a rotating team of journalists
27 Institution of proportional representation in city and state elections
28 City and state legislatures to vary in size as reflection of actual numbers of persons voting
29 Experimentation with a participatory legislative program analogous to the participatory jury system
30 National lottery

The Class Marshal election was over very fast.

When the student council barred her name from the ballot, an ad hoc committee of supporters challenged Dean Porlock and the council. Porlock replied simply that Sarah Galbraeth was "not a member of Harvard College." The committee called this a technicality. Girls had participated fully in all Harvard College classes and activities since the end of World War II. True, there were still clubs for men only, scholarships and fellowships for men only, football tickets for alumni and not alumnae. But these were private fiefdoms within Harvard—not Harvard itself—it was argued; and what was more, even they would eventually be integrated. In an inchoate way Sarah's candidacy had hooked into feelings that were sweeping the Harvard campus and all campuses in this last year.

"There's more at stake here than just the election of Sarah Galbraeth," said a spokesman for her candidacy. "Rank-and-file enthusiasm is mounting fast, and we have faculty support." Indeed, a couple of the wittier faculty members were composing campy campaign tunes for Sarah, with lyrics like "heterogene" and "farciful." (What else rhymes with "Marshal"?)

Sarah's student supporters urged the senior class to write in her name on the prohibited ballots.

Then, an hour after the polls closed on Monday evening, the

election committee chairman made an announcement to the Harvard radio station that no write-in votes would be counted.

In the *Crimson* a freshman was handing around sandwiches, consulting the scribbles on a paper bag, giving back change. "Thanks," Sarah said, unwrapping her egg salad. "This is beginning to get me down," she admitted to Michael. "I didn't realize that Wade LaMar Sterkin was running for Class Marshal too. He could at least have disqualified himself from the election committee."

"Oh, you know how Harvard politicians are," replied Michael from over his sandwich. Chris was of the same mind. There was no talk of appealing the student council's despotism. Boys like Michael and Chris had no truck with the Wade LaMar Sterkins of Harvard. Their own ambitions were expressed more subtly. Even as the student council took the upper hand the Crimeds felt pleased and smug, as if what they had set out to prove about Harvard had indeed been proven.

Joey ran in breathlessly, snow on his cowlick, from Adams House.

"Sarah would have qualified for the finals," he sputtered, "if they had counted her votes! *Everybody* was writing her name in!"

Nestor looked up drowsily from his seat deep in the leather sofa of the ed chairman's office. "What a sweet, gentlemanly thing to say." He flicked a cigarette ash to the floor. The new dimensions of Sarah's fame had definitely gotten on the actor's nerves.

Sarah looked at Joey. She looked at Nestor, who had his eyes closed. She didn't know what to believe.

Before dawn on January 18, 1965, the day of the run-off and final vote, Thaddeus Foote sneaked his friend Nestor Schwarz up into the top-floor Great Hall of *Lampoon* Castle, and there, in delicious secrecy, the two of them penned an amazing diatribe accusing women of giggling, being emotional, and having babies. Headlined "Down with Sarah," their joint creation was magically railroaded past *Crimson* editorial procedures and printed

anonymously, on the editorial page, where it became the de facto statement of official *Crimson* policy. "She didn't even participate in any
Harvard activities," the editorialists lied, pointing to the "Hi!" that
had appeared under Sarah's picture—and thus neatly turned the *Crimson*'s own ambiguous campaign strategy against her.

"Who wrote that goddamned ed?" Benjamin demanded an-
grily, blustering into the newsroom soon after the paper hit the dorms.

"Foote, I think," replied CFMcS with a weary toss of his paper
wad. "Look it up in the Closed Comment Book."

The day was also Sarah's twenty-first birthday. The *Crimson*
archly published this news in the weather slot in the top right-hand
corner of page one. For the first time in her life no one wished Sarah
"Happy Birthday" all day. Not even Michael, who was usually so
thoughtful.

Dean Porlock and Wade LaMar Sterkin and Wade's pal the
election committee chairman counted the votes in well-guarded secrecy. No press, no poll-watchers, no *Crimson*. Then they locked the
thousand-some ballots in the dean's closet in University Hall and announced four winners: a Jewish football hero, a Jewish swimmer, a
black born in Panama, and one old-time WASP aristocrat. The unorthodox male candidate had been eliminated, too; but he'd been allowed in the race longer than Sarah had.

Sarah felt sick to her stomach. She wondered if she had only
imagined that her friends had thrust her into the center of something,
and then abandoned her there. Where was everybody? Had she been
gaslighted?

Two or three professors and one Cambridge city councillor,
Alfred Vellucci, affirmed to male *Crimson* reporters that they thought
Sarah should continue the effort. No one asked to speak to her.

"I'm going to keep on fighting," she said.

Michael was against it.

"Absolutely right," chimed in the ubiquitous Nestor. "The
party's over. Don't beat a dead horse."

The two boys looked at each other. The *Crimson* editor, all sandy
hair and freckles and light, standing by his circular desk. The famous
Harvard actor, more menacing, of flashing chiaroscuro complexion,
sitting next to a typewriter, swinging his legs restlessly. Nestor got up.
He motioned first to Sarah and then to Michael. And the three of

them retired into the managing editor's office for a private conference.

"Poor to see smoke-filled-room politics," commented CFMcS, making a face.

On the bulletin board outside the closed door of the m.e.'s office, several letters to the editor having to do with the Class Marshal race had been tacked. One unsigned note—which Nestor had identified in one corner as having been written by "my irate friend The Snake"—read: "MIss GAlbraeth. Keep out of the Race if you no whats good for You."

Inside the managing editor's office they were discussing dead horses. Underestimating Nestor (and, like Sarah, having been only temporarily taken aback by that day's "Down with Sarah" piece, afterward laughing at it, giving it little thought, regarding it as a bit of *Crimson* irony), Michael had become the other boy's ally. Together they pursuaded her that to forge on pushily at this point, against all the powers-that-be, when everyone was *tired* of it already, would be, well, unattractive. It would spoil the fun. "It had a serious purpose," Michael explained solicitously. "But it works best in the form of a joke." The implications of their argument were frankly sexual. In order to remain her lovable feminine self, Sarah had no choice now but to pull out.

In about an hour the door opened, and the three of them walked back into the newsroom, Sarah looking drained. She made her concession speech with all the dignity she could muster. The *Crimson* printed it. People choked over their morning coffee. It was all over.

J anuary reinsinuated itself. As students sloshed up and down Plympton Street lugubrious and depressed, Sarah sat numbly in the newsroom chewing on a pencil. She hadn't seriously considered for a minute going against the combined wishes of Michael and Nestor, but now the consequences of her withdrawal were beginning to assail her.

It seemed there had been at least a few students who felt

strongly that she should have stayed in, even when the dean and the council and all were being so adamant, so imperative. Someone in the dorm had whispered that by conceding she had betrayed the cause. Someone, she didn't know who, but she suspected it might be Danny Matlaw, whom she hadn't seen in a long time, had tacked up a version of Robert Browning's "The Lost Leader" on the *Crimson* bulletin board, folded, penciled with her initials. As she read it, the tears came, and she had to retreat to the ladies' room. She left the yellow newsprint sheet unfolded on the platen of an Olympia:

> Just for a handful of silver she left us,
> Just for a riband to stick in her coat . . .
> We that had loved her so, followed her, honored her,
> Lived in her mild and magnificent eye,
> Learned her great language, caught her clear accents,
> Made her our pattern to live and to die! . . .
> Blot out her name, then, record one lost soul more,
> One task more declined, one more footpath untrod,
> One more triumph for devils and sorrow for angels,
> One wrong more to man, one more insult to God!
> Life's night begins: let her never come back to us!
> There would be doubt, hesitation and pain,
> Forced praise on our part—the glimmer of twilight,
> Never glad confident morning again!

In the little hutch of the women's bathroom Sarah flopped down on the hard cot, feeling so alone. She hadn't known how many people were behind her—if any. For once she had taken no polls. For all her feminist speeches it had been, in the end, a personal affair. She had shared Michael's and the *Crimson*'s perception that it "had to be a joke . . . to work"; but now she was beginning to see that if it *was* a joke, the joke was on her.

Her hometown newspaper had followed the election. They were excited at first: "Former MCHS Student Makes Good." But their third and final article had carried the heartbreaking headline "Sarah Gives Up But Not Mother." The *Eagle* had interviewed Sarah's mom. Even her mom had thought the race worth more of a fight.

Sarah shook her head and buried her face in the lumpy sack that served as a pillow. She felt so humiliated. Michael was being sweetly reasonable—she didn't know why the thought of him made her so angry. Chris, Joey, Benjamin—they would think her ridiculous if she admitted to feeling bad now. They had never given her license to feel as good about it as she had felt. She almost took comfort in Nestor's outright nastiness. At least his cynicism was a constant.

Sarah got up and peered into the polished metal sheet over the basin. Her reflection swam back at her, wavy and whorled as the metal, but undeniably there. She was glad to see her eyes hadn't migrated to the same side of her nose. An organizing principle was holding things together. She recalled a poem she had learned in Miss Demos's class in MCHS:

> Momentous to himself as I to me
> Has each man been that ever woman bore.
> This in a lightning flash of sympathy
> I felt; an instant and no more.

The face resolved itself into familiarity. It was a funny, but generally okay face. She threw some water at herself, and blinked at the cold wetness, and stepped across the bathroom threshold out into the stairway lobby again, stumbling. The rudder of her innocence was gone. A deeply felt and vital optimism about herself and society and Harvard had been demolished. The ache of this was so bad that all Sarah could do for the moment was deny it.

In the newsroom people were talking about exams. Michael looked up from his dummy and gave her a wink. One freshman candidate gaped at her. The boy's look reminded Sarah of Adams House, where she often ate dinner with the other *Crimson* execs. All semester she had loved that large, polished oak dining hall, that room hung with portraits of great former Harvard men, and she had entered it proudly, sure of herself, a comer making her way up through the hierarchy. But during the Class Marshal election someone had tacked up a poster near the Adams House dining hall entrance—a poster that said "All the way with Sarah" under a mildly obscene illustration. Yesterday evening after the results were in, after she had conceded, when she had gone as usual to Adams House for dinner with Michael and Chris Green and Joey and Nestor, her entrance into the dining hall had drawn applause and hisses.

Sarah drifted across the newsroom and let her glance pass over the various papers and posters pinned over the ledge. Before her eyes the notices flew apart, becoming discrete and autonomous, each attached to the wall by a different hand, each with its separate meaning and purpose, until the whole panorama of irrelevant, blank squareness had receded like a retreating universe into surreal dispensability. A couple of issues of *Veda* were scattered among the Comment Books. Sarah touched one. It was the maiden issue, edited by Foote, the issue about drugs. Sarah licked a finger and opened it, glancing at the splendiferous profusion of psychedelia, the fish-eye lens photo of the editorial staff, and closed it again with a sigh.

And a dark chaos rose up inside her at that moment to fill the nothingness, a horrible subterranean tantrum, a terrible squall of which the person Sarah had no real knowledge. Fire alarms and police sirens were going off in a distant place, and a single nerve in Sarah's brain-net committed suicide or died of the blow she had received. Her world transformed black for white, like a photographic negative, for a single instant. And where she had always hungered for the form of the good, she now began to lust after the patterns of evil. The syllogism that she was making in the very marrow of her bones, with her instincts if not with her intelligence, was: "If A to B to C is not correct, well, then, perhaps I should try Z."

That night in Stanton House anyone still in the dormitory wished she were out on a date. It was one of those crystal geometric wintry nights when the windows grow lace and snow is a thrilling promise. In that cleansing silence something was sure to be going on, romantic and electric, elsewhere. A few girls wandered around the dorm ashamed, in bathrobes, hiding from one another.

Sarah was in her room on the top floor with *The Confidence Man*, buzzing nervousness in her ears. The exam was in two days. Thirteen books. This was the third. Ten to go. Her door was closed; she couldn't face anyone.

Suddenly she realized that someone was moaning on the other side of the house. It was an extraordinary sound: "No . . . No! . . ." Sarah knew that this person must be in extreme pain, but still she kept herself silent. She let her sandals slip off her feet without a sound. She even held her breath a moment, so as to disappear into the dark night, the more to leave the sufferer alone in an empty dormitory.

When she had finished skimming Melville, Sarah tiptoed downstairs. Finding her personal shelf in the pantry empty, she stole some skim milk powder from someone else's shelf, mixed it with the collective sugar, and settled down in front of *The New York Times* to eat it dry. She had read two articles when Kievskaya appeared.

The big, dark girl looked more majestic than ever. Her long, thick, blue flannel robe was sashed at the waist and she walked barefoot with the sure stride of an African. The violet pools under her eyes were darker than usual. A strange pattern of lights moved around her face. She smiled at Sarah sullenly. But even as she watched, Sarah saw something creeping across Kievskaya's face like a wave, like something coming in from very far out. The lines around her eyes darkened further.

"You look sad," Sarah said.

And as she said them her words drifted off into word-limbo where they belonged, less living, less real than the strange irresistible thing that was happening in front of her eyes. By millions of tiny degrees Kievskaya's face was changing from the mask of polite caution with which we transact our business to something more open, more vulnerable, more terrible. The thing was sweeping through her like a tornado. Her eyes were growing darker and wetter every instant.

Twisting open her mouth then, letting out the cry, the bleat, the bellow, the howl that was the stifled orgasm of her pain, she began to cry. Tears ran over her face in sheets. She lifted her hands from her breasts forward, lifted her heavy arms.

And she turned away from Sarah and began walking up the swirling Victorian stairway in time to her own loud, horrible weeping, in time to silent music, her head always forward, clearing a path through the air with her tears.

Woman wronged was walking, weeping, up the stairs. Woman loving still where love had died. The tears were the only answer, the only true thing.

"I'm sorry," Sarah called up the stairs lamely.

"The simplest and cheapest, most nutritionally complete diet is peanut butter on whole wheat bread with whole milk," said Thaddeus P. Foote, sitting in the Hoare House dining hall with his sidekick Briggs Smith. Somehow the Indo-European languages expert had become an expert on nutrition as well as drugs.

Briggs was nodding. "Is that so?"

"Absolutely right!" emphasized the red-bearded man with a gesture. "The American diet of daily beef might have been appropriate on the frontier. But these days men rarely have to kill buffalo or pull their wagons in a circle to fight the Indians, and all that animal fat just goes to sleep in their blood vessels and eventually kills them. Which is not even to mention the additives—"

"Oh, God, the additives!" moaned Briggs.

"What are you agreeing about?" demanded his friend. "You and all your cheeseburgers . . ."

Briggs was stumped, but only for a moment. "Yes, yes, ha ha," he returned quickly. "You're not exactly immune to the madness of the palate yourself, Foote. What about your famous 'all oil' diet? Remember that? When you were chug-a-lugging a cup of safflower oil every day—!? That was pretty funny!"

"Hrumph, yes," said Foote. "It did make me a little oily."

For a while they chewed their blood-red roast beef in silence. The new master of the House passed by their table and nodded politely. All around them young men in spanking white shirts and narrow ties and well-cut suit jackets were making discreet, witty conversation, entirely insulated from the distracting presence of the female. Only the stocky, green-uniformed "kitchen ladies" marred this vista of well-to-do maleness, ladling out potatoes or salad or ice cream—their round arms disturbing no more than a boy's peripheral vision.

Hoare House was rather in the running against Eliot House in the misogyny department. The difference between them was that at Eliot House all values proceeded from and related back to the personality of the Master, one John Finley, an eighteenth-century gentleman in dress and manners and a classics scholar, while at Hoare the key concept to which all arguments and discrepancies were eventually referred was a more abstract "tradition." The tradition of Hoare House was based on an idea of the noble male collectivity, such as, for example, the Roman Senate. Masters of Hoare came and went, as it were, handing on the "tippet" of masterhood as they did so. But High Table remained. "Everything important in Hoare House happens after a big dinner," they said.

Now Briggs and Foote were discussing their friend Michael Verhoeven, who had made the mistake of moving into an off-campus apartment so he could be with his paramour Sarah Galbraeth. The boy did not seem to be doing well. When they ran into him now at the *Crimson* or wherever, he looked a bit peaked, a bit pale, not quite himself. Was the romance going badly? Briggs wanted to know.

Foote said nothing. He cared for Michael Verhoeven deeply.

"I wish there was something I could do," he said. "He's got to snap out of it soon or he'll find himself graduated and without a job."

"Well, there's not much chance of that, is there?" demanded Briggs. "I mean, doesn't *Vogue* or *The Paris Review* or somebody just snap up the editor of the *Crimson?*"

"Hm, I suppose so," said Foote. Unlike the other fellow, he felt not the slightest twinge of jealousy in regard to Michael Verhoeven, but only tenderness, as toward a baby brother.

"Did the thing about Sarah being Class Marshal upset him?" asked Briggs. "I mean: it upset me. God. It was so weird."

"No, no, no, no, no, no, no, no," replied Foote.

"What a changeable girl she is. I don't know how he manages.

One day she looks almost pretty, and the next time you see her, she's a terror. Completely different. Remember how all the clubbies were calling her 'Sarah-Gal'? I think some of them really thought that was her name!"

"He may be upset about coming to the end of his term as managing editor of the *Crimson*. That's been taking up most of his time for the past year, you know."

Briggs was energetically beating his vanilla ice cream into a mush. "Why are you so worried about finding him a job?" he said. "What about helping me? You think I want to go to law school?"

"If you go to law school, it's entirely your own fault," replied Foote disinterestedly.

"Will you write to me from Benares?"

"I never make statements about the future."

"What are you planning to study, again? You'll notice, I said: *planning* to study. Not: what *will* you study."

"Oh, just more of the same. Factor analysis of the Vedas. Hindu University has all six of the last Sanskrit scholars left in India."

Briggs took that seriously.

They continued talking through a leisurely dessert and coffee. Fred Aeschuylus passed their table.

"Freddy."

"*Thad*-deus—!"

The dining hall was slowly emptying. It was getting on toward 9:00 P.M., a delicious hour to be young, male, free, white, Ivy, and have a prosperous and stimulating future stretched out ahead of you. All across America a hundred million families were snapping on their TVs to watch "I Love Lucy" or "Gunsmoke" or "The Beverly Hillbillies," but at Harvard and so many places like Harvard the prime time of evening was a beckon and a promise to climb the ladders of self for a few more precious hours, until at last night, and under its wings sleep, once again descended.

As they carried their round plastic trays to the garbage chutes, Briggs and Foote were laughing at the idea that they might, all of them, enlist in the army and go over and be dogfaces in Vietnam. Variations on the theme of clubby mannerisms in a life-and-death jungle-war infantry setting amused them as they walked through the

French doors and out across the frozen path of the courtyard back to their rooms.

At the moment that they separated it struck Foote that Michael Verhoeven's angst and ennui were probably making him more than usually receptive to outside influences. The thought was like a bugle in Foote's brain. He was not a man to miss such an opportunity. Just so had he taken advantage of what he perceived as Binks's and Thatcher's mixed feelings toward the university their employer, to force that moment to its crisis. He didn't care in the least whether Binks and Thatcher were lionized or thrown to the lions. But the exercise of abstract power, for its own sake, devil take the hindmost—that was his life.

There was something he could do to alter Michael's situation, he was sure of it. If he could only think what . . .

Sitting at the managing editor's desk, his back to the newsroom, Michael was writing his name in large block letters on a sheet of yellow paper, and the number "2" in every possible typestyle. It was 2:00 A.M. Logically, he should be home asleep or studying, but all he could think about was the end of his administration as managing editor. The thought gave him a headache. Sarah wasn't home and loneliness had driven him here.

CFMcS was in the newsroom too, and the sound of his wads of paper lobbing into the garbage can was calming.

"And two for four, the famous McSilver still leading the pack, yes, and in." Charlie's voice droned on softly. Michael's lettering grew heavier and heavier.

Suddenly Foote's face loomed above Michael as he sat writing. "Verhoeven!" said the big, ruddy, hirsute fellow.

Michael jumped.

"Do you want to learn something about yourself?" began Foote, but Michael was already interrupting.

"I've told you, Foote. I'm not taking any of your drugs."

Foote was all smiles. "Ah, your remarkable conservatism. We can discuss that another time. What I have in mind tonight is just something very interesting I want to show you. All you have to do is open your eyes and look."

Michael put his fountain pen down wearily. "Well, I guess that can't hurt . . . much. What is it?"

Foote looked over at McSilver, who was all ears.

"It's difficult to explain . . . here," he said.

"Eat dork, turkey," said McSilver, and went back to his wadball.

"Do you want to come back with me to my room?" asked Foote.

"Why can't you show me whatever it is here?"

"Who's in the president's office?"

"I don't know. Somebody. Chris and Tui Burne-Jones."

"And the ed chairman's office?"

"Ford, Chrysler, and General Motors. I don't know. It's all sewed up.'"

"I suppose Art is downstairs."

"That man has put in thirty-five years of overtime! . . . All right, let's go up to the sanctum," said Michael, and rose, crushing the sheet with his name all over it and tossing it into McSilver's garbage can from fifteen feet. He trudged up the carpeted stairway ahead of his old roommate, casting a gentle glance at the pinup of Sarah as he passed.

Foote switched on a floor lamp in the black room, causing a little crimson pool of light to form on the worn rug. Michael switched on another. The long curtains were open and the night showed perfectly black through all the windows along the long wall. An oversized bound volume of *Crimson*s from 1955 lay on the cocktail table. This was a room for serious business.

"Wanna watch a little TV?" said Michael, grinning.

"Let's go out on the roof," suggested Foote.

The roof was very cold and very dark. Gravel and old snow crunched beneath their feet. "How in hell are you going to show me anything out here?"

"Astute as ever, my friend." Foote cleared his throat. They went back into the building as far as the upstairs sink. The filthy little facility was piled high with boxes, but Foote switched on a naked overhead bulb and made himself comfortable against a carton of gin. Michael put a hand on the doorframe and looked expectant.

"Is this confidential enough for you?"

Foote drew a manila envelope from the inside pocket of his Persian lamb overcoat, and from this he withdrew what appeared to be a slightly larger than regulation deck of playing cards. These he fanned out on the grimy washboard. There were elaborate illustrations on every face. "Have you ever seen these before?"

"Can't say I have."

Foote tapped the deck against the drain to align it. "These are Tarot cards," he said. "They're the great-granddaddies of the ones you use every night to play poker." He looked at Michael, who appeared disappointed and slightly irritated. "The four suits are here, plus an additional court card in each, plus twenty-two more comprising the Major Arcana. . . ."

"So?" said Michael, shifting his weight.

Foote sped on. "The symbolism of the numbers and the suits and the Arcana is partly cabalistic, by which we mean Sabaean, Gnostic, and Zoroastrian, and partly Christian, and some say ultimately derived from ancient Egypt where knowledge was preserved for thousands of years without an alphabet."

He paused. Michael said nothing.

"If you were a prisoner in a cell with no books," Foote continued, "and had only this deck of cards . . . and knew how to read them . . . you could reconstruct all the literatures of the world."

Now Michael had a fix on the situation. Mumbo jumbo. "Is this what you brought me up here for, Foote? To show me a fancy deck of cards?"

"Don't be so impatient," chided Foote. "Patience is the first requirement. But since I know you have some important work you have to do sitting alone in the newsroom at two A.M., I'll get right to the point. This is *your* card, my dear friend. This is *you!*"

And then Foote fumbled adeptly with his Tarot deck and with a flourish laid on the sink before the managing editor a large pasteboard with the legend "The Devil" inscribed in an odd typeface along the bottom.

The picture on "The Devil" card was of a horrible monster with claws and a tail sitting above the figures of a human man and woman, naked and beautiful, standing erect, with just a touch of shame in their expressions. The man and the woman upon closer inspection appeared to be loosely chained to the great beast. They sported, as it did, horns and tails, but theirs were small and cute, decorative, harmless. The whole was black and fiery red, laced with occult signs. Abruptly Foote switched off the glaring bulb swinging above them, and spoke to Michael in the darkness.

"You see, that is you!" he boomed, sincere and passionate, as if he truly believed he was making a revelation to his friend that would help him. "But it doesn't have to be like that! You saw: the chains are loose! The prisoners can simply lift their chains from around their necks—!"

But Michael had gone from Foote's dark kitchen and was already halfway down the carpeted sanctum stairs, whence passing at a fast clip through the newsroom past CFMcS, and continuing down the second set of steps, these rickety and wooden, that led to the printing shop in the *Crimson*'s basement. And there was Art Hopkins as always seated at his big linotype machine forging the recently cooled lead back again into the shapes of the letters the children wanted it to take. Foote's image had penetrated and terrified Michael—and the idea that Foote thought that that was who he was—and he didn't want to see Foote again for a long time or Tarot cards again ever.

Art greeted Verhoeven laconically. Nearby Robin Palmer was leaning over a nearly completed flatbed page, reading the backward print, fitting in the needed slugs of metal.

"Well, Sarah's really eating up that publicity you guys arranged for her," remarked Tui, serving a large steaming platter of butterfly shrimp.

"Don't look at me," protested Nestor. "It was your friend here who created the monster." And taking six of the fattest and largest of the succulent crescents, and forking one quickly into his mouth, he gestured with his fork and full cheek toward Christopher Green.

"Huh? Who, me?" protested Chris. The shrimp plate had somehow passed him by and gone on to Thaddeus Foote, who was helping himself genteelly, a nodding, enigmatic smile on his face.

"Not to worry," said Foote. "There is no place for a woman at the head of a Harvard College class."

The occasion was a little intersession dinner party. The dorm being nearly empty for term break, Tui had brought together Foote and Briggs, Nestor, Chris, and Nestor's friends the under-professor of social relations John Stone and his wife Hepzibah, for a bit of a feast in the Stanton House living room. The wine was a splendid Pinot Chardonnay Mâcon, "Le Grand Crystal," from the Caves de la Reine Pédauque, and the group fell quickly into the conspiratorial familiarity of a brotherhood.

Both Nestor and Foote were particularly brilliant this evening, brimming over with anecdotes, stories, accusations, and fascinating facts. The under-professor applauded the actor's remarks, particularly, with the heartiest laughter. But the red-bearded shaman seized an opportunity to take the floor, slowing the pace of the conversation an iota and lowering its pitch, so that, in his own register, he could spin a long tale about an absent friend known as Berndt Norton, "a superb artist with golden hair and a great golden beard and the most infinitely deep cobalt eyes!" Nestor listened with a smile of faint cynicism on his lips. He had not met this Berndt Norton of Foote's, and knew nothing of his merits, but it seemed to him that at one point Foote's story had a logical loop that invalidated it.

If this was so, none of the others appeared to notice. Chris, in particular, was looking at Foote "as if Foote has quite hung the moon." But then, "it's no concern of mine." Nestor lifted another forkful of shrimp.

At last the actor interrupted Foote's exegesis of Berndt Norton's male and female symbolism to raise a point about Buñuel's razored eyeball. This was more to the taste of the under-professor of social relations, who expounded portentously and at length on the meaning of meaning, until Tui was ready to pronounce him a bore. But then the under-professor made an aside (or was he illustrating a point?) about the drug preferences of a certain well-known talk show host, and Tui's ears perked up, and she was once again pleased with her own prowess as a hostess.

The shrimp being done, Tui made a dramatic entrance through the swinging doors bearing a silver salver on which were balanced seven silver dishes of Baked Alaska. The group expressed unguarded approval. Nestor quickly restored the customary acid balance of the evening with a devastating reference to Tui's possible Freudian needs in serving up such a dish. But the company did the exotic dish justice nonetheless, smacking their lips and salivating and swallowing the warm cake and cold ice cream and steamy meringue in big, impatient, needy-child gulps. The conversation slipped into silence. Nestor heard in his mind's ear the sound of an oboe.

Their sloppy ice cream plates stashed on end tables and chair arms or on the floor, beside dinner plates decorated with red-orange shrimp ends, half-empty wine and water goblets, full ashtrays, pouches of smoking material and pipes and a stray wallet or two, Foote was the first to waken from the slumberous ease that seemed to have overtaken the rest of the company.

"Do you want to meet Berndt Norton?" he was saying to Chris. "I believe he's coming to Boston in February."

Winter was over. The new term shimmered as fresh in the mind as the city's spires in the liquid of Mass. Ave.'s puddles. On the first beautiful day Nestor and Sarah found themselves walking together out the front door of the *Crimson*, across Plympton Street, and into spring. Sarah turned to look at him silhouetted in the clean air, and she felt exhilarated. The sun shone from behind his head. Giddy, she danced around in front of him, so that it would shine from behind her head as well. Warmly, Nestor said, "Hey, Sarah, you wanna go to the Chinese restaurant?" And his voice diffracted the sunlight for her, so she heard in his words a many-colored spectrum of sentiments.

In the Chinese restaurant Nestor put his arm around Sarah's neck with bearlike roughness. So gay, she began to analyze the Class Marshal election. How long ago it seemed. She believed herself to be quite articulate on the subject now. Nestor smiled as she held forth: "Conceived in a spirit of playfulness . . . the joke contained a fatal germ of truth. . . . The anachronistic rule of aristocrats was a target of resentment for intellectuals, radicals, proletarians. . . . We get a meat and potatoes equality here, but no dessert. . . . It was a fast curved pitch. . . . But though they resisted my actual, physical election, they can't undo the 'damage' that has been done. . . . The seriousness of the cause—or causes—lives an imperishable life in the humor that surrounded it. . . ."

Nestor had, of course, played his own considerable part in the event. But now, as he sat on the patched red vinyl seats drinking tea and eating almond charsue ding with Sarah, he smiled and smiled, seeming to become happier and happier as she spoke, almost as if he were hearing some good and flattering news about himself. Chris and Joey Green came into the restaurant then, and sat down at a nearby table, smiling hello. Sarah wished to prolong the moment. But Nestor was already turning away from too much joy. The last nut disappeared into his mouth and he wiped an embarrassed hand across his face and looked at her hard.

Over their heads the ceiling was thickly inlaid with ornate brass-and-wood double-dragon mandalas, forming a pattern of squares that reached down to form a frieze along the upper walls. Tassels hung from chandeliers faced with six watercolor landscapes. A chart behind the cashier's counter showed which years pertained to which animals.

Then Sarah became shy, and at length stopped talking. In the interlude Nestor languidly raised his right hand and touched the crown of her head, moving his fingers in her hair with an expression of poised attentiveness and concentration that revealed the very blueprint and naked lines of his own face. Sarah lifted her eyes to him with something like fear. To her surprise, she saw before her nothing of the Nestor Schwarz she had long known, not the actor, not the gamemaster, not the Pan of energy. For the moment her glance fell upon flesh that was opaque as an object, a hollow vessel his soul had left behind in its sudden impulsive flight toward herself.

In response she accepted the gift, abandoned her own flesh,

adored his fleshly geometries. Chris, noticing something of this, stared in amazement.

Joey began to say something across the booths to Nestor and Sarah about Lyndon Johnson.

But Nestor, still facing Sarah with that unseeing look in his eyes, ignored the others to say to her, "You look pretty. Let's have a romance."

Sarah had the strongest desire to put her hand on Nestor's arm, but she refrained.

They paid their checks and walked out again into the dazzling spring. Sarah smiled good-bye to Nestor outside the restaurant and turned the corner. The next moment she smiled hello at Michael. Michael and Nestor didn't see each other.

Later that afternoon, sitting in the ed chairman's office, Sarah and Michael settled down to one of their usual political arguments. Sarah would take a position like Dan's or Carolee's, as she understood them, on the war, say, or the distribution of wealth, and Michael would refute her. She would stick to her guns until eventually Michael would accuse her of naiveté or "infantile left-ism." In the past Sarah had often ended up crying, convinced by Michael's superior logic and abundant information. And their love would be reaffirmed, their respective roles recrystalized.

But on this first day of the new term, a simple chat about the ILGWU took a new turn. Sarah changed the rules of their dispute. She played dirty. She debated "straight negative," as she had done in high school. Instead of hanging respectfully on to each of Michael's carefully constructed arguments, she circled around him, jabbing wherever she saw an opening, merciless, obstinate, inconsistent.

Michael grew angrier and sadder. "You damn sophist," he said. "Why are you doing this to me?"

And only then did Sarah settle down. It wasn't that she wanted to win so much; she just wanted him not to be always right.

The night of the annual arts and letters awards dinner came sooner than Sarah might have wished, less than a month after the Class Marshal business, in a blur of nervousness and speeches and spilled champagne and certificates and gifts.

One by one the leading figures on the *Crimson,* the *Lampoon,* the literary magazine, two poetry cells, and the Harvard Dramatic Club filed into a trim little Colonial cottage behind white columns in the driveway of Lowell House that was the Signet Club. Drinks from their separate clubhouses still in hand, dressed in their best, they chatted self-importantly or perceptively, breathing the rich, strange gaiety of a gilt-edged Cambridge evening. Inside, black kitchenmasters prepared extra-thick slabs of rare roast beef for the literary and social elite. T. S. Eliot had been a member of the Signet. It was said that a copy of the first edition of his poems was in the bookcase here with the requisite red rose pressed in its pages. Sarah made a mental note to send her first book with a white rose—then quickly berated herself for the thought. No woman had ever been a member.

But this was no night to dwell on male privilege. The *Crimson* horde—so many of whom were public school people—Westerners—Jewish—even female—had rented the space for the awards dinner, and their presence was tolerated. The long arpeggios of male-female flirtation were blended this evening with the usual dissonances and grace notes of homosexual interchange, though echoes of the latter hung in the rafters like cherished webs.

Nestor and Tui had come with Thaddeus Foote, and in the Signet parlor their little clique was bantering about the incoming *Crimson* operations manager, a bold girl veteran of Mississippi, who was expected to move the paper in an activist direction. "Pish-tosh," scoffed Foote, making a speculation about this girl's parents' probable black maid. The terrifying Tui Burne-Jones turned away from Foote to laugh with Chris Green. And Nestor whispered that she had recently taken all her clothes off in the editor-in-chief's office, on a dare. JHC and R. R. Hodgson were joking in *Wind in the Willows* babytalk.

In the small study a varsity football player from the *Advocate* business board was toying with a monocled theater reviewer, fascinated to see how close he could come to the other while still retaining the upper hand. The reviewer was quite caught in the athlete's spell.

The athlete offered the reviewer a job in his father's corporation. The reviewer complained that he didn't know if he could trust the athlete. The athlete swore by his name. The reviewer made as if to scoff. Whereupon the football player pulled back, offended, and exclaimed loudly, "Hey, man! You're bustin' my chops!" At this, a nearby woman turned her head away, and the straight man and the homosexual continued their conversation or negotiation in a lower tone.

Sarah was wearing her medium-blue Jackie Kennedy dress. Holding a tall glass of Scotch in one hand, she felt regal and fragile. Soon after their arrival at the Signet, Chris Green had slipped a placard over her head that read OOTG. "It's true, I am one of the greats," she thought fiercely, and left the sign in place awhile.

At dinner she drank more table wine than usual but found it difficult to eat. Through the meal and the speeches she watched Nestor, sitting across from her and to the left, as he clowned and clowned, moved by a high glee. Michael, sitting at her right, did not notice that she was meeting Nestor's eyes to laugh. When her successor presented Sarah with a farewell gift of paperbacks on *Home Sewing* and *Home Cooking* and Dr. Spock's *Baby and Child Care* there was general merriment. Nestor laughed loudly and long, and his eyes caught Sarah's once again. Michael was not laughing. It would leave a gap in his life not to be managing editor. Last semester of senior year was a little late to begin getting interested in academics. But he stood up when the time came and gave a good speech.

When the lengthy ritual was finally done, Nestor ambled over to Michael and Sarah and stood near them uncertainly. "Wanna go for a drink?" he suggested. Michael shook his head no but Sarah nodded yes and they went. Michael held Sarah's little wool princess coat for her and the three headed down Mount Auburn Street, letting the crush in the Signet fade to a dimming hubbub.

Nestor was addressing himself now exclusively to Michael, who thawed at the actor's profuse attentions. He began to smile and even laugh at Nestor's jokes. After a while he gave a great open laugh, an unaffected, little boy's laugh, and teased Nestor back in the funny accent of his Dutch grandmother: "Why don't you get a job, *hanh?*" At this Nestor burst into explosive guffaws of happiness at Michael's happiness, and the threesome reeled exuberantly along the cobblestones toward the Brattle. They were by now quite drunk on Scotch and champagne, observing themselves from a slight distance, sorrowing to be seniors, ignorant of their own futures, soon no longer to be chieftains of Cambridge, and reluctant perhaps to leave this great, rich, famous fruitcake of an institution—without at least a sip of nepenthe.

Under the Brattle the Casablanca was dark as pitch. After a moment shapes began to emerge: drinking, laughing, the atmosphere dense and tangible, murky, charged. Sarah caught a glimpse of the poetess from the dorm at a table along the wall, but the girl, seeing them, appeared silently to pledge silence. They sat and Sarah ordered more Scotch, and then another, and then another.

In the blackness, Sarah's eyes were on Nestor. His long, slightly dirty hair was falling over his amazing eyes and into his face and he was saying something about whether or not it was possible to experience "a little naked spark of the divine fire." He was drinking a lot, too, despite his ulcer. Sarah was trembling. She lit one of Michael's Camels, though she never smoked. Coughing and waving it away from her face, she smoked it down and lit another.

This campus marriage that she had with Michael: It was a sacred, wonderful thing, it was recognized by everyone in this little world of Cambridge, it gave other people warmth and confidence. And yet, insofar as it was also the very current of her life's energy, Sarah was experiencing some kind of change. Like an ancient iron gate shifting heavily out of its lifelong position at the end of the path to a great manor house, creaking and complaining, Sarah could feel something most heavy and slow and portentous inside herself disconnecting from its ancient pattern and seeking a new one, reestablishing itself in a configuration of greater strength. Everything about Nestor compelled her attention tonight. The circuit between their eyes ran directly to her blood, shortened her breath, speeded the thumping in her chest.

Sarah was less conscious now of Michael as a statesman— though his heart was falling out of his eyes in questions and sadness— than of Nestor as an exile, a poet, offering her a new code, an invitation, a taboo. Out of step now with the rhythms of their conversation, she could feel her pulse beating in time with the faint and dusky forest sound—the jukebox, a low underbreath comprehending everything, condoning everything.

Extinguishing her cigarette, Sarah said something about courage being the source of knowledge. About the "epiphany" she had had walking up Garden Street one day, when she had tasted the seeds in the core of an apple she had just finished and was about to throw away, and found them good. Nestor was nodding sagely, but Michael made a face and muttered something about "harebrained theories." Good Lord! She was always doing it! Saying things like "Why do girls eat apples and boys bananas?" Maybe if it hadn't been the depressing night of the arts and letters dinner . . . But the sight of his lover talking to his friend in this crazy way she sometimes had, and his friend pretending to understand, suddenly gave him the most terrific pain in the ass. Making a terse excuse, he rose and left.

In the Casablanca the dark bar had vanished like a ghost, and

Almost limping with anger, Michael walked back home to his one-room off-campus apartment next door to the *Crimson*, back to the empty hallway, to the double-locked door, to the Blake print and the red bedspread and the jar of crunchy peanut butter that Sarah had bought standing forlornly on top of a softly humming refrigerator— and he felt horrible. He took his clothes off, leaving them in a pile on the sofa, and got into bed: naked and eternally weary.

In the Casablanca the dark bar had vanished like a ghost, and on the jukebox Petula Clark had begun to sing "Downtown," and Sarah was alone for the first time with Nestor (ignoring the poetess at the other table, who was only occasionally glancing at them), and in her teeming brain she was showing movies of *Wuthering Heights* and *Steppenwulf, Sentimental Education* and *Anna Karenina* and *Splendeurs et misères des courtisanes,* and Sarah imagined she saw some male version of all this in Nestor's big black eyes and on his pouting lips, and then he took her hand.

> Just listen to the music
> Of the traffic in the city
> Linger on the sidewalk where
> The neon lights are pretty
> How can you lose? . . .

"I have loved you for a long time," he said.

"Oh! I love you too!" she said tremulously. And then he kissed her hand, holding it tightly in his own thrilling black-fingernailed hand. And they collapsed with love and drink, guessing and including the end in the very first moment, into each other's arms, to kiss one another on the mouth in a kiss made fabulous by the surprise of absolutely synchronous beginnings—right there in the Club Casablanca, over a table covered with tortured cocktail napkins.

They walked home together in the chill spring night. Nestor stopped to kiss her mouth once more on the traffic island in the middle of Brattle Square. A taxi went by, beeping. Sarah felt happier than one is permitted to feel—like a movie star. At her Radcliffe door Nestor said, "No matter what happens—don't forget how wonderful tonight was!" and left.

Meanwhile, back at the Signet, the high culture had attenuated into the merest thought of itself. Two homosexuals had fallen in a kind of love with a tall, skinny, thick-eyebrowed, clear-skinned, graceful and confident young Irish girl from the yearbook photo board. Nothing in this complex social interaction was causing the girl even the slightest twinge of anxiety. One of the two men volunteered a critique of her appearance, whereupon the other, more drunk, rose to her defense. "Not this girl!" he slurred. He was nodding toward her and grasping her hands, her arm, his eyes swimming. The girl was relating enthusiastically to all the men present, the football player, the homosexuals, neatly ignoring the other women. Her chin was pointed.

Sarah wriggled into an enormous red flannel shirt and blue jeans and sat down with her little, lightweight Hermes typewriter. All through the dorm girls were communing. Two seniors in the gov department were in their bedroom drinking hot Tang and illegal vodka, sitting on the floor beside a low, round coffee table, telling each other the events of their day. In the living room Tui Burne-Jones and Virginia Morris were discussing the *Crimson* arts and letters dinner, and they spoke eloquently of "communication" and "drunkenness," but said not a word about R.R. or about Chris Green, who had whispered to Tui half the night about love and death.

Kievskaya and Rosa were curled into an upstairs window seat comparing notes on their Jewishness. Kievskaya's grandparents had separately fled the Ukraine at the turn of the century to avoid conscription and "pogrom." Rosa's parents had brought her safely through Russia and Germany when what was happening was a "holocaust." Rosa was explaining to Kievskaya that she had never wanted to know why they had not been killed in Europe. The "how" she understood well enough. Kievskaya did not follow. "I asked my father how he knew it was time to leave," said Rosa, "and he said, 'You just know.' "

> We hang here in this halfway place, this nowhere [typed Sarah], this agar medium. Everything conspires to feed us, to make us grow, and we wear ourselves out with not growing fast enough.
>
> There is food, and there is warmth, and there is diversion, but we grow sick on its sweetness. There is no ground. Nothing grates to tell us we are there. We hunger not for food but for a floor, for a rough touch, for something that evades us. We long for brick, and sand slides through our fingers. Until finally our very selves turn in upon us, turn hard, and scrape. And we rejoice crazily in this solid touch, this unnatural hardening of what should be soft.

Night fell once more. Somewhere two 'Cliffies were making love.

In the morning Michael phoned, hysterical with worry and jealousy. Sarah went to him. As soon as she saw his handsome face contorted with pain and disillusionment, she fell into his arms. They made love with a wild, biting, angry kind of fervor that frightened them both. Never before had hatred mixed itself into their feelings.

On the rumpled bedspread afterward, Sarah proposed what seemed to her to be eminently reasonable: that they stay together, but he let her have her "freedom."

"Freedom? You mean Nestor?" he shouted. "If you sleep with him for the sake of an adventure, it will change things between us forever!"

They screamed and cried for hours. They talked about the

problem from six different directions. They broke up and reconciled and broke up again. They made sweeping statements about youth and adulthood. Sarah said, "The danger of not having lived your life is greater than the danger of ruining your life!"

Michael fixed himself a Scotch and swallowed it in a gulp. "Don't you hear what you're saying, baby?" he pleaded. "I love you. I want to marry you. A real, traditional wedding. I want you to be my wife!"

Sarah thought about both of their parents. They had two happy marriages. They had been together many years. But Michael's parents had met in the ditches of the labor war and were, let's face it, thrilled that Michael had come to Harvard. Her parents had never even finished high school. Somehow the idea of marriage, even of good marriage, didn't reach up quite as high as the idea of Harvard. . . .

T he phone rang in Stanton House. Rosa, absentmindedly twirling her brown hair, first jumped in horror and then shrank in anguish. So often these days it was Nestor: but it was never her that he wanted to speak to. Usually it was Tui. Or Yvette. Now, it was even Sarah. Rosa felt so lonely. There was no one in the house she could call her friend anymore. Losing the intimacy of her girl friends was even worse than losing Nestor as a boyfriend, such as he was.

But no, it *was* for her. When Kievskaya called her name Rosa walked slowly over, carrying her tea mug, and slipped into the wooden phone booth closet, pressing the old-fashioned earpiece to her ear and leaning forward to speak into the mouthpiece.

It was Susie, her older sister, in Toronto. Just calling to say hello, and see how was she. A tear rolled down Rosa's cheek. She was grateful to her.

"Oh, Susie," she said. "I'm so miserable!"

Day after day Sarah lived at flash-
point with Michael, breaking up with and returning to him with renewed passion, hysterical and consoled, now refreshed, now despairing.
Tormented by his inability to control or predict the situation, Michael
threatened to leave school. Sarah was horrified by the possibility.

But she honored her own confusion. Night after night she settled in after dinner on the dorm porch, the chill blowing through her
flannel shirt, and explored the first and most perfect isolation she had
ever known, and wrote notes to herself, a letter to some future Sarah, a
closely spaced, voluminous, typewritten diary. In writing she felt she
was wrenching the maelstrom of her experience from out of the terrible
jaws of time and redeeming it. Utterly in the throes of emotion, she
told herself that the moments in which emotion hold sway are the
moments of truest life. The elements of her situation danced before
her: marriage, democratic socialism, politics, Harvard, drugs.

When the first rush of crystallization was complete each night,
Sarah would turn to the final draft of her thesis, "Simone de Beauvoir:
Prophet of the New Feminism." Phrases from the Frenchwoman osmosed into her thinking, as reflections of her loves osmosed into the
thesis. She wrote—diary and thesis—until at last, each night, her brain
simply refused to run a moment longer. And then she stopped, scratching her hip through her Levis, tired but not sated, as if after a long
afternoon of ice-skating when the leg muscles have finally warmed up
and are begging for more. Was there a limit to the powers of the brain?
Just to speak with Nestor was to strain her understanding. He was so
difficult to comprehend. But she experienced the confusion, the uncertainty, even the tension and strain, of his presence, as physical excitement. "Nestor is a smart, bad person," she noted. "He is intellectually
old, but emotionally young. His ego is not integrated." The question of
Nestor's "evil" fascinated her. She wrote the word "evil" again and
again in her diary—in connection with this person to whom she was so
irresistibly drawn—but she could not have said what it meant. She did
not, at root, believe in it. The question of Nestor's possible "evil" en-
tailed a contradiction. And yet, as she wrote these words to herself,
these frightening and only half-understood words, she felt no less de-
vouringly curious to learn what they might really mean, no less de-

vouringly eager to be with Nestor, to have him, to capture him, to incorporate him, to kill him.

And then, very late at night, Sarah would pack up her Hermes and the pile of yellow newsprint and move into the kitchen for a last warm drink. There around the Stanton House kitchen table she made exotic feminist speeches to the nightly parade of sleepy-eyed girls. Her life had an uncanny unity. Her loves, her schoolwork, even her conversations now with whoever would listen (however skeptical or dazzled or disgusted they might be), were all of a piece. She felt a terrible exaltation. As she spoke she drank dark black currant tea and pursued her new cigarette habit diligently. She vowed she would live her life "with a hard, gemlike flame." The midnight girls felt a tremor of excitement at the phrase. And Sarah felt an increasing distance from them.

Rosa looked at her shyly from across the table, as if she still liked Sarah but was afraid she might do something outlandish at any moment, like jump up and bark. Recently Rosa had begun to notice a number of little imperfections in her old friend. It was not entirely clear to her whether Sarah was talking about jumping off cliffs and under trains for love, like the heroines of the old romances . . . or whether she had in mind something more along the lines of an opium den full of painters and musicians. Perhaps Sarah meant something else entirely.

She inquired. Was Sarah favoring extremism?

Kievskaya spoke up. She knew what Sarah was talking about, she said, and she agreed.

So did Tui say she understood, and explained that Sarah was talking about people who went down South and risked their lives, like Carolee Davis and Tommy Cartier.

Sarah disagreed impatiently. No, no, no. Going South was wonderful, but she was talking about risking everything this side of death . . . for love. She would not limit herself to conventions and propriety and suburbia. She would have many lovers. She would bear the children of many men! She would live, she would truly live!

At this juncture one late night Yvette Serre breezed into the kitchen from a study date, her reefer coat glistening with precipitation, bidding hello to the others in their robes, shaking her perfection of form down into a chair.

"So what is Sarah talking about now?" she murmured. *"L'art pure et dure?* Living in the present moment and all that? The great yearning for the impossible, the new, the anarchic, the fantastic? Is that right, Sarah? Is that what you are promoting?"

Sarah scowled. She thought Yvette was being hypocritical. The girl had had *seven* love affairs that Sarah knew about. She was the original *hetaera.* And yet lately she was sounding like she believed in monogamy, fidelity, tranquil relationships. Why? Where were all the exciting third world and vis stud types that used to hang around here anyway? What happened to all those guys from Choate?

"Oh, what's the point of coming to Harvard," wailed Sarah, "if your goal in life is going to be moderation? We knew in Iowa that moderation was the right goal. They know it on the soap operas every afternoon." She looked back at Rosa for an instant, with a flash of scorn.

"A woman can satisfy her need for excitement and vanity by flirting," said Yvette. "It is not necessary to have an affair."

"But why stop there? Men search for themselves—for the truth— in sex. Men gamble. Women confine their risks to leaving dirty dishes in the sink and overeating and being mean to their kids. Why—really, I want you to answer this!—why does every little girl in elementary school have neat handwriting?"

Yvette knew what Sarah was driving at, but she was not inclined to pursue the argument. She just stared at Sarah with a rare and curious expression on her face.

"Men take risks with their lives!" Sarah continued. "They tempt the abyss. Women won't accomplish anything until they do the same!"

"Is that what you want?" said Yvette. "To tempt the abyss?" A delicate smile crossed her face for a moment, her eyelids tinged and a little weary, battered veteran of the wars and deaths and motherhoods of mankind. Sarah was still such a child. How could she be intelligent, and muck about Cambridge for almost four years, and still not know that the abyss hangs from your toes at the edge of every step you take for your entire life? And the trick is not to find it—oh, no! it is always there; so easy to find—but to overcome it once again, having found it, to scramble up the treacherous further bank.

Yvette looked at Sarah searchingly one last moment, shook her head, and left the kitchen with a shrug. Once upon a time Sarah had been influenced by and followed Yvette's example in the matter of the facts of life. But Yvette had always been a cool paradigm of a girl, and never preachy; nor did she ever consider herself a best friend to Sarah, much less now when it was a question of Nestor Schwarz. It was too bad: Yvette was perhaps the only person who had the information necessary to push Sarah back from the brink.

Virginia Morris had also been listening. She was never inelegant or unattractive, even in bathrobe and fuzzy slippers. She took the kettle of boiling water from Rosa and poured herself some cocoa.

"That's all very fine, Sarah Galbraeth," she said. "But what's your life plan?"

Sarah looked up at the house president dumbly. Life plan? She had no life plan.

"It won't amount to a hill of beans without a life plan," warned Virginia.

The next time Nestor called it was to invite Sarah out to Tui's chum's house on the North Shore. She accepted.

There, in the blue-and-brown-striped nautical-motif boy's bedroom, Nestor said, "I wish I was anything but the second man in your life."

Michael listlessly raised a forkful of eggs, his head aching and his shirt wrinkled from a sleepless night of self-hatred. He had let himself play poker again. Several of his long night's companions were seated around him now, glumly eating their eighty-five-cent Hayes Bickford Special Breakfasts. The coffee was cold and the cream was clotting nastily, but Michael drank the free second cup when it was offered.

"It's Tuesday, Michael," said Charlie.

"Yeah, that's right, it's Tuesday. Go fuck yourself." Michael wiped his mouth and stalked off to pay his bill. But he had to come back to borrow thirty cents. "Take it off what you owe me," he said to Charlie angrily.

Thrown into new despair by this latest humiliation, Michael staggered out into the drizzly Cambridge morning. It was too early for classes, being still that empty hour when only fatigued *Crimson* editors and local merchants in from Billerica or Danvers were in the streets. As he crossed to the little node of light and life at the newsstand, Michael felt his forehead hair slowly cleaving, lizardlike, to his skin. Goddamn rain. He shut his eyes in fury and manipulated the saliva inside his jaws. Only the wordy disorder of the newsstand could save him now. Would let him forget the poker game, the money lost, the night awake and the forthcoming day, pregnant and awful with illegal, irresistible sleep, missed classes, no money, and . . . and . . . Sarah! Much as he wanted to, he couldn't keep Sarah out of his mind. "Because I'm so tired."

He reached for the *Times*. The Chinese were doing something on the Indian border. J. Anthony Lukas. Russell Baker. Gay Talese. Somewhere on the earth today there were "Tons of Newborn Elephant." God! That almost put things into perspective!

Even before he had finished surveying "the newspaper of record" and turned to glance over the rest of the wonderful display, Michael was feeling decidedly better. Reading the paper, knowing how to read the paper, was like knowing all the batting averages when the Dodgers have just beaten the Yankees in four straight. A relic of childhood happiness brought a wan smile to his lips. He took a dime out of his back pocket and handed it to the man in the striped apron.

Then he walked off into the dreary dawn of Harvard Square, a paper under his arm and the faintest suggestion of a click to his heels.

"She agreed to see him every Tuesday," smirked Charlie back in the Bick.

"But why? I thought they broke up."

"They did. I saw her moving her stuff out of his apartment the afternoon of the *Crimson*-WHRB game."

"Yeah."

"Well, either before that or after that, I don't know, he and Nestor had it out. . . . And to prove his friendship, or *something*, Nestor said he would only screw Sarah with Michael's permission."

"Jesus."

"You said it. So Michael told Sarah he actually *would* give his permission—on the condition that she see him at least once a week as well. So she agreed. And Tuesday's the day."

"Oh."

"Holy shit."

"I still don't understand what all the fuss is about. I don't think she's that good looking. I remember when I first came out for the *Crimson* every time she walked in Michael would go batshit and sink into the sofa and just stare at her legs."

"Once a week! Holy shit!"

"Her legs are okay, it's true, but what about—"

Benjamin always felt uneasy when conversations became anatomical, and so he got up and left before he had to hear anything that might affect his veneration of Sarah.

As the St. Paul's bells pealed two o'clock (mi, re, do, *so*) Sarah slammed her book shut. Time for Michael. With a last peek across the row of heads obediently bowed to an academic Allah, down, down, and across to that wonderful tall blond with the beard and the pile of Gaelic texts, she swept her strawberry licorice wrapper into the trash and stood up. Coeducation is the only way, she thought, observing that the Gaelic blond had looked up absentmindedly.

She made her way out of Widener in a stately fashion, her back tingling where she felt boys were looking at her. Alone, female, in a thrilling ocean of male. "All different from me!" she whispered to herself. "If we were all sitting and walking around here naked" (she smiled with one corner of her mouth), "they would all . . . and I . . ."

Michael was pacing the floor of his one room. He glanced at his bed. Clean sheets for her. A new bottle of Scotch. Would she come? Her footsteps down the long hall filled him with terror. How different were their meetings now! How different from the days when she came gladly, unexpectedly, daily, the days when they woke up lazily and wasted the morning together, the days before. . . .

Without knocking she opened the door with her key and stepped in. Her hair was wet and wispy but Michael saw something of the old love in her eyes. But perhaps it was just a gleam of sport. . . . He grabbed her and buried his face in her neck.

"Oh, Sarah, Sarah, Sarah!"

"Oh, my sweet love! Oh, Michael!"

Something luminously pure in him surrounded them both with warmth. She began to cry. She half-resisted, off balance, but he succeeded in pushing or pulling her across the room. With a strange, lovable, ferocious expression he tripped her so that she fell backward over the bedspread. He laughed and fell on top of her, laughing and kissing her, pulling the barrette out of her hair and opening the buttons of her blouse. She let him undress her and lay back to feel the moist afternoon air on her body as he hurriedly undressed himself. . . .

N o no no no NO! And yes Now! Now! Oh! Oh! Oh! Oh! The alphabet aligned along the sides of the directional signal like iron filings, into a word she could almost read. Yes . . .

"**O**h, Nestor," she whispered, "I love you so much. God, I love you."

Nestor was sitting above her, immobile among the ravaged sheets, smoking. He stared across the room and out to the tree that filled the window. He was calculating that the leaves work the same way that capillaries work in people, taking in nutrients from the circulation medium (wind + air + rain = blood) and distributing them to the cells. So then a tree is a human being turned inside out. . . .

"Damn it, you haven't been listening to me." She tried to put some self-mockery into her voice so he wouldn't realize she was (it was forbidden) *nagging*.

"What did you say?" Nestor turned to her and blew smoke in her face.

The memory of him was still warm inside of her, and at the sight of his face she moved restlessly under the covers, trying to bump into him and disturb his remoteness.

"Mmm, c'mere," she whispered, reaching out her hand. "You were wonderful. Come . . . talk to me . . ."

"Wait. Let's listen to some music." Nestor touched his hair where she had touched it and swung around to where the shortwave radio sat precariously on a bridge chair. Hanging from the bed, he turned the selector meditatively and then settled back next to the tousled girl.

"Who's this?" he teased, taking a last puff and dropping his cigarette to the floor.

Sarah winced and rolled away from him to think. He was musically sophisticated; she was gargantuanly ignorant. The wind ruffled the branches of the sugar maple above the music for a moment.

"Beethoven?"

Nestor roared. "You idiot! You idiot! This could *never* be Beethoven. Beethoven is the last person it could be! Beethoven is the transition from classical to romantic and this, this, is the highpoint of baroque. Listen, stupid! See, it's Bach!"

He coughed a little to himself, amused.

Sarah made a coy small noise of self-deprecation and murmured that he would have to teach her about things like that.

"Sure I'll teach you," Nestor chuckled, and reached his hand down to poke her stomach.

The cowboy showed up suddenly one day, full of enthusiasm for the golden California coast, the silvery air over San Francisco, and the fun of heading a *New York Times* bureau. He held court for a bit in the *Crimson* newsroom among the younger fellows whose names he'd never learned; and when he'd had enough of that, he closed himself up in the president's office and telephoned Sarah.

"ABC here," he said briskly into the receiver, when she answered.

"Al!" she exclaimed. "Where are you?"

"Wa-a-al, some have been known to call this spot the center of the universe," he drawled happily, "but as for myself, I'd prefer a nice horsetrail on the shady side of the Rockies any day. But seriously—I'm fresh in from the Golden Gate because I heard you were in some trouble."

Sarah was astonished. She didn't for a minute believe that the cowboy had flown East expressly to see her. But such a melodramatic notion was in keeping with the relationship of high chivalry they had always enjoyed.

"Who—? Uh, how did you—?" she began.

"Well, it's not overly difficult for a crack investigative newshound to keep tabs on a little girl whose picture has been appearing on wire service dispatches coast to coast! . . ."

"Oh, you mean the Class Marshal thing?"

The cowboy cleared his throat ostentatiously. "Let's just say that I have several reliable independent sources of information on certain events the AP and the UPI have not yet seen fit to print."

Sarah could not help but be excited. How delightful it would be to see and talk to the cowboy again. He occupied such a special place in her life—not parental, not casual, not complicated by the carnal. He was chaste and admiring, a protector, a knight.

They made a date to meet that evening at the Casa B. The choice of the place was hers. Coulter would have preferred Cronin's or Fresh Pond.

When Sarah walked into the bar, dark and mostly empty at 6:00 P.M., the cowboy was installed at a corner table, stiffly smoking a cigarette and drinking a beer. A certain mechanical awkwardness spoiled his movements as he pretended not to notice her, then pretended to catch sight of her, and then underwent an involuntary tightening of a vein in his forehead as Sarah breezily sloughed off her jacket. As always, she felt wonderfully powerful in his presence. But for the first time her sense of power was mixed with something ominous.

The cowboy was seriously upset by what he had heard about Sarah and Nestor. He had lived through her refusal of his own love and her never fully explained selection of Michael Verhoeven—Coulter had thought Christopher Green the more "marriageable" of the two—with a depression that had edged on despair. But though that particular consummation had been itself illicit, a fall from grace, his own personal hell, he had at least liked and approved of Michael. And he had grown up among the furnishings of this generation. The campus marriage was to be tolerated. Sex might be enjoyed before the wedding ceremony by the trothed.

But this! This! This was an offense of a different order. He searched for the words with which to reach her now, desperately aware that if he failed, he could lose her forever.

"Al," she began peremptorily, looking into his face with compassion.

"Sarah Galbraeth!" he replied, nearly at a loss.

At this moment a waitress appeared insolently at Sarah's elbow. She was a slender and attractive young woman, dressed in a short skirt, T-shirt, and sandals, a "Cambridge hanger-on" who appeared from time to time in a Harvard play. To the cowboy she looked Continental and wanton.

He wished they had gone somewhere else. The fallen women and the con men and the brittle scraps of conversation that floated over from behind the bar made his own thoughts sound foolish to him. It was hard to keep a focus on one's identity in here. Sarah ordered a Scotch. The cowboy, pushing aside his empty beer glass, saw her that Scotch and raised her one.

"Sarah, Sarah," he said then. "You were my heroine." She blushed. "And now look what you're doing."

His directness caught her up short. So! He had no aesthetic appreciation for what she was going through. He disapproved. She felt disappointed. She waited for her drink and his double to arrive, and then swallowed half of hers in a gulp. "I know!" she replied, with equal histrionics. "It's crazy! I don't know what's making me do it! It's like an irresistible force—!"

"Bullshit on irresistible forces," said the cowboy. "It's not that mysterious. You've got to get hold of yourself. You're making a very, very bad mistake."

She sipped her drink and looked at him guardedly.

"Now I don't know what exactly happened between you and Nestor Schwarz. I don't know if you ran after him, or he ran after you . . ." •

Sarah wondered if he wanted her to tell him about that, but it seemed he didn't.

". . . But I know something about the kind of person he is."

Sarah sat back to listen. She could talk about Nestor forever. The jukebox had begun to play "Hang On Sloopy."

"Michael, and you, and I, and a few others I could name . . . Eddie O'Brien, say . . . are children of the Enlightenment. But Nestor Schwarz is something different. I don't know why, but he wants to take the thing we all value most, and make it his slave, and degrade it, and destroy it. I don't know why he wants to do that. I don't know what makes him the way he is. But that's what he wants. And if you're so all fired up to get yourself involved with him, you damn well better understand at least that much."

Sarah felt as though she were looking at the cowboy through the wrong end of a telescope: all parts perfect, but miniaturized. Far, far away. "The thing you value most? . . . You mean . . . me?" she said confusedly.

"Yes, you, goddamnit! You're not it, you're not the *whole thing!* But you'll do. You're handy."

Sarah couldn't quite grasp it. She took another sip of her Scotch.

"You and Nestor have nothing in common," the cowboy went on. "You want to be liked. You were the literary queen of Cambridge. You tried to become the political queen, but you failed. And in your disappointment over that fiasco, you're trying to become a sexual queen. It's the biggest mistake of your life!

"Nestor doesn't want to be liked. He wants the opposite. He wants to be feared. He wants to be a heavy, like Hodgson and Crichton and Weiss and the guys everyone always says are the 'all-time greats,' the geniuses. He'd never be good to you or take care of you. He thinks you're in the ring together. He speaks to the very worst part of you, to that part of you that doesn't feel pretty, that doesn't even feel like a good writer. And he attracts that, and cultivates that, and is himself attracted to that. . . ."

The cowboy trailed off, as if locked in eternal incomprehension of a man who didn't love what the cowboy considered the thing in the world most worth loving.

Sarah was stymied. She had always been impressed with the cowboy's ability to sum up a situation. But she was having a constitutional difficulty assimilating what he was trying to tell her now. Not only was he looking far away, and small, but he even sounded as if his voice were coming across a great distance, as if his urgent and sincere message could not be transmitted intact across some terrible media warp.

"Hang on, Sloopy, Sloopy, hang on," the music droned.

"So you think my getting together with Nestor had something to do with what happened in the Class Marshal election?"

"Well, isn't it obvious?" said the cowboy.

"Uh, I don't know," replied Sarah. "Maybe . . . I mean, it sounds . . . Uh, I'll have to think about it . . . No. No, it doesn't. The two things don't have anything to do with each other."

Coulter didn't like Sarah's tone any more than he liked what she was saying. She sounded so dazed and uncertain, as though she were drifting already into the never-never land inhabited by the waitresses in this place. This wasn't the little girl he knew.

"Don't you understand?" he said, with increasing urgency. "The bastards gave you some stupid shit in that Class Marshal deal, and you let them grind you down instead of spitting in their faces or at least shrugging them off like we always used to. And now you're reacting in the most childish way! It's perverse! There's nothing Nestor can do for you, or give you; he can only take away what—"

"Oh, Al!" Sarah interrupted, feeling forced to defend herself. She had the idea that this Nestor business involved something higher and more important than happiness and unhappiness or even sin and virtue in their usual sense, that what was sweeping her along was so much stronger than shame, or reason, or fear . . . that as she told the cowboy about it, and tried to explain it all to him, it was he who now felt the distance between them increasing; faster and faster, now, both of them were speeding away along a dimension the other could not share even though that other be the most trusted and dear old friend. But still she spoke, explaining, trying to use up the words in her brain.

"Sarah! Stop!" said the cowboy at last. "I know you've thought a lot about your feelings for Nestor Schwarz, whatever they are, and you have a lot to say about it. You have a very subtle brain. You can think rings around most people here. But you're an ethereal spirit, goddamnit, don't you see? That's what everybody loves so much about your writing. You've been levitating five feet above this absurd jacket-and-tie place for four years, sprinkling fairy dust down onto the bull-shit now and then, subsisting on rainbow juice. But don't you realize what will happen if you hand over title to—to Nestor Schwarz? Sarah! My God! He'll turn you inside out!"

Sarah was silent. They finished their whiskeys. From another table there was some desultory talk of hashish. Sarah's impenetrable vagueness had plunged the cowboy into a gloom he thought he would probably have to cross the continent to dispel. Long ago he had lost Sarah's heart. Now he saw that he had lost her soul as well. She was not about to be wakened from this dream.

"I don't know how I can explain it any better than that," he mumbled. "If you don't see it . . ." He paid for their drinks and they parted company outside the Casa B.

Nestor and Foote were planted like colossi at the top of the *Crimson* entrance stairway, engrossed in a lively conversation, telling private jokes.

Tui Burne-Jones made as if to ignore the two completely on her way in, looking for Chris Green.

"Have you heard about Thad's son Red?" said Nestor earnestly, stopping the girl with his hand.

"No," she said, feeling foolish. "What about him?"

A smile shot across Foote's face like a sunbeam penetrating a forest. "He's my son! Or I'm his dad!"

"Oh, you guys," said Tui fondly.

Zipping his violin carefully into its case, Billy hummed a snatch of the andante of Mendelssohn's *Octet*—to think: that Mendelssohn was only sixteen when he wrote this amazing, brilliant piece—and smiled smugly at Jims, who was stretched out on his bed eating dry corn flakes.

"Jims, you gigantic beatnik," chided Billy, "why don't you go out and get an ice cream?"

"Er, um, ah: I believe we've been through this before," was Jims's answer. He adored ice cream. He could have eaten a ton of it— he said. But he had his ancestors' solemn and terrible hatred of self-indulgence, in which category ice cream—indeed, all food—clearly fell. In consequence, he was very thin.

Billy chuckled a dry, crackly chuckle, a rebuking, threatening, loving chuckle, and went on putting away his music. Bach Society had been good. Things were going extraordinarily well with his new friend Yvette. Happiness was coursing through his blood from his chest to his liver and on to all the other major organs. Jims noticed the increase in his friend's happiness level.

"Besides tormenting me with thoughts of ice cream," he said, raising himself up angularly, "why are you so happy?"

Billy, unembarrassed, beamed another blissful smile in Jims's direction. "Cambridge is paradise," he answered. "Yvette Serre has offered her luscious, warm, feminine body to me."

This news was hard to resist. A smile cracked the surface of Jims's face like an ice floe. He was ready to put aside depression for his friend's sake. But there were still the ancient taboos. There were still niceties of logic and rhetoric to be summoned in defense of the body.

"Cambridge?" he repeated. "Do you really mean to say that

Cambridge is paradise? What about the Himalayas? What about Fiji? What about the claims of Lodi, New Jersey? And isn't every place exactly the same as every other place?"

Billy chuckled his dry chuckle once again. "Robbo's got the grant," he announced, "the Wilson."

"What?" exclaimed Jims, bounding through the door of Robin Palmer's bedroom.

"It's true," said Robin. "I confess."

Jims sat down on Robin's bed and looked glum. "Where are you going to go?"

"Tokyo."

"Hm," replied Jims. "I wonder if Tokyo will be exactly like Cambridge."

"Undoubtedly," said Robin, with a cherubic smile. A thick volume of winter-spring haiku lay open on the desk in front of him. He was the key to this threesome. Robin Palmer had some things in common with Jim DeWitt, and other things in common with Billy Clemens, and the other two might never have come together on their own. But unlike as they were, they accepted each other for Robin's sake, as if to say, "Ariel would never invite a fool to his dinner parties."

The golden-haired boy seemed to be turning back to the book of Japanese poetry.

"Uh, I'm going out," announced Jims, suddenly all restlessness. He reached for the wolverine parka.

"Good night!" "Night!" called Billy and Robbo.

"Perverse Jims," thought Jims to himself as he bounded down the entry steps. "Can't stick around to share in the good fortune of his pals."

Jims emerged into the green space between Kirkland, Eliot, and Winthrop, now patchy with snow, and stopped for a moment to consider where to go. Swimming in the IAB? Clots of boys were coming and going in the streets, ear tabs down, zipped up, scarves flying. Jims zipped up his parka and tried to determine where he belonged. A decadent movie at the decadent Brattle?

Without deciding, he let himself gravitate up the incline toward the Square. His way was blocked by a heavy-set man in an untidy overcoat, galoshes, and thick glasses, carrying an umbrella, who had tapped a student on the shoulder and was saying something intently to him in what sounded to Jims like gibberish. Jims skirted the fellow and quickened his pace.

Should he drop in at the *Crimson* at this hour? Nah, he wasn't a *Crimson* wonk.

The indecision of the moment irritated him. He didn't believe in pure being. He very much desired to be doing something. If he was doing nothing, there was nothing left of him, he was nothing. For tasks, for almost any sort of task—like rowing a shell—or rappelling down a cliff—or keeping the electrical wiring of the summer house in repair—he was adequate. But when things got quiet like this, and it was not at all clear what the nature of the test was, he grew uneasy, as if afraid some unconscious impulse might take the opportunity to explode out of him.

Coming into the dark and shiny nighttime Square, Jims moved toward the girders and cranes that dominated the southeast corner. No one was working there now, of course, and the gridlike hulk just loomed its eight stories starkly vertical and violently lateral: the mute skeleton of a future administrative center. Jims could see through the windows of the construction shed near the sidewalk. Inside, a man in a plaid shirt and overalls was sitting smoking the end of a cigarette, leaning over a copy of the *Evening Traveler*.

The tall Harvard senior paused and let himself be momentarily wafted to stillness by a dream of the normal. His father had been on page one of Foreign Affairs this issue. If only he, Jims, could be that man inside the workmen's shed, reading the papers, doing an honest job, safe from the clanging demands of history.

Then Jims noticed another pair of eyes looking in through a spectators' peephole in the masons' fence. Stepping around the corner to identify them, he hallooed enthusiastically. "Sarah!"

Sarah was wearing her broad-lapeled, red wool Anna Karenina coat, a bookbag slung over her shoulder. "Jims!" she answered, smiling. She was just coming back from thesis tutorial with Larry Wylie, she explained, when she had noticed this guy . . .

"What did you notice about him?"

"Oh, I don't know," said Sarah. "Maybe it's that he seems to exist in a different rhythm from Harvard Square. He looks so peaceful, and we're all so jumpy."

"That's right!" said Jims, genuinely pleased.

They had started walking together up Mass. Ave. Then Jims hung a sudden right, cutting purposefully in front of the traffic in the street, between a convertible and a station wagon, heading into the Yard.

"Where are we going?" said Sarah.

"To the piano in Mem Hall," Jims said.

"Oh, goody," said Sarah.

"It's for you."

David, the guy from across the hall, handed the phone to Nestor, who was napping. "It's *World.*"

Nestor eased himself out of bed and took the phone, closing his eyes as he spoke.

"Yello!" His socked foot felt around for his shoe. . . . "Um hmm, yes, that's right." . . . "Why, of course!" Now he opened his eyes and winked at David, who was still standing nearby.

"Friday the nineteenth. Yes. That's fine. Fine. Always a pleasure to be of help." . . . "Um hmm, bye."

He hung the phone up with a ping. David was looking at him with undisguised curiosity, eyebrows raised and an arch half-smile on his face.

"*World* magazine wants to do a big story on pot parties at Harvard . . ." said Nestor happily, "and we are *it!*"

Jims sat down on the red piano bench and with casual elbows played the opening chords of "As Time Goes By." The notes echoed through the enormous empty hall. All along the walls metal folding chairs had been stacked up in banks of ten or twelve.

"Hey, that was terrific!" Sarah said when he stopped in the middle. They were alone in a big barnlike space, a space sometimes filled with a thousand registering freshmen, and Sarah couldn't keep from staring at Jims, so tall and cool and fair he was, and detached as a prince. He seemed to be embarrassed by how good he was at playing the piano. He stood up as if to undo it, and smiled. Then he played something else, standing, that she didn't recognize.

"You don't know 'When Sunny Gets Blue'?" Sarah shook her head. So he taught it to her.

> When Sunny gets blue
> Her eyes get gray and cloudy,
> Then the rain begins to fall.
> Pitter patter, pitter patter,
> Love is gone so what can matter?
> No sweet lover man comes to call.

> When Sunny gets blue,
> She breathes a sigh of sadness,
> Like the wind that stirs the trees.
> Wind that sets the leaves to swayin';
> Like some violins are playin'
> Weird and haunting melodies.

And then the bridge:

> People used to love
> To hear her laugh,
> See her smile,
> That's how she got her name.
> Since that sad affair,
> She's lost her smile,
> Changed her style,
> Somehow she's not the same.

And finally:

> But mem'ries will fade,
> And pretty dreams will rise up
> Where her other dreams fell through;
> Hurry, new love, hurry here,
> To kiss away each lonely tear,
> And hold her near,
> WHEN SUNNY GETS BLUE.

Sarah had pulled a folding chair over next to the piano and was singing Jims's song with him. He looked so happy to be singing, lost for the moment on someone else's schedule. He taught her the Hi-Lo's tenor part for "There's No One But You" and "I'll Get Tired of You (When Birds Get Tired of Singing)." Sarah had never heard these songs, and hadn't the faintest idea of who the Hi-Lo's were, but she could picture Jims and his friends in black and white tuxedos and dress shirts and top hats singing them.

Suddenly he grinned. "I'll bet you know this one." Leaning back on the bench and rolling his spine a millimeter, Jims played a fanfare in B flat, then a stately and familiar chord progression. It was a rock 'n' roll tune from the fifties: "One Summer Night."

"Come on, you know it!" said Jims. He prodded her to sing the lead, and Sarah did so uncertainly, faking the words, but with real pleasure. He gave her a quick look as if he were measuring her against youth culture and reality outside of Harvard and approving.

"Good! Fabulous!" He seemed to be quite himself now, relaxed and at home, his wolverine parka and her red Anna Karenina coat thrown over a nearby stack of folding chairs. And they stayed there and kept singing, riding the freight trains of their minds across the melting pot continent ("500 Miles"), songs that Jims knew from his childhood and youth, from chorales and from records (Wes Montgomery's "I've got a baby on the East coast, gig goin' on the West coast, suitcase full of sorrow . . ."), until at last Sarah shyly suggested one of her own favorites, "Summertime," and they sang that with enormous gusto, Sarah crooning the old-new spiritual for all she was worth, Jims dropping the piano keys to accompany her with a whistle hidden behind his hands like a harmonica. . . .

When they were sung out, Jims picked up his parka with a shrug of regret and they walked back outside into the cold, dark, starry night. They leaned up against the western wall of Memorial Hall and looked at the sky.

"Oh, golden Harvard!" Sarah thought. Even in the dark of the night she could feel the aura of the golden men, the young senators, playing touch football on the wedge of grass between Mem Hall and the Common, could see the men and their girls, the girls in red and blue and green. "And Jims . . ." she thought. A thin scarf of cloud drifted across the moon.

"Do you want to go get a yogurt or something?" he asked.

"No," she said. Food was the last thing on her mind. Then without warning she blurted out: "You love me, Jims! Don't you?" She couldn't tell the precise tint of his skin in the moonlight, but she could see there was no change in his posture. Was it possible he was having no reaction to what she'd said?

Then Jims leaned forward and kissed Sarah on the lips, cool as an ice cream cone.

"Oh!" she gasped, quite unprepared for *that*. "That changes everything!"

"No, everything is exactly the same," said the tall boy, now only a yard away from her in the night. Far across the Common they could see a few lights twinkling from the Congregational and Unitarian churches, some beadle or curate working late. And closer by, more lights twinkled in the freshman dorms: sweet freshmen, lively collaborators, testing themselves and scheming and competing, even in the darkness.

"I love your energy and your creativity, Sarah," he said. "I envy them."

Her heart leapt.

"But you know, I could never marry you. I have to marry a woman of my . . . circle. Someone who will know how to entertain the way my friends must be entertained. Someone my parents will approve of."

Sarah didn't know if she had been flash-frozen or tossed against a wall or both. She couldn't find her voice on the wind. But then a spark of wrath sprang up to warm her.

"You prig!!!" she shouted. "You patrician!! You bloodless upper-class bastard! I don't know what I ever saw in you!!!"

She coughed.

"No, I do know!" she continued. "You're pretty. You're so goddamned pretty. Your ancestors looked out over their fields and saw my ancestors there, and thought that perhaps sheep meadows would be more attractive than us and our little houses—and so you—they—just kicked us the hell out!"

Jims was speechless with horror. He tried to think of something to say to calm her down, to make her stop.

"But, um, ah—" he interjected, but it was useless.

"You *lairds*!!!" she wailed. "With your long, silky, blond hair from eating all that good mutton all your lives—!"

Jims gasped. But he couldn't help but laugh at that. He took the step that closed the space between them and put his arm around her shoulders.

"Let's go for that yogurt now," he said. "Okay?"

"You can't be in love with three men at once," said Rosa Doe. "It's greedy."

"There should be limits on jealousy, not on love!" declaimed Sarah, paraphrasing Bertrand Russell.

Rosa put down her mug of tea and gave her old friend a dispassionate look. "You've gotten spoiled by being the only girl on the *Crimson*."

"I'm *not* the only girl on the *Crimson*," replied Sarah petulantly. "You know that! . . ."

"Well, you're the only one who's a star," said Rosa.

Sarah, in wicked delight, couldn't think of anything to reply to that. Yes, she was a star. She couldn't imagine herself any other way. She felt absolutely, cell-tinglingly content; like the angel on the top of the Christmas tree; as though some Benign Power had dosed her soul with potency and kissed her in her sleep with the dream of invulnerability. Loneliness was no problem: she could always confide in her diary. And what did she need girl friends for anyway, when she was living at the very capstone of the men's world?

To be sure things went smoothly, *World* magazine supplied Nestor Schwarz with money to buy four ounces of the choicest marijuana. Nestor invited Sarah to be in on the fun, and after just a moment's hesitation, she agreed. So Nestor gathered the Snake, and David from across the hall, and Tui one afternoon in March for The Famous Harvard Pot Party. Sarah came running in late from a seminar.

Nestor was in his element, grinning and laughing and standing at the fireplace and striding about the room. He waved the bag of *World* grass with a flourish, and then lit one of the skinny, pinched cigarettes he had rolled, inhaling it tenderly for a long moment as if he were kissing it. When the smoke was fastened behind his smile, he handed the joint to Sarah. She had taken a place on one of the two couches in Nestor's living room, beside one of the boys she didn't know and Tui. Charlie Schulte, who was now working for *World* in New York but had come back up to Cambridge to do this story, stood unsmilingly by the windows with Cadwalader the photographer.

Sarah was nervous. Drugs were a dark continent where Nestor presided. Since she had only very recently begun to smoke even regular cigarettes, she expected to choke on the dope and cough it out.

She inhaled. Coughed it out. Fear of not getting high chilled her like fear of sexual unfulfillment.

"Take another toke," said Nestor. "Don't waste it."

"Am I doing it wrong?"

"Let's see."

Sarah inhaled again, concentrating on filling up her lungs and holding the smoke there. This time the smoke remained inside, and Nestor nodded approval. David and The Snake and Tui puffed in turn. Sarah motioned that Schulte and Cadwalader should have some, but the two of them brushed off her suggestion irritably. The marijuana came back to Sarah once, and then again.

On the third puff, Sarah felt the smoke mysteriously coming alive inside her body, flowing up to her brain to dissolve some flimsy membrane there. She pictured the top of her head gently popping off, like a cartoon character's hat, with little puffs of smoke or cloud beneath to show the movement. She giggled. Nestor laughed back at her. "This must be *it*," she thought, as her internal orientation shifted abruptly from the "ABC Network News" to a softer and more ambiguous FM or possibly educational station. Her underclothes suddenly seemed terribly confining. She fidgeted.

Schulte indicated to Cadwalader that he should take some pictures. For some reason, the suggestion infuriated Sarah, and she adamantly refused to let her picture be taken. Looking around the room, it seemed to her that the dope-smokers all had pleasant and relaxed expressions on their faces, while Schulte and Cadwalader looked decidedly grim. Her fear and anger for herself fused into a hatred of the two of them, for some crime of exploitation or hypocrisy they were committing. "Fascist bastards!" she snarled.

Schulte pretended not to understand, hardly to notice, perhaps to take such an out-of-the-ordinary remark for granted in this setting. He settled even more deeply into his posture of grimness. Sarah began to see him as ridiculous and pathetic.

Nestor had made a joke at Tui's expense; so Tui attacked Sarah. "She's supposed to be the big feminist," the girl was saying, "but she calls Nestor up ten times a day. . . ."

Nestor snuggled up to Sarah, balancing on the arm of the sofa. But he seemed terribly cold. "You've given me so much," he said in a syrupy voice. "Do you have anything else to give me?"

"I'm a good listener," replied Sarah brightly.

"Don't you understand?" said Nestor, standing up again, "I asked that question hostilely."

Sarah did not in fact understand much of what was going on. She had not yet got a grasp of her situation, this new circumstance of dope. All she could tell so far was that it was something different, it was strange.

Then the mood in the room suddenly changed. For a moment everyone (except for Schulte and Cadwalader, of course) seemed terribly happy and carefree, laughing boisterously or even hysterically at something David had said, something Nestor had taken him up on. Sarah was absorbed in watching Nestor. He had bent over to laugh in a funny, tender way she had never seen before, almost like a little old man, and was laughing so beautifully, so childishly, almost tearfully. He seemed to overflow with affection for everyone, even Schulte, whom he was defending against Sarah's attack.

"What's so funny, Sarah?" said Nestor all at once. "Tell us what the joke is."

Sarah faltered. "Schulte's so serious," she ventured.

"No! No! We were talking about what David said, about where things come from. . . Tell her, David . . ."

"No, I said, 'Where did *he* come from?' " said the other boy. The laughter petered out.

Then Nestor declared that he had been laughing at a joke "on a higher level of abstraction" than everyone else. Their joke was not, in fact, risible. This realization or decision evoked a wave of sadness in great-souled Nestor, and manifested itself in everyone else (except for Schulte and Cadwalader, of course) as a signal of ominous personal defeat.

Sarah suddenly had the thought that her mind was erasing, that she was a nothing, a void.

Nestor saw the streak of worry flashing across Sarah's exposed and vulnerable brain. He came over and sat down again on the arm of her sofa. His hand brushing hers as he handed across the miniscule butt end of the cigarette startled her with the intensity of its thereness; it was like a distilled essence of him, invested with more personality than one expects in a hand. She groped for the layer of words that would cushion and protect her, but it and they were gone. And with them had gone the sweet barrier of reason. Her personality lay bare to the pressure of incoming sensation. She felt nothing but a great lust for Nestor, a great, thwarted lust.

"You don't love me anymore, do you?" he teased.

In moments like this, all of Sarah's resources mobilized in the attempt to figure out what Nestor meant, what he was feeling. He was capable of saying in a single breath: "I love you. No, I hate you. No, I love you," and Sarah invariably willed herself to make sense of this ambiguity. In throwing away the dream of the happy marriage with the good citizen, Sarah had also sacrificed Michael's moral and emotional clarity, the security of being loved. She had put all of that behind her. Nestor was to be her mode of enlightenment.

"Is your head spinning?" he asked wickedly.

"Yes, how do you like it?" asked a somber Schulte from the window.

Nestor and his friends often smoked marijuana. But they never discussed their reactions, outside of an occasional comment on dosage or the power of the drug. Usually they listened to classical music and laughed. Nestor looked at Sarah now to see what she would say.

She said nothing. Later there would be time for rationalizations, for dope wisdom, for statements about sacred space and additional dimensions. For now all that was happening inside of her was the most tremendous urge to fornicate with Nestor. The drug had made her think him more beautiful and desirable than ever, an artist, an immortal. She began hesitantly to say something of this, but Nestor anticipated the rest and cut her off. No such stuff was going to transpire at *his* pot party.

"Come on," he announced imperatively, "it's time for dinner." He pulled away from Sarah and strode toward the door without looking back.

Sarah grabbed her coat and followed, and the others came after.

"Hey—wait!" called Schulte, hard on their heels.

In the street outside, Sarah had the strangest impulse—one she'd never had before—to run in front of a car. A primitive might have said she was trying to scare the devil out from inside of her.

Once in the Conant House dining hall Sarah felt paralyzed and terrified. She went though the dinner line with Nestor and The Snake and the rest, and only when they had gotten their food and were looking for a place to sit did she catch sight of Michael sitting alone. He turned pale at the sight of her.

Then Sarah realized what a terrible idea it had been to come out in public under the influence of the drug. She was not proud of herself; neither was she discreet. Caught in the middle, she felt destroyed, demolished. Nestor and his friends sat down by Michael, but Michael would not meet Sarah's eyes all through the meal. She grew angry, bolted her food, and left. As she fled the dining hall alone,

Nestor was telling the punchline of a joke: "I come to seize your berry, not to praise it!"

By the time she got back to Stanton House Sarah was seriously depressed. Sitting down with her little typewriter, she banged out a list of twenty reasons for hating herself. She felt the pot party had been a failure because it had not led to sex with Nestor.

Nestor felt that having sex with Sarah had been a success because it had led to their taking dope together.

Sarah loved all the smells backstage: greasepaint, sweat, a hundred perfumes, the musk of exhibition. She peered into the cracked dressing room mirror and awkwardly painted on her mascara. She smoothed her dress, and felt a great, happy eagerness to be on stage again, to be dancing in front of people in the darkness. She had the nonspeaking part of a gypsy dancer in a Strindberg play in which Nestor was starring.

Ready, she rose, stood in the wings, waited for the cue, hearing nothing of the dialogue. Onstage Nestor, in the dress of an old man, was declaiming brilliantly. She watched him: maternal, proud. Then he exited quickly, past her. The dancers' music began. She and the other five gypsies plunged from the darkness into the glare of the white lights, to run and leap and hold each other's hands in the focus point of the invisible eyes. Was that Michael in the audience, in the last row? No, it couldn't be. The music played.

When the curtain came down, Sarah sought Nestor out in the warm, exciting tumult. She felt so pretty in her costume, her face flushed and radiant, her hair wild, but Nestor hardly seemed to notice her. He was busy in some kind of discussion about drugs with another one of the dancers. When that was done, he turned to Sarah with an ardent look.

"Come on," he said, with a roughness she adored, "don't bother to change. Let's drop in on your friends at the *Crimson.*" A chill ran up Sarah's back at the thought of walking all the way through Harvard

Square, from the theater to the newspaper office, across the Gold Coast, in this dress of a hussy and a vagrant, behind this painted face. Dared she show herself to the old gang purple-eyed, bespangled, cascading golden-brassy metal at every point where the blood throbbed or the flesh became delicate, turned something archaic behind this long skirt?

She looked up at Nestor, childishly proud, fearfully uncertain of approval.

"Come on," he said. "You look fine. Let's go!" And they took off down the cobbled streets of Harvard Square, a terrible recklessness beating in their blood.

Charlie McSilver was dancing around the newsroom. First he would fling a wad of paper joyfully into the wastebasket, then he would dance over to fetch it out, and then he would toss it in again from further back. "Atta way, Charlie, baby! You'll kill 'em in the Garden! And another eighteen for *twen*-ty five!"

"If you want to teach, *don't* go to the ed school, just teach." A group from the editorial board were leaning against the ledge arguing about futures, flipping the pages of the Comment Books, bemoaning the stupidity of the latest batch of candidates. One fellow was methodically obliterating the comments of another fellow with a rubber stamp that read: "Ho Hum. Baby Editors Always Scribble."

"Hello? Anybody there?" Sarah's voice tumbled up the stairs. The heads in the newsroom couldn't help but turn toward the wide entrance hall and register greetings.

Sarah and Nestor strode in. He had just told her that, of course, journalism was immoral, and she was beaming at his wit.

"What, is it Halloween already?" inquired CFMcS.

"Oh, this old thing?" replied Sarah coolly.

"How's the man?" said Nestor, slapping Charlie McSilver enthusiastically on the back and indicating with a ferocious glare from beneath his black and white eyebrows that the couple's outlandish get-up and preposterous makeup were not open for discussion. Two or three of the shadow cabinet turned from the Comment Book ledge to give Nestor and Sarah a disapproving grimace, and then turned away again.

Sarah put a quarter in the Coke machine and acknowledged the hellos of a couple of news board candidates. She wondered if it were just her imagination, or if the *Crimson* had really cooled toward her since . . . When Michael had been managing editor and she executive editor and they lovers, their entrance had used to elicit a kind of general rejoicing. . . .

"Just bagged twenty out of twenty-seven and never in better voice," replied Charlie. "Care to challenge the champ on his home court?"

"Tempting," said Nestor. "But we are here on serious business. *The Return of Dracula* is on *right at this very moment!*"

"Good to hear!" cried Charlie enthusiastically, letting his wad drop to the unswept floor to take its place with the rest of the debris. The *Crimson* was cleaned to the bones every other Friday morning, too early for *Crimson* editors to be awake, but for a long fortnight the boys and girls let it fill up slowly with crud like a sinking rowboat.

Nestor and Charlie, climbing the stairs to the sanctum from which direction the voice of Bela Lugosi could already be heard, came face to face with Michael Verhoeven carrying one of the heavy office typewriters downstairs. Involuntarily, Nestor Schwarz paused a beat on the landing.

Charlie, oblivious, hailed the former managing editor in a friendly manner: "Verboten!"

Nestor searched Michael's face for forgiveness, but saw none. He willed himself to continue walking, but his eyes in their frame of greasepaint had become blacker and more shadowy.

Michael willed Nestor not to exist. He just blocked him out of his vision, him and the air around him for three feet on every side. Nothing that Nestor put out in any form was going to affect him in any way. Alone of the three he continued his progress without breaking stride, without saying a word, as if he had passed nothing on the stairs but air.

In the sanctum Nestor spread out on the sofa to enjoy the show, forgetting Michael. Above the strains of vampire movie music, an occasional exuberant comment from McSilver could be heard. "Between the motion and the act . . . falls The Shadow!" he yelled once. And later, "Eyes I dare not meet in dreams! . . ."

Downstairs, Michael's and Sarah's eyes had met in mute confusion, longing, uncertainty. Without a word she followed him into the ed chairman's office, where he closed the door. They sat together on the ed chairman's sofa, his arm around her shoulder, his other hand holding her hand tightly. He said, "I love you, Sarah. I still love you, you bitch." And tears came to his eyes, and she wiped them off, and put her head on his shoulder for a little while.

"It's no use your even talking to me about it," said Sarah to Chris Green in the Midget Restaurant. "I've broken the thread."

"No, no you haven't," the boy protested. "You've just frayed it a little."

"No, the beautiful dream is gone," declared Sarah sadly but definitively. She was eating canned fruit from a little metal sundae dish. Chris was drinking coffee and eating an English muffin. The Midget was the perfect place to be having this discussion. It was so drab, so unlike Harvard Square. The waitresses were lumpy and out of style. It threw their conversation into a lurid orangey light.

"You've got to go back to him—!" protested the boy, with a kind of helplessness. His dimpled cheeks were almost childlike.

"No, I've punctured the dream."

"What dream are you talking about?"

"Oh, you know. A little house in the suburbs. A white picket fence. A rosebush in the garden. Two or three children."

"How does Sarah Galbraeth fit into that picture?"

"I guess I'd have a teaching job. Writing on the side."

"Which side?"

Sarah laughed. Chris was sweet to be doing this, trying to get her to reverse the major direction of her life. But when he spoke to her of love and marriage she felt their communication clouded by an un-acknowledged attraction between the two of them.

"I just can't believe you," said Chris after a moment. "You and Michael are . . . were . . . such a good . . . couple."

"Oh, I almost forgot: a swing in the backyard."

Ｅast of the Georgian Harvard Houses a great concrete monolith had arisen, chock-a-block with married students, decorated by José Luis Sert—an architect very much in favor around Cambridge these days—with broad panels of primary colors.

In the small kitchen of their new apartment, Dan and Katy Matlaw were eating spaghetti and gossiping about Sarah and Nestor. Dan thought Sarah had chosen the actor because he was a few inches taller than Michael, "and this society places a lot of emphasis on height in a man."

His wife agreed. The two of them thought Sarah's interest in Nestor was understandable and an okay sort of adventure. Katy was pregnant.

"I just hope she gets out of it alive," she said.

Dan was going for a master's degree in economics now, a field that still made no sense to him. He was also writing for *Ramparts,* a little magazine in San Francisco that was evolving from Catholicism to radicalism. He would sit in his input/output classes preoccupied with the points that didn't fit into the official version of the events in Dallas:

1. The head had jerked forward and then back with a velocity too great for it to have been a nervous reaction.
2. A TV newsman on the scene had reported seeing a shot come from the knoll.
3. The description of the wound in Texas differed from the description in D.C.
4. The CIA's Hunt had met with Oswald previously.

5. The *Life* photo had shadows running at inconsistent angles.
6. Was there a renegade group within the Agency called The Secret Five?

Danny took some notes he had made and went to his desk.

"I'm going to call Carolee about that SNCC file," said his wife. The women were still on good terms.

Kievskaya had indeed changed her major from biology to soc rel as Weiss had anticipated, but she wasn't sure she was any happier. She sat in Talcott Parsons's "General Approach to a Theory of Action" and took notes listlessly. With rather more interest she took part in antiwar demonstrations in Cambridge and Boston to protest the president's continuing escalation. She had aligned herself with "the action faction" of SDS, otherwise known as "the praxis axis."

Finally one day Kievskaya reached her saturation point in a gov seminar. The white-haired professor had invited a former Harvard faculty member to come speak—a man now consulting in Washington—and that very revered academic was saying that it was best America "punish" the Vietnamese . . . "up to a point" . . . for their communism—while offering "economic rewards" for choosing our side. The think-tanker was sure the Vietnamese would "come around," because it was in their interest to do so "as rational men."

Breaking out of her daze, Kievskaya rose, dropped her notebook with a thud in the wastebasket near the door, and, silent before the startled eyes of the others, simply left the room forever. Outside in the air she felt much better.

"I have to talk to someone," she thought. "Who can I call?" From a phone booth in the chrome and glass corridor of Boylston, she dialed Harold Weiss.

"Oh, God! I can't stand it!" she said, hardly waiting for him to reply. *"Harvard* is making the war! These people think the Vietnamese are children! Johnson's got a quarter of a million soldiers over there who don't know what the hell they're fighting for!"

Weiss was delighted to hear from her. While not at all sympathetic to her walking out of class, nor even to her feelings about the war, he admired her spirit. He spoke to her reassuringly. They made a date to have Friday night dinner in the little out-of-the-way frame house on Divinity Avenue that belonged to the Hillel Society.

Sarah stood in front of the closet contemplatively. Behind her Nestor lay dozing. It had come true, just as she had thought: sex with him had indeed gotten better after they started smoking pot together. Though he hardly touched or kissed her at all, still the act of sex with Nestor electrified Sarah, before, during, and for a long while afterward. He observed her strong reaction, while minimizing his own. Especially in the presence of others, he pretended almost not to know her. It was as if she were a secret, guilty pleasure, to be hoarded in private and publicly denied.

She turned and glanced at him and, satisfied he wasn't watching, got a pair of boy's dungarees out of the closet and hurriedly pulled them on under her dress. Then she slithered out of her dress. Over her white lace bra she pulled a white T-shirt; the short sleeves hung nearly to her elbow and the round neck became a drooping décolleté. The blue jeans stood away from her hips and the legs folded over her ankles as she swashed across the room. Puppyish, she climbed onto the bed and started bouncing.

"Cut it out." He raised an arm to shield his face.

"Morning! Morning!" she cried, standing up full length and still jumping. The bed was shaking horribly. "Gotta get up! No work, no food!"

Nestor smiled one eye open at her. "Be a good girl and GET THE FUCK OFF THE BED! Okay?" he asked.

"You've slept too long already. Gotta get up. Gotta get up." She sat down with a bounce and tugged at him.

"What do you mean, morning? It's . . ." (he rolled over, catching a glimpse of his wrist on the roll) "only four o'clock. No time to be awake. Go away. Let me sleep."

"Yay! Four o'clock!" she cried. She leapt up and flung open the bedroom window to let in a startling rush of afternoon air. The room was serene and alive in the clear light, but Nestor only turned his muttering gradually down lower in a passable imitation of falling asleep.

"Yes, yes, now go away, let Nestor sleep. Nestor is so tired. So tired. So . . ."

Sarah tiptoed out of the room and waited there breathlessly a few moments. Then she returned with a glass of water. She dropped a few drops in his ear. "This is really fun," she thought.

"*No!*" Nestor cried, raising himself up and lunging at her. With a shriek she danced backward out of the room. In the doorway, her glass still half full, she stared at him and giggled.

He propped himself back down and stared at her, a funny tolerance twisting his mouth and one eyebrow. How silly, how lovably silly she was. Silly. The word that had filled the whole sunny school in the mountains with conspiratorial hilarity. The word the starchy English teacher had tried to use against them, which they had dissolved in her face like a gumdrop. "Oh, you're so *silly!*"

She looked at him, her frightened glee dying down now that her mission was unexpectedly accomplished. What to do now? But what a wonderful-looking thing he was, propped there unbalanced in all his clothes. The open shirt, wrinkled and twisted off center, the unlaced sneakers, his long dark hair grown wild and rural in untimely sleep.

Suddenly she saw something change in his eyes, some hidden panel slide open. He leaned back and relaxed a couple of obscure muscles and she saw that he was calling her. He lifted one arm in just the barest, most invisible code.

She began to walk toward him slowly. . . .

They attacked each other. Fought like Indians. They bounced and kicked the sheets. They stopped to rest a moment and then began again. Sarah felt air running through her, like she was climbing the monkey bars behind Cerro Gordo County Central School again, hanging upside down by her knees, swinging so high. Nestor pinched her and she bit him and then he smacked her behind so hard she yelled

"Ow stop I really mean it!" and then Nestor grabbed her and pulled her out of the bed and came inside her against the wall standing up.

"Upstanding citizens," Sarah giggled, as they stood there after, their bodies still connected.

"We screw too much," said Nestor, pulling out. "It's bad for our relationship."

"Well, it's a screwy relationship!" Sarah looked at Nestor in comical childish satisfaction and fearful uncertainty of approval.

They collapsed back on the bed perpendicularly across one another, echoing occasional remnants of laughter.

At that moment there came the proverbial knock on the door. In seconds the couple had uncoupled, jumped up, dressed, and roughly made the bed. It wasn't good form to be discovered *in flagrante* even if Tiny Lench's place *was* a famous lovenest.

"Anybody home?" Tui.

Nestor replied with a loud nonspecific noise. Sarah strolled into the next room. The other two made entrance, Tui to the kitchen with a gallon of melting chocolate ice cream, Chris to an armchair in front of a television balanced on another chair. Tired and oblivious, he snapped on the set. But Tui took a look at Sarah's and Nestor's faces, at Sarah's hand stealing up to investigate her long reddish-brown hair standing away from her head, and looked away again with a laugh.

"And how have you two been?" she chuckled suggestively.

The four collected in the living room around Chris's chair, where he was already deeply engrossed in the Bruins. Tui handed him a dish of ice cream. Sarah watched for a moment but found it impossible to get interested in the hockey game, and so she sat down in another corner and typed out a fair copy of a dream she had had the night before.

Alone! I am running alone on a dark highway. Nothing on either side except a small strip of grass and a warning to stay off it. Nowhere to go but straight forward. Lights whiz by me, traveling as fast backward as I am traveling forward. But I must go forward. What country are we in now? What road is this? Faster. I must get there faster. On either side of me looms the silent, deserted city. Before me a tunnel in the mountain. Behind me I don't remember. I am afraid to look back, for I will see that I have been running forever, that there is nothing behind me, that I have come from nothing.

The others ignored her until Nestor lit up and offered his pipe around. Sarah accepted it and smoked. She put her writing things away. She moved to the floor by Nestor's feet and looked at Tui's little TV again with unseeing eyes, watching the changing play of the colors, especially the reds.

"I've never been hurt," she whispered dreamily up to Nestor, thinking that this was an odd and interesting fact.

Nestor looked down at her with aggressive detachment. "Sarah says she's never been hurt," he reported to Tui. Tui smiled. Chris looked over from the Bruins game with the hint of a frown. Nestor handed him the smoldering pipe and he turned away again.

"And you think I'm the guy who can do it for you?" said the actor, with a satisfied, lascivious smile.

"I guess so," said Sarah softly. She supposed that something witty had been said. They watched the game. Nestor ate two dishes of Tui's ice cream.

Later that evening as the four were setting out to walk the few blocks back to their dorms for the night, Nestor made a detour to thank their host. Tiny Lench was perhaps best-known for hanging an oar over his mantlepiece with notches cut in it. These days he was going around with a girl from Wellesley he called "Slit." They encountered him outside a run-down frame house with a gnarly elm in its front yard. A motorcycle leaned against the tree. The big machine looked precarious and powerful, all bulbous black curves and leering yellow faceplate, lowslung like a Hells Angel's hog.

Nestor pushed Sarah toward it. "Tiny here is going to give you a ride on his bike," he said to her. "Won't that be fun?"

And turning toward the tall heavy boy in leather jacket and mirrored shades, he added sharply, "Scare the piss outa her, Tiny!"

As Harold Weiss held open the door to the small house on Divinity Avenue, Kievskaya was involved in a long explanation of why being Jewish did not mean that much to her. It was a set of rituals, she said, a group of old, bearded men reading the Torah. Of Jewish history she knew only some isolated anecdotes from her long-past Hebrew school days. She admitted feeling that Yiddish and the rest of the old world Jewish culture had not proved useful as survival skills. She thought that her grandparents must have themselves decided—on some level—to abandon their Jewishness when they were forced so precipitously to emigrate.

Weiss nodded at her warmly, deeply interested.

Inside, about thirty Harvard and Radcliffe students and their dates were already seated around two large tables in the center of a comfortable living room, talking to one another. Chopped liver in small scoops dotted the plates in front of them. A woman Weiss recognized as the rabbi's wife greeted him and Kievskaya, and they slipped into almost the last of the empty chairs.

Kievskaya looked around. Bookcases lined three sides of the room to eye level, packed with large, thick volumes, singly and in sets, and collections of periodicals. Copies of *Mosaic,* the *Divinity School Bulletin,* and the *Crimson* lay on top. On a small round table at the head of the room two white candles in silver candlesticks were flickering, and their light reflected in the faces and on the shirtfronts of the students. Kievskaya had grumbled when Weiss asked her if she would please wear a white blouse tonight, but now she was glad she had. All the young men and women were wearing white shirts and blouses, and the effect was pleasant.

The rabbi of Hillel House—"the Jewish chaplain of Harvard"— was considered a popular fellow and well liked, though his circle of faithful was small. By design of the admissions committee, Harvard was about one-fifth Jewish. But most Jewish students, like Nestor Schwarz, were secular or even anti-Jewish in their orientation, and comfortable enough in the prevailing social climate of Cambridge. When they asserted themselves, it was in organizations like the *Crimson* and Tocsin, where they made up as much as half the membership.

The rabbi was now engaged in conversation with the boys nearest him at the table. He waved to Weiss, who smiled and waved back. Then the rabbi's wife came from the kitchen with a large plate covered with a multicolored embroidered cloth. Turning the cloth back she set the plate down beside the candlesticks, revealing two thick, braided loaves of fresh bread. The ceremony of separation of the community was about to begin.

The rabbi stood up, two books in hand, and the students stood up unevenly after him. In the respectful silence, the rabbi read aloud from the writings of another rabbi, Abraham Joshua Heschel, who had studied under the rabbi of Kautska and then at the gymnasium in Berlin. "Why is there a Sabbath?" he read. "The Sabbath is because of the holiness of time rather than space. The Sabbath is because we need a taste of that which is eternal in our lives. The Sabbath is because of the love and the pain that are resolved into joy by the Friday night wine."

Kievskaya felt a curious prickling sensation. She had never liked the printed prayers in prayer books. But what the rabbi was saying now made very good sense. She glanced at Weiss. He looked calm and almost transported, the candlelight glowing softly in his intelligent eyes. In a sudden intuition, Kievskaya saw the glint of the small flames as a tiny hope in a darkened, nearly lost, world. Something in her relaxed. She listened as the rabbi read further from Heschel, and then closed that book and read some melodious incantatory Hebrew from the other book.

Then the rabbi lifted a large silver cup of wine, said a blessing over it, and drank, and the students likewise sipped from the small glasses at their places, and something relaxed minutely in the whole of the assemblage.

Then the rabbi's wife said a prayer in Hebrew and English and led the ceremony of the eating of the bread. The meal followed. Conversation resumed happily, as the celebrants of the Sabbath shared familiar tastes.

"The rabbis teach that a Jewish woman has no obligations in time," said Weiss to Kievskaya over the main dish, "except for three. The first two are the lighting of the candles on Friday night, and the baking and first tasting of the Sabbath bread. By contrast a Jewish man has many time-bound obligations, involving doing certain things each morning and each night, and certain other things at different times of the year."

Kievskaya was strangely pleased by this view of the difference between men and women. She understood in her body that the times of a woman's life are different from the times of a man's.

"What's the third?" she asked innocently, but Weiss colored.

"I'll tell you about that later," he said.

They ate. The sounds of the evening were soft: occasional low notes of traffic from the avenue coming in through white-curtained windows; here and there a voice raised in emphasis; the clinking of silverware.

When the meal was done the students and the rabbi retired to an adjoining room where folding chairs had been set in rows to face a decorated box, and they conducted a traditional conservative service. Kievskaya let her mind wander, but the old Eastern European melodies were agreeable to her. Afterward they pushed the chairs against the wall and joined hands and danced more than one slow, graceful, Arabian-style dance, and then one wild, fast, and exciting dance in a style all its own. Many knew the Hebrew words to this last, which were about the excitement of the revelation on Mount Sinai.

It is not an old story
It is not an old story
It is not a dream of the past
Here is the foot of Mount Sinai
Here is the foot of Mount Sinai
The burning bush burns still!

Finally there was tea, and political discussions, and a relaxed drowsiness, and a pervasive warmth.

Walking home, Kievskaya told Harold Weiss that she had enjoyed the dinner much more than she had thought she would. Weiss was greatly pleased. He believed as Albert Einstein had believed, that the never-ending wonder of science reveals increasingly and in more detail the glory of the Creator, and he had been devoutly observant all his life. He looked at the smiling Kievskaya, at the wonderfully matronly form of her in her fur-lined overcoat, and he thought that perhaps, yes, she would make a good wife and mother of his children. Would it be possible for her to learn the laws she would need to know in this role? Would she be willing? He pondered the question of when and how to ask.

Nestor stared into the Signet Club's unlit fireplace. He felt with a sharp ache his own awful talent for wasting love. He realized, though it didn't help any, that he loved Michael more than he loved Sarah. Michael was one of the most humorous, and best-humored, persons Nestor had ever known. He wanted terribly to keep his friendship, on virtually any terms Michael might suggest. He had written the other boy a note apologizing for what had become of their friendship; indicating that he had not known what was going to happen, or intended it; suggesting a rapprochement. But he wasn't sure the letter was good enough. The pain around his throat and lungs increased, and he pulled the adrenalin inhaler out of a pocket and tried to quiet the choking that was rising inside him.

From a slumped-over sitting position Nestor rose and went over to put Purcell on the Signet's record player. Then he dragged several logs from the woodbin over to the hearth and lit a fire. Wearily, he sat down again to watch the small, flickering flames and listen to the music.

> Come, come, ye Sons of Art,
> Come, come away!
> Come, come, ye Sons of Art,
> Come, come away!

As always, the happy ode recalled to him his prep school girl friend, who had liked to sing it. That had been a time! Once she had screamed at Nestor, veins standing out in her neck, "You're killing me!" What he had done was confuse her into thinking she might be pregnant, though their lovemaking had never been consummated.

To exorcise this horrible dream of cruelty and breakdowns (had he really been cruel to her? he couldn't remember; though that had certainly been the consensus at the time), Nestor now occupied his mind with the question of when, exactly, in terms of which cut on the record, the big log on top of the pile would burn through and come crashing to the fireplace floor.

> Strike the viol!
> Strike the viol!
> Touch touch touch
> Touch touch the lute.
> Wake the harp!
> Wake the harp!
> Wake the harp!
> Inspire the flute!
> Wake the harp!
> Inspire the flute!

Michael had written back:

> You stupid, babyish, homosexual bastard. Now you want more attention? You want me to say it's all right and I still love you? Well, you can forget about that.

The big log crashed to the ground at precisely the start of the "These are the sacred charms" bass solo, as Nestor had predicted.

At that moment, too, Michael came through the door of the Signet Club, walked over to Nestor in his crimson leather armchair, and punched him hard in the jaw.

In Georgia in the summer of 1965, SNCC staff member Julian Bond was elected to the state House of Representatives as a result of the Supreme Court's "one man—one vote" reapportionment decision. In Alabama, a legal loophole made possible the creation of the Lowndes County Freedom Organization—in an acutely poor black area, known for Klan violence—under the sign of the black panther. And from Atlanta, and later from Montgomery, *Crimson* editors and their colleagues on *The Southern Courier* reported on all the latest-breaking stories of the civil rights movement.

In Jackson, Mississippi, the state legislature was holding a special session to liberalize the state's voting requirements. SNCC leadership saw this as "a blatant attempt to take the edge off the arguments presented by the Mississippi Freedom Democratic Party in their legal challenge to the seating of the five racist congressmen and their demand for recognition." A demonstration was mounted.

Eight hundred people were arrested and imprisoned.

Among the arrested was Carolee Davis. In her jail cell, she met and spoke at length with a young woman from the Bay area. To her dismay, she learned that a friend of this woman's had recently married Carolee's old boyfriend from Stanford. Carolee ground her teeth and wrinkled her brow and resolved to work harder to create a world where she could live and be loved.

That summer too, on an isolated campsite in northern Michigan, SDS held its annual convention in an atmosphere quite unlike the group's four previous conventions. Nearly all the participants were wearing denim outfits and boots. Many of the men sported droopy Pancho Villa mustaches. Marijuana was smoked for the first time.

Kievskaya, one of the Harvard delegates, didn't like the feel of things. A loud "new breed" from the West and South was highly suspicious of the current leadership, and arguing forcefully for "decentralization." What this meant in practice, as far as Kievskaya could see, was that general meetings were badly chaired, by persons chosen at random, and without regard to parliamentary procedures. Statements previously submitted for consideration were scrapped. No plans were made for the future. No national officers were elected. Hungry for justice-or-destruction, the group could agree on only one thing: to liberalize their membership requirements.

Something in Kievskaya snapped. The new left was not for her after all. She would tell Harold Weiss yes.

The summer after that, Charles Whitman took a rifle and some personal effects and climbed a tower at the University of Texas and murdered a large number of people at random. Charlie Schulte was an ace cub reporter for *World* magazine at this time, and so his editor put him on a plane for Texas with instructions to get hold of mug shots of all the Texas tower victims, so the picture magazine could run them en masse for a macabre yearbook effect. Schulte agreed.

But it turned out that one of the families of one of the victims was not willing to go along. They didn't think their daughter should be treated that way.

Schulte phoned the problem back to New York. "Not good enough," the editor barked. "We need them all. Else we can't do the story."

So Schulte turned back to the task. He had no temperamental aversion to it. He was of the kick-the-door-down school of journalism. He believed that when people were reluctant to speak it was usually because they had something to hide. At last he told the parents of the murdered girl that *World* magazine had in their possession a photo of her bloody corpse, and that they would print that, if the family didn't supply them with the head-and-shoulders photo requested.

The murdered girl's father agreed to meet Schulte in the hallway of a local high school, to exchange photos.

The rendezvous took place. As soon as Schulte had the photo of the girl he needed in his hands, he admitted to her father that he had been bluffing.

The bereaved man took a step backward and looked the young reporter full in the face, taking in the arrogance the boy had polished to perfection at Harvard.

"You scum!" he swore. And he turned away to weep.

Schulte felt the curse ripple through his entire body. His career flashed before his eyes, and the chief features of that "journalism" that he had placed before everything.

Soon after, Charlie Schulte quit the *World* staff. He made a good marriage with a cultured and attractive woman, and found himself a job he could stomach, buying movies from the BBC to be shown on American educational television.

By 1967, the country was in a serious state of flux. In San Francisco a colony of LSD veterans under the spell of Buster Thatcher were claiming to have created a New Jerusalem. Reporters were dispatched from the East Coast in early spring to interpret this chaotic euphoria back to the national establishment; among these was Michael Verhoeven, on assignment from two quality journals. By summer "the scene" was being elaborately orchestrated by Thatcher and his people; the "hippies" had been labeled and defined by the media (though few reporters were as perceptive as Michael and the earliest observers); and the mob had begun to move full scale into the market with "speed" and other drugs.

Sarah and Nestor spent the "Summer of Love" in New York City. They were full of theoretical enthusiasm for the changes that were sweeping the country, and believed themselves to be mixing in the exciting cultural and social life of New York. And yet their sphere of action was curiously limited, and they projected a barrier around themselves, a smokescreen thrown up by the drugs they were using now more and more frequently. Nestor was picking up a little money acting, and Sarah was occasionally writing articles, and there were still some funds saved from college allowances, and smaller bits that could be begged and borrowed from brothers and uncles—though these connections were suffering badly from Nestor's determined rudeness.

Sarah told herself that she had entered a new, "disengaged" phase of her life. She wondered if she would ever love in the old way again, believe in morality again, in other people, in God. Nothing was certain to her now, not one thing. She lived from moment to moment, listening only to her own impulses, attending seriously only to Nestor Schwarz.

Many evenings they sat at home together in a beautifully elegant sublet apartment in the Village, and Sarah imagined that her red velvet plush armchair was a bower in a rain forest. High grasses seemed to wave and grow by her side. The high ceiling hung low and viney overhead. Eyes closed, she inhaled the gentle scent of a vast unbroken waterfall roaring through a break in imaginary trees.

Nearby, Nestor would be smoking Tibetan hash in an ivory pipe, listening to a tape of Jackie DeShannon singing "What the World Needs Now Is Love."

When the tape ended, Sarah would blink her eyes open. Abruptly, she remembered the world of people her body had almost succeeded in abandoning. The Harvard urbs. Ego problems. Nestor. So she was only one station stop out of the central terminal after all.

"Do you think 'higher' is necessarily better?" she asked, wishing Nestor would relax and join her in the tropics.

The question irritated him. Of course higher was better, by definition. Some magic in the weed was capable of scratching a psychic itch. Laughter and self-love awaited on one chemical plateau, and a heady, divine oblivion beyond that. Nestor could not restrain himself from wanting always to be "higher."

"What do you think?" he answered.

"I think there are stages of being only slightly 'high' that you shouldn't waste," Sarah said. A nagging voice inside of her had never stopped denouncing drugs. It pained her that Nestor wanted always to be "higher." She didn't know what he meant when he called for "deliverance," for "relief." And yet, if one were going to sin, surely Nestor's was the correct way to do it. She smoked to be nearer him. And for his sake, and in a moderate way, she defended drugs.

She expected Nestor to understand this difference between them, but the truth was, he didn't see himself as an existential hero. "I am not an insane beatnik, Sarah, my pet." He smoked the damn marijuana with passionate intensity, and considered it part of the disorder of his life. But he would brook no pronouncements on the subject from Sarah. It was not *her* administration.

"Sarah the big dope expert," he grumbled now.

She shifted in her chair.

"Come on, you know I'm terrifically jealous of you for all the drugs you've taken."

"Yes, I know," said Nestor, trying to smile. Her refusal to take offense reassured him. At first he had not wanted to hurt her—and that was a good feeling. But in time that stage had passed—"all things fly apart"—and these days Nestor considered that the two of them were still together because Sarah was strong and healthy enough to take his shit.

"Put on Dylan," said Sarah.

"No," said Nestor. "I don't think you have a healthy attitude toward him. You carried on all night about how witty it was that he said 'ho' when some schmuck said 'hi' to him." He put the record he was holding down onto the turntable and dropped the finely engineered tone arm down onto the outer groove with solicitude. Red, yellow, green, blue, and violet circus sounds exploded like toys into Sarah's rainforest.

It was twenty years ago today! . . .

"It *was* witty."

"*I* can write as good as Dylan. You could maybe write as good as Dylan. He's not such a great poet."

"Are you kidding?"

"Do you love him more than you love me?"

The Beatles continued to pour out their delighted enchantment, their permanently happy, brilliant, talented unity in the cause of universal pleasure. Their radiant faces and fairy-tale costumes beamed from the cardboard record sleeve at the two stoned lovers.

"Uh, I love Dylan more," said Sarah.

"Sergeant Pepper's Lonely Hearts Club Band" made its heart-breaking musical transition to "A Little Help from My Friends." Nestor had pointed out to Sarah how some verses in this song were a reference to the new sound coming out of San Francisco.

Sarah got out of her armchair and went and sat down on the Oriental rug at Nestor's feet and hugged his knees. She knew it would look silly to anybody else, but it was just how she felt about him . . . and he liked it, too. He smiled down at her, gracious as a prince.

"I'm better looking than he is," said Nestor.

"Yes, you are," said Sarah. Under the influence of the drugs both Nestor and Sarah had grown ethereally slim. The long dark hair that now framed Nestor's face gave him the look of a pensive John Lennon.

"How much better?"

Sarah loved it when Nestor showed her his most intimate needs, cloaked in a vulnerable, childish hesitancy. They were alone together now in a very real way. Christopher Green had tried to convince her to break up with Nestor and go back to Michael before they had left Harvard, but he had finally given up, and had himself married Tui, for no reason Sarah could understand; and Tui having decided that she wanted nothing more to do with Mr. Schwarz, the two couples had not remained close. Many of their old *Crimson* friends, indeed, had now turned against Sarah and Nestor for Michael's sake, or concluded that she was being so foolish there was no hope for her. There were in fact no friends at all to back them up, no family to wish them well (how Sarah's parents hated what they knew of this boy!), no society outside the two of them any more at all. Honing this aloneness to a fine point, Sarah had become reckless with the feelings of everyone in the world besides Nestor. When old pals infrequently came around and told her they were "a bad couple," or that he was not treating her well, or that she was "affecting cynicism," she waved them away.

She enjoyed this preposterous question, about "how much better looking" he was than Bob Dylan. To think about Dylan and Nestor in the same breath made her dizzy with theology.

"Um . . . it's not exactly clear . . ." she replied.

"Well, Dylan works harder than I do, that's clear," said Nestor. "If I could only make myself—" he broke off in midthought. Speaking about not working was painful. They listened to the music.

She's leaving home,

the Beatles sang.

Bye bye.

"You have a better education than he does," Sarah said softly. "You're a cultured fellow . . ."

"Goddamnit! That's the trouble! All my diddly-shit education! I've had input up the giggy, but I still have nothing to show for it! I feel like—like I'm hanging over the edge of a cliff, all wrapped up in a Saran Wrap baggie! . . . And I'm twenty-three!!!"

"You'll be as great as Dylan. You're as smart as he is," said Sarah soothingly.

"I don't want to talk about him anymore."

Sarah was still. She knew that Nestor took this matter of accomplishments, of work, in deadly earnest, more seriously than he took anything else. "When my wife is dying of tuberculosis, my children begging in the streets, my house being repossessed, I will be emoting like Lear, thinking of nothing—do you hear me? nothing!—but my chest-cavity resonance!" This was Nestor's proud boast. And it was Sarah's job to support him in this.

Now she reassured both of them by reciting some of the best compliments others had paid him, potent compliments to his looks, his talent, his intelligence. She reminded him of all the love Tui (now married to Chris) and Rosa (now close to receiving her Ph.D.) and Yvette (now blissfully happy with Billy Clemens) had had for him, feeding the hearts of her former friends to him like a citizen of old Tyre trying to appease Moloch.

Nestor listened, gratified. He leaned back in his velvet chair and closed his praised eyes. He had some good compliments for Sarah, too, that he unspooled cautiously when it was clear she had finished with hers. He said she had a "fabulous sensibility." He told her a dream he had had of her flying to Hanoi with Hayden and Lind and Aptheker because she was always so much in the center of things. She was not just in the center of things, she was "in the absolute *nuclear* center of things!"

"Oh, Nestor," Sarah sighed. "Do you realize how happy it makes me when you say things like that? . . ."

"Yeah, I realize. I'm just wondering who the terrific guy will be that you'll fall in love with after me—"

Sarah gave Nestor a hurt look, and rose and walked away idly toward the record player.

"Come on! Sit back down! I'm only kidding! Usually you would just laugh at that kind of stuff."

Sarah looked at Nestor shyly, and came back to him, and they smoked some of the hash together. Then Nestor switched out the lamp, and put a *Ravi Shankar in New York* evening raga on the stereo, and they went into the curtained bedroom, their bodies touching, and relaxed together once again in the copulatory mysticism of the East.

When she woke very late the next morning, the drone of Nestor's habitual WNEW-FM in her ears, a dim haze of rain visible beyond the heavy curtains, the room disorderly with the excesses of the night before, Sarah's first feeling or thought was of apocalypse. Apocalypse and disaster. Epiphany.

It was an aura that emanated from the exploding brain of Nestor Schwarz, even as he lay there beside her still asleep.

She looked at him with a long, immaculate fondness. She felt the suspenseful promise of his talent just as he did, a rope precariously hanging from Everest. His deep understanding of the horrors of fate made life with him seem worthwile.

She tiptoed out of bed. Perhaps she would attempt an onion omelet.

Late 1967: a coffeehouse in a small town just outside of a U.S. army base. The soldiers, off-duty, are relieved to be able to come in here and relax, to find sympathetic antiwar waitresses willing to listen to their gripes, to drink coffee and pick up a counterculture newspaper and maybe look around to see how many other GIs are in the same boat. . . .

Katy Matlaw is one of the antiwar waitresses, her red hair flowing like a waterfall down her back. Her infant daughter runs precociously around on the wooden floor.

And at the back of the coffeehouse, on a small stage, Dan Matlaw has picked up his guitar. Tougher and more leathery than ever, he's going to do some ranting rock 'n' roll, vehement and literate, and some of his pals are going to back him up on drums and bass and a wailing sax. . . .

> So back to England Paine goes and keeps fighting,
> He writes THE RIGHTS OF MAN and gets charged
>   with inciting
> To Mutiny and Sedition, but on the night they
>   come to bust him
> William Blake has a premonition, Tom Paine has
>   the sense to trust him . . . !

In the winter of 1967–68, Sarah and Nestor's money ran out. They moved out of their pleasant West Village sublet to a single room with off-plumb walls and slanty floors on St. Mark's Place in the East Village, and Sarah got a job writing for the *East Village Other*. By this time the drugs that they had taken together had enabled Sarah to quite reprogram her brain to suit Nestor, and she could no longer honestly say whether she was happy or sad. In consequence, when she thought about the evolution of her fortunes with him—and she scribbled her thoughts down in notebooks incessantly, for her mind had not stopped working, for all that her old emotional connections had become unstuck—she thought of their life together not so much as a decline in prosperity, but as an increase in aestheticism. Hadn't that been the point of a good deal of her Harvard education, after all? That the truly great artists died young and miserably, or committed suicide, or burnt themselves out tragically in the fires of their genius?

Nestor was having some erratic success as an actor. His career was not helped, however, by the fact that, after a brouhaha over the Dr. Faustus screen rights, he had jettisoned his Harvard connections in preference to those he was making in the city's teeming drug culture. Nor was his brilliant viciousness as useful as it had been in Cambridge; he had already quite badly offended some of New York's key theater people. Though their poverty and the uncertainty of his status depressed him, Nestor kept a good face on it. He decorated their little apartment with a gigantic poster of Marlon Brando in *The Wild Ones,* and accumulated and hoarded his possessions (among which was a collection of more than three hundred ties he had been bequeathed by a dead man); all the time Sarah's belongings were diminishing till they barely filled one smallish suitcase.

They still listened to rock music on the FM radio day and night. But lately, following necessity and a certain fashion, they had stopped dining on imported liver pâté and Crema Danica cheese and spent many evenings in the neighborhood Paradox restaurant drinking unlimited free tea in the backyard with beat, hip, and zen luminaries, and eating rice and vegetables sautéed to a monochrome in soy sauce.

At first Sarah found it difficult to sleep so close to the noise and bustle of St. Mark's Place (and the low ceiling, and the out-of-plumb walls, and the failing radiator were no help), but after a while she put herself on a "free running" sleep schedule—grabbing a nap any time of the day or night she felt tired, and likewise waking, rising, eating, writing, any hour of the night or day—and this seemed to suit, even to exhilarate, her.

She had become extremely thin. Nestor was a hard taskmaster in this regard. "I hope you die!" he snarled at her one night in the Paradox when she reached for a dish of string beans he thought unnecessary; and when she modeled a pair of baggy trousers he sneered, "You're ugly enough with *that*." And she focused her wardrobe upon skinny Levis, a pair of open-toed old-lady shoes, and multiple strands of Indian prayer beads.

And though Nestor was harder and harder to live with, all the time, and spoke admiringly of de Sade, Sarah's passion or obsession for him continued unabated.

They played at rough sex, Nestor spanking Sarah with a French hairbrush. He criticized every aspect of her body, her life, herself, unmercifully.

And yet, when she lay finally in his big clutches on the mattress on the floor of the tenement, Bob Dylan or the Beatles or the Temptations or Dionne Warwick beaming steadily into their ears like an extraterrestrial consolation or communiqué, Nestor quite worn with the effort of his prolonged, determined thrusting until, in mysterious silence, he climaxed, and was spent, and remained inside of her inert and detumescing, Sarah always saw her way to the deep madness of the shivering fit, the moment of uncontrol that appeased at the same time that it repelled him.

Sometimes she lay like that with Nestor, trembling, for a long time, a fragile bell that had been too hard struck. She loved this strange new body that this man had given her—this body that was all skeleton and nerve and shivering flower—loved her new self in purest solipsism—even as she realized that she had put the old Sarah Galbraeth far, far behind her.

The girl's sexual satisfaction had become a source of some discomfort to the boy. "Yvette and I always had simultaneous orgasms," he said one day, topping her.

"Yeah, I bet you did," retorted Sarah. She was convinced that no one but she could save Nestor, could redeem him with the greatness of her love, could permit his genius to live and thrive.

In the long afternoons of artists hanging around the house, Nestor liked to engage in an exotic and difficult Japanese pastime called "Stop." "Hey, Sarah—wanna play Stop?" he would intone in his deepest voice.

And Sarah would always shrug and say, "Okay."

And so they would set up the thick wooden board on a shaky bridge table, and take their respective stones, and play: Nestor at first just serious and solemn, then lapsed into a preoccupied tender sadness Sarah believed was the very root of him; Sarah bored and easily distracted. And their territories advanced and grew complicated, encircled and were in turn encircled. No heroic or hierarchic characters held the day, as in chess. The man and the woman, with their handfuls of black and white pieces, rather participated in a slow and orderly progression from an infinite periphery toward an absolute center.

The little discs filled the crosshatchings of the grid with graceful, poignant geometries, until the moans and shadows of the East Village evening sifted in through the window past a dying avocado plant and fleeting nightmares troubled the pavement.

These were Nestor's happiest moments. Usually he won. Truly pleased, he would exult, and announce himself a tactical genius.

One night Sarah said, "You can win at this little game, but I'm really smarter than you. You don't do any original thinking."

"Be a good girl and draw water and hew wood for me, will you?" replied Nestor, picking up the black and white pieces and putting them back into their two boxes.

"I wash your T-shirts and make food for you every now and then, don't I?" said Sarah.

"You always get shells in your omelets. But let's not get into that. Figure out what game you're playing and then play it, Sarah. Don't vacillate so goddamn much."

Though they were both moving about now in the cultural "underground," Sarah's and Nestor's social circles were actually very separate. She spent long hours in the funky *EVO* storefront with fellow *Other* writers Tosches and Meltzer and P.J., while Nestor went out to parties nearly every night to which he saw no need to bring Sarah. One time at Andy Warhol's loft on Union Square, Nestor had apparently gotten into a flamboyant battle of wits with the pop artist, accusing him, Andy, of having copied his, Nestor's, hair. But hearing the story only from Nestor, Sarah had no way of knowing who had won.

When the Richard Lester antiwar movie starring John Lennon opened up, Sarah and Nestor were the first on line at the theater. That was why they lived here, after all. All arts led to Manhattan. It was a clear, sparkling, exciting New York City night, and Sarah imagined the lights of midtown illuminating the sky all the way back to Cambridge. Nestor was expounding with pleasure on the work of Jasper Johns, and Sarah, her enthusiasm a visible gel under the surface of her hollowed face, was giving him her undivided attention. She was wearing a long feather boa and her customary old-lady shoes; Nestor was wearing dark glasses.

They had purchased their tickets, and were walking away from the theater to kill an hour before showtime, when a young man in a jacket and tie caught Sarah's arm.

"Aren't you Sarah Galbraeth?" he said. "The author of 'An Analysis of Coeds as Ice Cream'?"

Sarah blinked happily and nodded. It seemed like such a long time ago. She was amazed that anyone would still recognize her.

"Someone showed me your piece in the *East Village Other* about WBAI," he said, smiling, "and I thought it was really good."

Sarah was biting her lower lip prettily, but she couldn't think of anything to say.

"I recognize you from Cambridge," the fellow explained, now almost apologetically, discomfited by her silence. "Well, keep writing!"

Nestor was glaring as they walked away and down the street. Sarah was not letting herself bask, or gloat, but it was as if she had heard the song of sirens. She tried to make a joke of it.

"Did you get that fellow's name and address?" she asked, looking at Nestor mischievously.

The boy exploded. "What an ugly, *ugly* thing to say!" He turned to her with hatred in his eyes. "You will never be able to understand *anything* until you get it through your head that you are *dogshit!* I am dogshit too, it's true. But you are even dogshittier dogshit!"

"No," said Sarah calmly, almost used to Nestor's language by now. "I'm one of the greats. We're going to be a great and famous couple. Like Jean-Paul Sartre and Simone de Beauvoir . . ."

"And aren't you over that Simone de Beauvoir shit yet?" bellowed Nestor. "If you're still thinking about Simone de Beauvoir, there's really absolutely no hope for you! You were so intoxicated by the idea of yourself as Class Marshal, it was *disgusting.* You were like some fat girl prancing around saying, 'Look at me! Look at my pretty dress!' when all the time she's really naked and greasy and rubbing her smelly armpits into people's faces, her disgusting smelly cunt. . . ."

Sarah felt herself recoil to the very cells of her body. There were still some words that had the power to pierce her. There were still some quirks in Nestor she could just not quite bear. But she felt paralyzed and unable at this moment to act. She let the matter hang. They went to the movie. They rode the subway back downtown in silence.

Home in the tenement, Nestor shrugged his jacket off and kicked his shoes in the direction of the closet. Trudging across the slanting floor in his socks, he grabbed an open jar of macadamia nuts from the top of the stove and sank into the apartment's one easy chair to eat them. His arm moved mechanically; between his teeth the nuts crunched. After a few minutes he had a better idea. Setting the jar down, he rose with some purposefulness and approached the bricks and boards bookcase, scanning the shelves for a certain title.

Between Huysmans and Spengler he spotted the antique, gold-edged copy of Goethe's *Faust.* This was the Faust who went to heaven, unlike the Faust of Marlowe, whom Nestor had portrayed, who went to hell. The boy withdrew the volume eagerly and settled himself back in the overstuffed, shabby chair.

He sighed, taking a breath in anticipation of delight. The binding and cover of the book were of rich dark leather, with the names of the author and work embossed in gold Italic. He held it in his lap for a moment as if weighing it, and let his shoulders drop.

Then, like a surgeon or butcher, he abruptly separated the front cover from the back, throwing the central pages open to his gaze. In the well where the story might have been, dross paper had been carved away with a knife, and there lay, for Nestor's keen appreciation, a small plastic bag bound with red elastic, containing a scraggly green-ish-brown plant substance.

Nestor took some papers from the drawer of a rickety table by his side, tamped the crushed leaves into them, lit his creation with a match, and dropped Goethe to the floor at his other side without a second thought.

And soon there was only the out-of-work actor sitting far back in his chair, his long hair resting on the torn bolster, his eyes partly closed, his mouth in a half-smile of unearthly profundity, and the sweetish aroma of the marijuana circling through the room and out under the police-locked door, and Sarah, at the sink, washing dishes.

She let Nestor smoke for a while, and turn on the radio, and sink back into his chair, as she finished with the dishes and kicked his shoes into the closet. Then she asked him for some of the marijuana (he was by now on his fourth joint), and took the half-smoked cigarette he gave her, and went with it to sit, in the cold, on the fire escape. The view that offered itself to her gaze was of broken cement and some bare, tangled ailanthus, the city weed-tree, in a narrow space between the backs of the buildings on St. Mark's Place and Ninth Street that was more of a cul-de-sac than a courtyard.

With the very first taste of the drug in her mouth, Sarah got a feeling about it that she had never had before. In its taste, in its smell, she scented death. "The sacred and ceremonial herb is a poison," she thought or realized with a frightening clarity, and the certainty of a truth stretched out in front of her like a wide road for her to walk along; "and in poisoning ourselves with it slowly and methodically, we court the excitement of our own death throes, and savor our body's frenzied attempt at self-defense. That's all it is," she thought, as the winter wind shivered in the scraggly trees. "This is death." Having taken a single puff, Sarah flipped the remains of the cigarette into the space between the buildings with a keen horror.

She stood against the doorframe at the back of the apartment and addressed Nestor softly. "Is that what your big attraction was for me at Harvard?" she asked in a surprisingly detached tone (considering the squall they had had outside the theater and the silence that had followed it), "that you were the local dope connection?"

Nestor laughed. "Sure, honey. Plus you thought I was the genius of the age."

"I thought that? I wonder why."

"Now you realize I'm an imbecile?" said Nestor, with a carefree grin Sarah didn't remember having seen before.

"An imbecile?" she repeated numbly.

Her thoughts turned back to Mason City. In those days things were so clear, so easy. She saw or hallucinated the faces of her father and mother, her brother, her sister-in-law, her little nephews, Dr. Abramson, Miss Demos, Marianne Reuss and Marianne's new family, the kids at the Sunday school, Mrs. Crane who had sent her off to Harvard. . . . And it was as if they were all staring at her with shock and disappointment . . . as if they scarcely recognized her any longer . . . as if they were accusing her. . . .

And from Mason City the channel of her mind flowed smoothly on to Cambridge. Once the drug life—the inconsequential and ridiculous scandal over Binks and Thatcher—had been merely a picture on the wall of the mansion of Harvard. But since then Sarah had passed through a knothole in time, a path between universes, and fair Harvard, great Harvard, splendid Harvard—the wonderful precincts and manners of the *Crimson* itself—had all become no more real than a picture on a wall of the drug life. Her life. She had bought into "highness." She had not been quite sophisticated enough. "It's not love that's been my disease all along," she thought, "but dope. Just as everyone said. If only I'd been able to hear them." She thought of the golden girl she had been, who had had no need to listen to the earnest entreaties of friends, who had not taken the time to weigh and consider and measure and judge, as everyone must, but had instead plunged headlong, blind and deaf, enclosed in self-love, toward her doom.

And now, for the first time, she could hear again the voices of Harvard, and of the *Crimson,* calling her—though it was from a great distance, and as if already embodied in an artifact—"We offered you an education based on freedom and rationality, and you chose to be educated at the hands of Nestor Schwarz."

"Why were you always so jealous of my life on the *Crimson,* anyway?" she asked Nestor then, as if in a dream. "You were doing okay in theater. But you hardly even cared about that. You spent most of your time digging yourself a pit. Isn't that right? Did you ever do anything with enthusiasm besides play pool and poker and drink and turn on?"

"Not with my whole heart," laughed Nestor. "I take my games seriously, but not my life. Just the opposite of you."

Sarah took a step toward him. "No, wait a minute," she said. "You *did* do something real once. It was unsigned, so I didn't know at first who'd done it. But then I saw it in the Closed Comment Book with your initials at the top . . ." She groped to remember. "But then I guess I forgot about it right away again. . . ."

Nestor lifted his two-color eyebrow. "I'm sure I don't know what you're talking about. . . ."

But Sarah cut him off with an expression of building fury. "You wrote that Class Marshal editorial thing telling people not to vote for me—!"

"That's right," said Nestor easily. This was so unimportant. "In *Lampoon* Castle. Everybody knew I wrote that."

Sarah's insides sank. "I didn't know it."

"Maybe you didn't want to know it."

It was at this moment that loathing chilled the blood in Sarah's veins. She gazed with icy eyes at Nestor standing in front of her. And the personality that had ruled her dreams for so long fell bit by bit apart and into tiny pieces. His hand, with its long, unclean fingernails, holding onto his beloved little plastic sack of vegetable debris, was unutterably hideous. From his perversely tinted eyebrow a brooding darkness, an unforgivable, guilty premeditation, enveloped the whole upper half of his face. She looked at his supercilious mouth, at his slumping back, at his long feet hiding like cowards in their even longer socks, and she felt no further connection with this man.

And the ice broke Sarah's heart, and the dream sprang forth in a flood of wrath and hysteria and tears.

"God damn you! God damn you!" she cried at the top of her voice, rushing toward him, her hands grabbing for his head.

Real fear transformed him. The obsession of genitalia, the agony in the stomach, the pledge of contemptuous control rallied together to repulse his attacker, to repulse the attack he had waited for and expected for so long. With the sureness of long fear he tossed away the dope and grabbed her hands and wrenched her arms down in front of him.

"Sarah," he said, with a fondness that softened his terror—for this was the woman he had long wanted, this avenging, exploding angel, who would destroy him for the sin of being alive—"control yourself."

Tears were streaming down her face.

"You slime! You vermin!" she screamed. "You louse!" Sarah sobbed, and tried to break free of Nestor's grip. "You ruined me!"

The sadness now on Nestor's face was authentic. All that sweet love she had had to give him, all that joy: finally it had come to an end. Now for the first time he felt he could touch her true self. A tentative feeling like love awoke in him.

But it was too late.

Her screaming had hurt her throat. She paused. "God damn you," she said in a lower voice.

"Come on, honey, take it easy," whispered Nestor tenderly. "Maybe I distracted you a little when you were deciding on the game of your life."

At this Sarah began to cry again, sobbing and pounding as hard as she could on Nestor's chest with her fists locked in his own.

"You ruined me!" she cried as if with her last breath. "And I let you do it!" This final realization (more than anything Nestor could say to her now) quieted her, and she let her hands fall away from the boy and stood looking at him blankly, as if at a stranger. She understood that she had made a bargain with him. A terrible bargain. And that it was too late to undo it. Too late.

Too late . . . The cold ghost of time touched Sarah's spirit and she fell back from it, alone and miserable. How long had it been now since she had been happy? Since she had been "herself"? She thought about how once upon a time she had felt herself to be a starchild, blessed with grace and invulnerability and strength; and she thought about what she had become; and the tears flowed down her cheeks unnoticed as she turned and walked to the end of the room.

Leaning uncertainly on the now-clean kitchen sink, Sarah whispered, "Get out of here."

This did not frighten Nestor. He cocked his head and looked at her coolly. Was it really possible that Sarah was going to renege on her unspoken agreement to love and preserve him even if it meant the sacrifice of her own interests? He shouldn't be surprised if she took that tack; common sense would be on her side. But from the very beginning he had had something even more powerful on his side. He had had magic. He wondered now idly if the magic had run out at last.

"Hey, baby, I got this place through *my* connections," said Nestor drily. "But if *you* want to leave, I'll tell you what I'm gonna do: I'm going to give you a nice ride out to your mom and dad's place in Iowa on the Honda."

"No, thanks," said Sarah, throwing her few things into the small suitcase, sitting down on the mattress on the floor to phone the train station, walking out.

Nestor stood looking at the door that closed behind her. If, indeed, it were true that Sarah was leaving him (and he could not really be sure, even now, since she had faltered in her faith before and been persuaded back by means of the unanalyzable magic of sex), if this were, indeed, the end of the two of them, the expression of an act of will on her part (that he wasn't at all sure she was capable of) tantamount to denying him—renouncing him—well, then, it could mean only one thing. She had seen and shared too much: she could not be let back into the world an impartial witness. They would be enemies.

Then it was as if his breath just stopped coming. He wheezed once. And coughed. And wheezed again. And grew anxious with the long-familiar dread of asphyxiation.

"Shit," he thought, closing his eyes and groping for the inhaler.

I t was not long after Sarah had arrived back in Iowa that she got the long-distance call from Michael. The conversation was brief and awkward. But it seemed only right, he said, that he be the one to tell her. Nestor had cracked up his bike and himself in a nighttime accident with a truck on the turnpike just outside of Cambridge. When they got to him, his head and his feet were a hundred feet apart on the opposite sides of the road.

"Nestor dead?" thought Sarah, as she sat up in her old bedroom. A colorful button still on the bulletin board read: "I Boosted MCHS G.O."

Her mother came up the stairs and hugged her, as she had been hugging her every day. "Everything's gonna be all right. You'll see. Those big guys at Harvard should never have let a bastard like Nestor Schwarz into their school. If that's what they considered 'intelligent' . . ."

"Nestor's dead, Mommy," said Sarah, her eyes full.

Her mother looked startled for a moment. But only for a moment. "And good riddance, I say!" proclaimed Mrs. Galbraeth loudly. Now it was for Sarah to be startled. "You know there's blessed few people in this world I would say that about," she explained. Then her mother went back downstairs to make supper for her father, and Sarah sat and reflected, as she was to do again many times.

"Nestor is dead. And I am not what I was," she thought stoically.

After a while she heard her mother's voice calling the family to supper. But she felt no more hunger in her, neither for food nor for experience. It seemed to her she had pushed her curiosity, or her spite, or her silly, vulnerable, childish pride, behind a veil from which there was no returning, and might have to spend the rest of her life forgetting what she had found there.

But exhausted and weak as she might be, as deathly tired and discouraged, there were still a pair of purple grackles hopping about on the lawn outside her window, still a glint of sunlight, still a breath of cooking steam in which her mother had invested love. She needed time and rest, but she was alive. And she would heal. She would pick up again the thread that she had dropped.

Sarah went downstairs, and kissed her old father lightly on the forehead.

Cont'd. from page iv

York, N.Y., used by permission, all rights reserved. "Dancing on the Ceiling," by Rogers & Hart, copyright 1930 (renewed) by Warner Bros. Inc., all rights reserved, used by permission. Excerpts from *The Second Sex*, by Simone de Beauvoir, copyright 1952 by Alfred A. Knopf, Inc. Excerpts from *Doctor Faustus*, by Christopher Marlowe, edited by Sylvan Barnet, and *The History of the Damnable Life* (English translation), New American Library. "Downtown," words and music by Tony Hatch, copyright © 1964 by Welbeck Music Ltd., London, England, sole selling agent MCA Music, a division of MCA Inc., New York, N.Y., for North, South, and Central America, used by permission, all rights reserved. "Hang on Sloopy," by Wes Farrell and Bert Russell, copyright © 1964 by Picturesque Music Publishing Corp. & Robert Mellin, Inc., published in the U.S.A. & Canada by Morris Music, Inc. (Chappell Music, Admin.) and Robert Mellin, Inc., international copyright secured, all rights reserved, used by permission. "When Sunny Gets Blue," by Jack Segal and Marvin Fisher, copyright © 1956 by Marvin Music Company. "West Coast Blues," by John L. (Wes) Montgomery, copyright © 1960 by Taggie Music Co., a division of Gopam Enterprises, Inc. "Come, Ye Sons of Art," traditional words, music by Henry Purcell, copyright © 1974 by G. Schirmer, Inc., used by permission. "Sgt. Pepper's Lonely Hearts Club Band," by John Lennon and Paul McCartney, copyright © 1967 by Northern Songs Limited, all rights for the U.S.A., Mexico, and the Philippines controlled by Maclen Music, Inc., c/o ATV Music Corp., used by permission, all rights reserved. "She's Leaving Home," by John Lennon and Paul McCartney, copyright © 1967 by Northern Songs Limited, all rights for the U.S.A., Mexico, and the Philippines controlled by Maclen Music, Inc., c/o ATV Music Corp., used by permission, all rights reserved. "Tom Paine," copyright © 1979 by Leaves in October.